PRAISE FOR HOLLAND KANE

Morning Light

"a poignant novel…examines long-buried memories and unsolved mysteries…[that] comes full circle from loss and longing to passionate, obsessive love and, eventually, a sense of self."

— D. Donovan, *Midwest Review of Books*

"In this exploration of a modern woman's search for love and fulfillment, Holland Kane sheds light on the dark places our dreams can carry us, places we never meant to go."

— Carol Orlock, award-winning novelist

Winter Reeds

"Kane spins a fascinating web of discoveries and intrigue, and the surprises don't stop until the very end. A gripping tale of how some secrets can't be buried."

— *Kirkus Reviews*

"Holland Kane writes fiction that will make you think."

— Billy Squier, American rock musician

"Kane shows sensitivity to language and story in this revealing book—I couldn't put it down."

— Ina Bray, librarian and former chair of the King County Arts Commission

morning light

HOLLAND KANE

Also by Holland Kane:

Winter Reeds
Deer Creek (forthcoming)

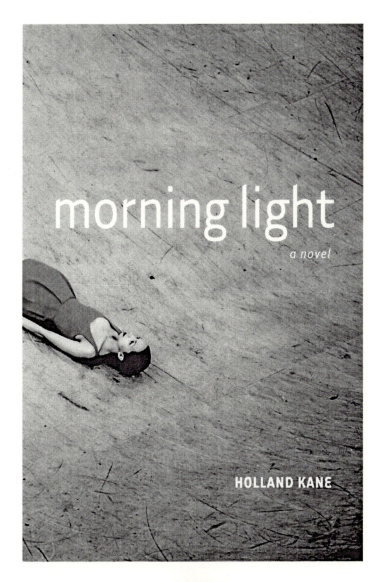

morning light

a novel

HOLLAND KANE

rumor house books

Morning Light

RUMOR HOUSE BOOKS
6029 95th Pl SW
Mukilteo, WA 98275

For more information about the author, visit www.hollandkane.com.

Edition ISBNs
Trade Paperback: 978-0-9858293-3-9
E-book: 978-0-9858293-4-6

First Edition 2013

This edition was prepared for printing by
The Editorial Department
7650 E. Broadway, #308
Tucson, Arizona 85710
www.editorialdepartment.com

Cover photograph ©iStockphoto
Cover design by Kelly Leslie
Book interior design by Morgana Gallaway

A note on the type:
This book was set in Bembo Book, a digital-friendly version of the classic Bembo cut for the celebrated Venetian printer Aldus Manutius by Francesco Griffo.

For Dana

Far out there—that
Soft line where the air meets
The sea—it is as incomprehensible as
existence—it is incomprehensible as
death—as eternal as longing.

Edvard Munch

chapter 1

In the spring of the year that Emily's husband told her his religion barred him from sleeping with her unless she quit using birth control, the crocuses and the hyacinth had already bloomed and I was living in a house in Brooklyn. The startling development in an otherwise warm marriage upset her. She wasn't opposed to having children, but at her age she was nowhere near the dreaded advanced maternal age, code AMA that some nurses posted on the doors of delivery rooms, and she expected to wait several more years before starting a family. She recorded the date they stopped having sex in her journal—on her twenty-fourth birthday.

Rick's abstinence—he was a Roman Catholic—seemed to alter the location of the earth's gravity. She was mystified how his faith could suddenly turn her into a source of sin. She blamed their recent personal bankruptcy and the collapse of his career for his sudden charismatic return to the solace of his religion.

I was too young at the time to understand the events unfolding before me. I did not know at the time that Rick was denying himself the physical intimacy of sex with the only woman who had ever mattered to him, nor could I fathom the depth of Emily's frustration. She wrote in her journal that an element of shame entered her life, something she had never experienced before, the shame of thwarted intimacy, the shame of being spurned—and in the midst of this shame my mother's friendship became all the more important to her. She wrote in her journal that Sara became *as vital as air, as essential as breathing.*

My mother became the North Star guiding Emily's uncharted American life. Sara was an artist who'd always wanted to have a daughter. But she had only me, a boy. When she first met Emily, a dancer and choreographer, at the time only a sixteen-year-old Lithuanian immigrant girl brought to the States illegally to work as household help, Sara knew in her heart she had found the daughter she had always wanted, and Emily found the mother she needed. The years went on—Emily's first boyfriend and breakup, and then her marriage to Rick.

My mother and Emily discussed everything, made and changed plans, each advising the other and weighing a multitude of small decisions. Their attraction for each other could only be described as love. This affectionate relationship suffered in the last year of my mother's life, in part due to her declining health, but also due to Emily's self-censorship—she could not reveal to my mother the secrets she examined daily in her journals.

In the same year that Rick doubled-down on his resolve to remain true to his Church's teachings, Emily was invited to perform at the Jacob's Pillow Dance Festival. This was a huge breakthrough for her as a choreographer, a chance to dance before large audiences and meet the best performers in her field. She liked to choreograph opposing moods, and then arranged these moods into movements. A pattern that was both simple and pleasing to audiences; a contest between clearly defined opposites—good and evil, love and loss, trial and testing—a pattern used since epic stories from the past. But who, or what, could have been the antagonist to take down her good marriage? Rick was neither a tyrant, nor stupid. He loved her and continued to love her—the loyalist in her corner, an honorable man who had become unbending in his newfound principles. She saw his good qualities, and she loved him, too. But months into his abstinence regimen, willy-nilly, she found herself attracted to me, then a seventeen-year-old boy.

In her journals—the journals she had refused to show me—she questioned her emotions, her abilities and talents, her lack of formal schooling and her wayward mind. Her doubts ran so deep that this beautiful woman decided she was no longer attractive.

I wouldn't understand the depth of her questioning and the complexity of her emotional life for another twenty years. By that time I had directed many plays. She came to the opening night of one of my productions, her eyes, a lustrous blue, were as vivid as ever. She was as trim as when I had last seen her, and her hair remained thick and rich and auburn dark. She had read in *The New York Times* about the Seattle theater scene and my recent appointment as Artistic Director. The reporter had noted that my first love wasn't directing but writing plays, but I had not staged my own work because *Maya*, the play I'd started to write in my youth about a secret love affair, had blocked me. I knew very little about sexual life in any form when I was young—let alone the rich and capacious ways of adult love. I groped around in the shadows of desire. My inability to explore the truth blocked every successive effort to finish the play. Some elemental thing was missing from my makeup, and my failure prevented me from becoming a playwright.

The unfinished script was like a question waiting to be answered.

I had told the reporter that I had wanted to script a romance, a story with a happy ending, and I kept coming up with tragedy. He was amused, and made a joke about the melodrama of young lives. I didn't tell him it was based on anyone remotely close to me. I explained, too knowingly, too convinced of my own truth, and too full of creative pride and prejudice and deceit, that imagination always trumps autobiography.

But from afar Emily ignored my confident self-assessments and guessed the truth—I had been writing about her and couldn't finish the work or advance as a playwright because she had refused to hand me the unedited version of her journals.

I was with a group of friends at intermission when she came over. Her beauty bowled me over and our love affair marched into the present. But the past, the past, our painful past...

My friends were baffled by my uneasiness. They didn't know that she'd left me, and that for years I had searched for her. I now introduced her as "my friend" and we chatted amiably about the awful rainy Seattle weather, when suddenly she retrieved a box she'd brought but had kept out of sight in a Macy's shopping bag. "Maybe you can make something out of these journals?" she asked. I took the box, a handful of writings recording her intimate life. She turned to leave.

"Wait, please wait," I said.

She hesitated, and I expected she'd wait. My friends were a boisterous bunch, and more of them joined us. I held up a hand to indicate to Emily that I could visit privately with her if only she could stay. I motioned for her to follow me as we headed for the open bar, but she smiled and said no.

There were so many aspects to her. She was a woman and a child; she was a tomboy and very sexual. A girl who loved fantasy, a woman with talent, and a child who couldn't give up her ideals. She was good to me, and guided my coming-of-age. She believed she was bad. I had missed her all these years.

I drank only half of a glass, the minimum I could get away with without offending my friends, and then I went looking for her. I asked several ushers for help. "Auburn hair, beautiful"—but my words were useless among so many beautiful women attending that night. I went up and down several aisles searching for her, until the lights dimmed and I had to accept the inevitable—she had left at intermission, departing as abruptly as she had earlier.

The play that night won plenty of applause and I should have stayed to celebrate. Instead, I apologized to my friends (headache, post-performance tension) and skipped the celebratory late dinner. At home, I pounced on the box of journals with the ferocity of the ravenous. I had wanted her to love me. I had wanted her to stay with me. I wanted her. No matter how uncommunicative we'd been at that point in our lives, I felt we had a conspiracy going. I now held the journals I had always wanted. I was as excited as a trespasser might feel walking into someone's private life, but something new had been added—I was once again a voyager exploring my own unexamined emotional life.

chapter 2

I launched a new project the same night she gave me her journals, sorting through the small events and loopy incidents we had experienced together, blending the truth she revealed about herself in her journals with my own memories that had migrated over the years for my own self-serving needs. *Morning Light* is an opening into that time, and what follows is not only the history of a play, but also a season of passion that had lasted a year—our time together, our efforts and failures and trials in the watershed year that set all our lives in motion toward an irrevocably altered future.

Although she was seven years older than me, she still retained her rural Lithuanian innocence that trailed her like a worried puppy. She was brought to the States by a Lithuanian fixer and her life would have been cast in the supporting role of good people doing menial work if she hadn't met my mother that same year. Sara yanked her away from the fixer, fought off his threats by hiring a lawyer who eventually prevailed in winning Emily legal immigrant status.

From then on Emily was too busy to reflect on anything beyond the immediacy of her ambitious work ethic. "Life is my teacher," she announced, and like others who favor this ancient sentiment she would come to realize that life is a very clumsy and dilatory teacher, and you could spend all your youth learning what others learn in a fortnight.

The day that this became obvious was sunny and warm, the cherry blossoms were blooming at the Brooklyn Botanic Garden, and the starlings were glittering with coal-black iridescent plumage. In a mood for intimacy, she had bought a copy of *Cosmopolitan* magazine with all the furtiveness that a boy my age at the time would have displayed buying *Hustler* or the tamer *Playboy*. It was the love issue, and along with a beautiful woman on the cover, it promised to reveal "Crazy Hot Sex."

Emily was in the dark about the libidinal economies in America. She wondered how a man or a woman could marry four or five times in quick succession with no one taking much notice, mating with as many sex partners as one could attract into serial monogamous marriages—and no one called this sleeping around, but sleeping between single unmarried people wasn't accepted because, supposedly, it didn't support family values. The country's social habits baffled her.

She rummaged through her bureau, fingering lingerie, torn warmups, leotards, and checking out several pairs of jeans to see which outfits did justice to her long, narrow waist and sculpted figure. She decided on a white caftan with a plunging neckline and chose tight jeans. She looked wholesome and yet as if of another era, Etruscan perhaps.

Rick had just gotten out of the shower and was shaving. He had a bath towel wrapped around him. She liked his masculine early-morning routine, the eager-beaver get-to-work process, and the pleasing smell of the shaving cream. She admired his firm chin, and the tender and vulnerable neck. His tidy and slim body was scaled to her own fine proportions. In heels she was as tall as he was shoeless. Her ideal dancing weight was 110 pounds, and he scaled at medium weight for a guy. His razor cleared a path through the shaving cream. Steam and the humidity added a sultry air. She wrapped her arms around him and leaned her head on his shoulder.

He stopped shaving. "What's up, angel?"

"Can't we, you know, can't we *celebrate* our marriage?" Her uplifting tone pushed against their shyness around the subject of sex.

"Now?" he asked.

"Don't you want me?"

"I can't," he said. His remark was heartfelt and off-kilter. He pulled on the razor. She sensed that he was frustrated that her hug was delaying him.

"Let's take a chance," she said.

"Uhm." He cut himself. A reddish stain mixed into the shaving cream. "How do I know that you're not on the pill?" That morning he had no intention of violating his Church's moral rules on contraception, laid out in a papal bull back in 1968.

"You no longer trust me?" she asked.

He whistled in a friendly way. "You might take the morning-after pill. Either way it's killing babies." He dabbed his chin with a salt stick. Despite his casual manner, he appeared to be as conflicted as Saint Augustine, who'd wanted to stop having sex with his common-law wife and the mother of his child in order to purify his soul.

"I can't," he said. "Not unless—"

She pushed away. He finished shaving and soon left for work. The peculiar embarrassment that comes from intimacy rejected subdued her sparkling mood.

When I read this passage in her journal I was struck by the intimate sadness I did not hear in her voice when I was young and self-absorbed. Big questions never troubled me—good and evil, love and marriage. I had instead a promiscuous instinct, an animal knowledge, and now, years later, after having learned that my instincts weren't always my best guide, I saw as if for the first time how confined Emily and Rick had been to the lunatic fringes of unrequited lives. But for them at the time, it didn't appear to be a fringe at all; they felt they were part of the mainstream.

She changed into her workout clothes and went over the day's schedule. The invitation to perform at Jacob's Pillow was like a helium-filled balloon lifting her mood. Surprise and variety had ambushed the orderly routine she had known—teaching, gym, workshops, rehearsals, small-venue performances and part-time work—and replaced it with busy anticipation to perform at Jacob's Pillow.

She slipped *Cosmo* into her gym bag and left for her nearby studio, walking fast to subdue the sense of frustrated desire. *What's the matter with me*, she wrote in her journal. *Does anyone like me?*

Rick had grown up to be uncomfortable around sexually

aware women. Claim-jumpers, he called them. She adopted the opposite pattern—that of extreme politeness, reticence, stoic acceptance, an excess of patience in her personal life. She wasn't sure how to grow in her personal relationship with Rick. He wore a Brown Scapular next to his chest—it had a beautiful image of the Virgin Mary on it. This symbol of devotion was weighed with indulgences that guaranteed a person's early release from purgatory after death, and it honored the Blessed Mother for her virgin delivery of Jesus. This constant reminder of the virtue of virginity made Emily feel as if a disapproving lady spy, critical of "carnal knowledge," was watching her as they made love. She wasn't sure how to prevail over his devout Marian practice.

On stage, her work was shifting toward a rebellious energy, bold and assertive, but at home, facing Rick, facing his devoutness, his college education, his former success as an executive, his speaking skills, she felt corralled into a relationship she'd never anticipated—the other, the female, the woman. The marriage of nature and desire that she had wanted and believed in had become weird, bound in knotty ways by invisible, pious, shackles. Silence ruled over personal issues, especially matters about sex. The rhetoric and practice of psychological professional help, the language of therapy, was absent from their lives. Rick depended on faith alone. She didn't know how to defend herself against silence—against the thing never said.

Cheerful by habit, the habit failed her that morning. *So what? It's only sex*, she wrote in her journal, determined to be happy. She entered the studio and opened the storefront window shades. But the emotions that had prepared her for seducing Rick now loitered on her skin. She took out *Cosmo*, it contained—"epic confessions, a cheater's diary, weird stuff guys Google about you"—and advertised it on the cover. She would have been embarrassed to read the articles at home with Rick nearby, which was why she was taking the magazine to her studio. She checked out the article on "fun, fearless lingerie" and got as far as "I'm marrying my gay best friend," when I dropped in at the studio that morning.

"What's up," I asked.

She slipped the magazine into the gym bag. "I'm working on a new dance that Sara had inspired."

She took in my curly hair, the tiny ridge under my eyes. She liked my voice. She liked that I talked slowly. She liked that I was taller than she was. Her mood shifted toward lightness whenever I was around. Her journal described a warm sensation, unexpected, sexual, and instantly regretted, passing though her body.

She caught a glimpse of herself in the mirror. She was wearing her husband's sweatshirt that she had artfully shredded to give her a disheveled waif-like look. The neckline was cut low and wide. She checked a bandage on her foot.

"You should be in school," she said.

She sat on the edge of the studio daybed and unwound the bandage, and looked closer at her foot. It was slightly swollen. She wiggled her toes and got up and took several steps to make sure the injury was healing. "How is Sara this morning?"

"I had to help her up the stairs," I said.

Out of a quarter of a million women my mother's age, only one would be diagnosed with breast cancer, and she would most likely survive if the disease could be detected early. But my mother, stubborn, forceful, brave, as energetic as Emily, had waited too long to make an appointment to have a lump looked at, and by the time she did her doctors discovered not only the cancerous growth but also several infected lymph nodes. The invasive journey from a suspicious flu to a devastating diagnosis had been discouragingly fast.

As an artist, Sara's goal had been to make art out of her own life; the rest was process, a living process, a changing process, additions and subtractions, items to fortify love, to make something out of hope and uncertainty. She did photography, made objects and conceptual pieces. Her soft sculptures and works-in-progress were stored in the studio, and Emily, who liked to work at least six hours a day on her choreography, felt all the closer to my mother because my mother's art was present. Our lives had a rewarding urban closeness—my mother's house, the studio, my high school, the diner where Emily and I worked part time, were all within walking distance. And Sara had been the source of our communal energy, the fire behind our lives.

Emily completed her ankle inspection and did several stretching routines. "She'll get better."

The fact that my mother was dying, that her moment in our lives was passing, had not yet soaked through our being. We were denying death's willfulness, and bouncing like lunatics between reckless optimism and false cheerfulness. Emily, usually as truthful as a saint, began telling small lies in the pursuit of hope for my mother's recovery. But there's only so much happy fakery you can do under bad circumstances.

Emily smiled, I smiled, our eyes filled with tears. An internal quake seemed to shatter our stability, our confidence. We embraced just to hold on to our lives.

I held her and held her, holding her longer and tighter and closer than she felt comfortable having me hold her. She pulled away and a shadow must have crossed my face. Disappointment filled my heart. I needed her touch. I needed to hold and to hug and to linger. I felt rejected, hurt, and turned-away. With my mother close to dying, I was as close to being an orphan kid as one could find in Dickens' novels. But my narrow self-regard failed to take Emily's emotions into consideration—she was devastated by my mother's illness.

Outside, a truck rode over a manhole and sent a shudder underfoot. A couple of men who worked as sheet-metal fabricators nearby were on their way to work. She recognized their trade by the shoes they wore: oiled-leather, and pronounced bulbous uppers that had been ripped in places to expose the steel shell protecting their toes from being severed by falling metal objects.

The men were solid. Their steps were short, abrupt and fast. She wrote in her journal that she felt inadequate when comparing her own passion for dance—its ethereal gestures and fleeting moments—with the practical, helpful, repetitive, common good things that men and women do to keep the world upright.

She had none of the pretensions that made some artists critical of the get-to-work crowd, the much-criticized bourgeoisie, or middle class as we call it today. Few among Oscar Wilde's aesthetes would have been her favorites, although she was in favor of gay marriages and relationships, for which Wilde went to prison. What confused her, what she had never completely learned in Lithuania, was the nature of chaotic desire that fueled her self-discovery through dance.

I was feeling my own chaos. In fact I was on fire, my body electric. I wanted her in the way I dared not explain to her.

Years later I would learn that Thanatos and Eros, death and erotic love, have a tangled, incestuous relationship. I wasn't capable of such sophisticated thinking when I was young, but I realize now that back then, in the midst of grief over my mother's prospects, I was consumed with a raging desire for Emily. I wanted her to love me in the way a woman loves a man. I wanted her to take me as she would take a husband.

"What are you doing?" she asked.

"I'm rolling down the window shades."

"I don't want to be in the dark with you."

"I'm ready, and—"

"Please, don't," she said.

To distract me, to delay and obstruct the fire she saw rising within me, coloring my face and flashing in my eyes, she danced a phrase from a sequence she was choreographing. I let go of the rollup shade and squinted at the morning light, and then at my mother's artwork. Sara had made a series of large-format photographs of Emily. Some of the photos were similar to Cindy Sherman's work, and there were many of them—more than those my mother had taken of me.

I waited, entranced by Emily's dancing. Her thick hair, the lovely eyes, lissome arms, and the beautiful mouth—this was my tipping point, unmet desire.

But she wanted to avoid the whispered secrets told in the intimate shadows I was offering. She wanted to use her vitality to transcend darkness; she wanted to dance with clarity and light, and anything as unruly as desire got in the way. Writing in her journal, she would soon discover a sort of negative capability: "Today I didn't even *think* about David." But that morning she was thinking about me, and unable to stop thinking about me.

She danced a sequence more violently as if to punish her body. The control she had over her movements collapsed into a state of uncertainty. She stopped.

"I want you," I said.

She remained silent and went to work on another dance. I became intensely aware of her steps sounding on the boards. Several more workmen passed in front of the store.

She wrote in her journal that when she saw me walk across the boards to roll down the shades her desire registered as quickly as heat on an instant-read digital thermometer. She stopped dancing and said, "If you close the shades, I'm leaving."

I closed the shades anyway. I waited. She stepped behind a shoulder-high privacy screen to change into street clothes. I didn't know then that she, too, was simmering with emotion.

She couldn't admit her complicated feelings toward me to my mother—instead, she filled pages and pages with rare intimacy. The journal became the confidant she needed, and she wrote in it as if speaking to a friend sworn to secrecy. But she often wrote in circles, repeating scenes, adding dialogue, revisiting what she'd written and adding new opinions.

Some of the entries had the repetitive genius of Gertrude Stein, and at other times the laconic structures of the artist Sol LeWitt.

"What's taking you so long?"

"I'm trying to decide what to wear."

We listened to the mournful sounds of a bus with bad brakes stopping at the corner. I waited an edgy long moment before she came out from behind the privacy screen dressed in white underwear and a black tube top. On a summer beach her shapely appearance would have been a bikini-clad public pleasure. But in the privacy of the moment, the same amount of exposed skin shifted the mood from beach-like vitality to intimacy. She was holding two pairs of jeans. "Which pair do you like?"

I didn't care which pair of jeans she wore.

She came closer and we stood in the shade-filtered honey light. I could almost circle her waist with my hands, and I did. She felt my blood run high as I held her. The top of her head came up to my shoulders, and there was now a bead of sweat on her forehead. A chorus of angels had to be screaming at her.

She counted four buses passing at long intervals as we made love on the daybed. She heard the brakes each time. She didn't want to stop, but when we had to stop, and when there was no other way left except to stop, I thought of her modesty and told her to wait while I went to get her underwear. She smiled and said that Rick might have done the same for her. I couldn't bear to think that Rick and me—that the both of us—were cut from the same cloth. That morning she realized that she was attractive to me and must be attractive to others, despite Rick's flight into abstinence. This discovery, odd as it may seem, that a beautiful woman never knew she was beautiful, burned in my memory a generation later.

chapter 3

Ten days after we had made love she tested herself with a store-bought pregnancy kit. The result was alarming: a shimmering blue crossbar completed a plus sign. The test, which the manufacturer claimed was 98 percent accurate, indicated pregnancy.

Only once with the boy, only once in her life that she had ever cheated on anyone, and she was now pregnant? How unthinkable, how unfair and unjust and crazy and severe her bad luck—it sent a tremor through her. She heard Rick moving about in the apartment as he prepared to leave for work. She wrapped the popsicle-size tester in toilet paper and took it to her dresser. He came in and was holding a newspaper. His kiss felt hurried.

"Angel, I'm becoming the bow-wow boy at Auto Max. I jump and bark and play tricks." He had taken the auto sales job after their personal bankruptcy and had been unhappy at work. He glanced at the tissue-wrapped pregnancy tester. She covered it with her hand.

"Can you afford to quit?" she asked.

"Yeah, yeah, I know. Hang in there."

"Something else will come along."

"I'm networking like crazy, schmoozing, kissing up. I even humbled myself and went to see your old boyfriend, Jay, to ask him if I could work for Bradbury Corporation again. I hate the bastard. 'Any work,' I said. 'Give me a shot.' I was the pleadingest son of a bitch you ever heard beg for a job. I'd sweep his fuckin' office floor to get back in." Rick said it airily and irritably and bitterly.

That was exactly how Emily had reported his conversation in her journal. To those who are uneasy with language the *New York Times* does not print, I need to make several apologies. Rick swears a lot, the only person in this history who does swear. I've considered putting in asterisks, as in f★★★ and ★★★★ing, where it was appropriate, but that would have mystified the account, and fooled nobody, so I didn't.

"His dad trusted you."

"Poor ol' Bradbury Sr."

"He was going to make you the CEO." She was wistful.

"And now, with his son in charge, I don't even *dream* of getting back my VP title." His eyes lit up in the hope that he was wrong and it could happen, but his jaw tightened as he went on. "Jay's wife, Page, is on the board of trustees, and she's rooting for me. Thank God I got to know her when she was his dad's admin manager. She always liked me and said I had a nice smile." He paused. "I hate to say this, but Jay is nothing like his old man. The old guy was fun to work for. Shrewd. A relentless, ruthless son of a bitch, but fun. He would screw anybody and everybody to get ahead, but he took care of his employees. He wasn't doing the Cayman Islands shit. No Swiss accounts, as far as I know, but Jay Jr.? The big asshole? He never had to work for a thing in his life. And then"—he raised his finger—"then he becomes the shoo-in guy to take over his dad's job that I'd expected to get. Me and my shoeshine are out on the street."

Rick threw a couple of mock punches. "A third of the guys who work for Jay think he's great, a third think he's an asshole, and the rest don't dare say what they think so long as they get a paycheck."

"You're lucky Jay is thinking about rehiring you."

"Oh, he can kiss my ass."

"Please calm down."

"Yeah, I guess. What the hell? Who knows? Maybe he'll hire me. He sometimes acts like he's my best friend. He asks about you. He always asks about you. The son of a bitch. He says I can use his sailboat whenever I want to take you sailing. He says that even though I can't afford the goddamned diesel the auxiliary engine eats." He punched the palm of his hand. "When it come to you, he's as transparent as a Ziploc bag full of hot air. He wants to show off his toys to you. He wants to show you what he's got. What he can afford. A big fuckin' boat. What you missed by throwing him over for me. The asshole."

"Stop being so volatile."

"You'd think he would have bought the vessel with his own earnings. He fixed the pay scale so he gets a hundred times what he deserves. Not a chance he's going to use his own money. How many of us get to pay off a big boat as a company expense? Charging it off as a 'training' expense. You should see the *Miscellaneous Expense*, a sailor's dream. I love it. The cost of the electronics on it could buy us a house."

She had left Jay for Rick five years ago, but the past lingered on. She wondered if Rick had quit the Bradbury organization on account of it. He kept pacing behind her back, apparently retracing each step leading to their recent personal bankruptcy, analyzing his missteps with the tedious and agonizing imprecision of someone scrutinizing a broken love affair.

The sudden papery smack of his newspaper coming down on her dresser brought him to a new conclusion about his bankruptcy: "I should have held out for a fuckin' Chapter 11 reorganization. We could have bootstrapped our way out of it."

She listened patiently. She always listened. She was worried for him. He was pale and had lost weight, but he always dressed neatly, his clothes immaculate.

"I just fucked up. I didn't do my SMART."

She gave him an inquisitive look.

He repeated the management guru's goal-oriented calling card: "SMART—Specific, Measurable, Attainable, Realistic, and Time-bounded goals." He stopped to touch her shoulder.

"Jay isn't so bad," she said.

"He sucks."

"Please don't get hung up about Jay and me and our past. He married Page. He'll do you a favor."

"I don't need favors from assholes."

"Don't be rash."

"Angel, it's easy for you to say what I should and shouldn't be doing, because dance has always been the only thing you wanted to do." He picked up a publicity picture that she used to advertise her dance classes. The photographer had made her eyes look enormous, and the eye catch, the bright reflection of light in them, mirrored a dreamy longing, her trademark. She was adorable, every man's dream, and every boy's fantasy.

Yes, she was dreamy, she admitted in her journals. But her dreams had always been reasonable. And now the reasonable person she'd known herself to be, and others had praised her for being, had gone off and done an extremely unreasonable thing by sleeping with me.

Rick looked at his watch. His manner was springy, optimistic, carrying an American casualness that appealed to her and to her Lithuanian friends who had also married American men. She attempted to gauge his mind—the unspoken, the unruly, the ever-changing noisy inner traffic. After months of resolute self-denial and physical distance, he wanted her. His attention shot a bolt of uneasiness through her. She had tried to seduce him the other week and he had treated her as a derelict sexual deviant. The sudden change pleased her, but the faint smell coming off the pregnancy tester worried her. Outwardly calm, she was shivering inside and her breathing was shallow.

"Won't you be late for work?" she asked.

"To hell with work."

He was smiling.

"You're okay with contraception all of a sudden?"

"I'm a sinner."

Rick waited for her to say something else, but they'd been in a sex-free zone for too long to get over it in one morning. She hesitated.

She had something to hide from him, and it made matters worse. As far as she knew, Rick had nothing to hide. There were no secret desires or fetishes in his past or his present. No hidden cache of a former girlfriend's nude photographs. No sexy pinups. No lurid e-mail exchanges as far as she knew. No meetings in park bathrooms for sexual liaisons. No mistresses or gambling binges to uncover. No affairs. His drinking was out in the open and not in a closet. Nor was he a closeted gay man, though she might have preferred him to be gay to excuse his avoiding sex with her. He was overzealous in his piety—but neither sex nor gluttony nor greed for fame or money or power made his A list. There was no B list.

"But you hate birth control?"

"Yes."

He started pacing again. He had once said to her that he would go out of his way to avoid a girl he especially liked if the attraction had the potential to hurt his marriage. This lack of waywardness might be boring, but it made her feel safe, and he usually made up for his physical inattention with many boyish passions. He was licensed to fly single-engine aircraft, he drove a motorcycle, and he was a competent sailor.

An awkward moment asserted itself. "Yeah, dammit, I've got to be the breadwinner. No fucking around for me."

His devotion to the papal bull forbidding contraception led to many journal entries—cryptic comments in the margins, annotations, checkmarks of approval and disapproval. In separate encounters with her journal she was amazed at herself and Rick, troubled, encouraged, confident, eager, adventurous, or disappointed, adding triple exclamation points, triple question marks.

Not certain what to do next, she kissed him goodbye. The slight scent from the testing stick caught his attention. "Are you sick?"

A tiny muscle above her cheekbone jumped and her eyes darted between the tester and his face. Rick had talked many times about starting a family. He had talked and talked and talked about it. Rick wanted to have a child with her, two children, three children, four children, and even five. Women have only four hundred eggs to squander in their entire lifetimes. Sperm, it turns out, are countless, millions of them, aggressive, greedy to make use of their fleeting lives. But Rick was a nurturer, too, and would have made a good dad to a dozen kids had he been wealthy enough to have them, and had a harem to carry them to term. He picked up the tester that was concealed in toilet paper and could pass for a thermometer. "Fever?"

"A girl thing."

He dropped it. He was uneasy with girly things. She gave him another kiss and he set off for work, closing the door behind him. "Have a good day," she whispered.

chapter 4

Her journals reveal a woman who had fallen into a huge nautilus shell that was going to echo regret for all time. She wanted her affair with me to end immediately, with no damage done to anyone. The following day, however, I dropped in at her studio again. My hair was wet from a shower. Had I been a dancer, I would have made a good partner. I had a long back and strong legs and good shoulders that could carry her across a stage flawlessly.

I saw Rick's Army .45 left on the lateral file cabinet that also held my mother's photographic portfolio. He had been licensed to keep the semiautomatic and insisted on leaving it in Emily's studio "just in case" she ever needed it. I picked it up, juggled its weight in one hand, turning it over.

"Has he fired the gun?"

"Not in years."

"The clip only holds seven rounds and the hammer is chipped." I ejected the clip and pulled back on the breech to its rearward position. She didn't like the clicking sound, which had a deadly, industrial urgency. She took the gun and touched the grooved slide. The semiautomatic, WWII vintage, wasn't like the sleek 9mm Glocks people saw in movies. James Bond would have been afraid to use this gun. She was afraid of the gun, too.

"Rick left it for my protection."

Casting doubt, I said, "It can't be a hot seller at gun swaps." My assertiveness bordered on arrogance.

"He isn't your rival. He's my husband, a man fighting for a paycheck."

"He's losing the fight?"

"Shut your mouth. Shut up, please."

"You're so beautiful," I said.

She forced a laugh. She'd had no premonition that this was going to be a day of surprises. "What do you know about beauty?" She wore a long-sleeve dance costume with lots of buttons.

"I'm reading Ovid. *Amores* and *Remedia Amoris*. Love and cures for love."

"What's that have to do with me?" She stepped back abruptly. It was maddening for her to lose the thread of her life. The latest e-mail I had sent her had the image of *Mother and Child* attached, a work by Egon Schiele, a guy who couldn't put pencil to paper without Eros riding the tip.

"You're messing with me," she said.

She faced the rural person inhabiting her skin—a modest and unassuming person, a person fearful of vanity, an affectionate person who believed against all gathered historical evidence that every problem had a solution, that every couple could save their marriage, and every situation carried some positive twist. She had grown up on rural earnestness, and even though my mother had given her a cosmopolitan polish, she remained beyond irony, intensely sincere, a believer filled with cheer.

She danced a confined, angular piece, erasing the comic style associated with her earlier work. She paused, her stance taut. Her legwarmers were new and dyed pink. Her breathing had become hinged on something inside her. She had choreographed a political piece, but on seeing my reaction, she was thrown into doubt.

"You do sensual moves better than politics," I said.

She looked at me carefully.

"You just want to sleep with me," she said.

"Why not?"

She switched to another dance and danced *Waterboarding* in a work inspired by Joost's *The Green Table*.

She stopped. "You look mystified."

"Yeah. Something. I don't know what. Your choreography looks hard."

"Everything challenging is hard."

"Why do you do it?"

She handed me a copy of Paul Taylor's essay that she asked all her students to read, "Why I Make Dances." She recited a portion from memory. Taylor wanted to make dances because it freed him from coping with the real world. He wanted to inhabit a universe of his own making where everyone would have honest insights into the human condition.

I listened absentmindedly, my mind on a separate track. Her neck was beautiful and her shoulders perfect. I ran an imaginary hand along her abdomen. I didn't know then that she was pregnant. I wouldn't know that for a long time, not until I read about it in the unedited journals that she handed to me in Seattle. Had I known that a just-fertilized egg was multiplying cells to give life in her body, just as my mother's cancerous cells were multiplying to bring death, I might have acted differently.

"Mom is not feeling good today," I said. "But she told me to tell you she's okay."

"We'll get Sara into Hutchison in Seattle for a bone marrow transplant." They'd been working on this last-ditch effort to persuade her physicians that Sara was worth the cost. "She'll get better. She will."

"She called you her daughter."

"You keep messing with me."

Her journal revealed there was something new going on to trouble her—she was now beginning to worry that she might not remain attractive to me. This was the beginning of a seesaw experience for her. The petals of a daisy were being pulled off, does he, doesn't he…She couldn't tell what was going on in my head. Her journals soothed her nerves and untangled her feelings. That year she was happier making dance than she had ever been before. She also said it was the saddest year of her life. She couldn't see the way forward, how to keep Rick, how to deal with her forthcoming appearance at Jacob's Pillow. For my part, I couldn't forget the daybed we'd shared. Everything else felt like a distraction.

I made the first move. My fingers were steady as I reached for the buttons on her costume. I felt her heart beating. We faced our reflection in the mirrors. She noticed again how attractive she was, something her husband seemed not to notice enough. She noted in her journal that my shoulders looked like angel wings protecting her. "I love you," she said, and shivered.

I wasn't prepared for the next thing she did: she stopped me cold and told me to go home. I must have looked flustered. A flash of anger might have shown in my eyes, but I left.

chapter 5

Later the same day she was writing an apology in her journal, apologizing to Rick. She loved Rick, too. But how do you love a saint? The journal's emotion-packed cries and whispers continued:

> *Rick, listen to me! I feel desperate to have failed you. I don't know why I did it, what anger grows inside me, what hopes lie simmering, please please let us someday talk about it. Let us live, let's even have a quarrel, fight like crazy, speak our minds and live our lives out in full.*

She heard Rick knock and she put away her journal. He entered beaming. "Angel, Jay wants to loan me his boat this weekend."

"He's ordering you to use the boat?"

"He might give me that job."

She didn't want to see her ex-boyfriend, even though the

charitable Bradbury foundation had given her a grant. "Is he going to be onboard?"

"No, it's just you and me and the sea."

Rick was alive with renewed enthusiasm and hungry for sunshine. That weekend she and Rick carried provisions down the marina walkway to load aboard *Miscellaneous Expense*.

The masts were enormous, and the electrically powered stainless steel winches could have passed for polished works of art. The vessel had been designed to sail single-handed across an ocean and it could also sleep eight. They got underway in a light breeze. Rick checked the wind vane on the mast. "Calm seas for now."

"Not for us."

She said it cheerfully, meaning to amuse him, entertain him, and raise the banner to ride out the storm in a difficult journey. But Rick took things literally. Metaphor and simile hadn't yet been posted in his operating manual. He didn't understand why she had said what she had said, but the cheerful sound of her voice disarmed him.

As I read her journals and witnessed her effort to keep their vessel afloat, I saw her often second-guessing what he had left unsaid, and in parts of her journals this got very tricky. She was the person closest to him, and knew a lot about him, but some of the transitions that she provided in her journals seemed strained, or incomplete. Where I needed to edit them for clarity and meaning, I did. I also considered putting in a disclaimer, "The opinions expressed here belong solely to those of the people speaking." But most readers who read this history will probably know this.

At any rate, back on the *Miscellaneous Expense*, Rick assumed Emily was questioning his attitudes toward contraceptives. He couldn't stomach their use. It literally pained him. He took a deep breath, and he must have decided on the martyr's path. "I love you no matter what."

"No joking," she said. But it didn't sound funny.

"It's a strain on us."

"There must have been a reason the Virgin Mary avoided sex."

"Avoided it?"

"Yes, avoided sex."

His tone slipped to a lower register. "Let's not be profane. What's wrong is wrong. I even asked Father Dan on the hush-hush to confirm it. I'm not just some crazy solo believer."

"And he said?"

"He bunted. He didn't give me a clear answer."

"Rick, as far as I know, our bishops are fools. As many Catholics use birth control as the general population. What's the big deal?"

"My conscience is a big deal."

"Your conscience?" she said it all in a rush. "How about my body? My career? My hopes and my future?"

"You'd make beautiful babies."

She snorted, and a violent thought seized her. "I'm not a baby factory."

"I just paid you a compliment."

"That was sweet talk?"

A reproach gathered in the corners of his mouth. "You haven't been listening."

"To make babies."

"Yes. What's wrong with that?"

"A blue-ribbon prize breeder."

"It was a compliment, fuckin' praise, a compliment for God's sake."

"You don't want to sleep with me for the fun and the pleasure?"

He reeled a little. "I'd like to show you that I'm a man."

She was amazed. "Don't you know that already?"

"Well, you know, it's like, it's—"

Upset by their inability to understand each other, he made a show of inspecting the rigging. She went below to go to the bathroom, which is called a "head" on a boat. A plastic sign above the air-powered toilet reminded her not to flush sanitary napkins into the holding tank. *Not to worry. Not for many months.*

There was something in the back of her mind that she was unable to make clear to herself, or understand, or quarrel with it. She honored the people who wished to believe what they wanted to believe. And now the tables had been turned on her in a weird way. Rick didn't like her beliefs. He couldn't stomach them. She wasn't given the freedom to believe what she wanted to believe.

She'd come to think of the Church as *his* rather than her church. The clergy of *his* Church had come to believe women's bodies soiled quickly, or had short shelf lives, or needed extra-protective coverings, or preservatives, or something. Women had to be governed for purity. Men were okay, dirty or otherwise. Men gathered at synods to see what had to be done. Laws were passed, rules issued, directives enforced. No one seemed to get as excited about ruling men's bodies with the same passion as they ruled over women's bodies. Early on, Christian men invented chastity belts to bolt on women to protect men from doubt that their women's purity might be adulterated, and now they were demanding that women carry babies to term for the men no matter how vile the man, or unlikely the baby to survive.

Romance and childbearing, love and property ownership, all piled onto sex and marriages and passion, all discrete units with their own identities, were enough to confuse anyone. My mother kept up with current writers and artists, and she would've read books from my grandmother's generation—Firestone's *The Dialectic of Sex*, Becker's *The Denial of Death,* and she'd studied Otto Rank, all of which would have been hocus-pocus to Rick, and risky reading for an immigrant woman like Emily, but I think it was in my mother's library that Emily first discovered other ways of thinking, and began to separate from her former self in order to grow as an artist.

Wave after wave of feminist literature washed over her as she built her own mental and social church. It was a pleasant church, unisex, classless, communal, welcoming and scented with incense, lit by candles and brightly illuminated in gold. Very pretty, like a lovely ornament she would wear on occasion. She had no quarrel with palm readers, she liked mystics, and studied astrology. Her church was more peaceful and, in effect, truly pantheistic.

Rick's Church was a colonial power set on conquering and holding territory. Souls, for one thing, needed aggressive help.

And special attention had to be paid to women's reproductive lives, to keep them productive in creating those souls. But the way his Church went about it was more like exploiting a resource, mining an asset, making it work harder to enhance productivity, to be "fruitful" as they used to say, and if you had to trick a woman into thinking that romance was the path, as Anna Karenina believed, then let them think that. A number of women started to believe this, and grew into multitudes, and no one wielding ecclesiastical authority wanted to inform them otherwise, not when a world made up of future little Catholics was at stake. My mother had a different view and must have mentioned it to Emily.

I don't think Emily truly studied the matter. The world was her teacher, she'd said several times, and she had a more immediate problem to solve. She didn't know how to overcome Rick's feelings of sinfulness when he wanted sex for the mere pleasure of sensual excitement. But she understood that something huge was at stake—their life together, his freedom, and her freedom, too.

She was determined to separate herself from priestly expectations, and she wanted to mark her independence. Ron Athey came to her mind, an extreme performance artist she had seen at the Performance Space 122 in the East Village. The boldness of his act—a ritual scarification—had terrified her.

It was now or never, she wrote, *my break with convention*. She searched the medicine cabinet in the head and found a box of single-edge razors. Holding her breath, her heart pounding, she took a razor and cut an inch-long line on her left forearm. Mesmerized by the sight of blood, she became slightly nauseated but felt no pain. She was amazed by what she had just done.

Her journal recorded that the first cut—symbolic, iconic— was for my mother. She then made a second cut on her arm for me. Her tribal scarification was meant to show everyone else that she was different, special, not just the same old, same old, a beautiful girl among many beautiful women. She wanted a permanent bond with the people she loved, intimacy until death do us part. It was in that instant that she understood why fate had possessed her body to make her pregnant: it wasn't the poltergeist she had first imagined, a sexual whore, but a good spirit that had come to guide her toward having a child, a living offering to the memory of my mother.

She would keep the baby for Sara.

This recognition came as a sudden and powerful revelation—a vision, an enactment of a bright future. Once this was settled, she couldn't shake it, and it changed everything that followed. She would have the baby. She would keep the baby. She would have to come to terms with Rick and let him know.

She activated an air-powered flush to warn Rick to stay away while she finished cutting to mark the loves of her life. Her forearm tingled and her breathing slowed. Bracing her arm, she made a third parallel cut and then a fourth. The last two cuts were for the unborn baby and for Rick. She couldn't leave Rick, abandon him, in part because she loved him, in part because she saw him precious, in part because he was such an innocent swept up in the carnival of faith, and in some ways he seemed incapable of handling life on earth.

She took the razor and a box of gauze pads and seated herself in the main cabin. By now she was drifting into a zone of disassociated feelings. A little woozy, light-headed, tingly. Not quite lucid, no longer in perfect control, but happy, relieved—she had decided to face the inevitable. She had done the worst possible thing to her body, disfigured her forearm, and she was no longer afraid. Not afraid of public embarrassment or uncertainty, not afraid of being exposed.

chapter 6

The click-click sounds of the autopilot gears at the rear of the boat barely registered on her. She was in a free-floating state. The porthole alongside her head had a streak of blood on the rim where she had touched it accidentally. The swish of sails and the clatter of blocks on deck diminished and the whispering hull resumed its progress across the sound. She listened to the overlapping waves curling on either side of the boat and watched the blood from the four cuts mingling.

"Angel?"

She didn't startle. She looked up, she was doe-eyed, misty with affection, and saw his boat shoes, and then his drawn face. She had not heard him step onto the companionway. His eyes were hollowed-out bright and his face was ashen, aging by the second. She placed the razor on a piece of gauze and used another square to sop up the blood on her arm.

"What's going on?" Rick asked.

His voice choked but his coloring returned, and then came a softer look. Rick could not read the fine and elusive in her, the circular moods that kept them together. She wasn't much better at reading his moods. He went on, whisper quiet. "A tattoo would have been less disfiguring."

The boat took a swell and fell steeply into a trough. They grabbed handholds to steady themselves, and Rick, letting go of his hold, embraced her. She met his eyes, his innocent eyes brightened by fear, and touched his smooth skin and light eyebrows, and tried to soothe his disquieting innocence. He had surrendered too much of himself to his faith. He said something, murmured it, but she wasn't sure what he was saying. It seemed so fuzzy, so tone altered, hanging in the injured air between them. Maybe he wasn't speaking at all, maybe she was only dreaming about hearing him speak, and then she heard her voice, or possibly not.

"I'm pregnant," she said.

She would replay the next few moments for the rest of her life.

"What?" he whispered.

"I'm pregnant."

"We haven't slept—"

His eyes were alarmed and vacant at once. There was nothing looking back. No criticism, no judgments. Rick started to beat his forehead against a cabin locker, louder and louder against the teak trim. The rapture and abandonment and extreme emotion she had wanted to choreograph from the safety of a safe marriage had invaded her personal life.

The wind was up and the vessel sailed on. "The boat," she

said. It was sailing on autopilot without its captain. He didn't hear her. "The boat," she pleaded. He was the ship's captain. "You have to go back on deck."

He still didn't hear her. He was trying to destroy his forehead. She had misjudged him. He was suddenly different, deranged. He was trying to kill himself because she was pregnant.

A steady blast from a sea horn stunned them. His forehead was bloodied and the blood from her arms had smeared blood over the both of them. The sea horn was wailing, warning of a collision. He lurched and grabbed both handrails to pull himself upward on the companionway stairs. He disengaged the autopilot and swung the wheel smartly starboard. The vessels passed several feet apart and it was quiet again, except for the susurrus wind and the sea.

She couldn't ignore his bloodied forehead and tried to clean it with a towel and water from a water bottle. What insanity had possessed her to reveal her pregnancy? What could she have been thinking?

"Pregnant," he said.

"Did I say that? I was dreaming. I must have zoned out."

"I heard you."

"I—"

"Pregnant!"

Almost imperceptibly, she nodded her head. "What are we going to do?"

Rick looked up at the wind wane and the radar on the mast. "Dear God," he asked the sky, and then as he turned to face her a chilling formality came to his eyes. "You're with child."

"You have every right to be angry."

"Get it adopted."

"You want me to give away my baby?"

He tightened the jib. "It's going to make somebody happy to have your kid. I'll borrow the money to send you to Lithuania. Have it in secret, your love child." His low voice made her cringe.

"You're ashamed of me?"

"No one will know. I'll tell them you're on tour."

The fact that she was Lithuanian rarely intruded on their lives because she had changed her name several times and spoke colloquial English. "You won't love my baby?"

"If they don't do adoptions then—"

Her chest felt a weight; her mind seemed detached. Her own sins were no longer so urgent. She had a new responsibility—she had to protect her baby, Sara's grandchild. "My baby will be born American."

"If you don't give it up—"

"Don't—"

"We'll never be close again. You'll look out for *your* kid and think what you've missed with the other guy."

"I'll never stop hating you if you force me to give up my baby."

This stopped Rick; in fact, it stunned him. "Hate me?"

"Hate you every day of my life left."

"Ah, ahhh, I'm—" He gagged, and then continued. "Hate me on account of the guy who dumped you?"

"There's no other guy."

"The Immaculate fuckin' Conception."

He got his dogma wrong. The Immaculate Conception had nothing to do with sex. It meant that Mary, Mother of Christ, was born without original sin.

"The Virgin birth!" he shouted.

Her own fury now blazed. "Don't say any trash thing you'll regret."

"A fucking bastard kid."

"Just one more creepy thing—"

"Jay Bradbury, that fuckin' son of a bitch."

This stunned her. Her mouth was open. Of course, he would think she was carrying her former lover's baby.

"I'll kill the son of a bitch."

Why were the stars so desperately aligned against her? She spoke without thinking: "Say another evil thing and I'm outta here. Gone from your life."

Her warnings finally caught his total attention. "Gone from my life?" he said, quivering with tension, disbelieving. It was inconceivable.

"Gone."

"Don't say gone."

The man was devoted to her. He couldn't bear to lose her. She was the most beautiful and lasting connection to life he'd ever experienced.

"Gone," she said.

He became meek, ready to reconcile. He let loose the sheets controlling the sails and set the sails flapping. The terrible noise made talking impossible and he let the sail flap for several minutes before altering course and allowing the sails to billow downwind. They sailed on with a new acceptance for each other's differences that could have been mistaken for a cease-fire; they shared a mutual wish to hold steady in rough seas. Her journal revealed that they anchored overnight before sailing home.

I tell him again that Jay isn't the baby's father and then submit to lovemaking. The sheets are damp and humidity clings to our naked bodies. He says that he'll never leave me. It runs like a mantra: Never, never, never. There's a change in the warm air as he says this, and I'm happy he doesn't mention Jay again. We sail home in a strange mood of closeness, more silent than usual, paying greater attention to the sea things around us, an eddy, a flood of choppy, irregular waves, the seagulls, the distant clouds, and we dock without further incident.

chapter 7

She was excited to take her first steps toward a good birth and called Dr. Wilson's office to make an appointment. The doctor was Rick's friend and she got in right away even though she hadn't told the receptionist why she wanted to see the doctor. She wore a long-sleeve blouse to hide the healing welts on her forearm, and having arrived early, she fidgeted, crossing and uncrossing her legs. At last she was directed into Dr. Wilson's inner office. He had stacks of a diocesan magazine on his desk. A mock-up for the new issue was open to the blazing headline "RU-486 Abortion: Satan's Morning-After Revenge." And another, "Misoprostol Condemns Women to Hell."

Misoprostol was an anti-ulcer drug that could also induce medical abortions. The doctor asked her to take a seat but his attention was focused on the magazine layout in front of him. He financed its publication and was known for his support of the Latin Mass. His devotion to moral positions was so unbending that he had become a source of diocesan gossip. Even Sister St. Ambrose rolled her eyes to indicate her uneasiness with Dr. Wilson's ironclad convictions.

"I'm not sure the headline works," he said. He was a tidy man. Physically fit and balding, he looked like a monk with an oversize tonsure.

"How about, 'The Morning-After Pill: Is it Right for You?'" Emily asked.

The doctor leaned back in his huge executive chair. "You're being ironic," he said with a burst of laughter and appreciation. "We Catholics don't do irony."

"That was a straight-up suggestion."

"Oh, no? Don't tell me? Please. You're not one of those liberals?"

"Progressive?"

The word was distasteful to him. "I wouldn't prescribe a baby-killer pill to anyone. I wouldn't do it even if the law says I had to." He steepled his fingers. "We need tougher bishops in this country. Tougher laws, too. His Eminence in Brazil excommunicated the mother of a nine-year-old because she authorized a physician to give her child an abortion."

"A nine-year-old?" Emily was a horrified.

"Rape, incest. Who the heck knows? God sees everything. Forgives all."

No matter what position God took, Emily didn't approve. Besides, where was the equal treatment she expected under God's law? It appeared that God gave men more slack in the sin department. The doctor shrugged. He praised the bishop of Phoenix, Arizona, for excommunicating a hospital

administrator, a Sister, who authorized a medically necessary abortion to safeguard the mother. He went on to praise
Ireland, where all abortions are illegal. "It's the principle of the
thing—life is precious."

A woman in one Irish hospital pleaded that doctors save
her life by inducing labor. They refused. The baby died and
the mother died a slow, agonizing death. "That was a tough
one," Dr. Wilson conceded. "Mother and child went to meet
their Maker in heaven." The woman wasn't even a Catholic,
The Irish Times reported.

In Chile, where all abortions are also forbidden, women are
forced to carry abnormal fetuses to term. The state doesn't pro-
vide financial aid to support the unfortunate life, and the burden remains with the woman. But if the woman aborted then
she could be jailed for five to ten years thanks to laws passed by
the dictator Gen. Augusto Pinochet.

"Enough of that. How's Rick doing? All the guys feel
badly for him going bankrupt." Rick and Wilson were members of the local Knights of Columbus council and frequently
worked alongside Father Dan on charitable undertakings in
the parish. "Going bust like that, flat-on-his-ass, broken-bum
bust, so unexpected. Bankruptcy? Nerves and depression, and
unable to sleep? It's the pits. He's a proud man, so he didn't
approach me for help. I'm assuming that's why you came to see
me. To talk about him."

The altered course of their conversation caught her by surprise, but it also gave her an escape. "That's right. It's about
Rick. He's stressed and overworked." She had come for an ob-
gyn referral, but now she wanted to flee.

"Darn bad luck. Bankruptcy could give anyone a jolt. Makes guys tighten up." The doctor reached for his prescription pad. "Notwithstanding the ads for Cialis and Viagra, some guys are afraid to ask for help."

"Yes, I like the bathtub ads. Very romantic, relaxing."

"He's really tight, really bad?"

She made a so-so gesture with her hand.

"How many times do you guys get it on each week?"

She smiled and didn't answer. The doctor pushed on, advancing his curiosity. "Change positions?"

"Hmmm." She was repelled by his intrusion into her private life.

"Variety," the doctor suggested. "That could loosen Rick up."

"Yes, loosen him up."

Sara had taken Emily to see the artist Matthew Barney's *Cremaster* film cycle, named after the cremaster muscle, which raises and lowers a man's testes in response to temperature variations.

"Up and down," Emily said. She covered her mouth to stifle a laugh.

"It's not funny to guys," Dr. Wilson said.

Silence held them a moment. "Rick doesn't want me to talk about it."

"Yes, it's unfortunate," Dr. Wilson conceded. "I understand where you're coming from."

She hadn't said a thing about herself; he had no idea where she was coming from, and she was beginning to dislike him.

He nodded his head. "Truth is, I don't prescribe sex-performance drugs for recreational male use, but I've known Rick since he was a kid. You guys want a family. I know he wants a family. Not just, you know…not just, well, it's best left unsaid. No matter how bad times are for you guys, I know he wants a family." She forced herself to remain still. "He wouldn't want my help just to have, you know, just for fun. That's not in God's plan, I'm saying."

"You're saying."

He wrote a Viagra prescription for Rick and leaned back in his chair. "This will help you, too."

She slipped the erectile dysfunction prescription into her bag.

"While you're here, please give me your take on this." Dr. Wilson showed her a letter. "I've just asked Sister St. Ambrose to organize a cadre of our best kids to keep an eye on their schoolmates' sexual activities. A sort of peer-to-peer oversight group."

"Looking for sex?"

"Well—"

"What's wrong with the kids?"

"The Internet."

"A faith-based school surveillance program?" She could hardly believe it. If God was watching out all the time for sin, why did He need to have a gang of kids helping Him?

"We have to do something. Sex is rampant today."

"Wasn't it, uhmm, rampant before?"

"We're sinners."

"You want me to say it's okay to teach kids to spy and tattle on each other?" She had been born in a country that was once authoritarian; she was sensitive to the ugliness of nations built with the help of citizen spies. "How about sex education?"

"I can't believe you're saying that."

His tone irritated her. It was dominant. Confident. Convinced. Confirmed. He had made a fortune with a private clinic upstate that treated priests and Catholic laity for sexual disorders. He noticed her readiness to leave. "I've been talking with Father Dan about David."

"David? Why David?"

"Yes, Sister's 'Spoza'. We have an obligation to reform his spiritual life."

"David is Jewish."

It's true. My father was a gentile, but according to Jewish matrilineal tradition I was Jewish, and according to my mother's tradition, nonobservant. My grandfather on my mother's side had provided medical services to Catholic hospitals, and the diocese remembered him gratefully after he'd died by granting his daughter's only son, me, a tuition-free ride at Holy Redeemer High School.

"Well, we can work on that." The doctor clasped his hands. He mentioned an organization called Jews for Jesus but didn't push it. They chatted amiably for a few minutes about the upcoming school auction. Then, Dr. Wilson stood politely and they said goodbye. Out on Fifth Avenue she tore up Rick's prescription and tossed it into the city trash receptacle.

r. Wilson's invasion into the private domain of faith and marriage intimacy upset Emily, and she hadn't gotten the ob-gyn name she needed. She went to see my mother hoping to find relief; instead she found a woman coarsened by illness and pain. The good news was that Sara had been admitted to the Fred Hutchinson Cancer Research Center in Seattle. Emily asked if she wanted her ex, Alex, my father, the man who had dumped us to pursue his own dreams, notified of her illness.

"Babe, the only thing Alex and I agreed on was that our marriage was a disaster and left us with broken furniture."

My mother didn't want to be morbid, but insisted on taking care of several issues just in case the worse would happen. They talked a long time. Emily promised to see to it that her MoMA PS1 retrospective art show would go on as scheduled. She also agreed to act as my mother's executor and arrange for the sale of her artworks to help pay for my education in the event the Hutchinson treatment failed, and she agreed to become my legal guardian, if that was what was finally and unfortunately needed.

There were housekeeping issues, too. Emily said she'd persuade Rick to rent an apartment in my mother's brownstone to help Sara's finances. Emily agreed to everything, and had my mother asked her to jump out the window, I think Emily would have agreed to do that, too.

There was plenty of love in these designs and instructions, lots of hope, a future, a bond to connect them. Her relationship with my mother had an intimacy that was closer than the closeness offered by a shared bed, because they shared each other's dreams. But more disturbing, at least from Emily's side, was Sara's insistence that from that time onward they had to stop visiting and speaking to each other in order to let Emily concentrate on her choreography and dance preparations.

"It's the least I can do for you," Sara said. She wasn't afraid to show weakness confronting her own death. She'd hoped for the best and could accept the worse. She quoted Jean-Paul Sartre preparing for death: "…certain that the last burst of my heart would be inscribed on the last volume of my works, and that death would be taking only a dead man."

At any rate, Sara didn't want to distract Emily from her career. That was the deal, my mother's contribution. "You have your Alaskan tour coming up, you have Jacob's Pillow." She waved a hand in annoyance at Emily's objections. My mother wasn't going to complain about injustice, bad luck, or the worst part when the end is prematurely near, have anyone hear her cry. "I want you to make dances for me." That's how their vow of silence was sealed. She demanded that only text messages and the occasional recorded voice mail pass between them until Sara was in remission. Emily pressed her hand in agreement and they held each other, hoping that my mother would live longer than the seven months one oncologist had predicted.

Emily's sleeve got nudged higher, exposing the tribal cuts on her forearm.

"What has that guy done to you!" Sara exclaimed. She seized Emily's arm to see the cuts.

"I, well, I, you see—Rick isn't to blame."

"You're into *cutting* yourself?" There was panic and anger in my mother's voice. "You foolish girl!"

"Please—"

"Punishing yourself, hurting yourself? That's pathetic. That's psychotic. That's Rick's Catholicism poisoning you. Get rid of him! The tortured soul. Alex, my ex, was a Catholic. He was into torturing *me*."

"I don't want to talk about it."

My mother calmed down and apologized for speaking disrespectfully about another faith's derelictions and dispositions. They kissed and hugged, and Emily fought off a terrible premonition that Sara might not survive.

chapter 9

Emily went to work her regular shift at Sam's diner. The diner's owner was a gregarious man, large and energetic, and a knowledgeable fan of dance. He paid her more than the rate he paid other employees. He boasted that the extra pay was his contribution to the arts. No spendthrift, he also employed me at minimum wage.

On that day the cook had to run out to buy parsley and the boss had left to help his son out of some trouble at school. Emily checked to see if we had enough egg salad to last through the lunch rush and finding the supply low, started to make a fresh batch. She shelled the boiled eggs and broke them up in a bowl. She added the mayo and chopped the tiny pickles and then diced some onions and added a few capers. I was outside the diner sweeping the sidewalk. She admitted in her journal that she felt close to me and yet at a safe distance.

I swept the front of the diner and gave the broom a couple of good whacks on the curb to dust it off. No slouch and no slacker, I was somewhat like Rick in that I was serious about my work. I finished sweeping the sidewalk and went inside to clean the grill. I moved the cleaning block exactly six inches every time, cleaning one swath after another, steady and regular, blending the silver trails. As I worked, I told Emily the play I'd been writing to impress my high school teacher, Sister St. Ambrose.

"I'm dealing with a priestly character. My guy is a straight shooter like Rick."

"You're a Jewish kid. You're supposed to write what you know. Why would you want to do a priestly play?"

"No one asked Shakespeare why he wanted to do Cleopatra. No one said he was a cross-dresser."

"So now you're Shakespeare?"

I said nothing.

"Stick with what you know."

"And remain ignorant?"

"Rick says the truth was discovered centuries ago. He's not going to root around reinventing it."

"That would be stupid."

"He's got a lot of smart things to say."

"I like him—too bad he doesn't like me."

"He thinks you've been spoiled by Sara."

"What's wrong with me wanting to explore what it means to be one of the divinely anointed in a skeptical secular world?"

"Is Sister St. Ambrose encouraging this?"

"I'm within my rights as a Jewish student. The Christian Bible is three-quarters Hebrew Scripture."

Emily said nothing. I said nothing, and we kept working.

Sister St. Ambrose had given me a playful nickname. "You know why Sister calls me 'Spoza'?"

"Something to do with Lollapalooza?"

"Music? She's not into music. She took *suppose* and smashed it up against a clipped *Spinoza* and got *Spoza*." Unashamed and a little arrogant, I knew only odd pieces of history; overall, I was better informed than kids in school, but I pretended to know a lot more than I did.

"Why don't you ask me about Spinoza?"

She shook her head no. She wasn't interested. She had the spatula in her hand, determined to mash eggs. I went on anyway. "Spinoza got kicked out from the Amsterdam Jewish community for 'abominable heresies and monstrous deeds,' which turned out to be his denunciation of 'bondage' to religious zealotry and his rejection of the idea of personal immortality in the hereafter."

"Could you get me the onions?" She pointed to the storage area.

I went to get them. "He totally believed that organized religions were organized superstitions, and that the Bible wasn't the word of God but a 'corrupted and mutilated document' passed down from human writings." I was Sister St. Ambrose's smartest student and her most vigilant provocateur. Half the time Emily didn't know if what I was saying was truth. She blew a lock of her hair out from in front of her eyes. "Why be a pest?"

This was a good question. Why did I want to be a pest? Maybe I had an underlying need to sabotage my relationships. I never learned why, or what to do about it.

"I love Sister St. Ambrose," I said.

"Then do something uplifting for her. Mention her involvement with the Leadership Conference of Women Religious."

"I got a title: *Nuns Riot*."

Emily kept working.

"The Leadership Conference of Women Religious would be a good background for your play."

"But I'm not into that."

"What? What are you into?"

I was into Emily, but I couldn't say that. I said, "I need a man to use as a model, a man I could learn to embrace or avoid, you know, like everybody needs models, a man model for me, a strong guy or a weak man, a good guy or bad man, just a man, any man."

"Ask Father Dan to help you."

I glanced at her skeptically.

She had little interest in all that, and showed less patience with me. "Okay, then talk to Rick."

"He could have been a priest."

Now we were at the heart of her complex marriage. Rick had chosen the wrong calling. He shouldn't have married. He was compassionate, dutiful, devout, and eager to help the poor and disadvantaged, if only he had the money to do it. But as the son of immigrant parents, he had pursued business and management as the only reasonable way for a guy without wealthy mentors or a powerful family to get beyond the work-ingman's hand-to-mouth existence his parents had lived when he was growing up.

A lover he was not. He would have made a fine priest.

I finished working the grill. "I saw a great movie last night. This guy in it says, 'It's not good to meet the right person either too soon or too late in your life.' Kinda like us. You know what I mean? Like, well, like me being too young for you?"

Our difference in age back then had seemed enormous to me because at twenty-four she had been the "older" woman. Today, the seven-year difference amounted to an absent-minded flicker of time.

She didn't know how to answer me. She could scold me or she could remain silent. She knew that I could betray her. Tell my mother. Turn her over to the cops. Our lovemaking had altered the sexual landscape and tilted power in my direction. My gaze loitered on her hair as she tried to purge the warm feeling inside her.

I pushed on. "I'm older than Juliet was in *Romeo and Juliet*."

"So what?"

"I'm older than Romeo, too."

"There are other things to think about."

"Just because my age makes me illegal in some states and legal in other states—"

"You're going to tell me that Juliet was thirteen and Romeo was sixteen and Shakespeare only knows what age when he wrote that play."

"His heart was young."

"My heart betrayed me."

"It doesn't feel bad to me. Not in *my* heart."

That was an understatement.

She had seen me grow from a gawky adolescent to a new adult. It would have been difficult for anyone to think of me as a child who needed the government's protection. And now that I think about it, yes, young boys and girls need protection—mostly they need protection from predatory males. But boys my age and my size eager to love a woman shouldn't hazard a woman's prosecution and jail time.

"I'm old enough to give my consent." I pushed on. "Rick doesn't satisfy you."

This was possibly the worst thing I could have said. Secrets and silence are the twin guards around people's sexual lives. Her face turned red. She didn't want anyone to know that she wasn't living up to lovemaking standards reported by *Cosmo*.

At any rate, she was unprepared to deal with my dramatic queries, my wordiness, my blog throwaways and Twitter provocations. And since I brought up Twitter, which even the Pope has used, I should mention that I've taken temporal narrative liberties to describe the making of *Morning Light* by foreshortening and juggling the order of scenes to eliminate dull moments and to emphasize contemporary events.

I hope you don't mind.

My license comes from many sources. I picked up my know-it-all but reliable Stage Manager outlook from Thornton Wilder's *Our Town* Stage Manager, and I got the rest from Luigi Pirandello's *Six Characters in Search of an Author*. By using both of these playwrights as models, I latched on to the postmodern method—if that's what you want to call it, but just so you'll know, this so-called postmodern way to tell a story is as old as Laurence Sterne's *The Life and Opinions of Tristram Shandy,* written back in 1759.

Anyway, I tried to rescue Emily and me from a quarrel by quoting Thornton Wilder describing Shakespeare as "one of the few writers in all literature who could present a young woman as both virtuous and interesting. He fashioned nine of them and they continue to affect the spiritual weather of the world."

"Virtuous and interesting? You're criticizing me?"

"No. I was just talking."

"Just talking and criticizing."

Emily walked to the fridge to find more eggs and took a carton out of the fridge. "We didn't, I couldn't, I shouldn't. I'm sorry."

"You want to, I want to."

"You're a border-crashing culture-shocking collection of youth-colored opinions I'm beginning to dislike."

"That's very good," I said. "May I use the lines in my play?"

She laughed uncomfortably. I was over-the-top and I was poking fun at her, prying into the special recesses of her character. She resisted, and pointing at her chest said, "This is *me*, with egg salad." And then she gestured to the wall mirror. "There's me on stage dancing. I'm seductive, alluring and sexy, strikingly photographed, and attractive to you and to strangers and who knows what? Some wretched serial killer among them."

"That's awesomely negative."

She smacked a spatula against a steel bowl. "You'll never let go of me? Never let go of what we've done!"

"Are you angry with me?"

"No, I'm flattered. Or I was flattered and I shouldn't have been flattered."

"I can't stop thinking about it," I said.

Her face was flushed, and her hair highlights seemed to glow. I looked at her reflection in the mirror. She had dancer's legs, grace and lightness on the boards. Her strength was in her torso, shoulders, and ankles, flexible and strong, carrying her through four and as much as six hours of practice every day.

"I'm sorry," she said.

"You said that before."

Her journal said that the attraction lingered. She knew it could ruin her marriage, wreck her career, and send her to prison. She gripped the spatula and blended the chopped celery and onions into the salad. "It's all just growing up for you, this sex thing, play-acting, theater. The theater of the absurd. You don't want me. You want sex."

"I want that, too."

She pushed the salad closer to me. "Eat this before the lunch crowd hits us." Her voice was brusque and businesslike. She expected the cook to return any moment, and a waitress was scheduled to start her shift. "I'm not going to live a divided life between you and my loyalty to Rick and Sara, divided in what I think is right and wrong."

I looked at her. "My life is going to be all of a piece."

She wished she had my confidence. I was athletic, fine nostrils flaring, my face vaguely feminine yet unmistakably male.

Just then a foursome of early lunch customers came in. Two of them wanted egg salad sandwiches, and two asked for the daily omelet special. I set up their drinks and Emily prepared the dishes. Her movements were quick and precise, mine equally so as we did the grill work, plated the sandwiches,

added the relish, and dished up the omelets. We were like dancers in the narrow space between the grill and the counter. With
a coffeepot in my hand, I needed to slide past her to give the
customers a refill. I stopped and paused and waited. We were
pelvis to pelvis. I didn't think this pause and step-in-place jostle
was overtly sexual, but in retrospect—it was.

The customers quieted. "Excuse me," one of them said.

From her journal I learned that Emily's heart was racing.
She was transfixed by an inward flush that coursed through her
body. I gave her a casual bump and spun away. The customers
finished eating and settled their bill at the cash register. Emily
was clearing their plates and saw that they had left no tip, but
one of them, a woman, had inked a message on a napkin.

"You slut!" it read.

She stared at it, disbelieving the words. I smoothed the
wrinkled napkin on the counter until we could see the expan-
sive handwriting more clearly. *You slut!* My first impulse was to
laugh but Emily recoiled as if a car door had slammed the side
of her head. She accepted the blame. *You slut.*

chapter 10

As I looked over her journals, I understood my job was that of a librarian and curator. I had to select, rearrange and organize as if I was handling an artist's midlife career retrospective. There were patterns and events that repeated and duplicated. I kept a number of repetitions. It was a sort of call and response, will against nature. With each circuit past a similar event, she was learning more about herself.

The day she went to a Holy Redeemer annual fund-raising campaign meeting, Page Bradbury, Dr. Wilson, and Jay were present. She smiled warmly at Jay. She didn't dislike him, and the smile was honest. She understood now that he had been too wealthy for her, and that she had been too young and unpolished to be his girlfriend. At the end of the affair, she'd left him with her conscience intact.

Jay was part of the male world that was so privileged, so endowed with financial gifts they didn't have to earn, so entitled and so uninhibited in their expectation that the world belonged to them, that she couldn't have understood it when she was a teenager. His parents launched Jay at twenty-five with a trust fund in excess of twelve million dollars, and now that he was in his fifties, married to the much younger Page, he believed he deserved everything that he'd gotten from his parents without having to work for it and railed against "death taxes" as a socialist idea to diminish his inheritance.

During a break in the school budget presentations, Jay whispered an invitation to Emily to join him for a chat in the school cafeteria. They sat at a folding table across from each other. Her original attraction to Jay had to be one of the mysteries of her life. He was much older than she was. She didn't think she had used him, despite a niggling doubt that she might have. And now, as she cruised the private territories of her mind, recalling that Jay had asked her out when she was an impressionable girl, a foreigner, a teenager, and easily awed by a man who was forceful, arrogant, and wealthy, she forgave herself her youthful misdemeanors.

She listened carefully, trying to be engaging and attentive even though her mind wandered. His salted hair was closely trimmed, and he used lots of product to make it stand; his eyes had a flickering quickness, as if they were throwing small jabs at you.

"So I hear you're mutilating yourself," he said.

She was stunned, unable to speak. "Mutilating?" she finally said. "You think I'm crazy?" She made sure her sleeve covered her forearm. Apparently, the scars on her arm were a threat to the common order; she had become an outlier. Cotton Mather would have considered her a witch. "Is this about me?"

He shook his head. "You left me so suddenly."

"Are you still bruised?"

"A little battered."

"You're married."

"So are you."

She'd meant him no harm. "You never asked me to marry you."

"I was thinking about it."

"But you married Page."

"On the rebound." He looked unsure of himself. "Would you have agreed to marry had I asked you?"

"Oh, Jay. I was too young for you. A silly girl." She felt like kissing him on the nose.

Her journal had a confusion of notes to mark this incident. It wasn't clear when she added the marginalia, a gloss on what she'd written earlier. I suspect that it might have been before she married Rick. This marriage thing kept repeating in her journal. Today people do and don't get married and live together, having and raising children. But she was from the Old World and traditional marriage remained big in her mind, even if less certain. One thing is clear, she'd picked up a copy of a novella written by Jane Austen, *Lady Susan*. It's hardly known today, and rarely discussed. It's not clear where Emily got it. Possibly from the Strand bookstore, or maybe from a Village street vendor selling books the NYU and New School students had gotten rid of at the end of a literature class. Jane Austen was nineteen when she'd written the book, but it wasn't published until fifty years after her death.

The suppressed work is the antithesis of the Jane Austen proto-feminist, middle-class "lady" novels we learned to admire. Written in an epistolary fashion, it revealed the working mind of a scheming, intelligent, and sexually adventurous woman, the aforementioned Lady Susan, an attractive and witty widow in her thirties who won her title from an aristocrat she survived. Susan was anything but morally scintillating in her liaisons. This was the young Jane Austen writing? What could she have been thinking? Lady Susan was so different from the moral archetypes portrayed in her other novels, it could have been written by Anaïs Nin when she was dating Henry Miller. In any case, from this book, Emily had copied and underlined the dialogue of a woman criticizing another for marrying an older man, who was "Too old to be agreeable, and too young to die."

I wondered if this singular line, like the word *Rosebud* on a sled in Orson Welles's *Citizen Kane*, was the secret emotional wisdom that led to Emily's breakup with Jay. The bad feelings Jay had experienced over their breakup were not truly visible, and she wanted him to hire Rick. Jay's vigorous style remained seductive. She smiled.

"Thank God I won't have to use a sledgehammer to get a smile out of you," Jay said.

"Not a sledgehammer," she promised. After all, their breakup had been a no-fault event, and she was fond of him in the way she could be fond of a grandfather. They both looked past each other. She was thinking about interviewing male dancers, her schedule, her appointment with her ob-gyn, costumes, and Sara's longing to live.

"You sure chat up a storm," he said.

But he didn't seem to mind that she didn't chat that much, and he made up for it with his own urgent need to speak uninterrupted. He had married Page and he was running his father's company. Then, perhaps sensing her boredom, eager to get closer to the past he had shared with her, he said he had recently bought a painting of Narcissus and Echo that was painted in the late Renaissance, though the painting's provenance was uncertain.

"I was thinking of you when I bought the painting."

She tried humor. "I'm such a waste of your time."

"I've never gotten over you."

She was pleased. A win. Maybe he'll hire Rick.

"I'm a strange duck," she said. "I'm not that interesting."

"I was hoping we could be friends again."

"Jay, we are friends."

The unexpected and unplanned. She plunged into a small deception. "Rick and I are *both* your friends," she said cheerfully. "He thinks you're terrific! He would *love* to work for you. He thinks you're a great guy!" *Dear God, please please forgive me.*

His voice dropped a register. "I'll hire him if you ask me to."

The sudden tension caught her cold. "Yes, I'm asking you. Please. And I'm asking you to keep this private between us."

"A secret?"

"A small one."

"I'd like to see you more often."

She realized where this was going. He wasn't a man used to asking anyone for a favor. He bought things, he paid for services, and now he looked away, embarrassed because he had asked for something he could not buy, and that could be denied to him. His profile seemed to melt; his age was showing.

"We can have coffee together," she said.

"Look." He glanced at the door. "I'm too quick and too demanding. It's no way to make a sale." He appeared uncertain of what to say next. She let the moment of ambiguity slide.

"When can Rick start work?"

"I'll have a letter in the mail to him tomorrow." He was abrupt.

She thanked him, and remembered to ask how Page was doing. But he didn't want to talk anymore and they returned to the meeting.

Emily described to me Jay's changing taste in pictures. I was doing my homework on ancient Greek playwrights when she told me about it. By then I'd taken many of Sister St. Ambrose's classes steeped in ancient classics, and had followed up with independent study. I was proud of my knowledge.

"You've heard the story of Narcissus and Echo?" I asked.

Emily was pleasantly mystified. "Go on."

"Narcissus doesn't love Echo, you see, because, he's like too busy loving himself. So Echo, who of course loves him like crazy, wastes away and when she dies only her voice remains, echoing his."

"That's it?"

I rubbed my palm, searching for another thing to say,

another way to intrigue her, keep her interested in me, and keep her with me. "There are two more versions."

"Happier, I hope."

"I'll let you decide. In one version Pan plays a flute so sweetly that trees in a grazing area used by shepherds start to dance to his music. Echo spurns him in favor of a satyr full of another kind of life. Pan wants revenge, so he drives the shepherds mad with his music and they tear Echo to shreds, leaving only her voice."

"It's all about Echo?"

"Yes."

"I'm Echo?" She was cheerfully curious.

"Okay, there is another version many people like best. Echo gets her wish to be with her lover, but they're reunited only in longing and not in the body, her voice echoing the last two syllables of his cry for her before he loses her."

"How sad."

The last Echo story reminded her of the Catholic version of love, borrowed from the Greek *agape*, ethereal rather than physical, selfless love, all of it in the spirit and the body condemned to melancholy longing.

"Do you like the last take on Echo?" she asked.

I had little insight into my own youth, but that one I got right—"I'm too young to like the sexless version."

chapter 11

That weekend Emily boarded the *Miscellaneous Expense* again. She hadn't planned to go sailing so soon, but she couldn't avoid it either. Rick said he needed her company. He gave her a peck on the cheek. "I'm worried," he said. "You're turning into a stray soul."

"I've strayed all right." She smiled at her joke.

He stroked her hair. She had done the math and knew she could make it through Jacob's Pillow before the end of the first trimester. The cuts on her forearm were still puckered.

"Angel, please sign in at Wilson's upstate clinic for a rest."

The idea repulsed her. The doctor's sexual probing had been repellent. He wasn't like the team of Masters and Johnson, famous for their groundbreaking studies in human sexual response. He was just a nosy guy. She was reticent about such matters and wouldn't have been a good subject anyway. She confided only to her journal. Her choreography was in transition and unfinished. She was overcommitted, and at times jittery. She now wished that she had not agreed to perform at the Midnight Sun Festival in Alaska.

"Angel, Dr. Wilson can help you."

"I don't like Wilson. I don't know what you see in him."

"Wilson is one of the finest men we have in our circle."

"I don't know what he does with his upstate patients, but I've heard awful rumors." And then it dawned on her. "You want me to—" She cringed at the insult. "He treats sexually obsessive people, doesn't he?"

"Yeah, he handles a few priests. But most of his clients are laypeople."

"It's about sex. That's why you want me to—"

"Don't take it in a bad way. You could use a break." He was holding both her arms in a way that was meant to be affectionate. She yanked herself free and brushed her forearm against the stainless steel rigging. A scab sheared away. The cut started to bleed and Rick rushed to find bandages and antibacterial cream. He treated her arm, and she felt again the closeness they had once shared. He glanced at her stomach.

"My friends, if they knew—" he stopped.

He wasn't angry, however. She was pregnant and he didn't have to worry about killing babies with contraception. Their sexual life had been restored to a degree.

She watched him disengage the autopilot and tighten the sheets to sail closer to the wind. The fresh air exhilarated her and she liked his suggestion that they go fishing near a spot they had once visited. They anchored in a cove and lowered the whaler at the stern of the boat. Minutes later the whaler's white wake fanned out behind them as they docked to buy bait at a shack. Broken sand dollars and parts of horseshoe crabs and shells tumbled below the bow as she waited for him to return. She felt a new excitement, happiness, and the courage to go in a new direction. She felt the sun and the breeze blowing onshore. Maybe it'll all work out—this was her hope put down in her journals several times, and sometimes followed by an exclamation point.

Rick returned from the shack and handed her a bait box. They pushed off, and the whaler clipped along until he killed the engine. They started to fish. He caught a flounder and then a rockfish and threw them into a catch pail. Buzzing insects brokered the silence between them. He jiggled his line and her line as well.

"When are you going to start to show?" he asked.

"Maybe not until two more months if I'm lucky. I probably won't feel it moving until after fourteen weeks. That'll get me past Jacob's Pillow."

He busied himself with the tackle box. His head was down. "I wonder what the hell I did to offend God to get this crap thrown in my face." He was thinking of Job.

She was startled. "You didn't do anything wrong. I didn't say you did anything wrong."

The fish were flopping in the pail.

"Aren't you going to kill them?" she asked. "They're suffering and desperate."

Rick's face seemed to go blank. "I'd like to kill the son of a bitch who fucked you."

The switch from calmness to violent words was so unexpected that she didn't have time to react. He grabbed a fish mallet, seized the pail, and spilled the fish out on the sole. Shouting a guttural cry, he whacked the "fucking" flounder.

"Stop it, Rick!"

His chest was heaving as he tried to catch his breath. The mallet was shining scarlet and silver. He shattered the rockfish next, scattering scales and bone and splintering the surface of the fiberglass bottom. He tore at the Brown Scapular he wore around his neck, the Scapular of Our Lady of Mount Carmel, but the leather straps wouldn't tear and he was as near strangling himself. His face looked stitched together and ready to burst.

"My God," she said. She stared at the slithering mess coming off the gunwale. "You were never violent before."

"I was a wussy, a pussy, a fuckin' dumb asshole." He was breathing heavily, gasps coming fast. "When did you fall out of love with me?"

She loathed his violent speech. "Leave me," she demanded.

He was suddenly docile. "I could *never* leave you."

He picked at the scapular and she searched the horizon above the marsh grasses. The smell of the grasses and the seashore were exhilarating. She remembered how peaceful they had once been, and she remembered how she hadn't wanted the world to intrude. And how everything had changed.

chapter 12

The following Tuesday Rick's face lighted up on seeing Emily arrive at the Auto Max salesroom. Her hands were sweaty, excitement and enthusiasm percolated along the surface of her skin, and she smiled extravagantly, a knockout smile. She slowed as she approached him. He was on one knee alongside a desk while helping a woman fill out a credit application. He mouthed a silent message that he would be free in a moment.

He had to *kneel* to do good work selling cars?

Emily composed a brief dance in her head. Her dancers take abrupt steps. Their hands flutter as if in fear or in pain, and they grimace. The music composed of sudden skittish outbursts, incomprehensible high notes, tortured, malignant, everyone dancing for the money, green bills falling, green cascading, sweeping up in a green swirl. The dancers' bodies first appear beautiful, then a little weary, a little cramped, slightly painful, bending awkwardly at the knees and the hips, and still dancing for the money. The dancers are now no longer beautiful, more stark, and stumbling, holding on to the props.

What was Rick doing now? Was he actually touching the customer's hand to close the deal? Skin-to-skin commerce—how could the woman allow this? How could Rick do it? Pitching fondness in the cause of selling a car. He was slow to touch others, reluctant to hug unless he really meant to be warm. He couldn't lie with the ease that some people managed. Politicians especially. In his business practice there was virtue to be gained in silence, but he hadn't learned the virtues of mendacity otherwise. He hadn't read the Latin scribe who professed that "he who doesn't know how to lie doesn't know how to rule." So the very sight of his touching someone in feigned affection to sell a car was repugnant, a social lie as insidious and untrustworthy as lies made of words. She took an admonishing step toward him. Clutching Jay's letter offering to hire him, she pointed to the BCC logo.

"Bradbury hired me?" Rick asked. He was still kneeling, consumed by a need to earn a commission. She nodded enthusiastically. He looked disbelieving and then grateful, and then elated. She gestured for him to get off his knees. He got up and embraced her. It felt as if they were renewing marital vows, off on new beginnings and bound to new hopes rising. The helium-filled balloons attached to the cars in the front of the store seemed to float higher.

She was thinking of this happy moment later, after Rick had started working at Bradbury Corporation. She had asked him to meet her at an East Village café after her ob-gyn exam. The results had been as expected; her nurse technician said that

all was going well but the embryo was too small for a sono-
gram to determine the sex, which was just as well because she
wanted the suspense, the anticipation and excitement of something welcome but yet unknown.

Rick strode in. The executive on the go, he was a changed
man, more intense, somewhat abrupt and deeply absorbed by
Bradbury company problems. He looked especially crisp in his
smart new suit—a man she could depend on. She raised herself
a few inches from her seat to accept his kiss and felt almost
giddy as she blurted out that her baby was developing nor-
mally. She asked him to pick a name for the child they would
raise together. A name for a girl and one for a boy.

"Why should I pick a name?"

She ignored the slight resentment she heard, but seeing that
he was sincere, she went on. "But you love me, don't you?"

"I've loved you too long to stop now."

She wondered if that was a demotion. "We can participate
in parenting?"

"But your kid won't have my blood."

"Couldn't you love my baby?"

"I'm not the uncaring guy you make me out to be."

"I've never said you're uncaring." Things were looking up.
"I'm going to convert Sara's guest room into a nursery."

"Who said we're moving into Sara's place?"

"You know, when she gets back from Seattle, from
Hutchison, when—"

My mother had kept their mutual promise, the vow of
phone silence, but texting was okay. Sara had texted that her
doctors were hopeful.

Rick swung his head adamantly to say no. He didn't want to live in Sara's place when they had their own apartment in Williamsburg.

Her mood took a dive. "You don't have to live with me."

"Angel, we can't separate. Not in your condition. I'd hate myself."

To separate or not, to live apart or not, for days on end this subject would haunt them, repeating itself. He looked at his watch and said he was late for a union contract meeting. He cracked his knuckles and she felt shadows enveloping them. Getting up, he hugged her carefully, as if hugging someone in danger of falling apart. She watched him strut on the way out, commanding the space in front of him. He was once again a boss at Bradbury Container Corporation and didn't have to kneel before customers to get them to sign a financing contract.

chapter 13

A happy normality took over. Her day began early. She pulled on her faded jeans, stonewashed in all the right places, adjusted her sweatshirt, tied her Nike cross-trainers, and grabbed her bag filled with legwarmers, tights, leotards, and extra sweats. There was now a fast-paced momentum and an impossible schedule to deal with—she was not only over-committed but also approaching exhaustion.

Rick spent a lot of time out of town on business and at work at BCC headquarters in the Red Hook section of South Brooklyn. He was so busy that her pregnancy seemed to occupy only a small corner of his mind. She was grateful for that—it suggested that a peaceful passage might follow, a stage of reconciliation where adult love bloomed anew and the revelation that she was carrying another man's baby could be reduced to the level of a misunderstanding.

Her ob-gyn in the East Village was encouraging, and Emily, her mood steadier, felt more at ease. She was careful about the food she allowed herself. She declined to have an amniocentesis—she'd heard that the procedure caused miscarriage in roughly one out of two hundred procedures. She worried that the enormous physical demands of dancing might be harmful to the baby, but the doctor assured her that that wasn't likely for a person as fit as she was.

She rode the subway to get to her studio, a large white box. The wooden floor was mounted on sturdy beams and provided an excellent and resilient surface on which to dance.

My mother's uncle had moved into her brownstone to stay with me, and I often dropped by to see Emily at her studio before going to school. We would discuss each other's efforts—I was working on a new satire. I no longer saw her at the diner. With Rick's higher income rolling in, she'd quit, and was getting ready to leave for the two-city Midnight Sun dance event in Alaska.

"I'm going to escort you," Rick said.

She'd not expected it. He seemed sincere, but he was always sincere—sincerely upset with her, and sincerely earnest to make the best of it. Sometimes he praised her to the point of embarrassing her. She was not only his better half—she was now his rock, his soul mate. She was the best, the finest.

He wrangled a few days off at Bradbury to escort her on her trip to Anchorage and Fairbanks. They'd taken a commercial flight to Alaska, and on arrival he'd rented a private plane from a flying club to fly her between the two cities. They'd made the flight to Fairbanks and were now returning to Anchorage. She watched the dual flight controls moving in tandem, suggesting two people in sync with each other. Below, the mountain streams ran silvery toward gray-green foothills. The more distant mountains were covered in a magenta hue.

She suspected that Rick, though he wanted to help her, had taken the time off because he didn't want to let her out of his sight. That aside, my mother's health was the larger problem. I knew from my uncle that the bone marrow transplant had failed to generate as many new cells as they had hoped. My mother was returning to Brooklyn early and she wasn't taking calls from any of her friends. She was on a final journey.

At the time, I didn't know about my mother's and Emily's vow not to speak to each other. Nor did I know that my mother was essentially sending Emily optimistic bullshit texts to keep her focused on her dance career. Sara had dismissed "death talk," as she had called it. With so many wonderful lies in place, Emily shook off the ominous implication that my mother's unscheduled early return to Brooklyn was bad news. She placed the tip of her finger on the cut she'd made for Sara, the first one, and gently rubbed the talismanic spot to wish my mother good luck.

The four-seat aircraft that Rick was piloting slipped past the darkened root of a cumulus cloud blossoming toward a white top.

"I'm performing my new dance in mint-colored body tights," she said.

"Hot."

"Why hot?"

"Those things make you more naked than skin."

Another dancer had called her a flower with interlocking petals rising toward her breasts. Be that as it may, she wanted to be judged on her choreography. Of course she liked it that men liked the way she looked, but that was secondary. She glanced at her husband. "I'm aiming for psychological nakedness."

"Christ," he said. "Your earlier work was a winner for you. It didn't carry anything confusing to audiences. You should stick with the winners."

"Romance. It was all about romance."

"Sticky physical crap makes audiences cringe."

"Rick, there are many bad things in life, but sensuality isn't one of them."

"Love and marriage go together."

"Like a horse and carriage?" The popular song was ancient.

"Nothing wrong in that."

She tugged on the sleeve of her sweater to expose the four chevrons she had cut in her forearm—my mother and me, the baby and Rick embodied in flesh, each a mystery, each known in only small ways. She glanced at the artificial horizon on the instrument panel. The Cessna's wings were banking sharply to the right. She was happy with her new direction in dance. The invitation to dance at Jacob's Pillow affirmed an exciting future.

A gust hit them broadside, sending shudders along the aircraft's aluminum skin. They were inches apart and she felt again the heightened sense of unease coupled with excitement that was new in her life. Her breathing quickened, each breath a shallow lick as the plane slipped through the air, spinning a little on its axis. The glare from the curved windshield blinded her, and the cabin heater warmed only her legs. She strained to keep her eye on the horizon.

"Are you trying to kill us?" she said.

"This is living, angel," he shouted above the engine noise. He was clowning for her, showing off. He pulled the plane's nose up. The control wheel quivered in his hands as he kept the aircraft in a nose-high attitude. The wings lost their bite and the aircraft started to fall to earth. "I'm doing a controlled stall."

"Stop it, Rick. I'm getting sick." He straightened and banked the Cessna to give her a better view of the glacier they wanted to hike before returning to Anchorage. He pulled down the aircraft's flaps to allow for a steep decent and they landed on the gravel landing strip nearby. He taxied to the tie-down area, and as they were getting out, he said it again, repeating himself, "I'll never leave you."

As I read this in her journals, I saw how much of their daily life repeats itself; doesn't everyone's life repeat itself? So many words said again, so many love songs, and none of us are able to live without them.

They approached the glacier, and she pointed to the faded warning signs telling them to keep out. Rick was fearless and said they could safely ignore the sign. A huge ice slab had broken from the glacier and the center of it glowed with a dirty yellow-blue light as if lighted by stage lights.

They climbed thirty yards and crossed a chasm and found a footpath on the outcropping. Below, she saw a flower making the best of a short growing season. She was struck by the isolation of the single bloom in the rock field, and according to her journal, she was thinking about me. I was coming of age in startling leaps. Abandoned by my father and worried about my mother.

A few stones tumbled along the sunny side of the chasm into the fast-moving glacial river. Rick was thirty feet higher on the climb, and backlighted by the sun. He signaled to her, but she couldn't hear what he said because of the crashing water noise from the gorge. The hillside seemed to inhale and she realized he was shouting a warning. The rocks underfoot started to move. The hill was alive and time rushed away. She didn't think they'd survive the avalanche, and she didn't mind dying, except for the fact that the baby would die, too.

All of a sudden she saw Rick hurtling toward her, his mouth wide open. He was midair, twisting frantically, sudden death in view. Their eyes locked. A jolt shot through her spine as she snatched a strap on his backpack and swung him toward the cliff.

Looking dazed, he was bruised and scratched and had a nosebleed. But she had saved him. Only then did she hear her own breathing. They did not speak for a while. The thundering water below kicked up a fine mist. They started to climb cautiously higher to the quiet side of a ridge. The rushing sounds fell away.

"You saved my life."

She looked straight ahead. "I think I need to move out."

"What for?" His cheeks were ruddy.

"I can't put you through this torment."

"I can handle it."

"You're deceiving yourself."

"We're not going to separate." He checked his watch. "Just because I was foolish in business and bankrupted us is no reason—"

"The baby?"

"—to separate?"

"What, then?"

They were deep into an emotional quagmire. Her journal entry described it:

> *I tell him I'm dreamy, and dreams can confuse, and yeah, sometimes I stumble, but my pratfalls are part of life lived and I pick myself up, change my ways. I'm tribal, my baby stays with me. I'm nature, but not all nature is good. Not violence, not illness. Sara saw the changes in me. She says we have culture to keep nature in check. But Rick can't change as easily or as quickly. I wonder how long we'll last together, though I'm the side of longevity. He's committed to making his way in the world. No man ranks anything without money, he says. I'm all about dance, about movement tied to emotion. I earn no money. The cost of such freedom is often paid in poverty. I can see myself dancing that way forever, but I'm afraid he will shatter.*

The vastness of the bleak gray-green foothills surrounded them with isolation, and the ragged white peaks made it seem that their place on Earth was awesomely small.

"Yeah, we'll do okay," he insisted. "Have kids of our own."

"Another child would be hard on us. You know, like now, like we have new responsibilities." She stroked the talismanic cuts on her arm and spoke faster. "I was waiting for the right moment to tell you. You see, I agreed to be David's guardian. That along with the baby—"

"You didn't sign anything?"

She felt a sudden darkening mood she wished she could dodge. "I did, a while back. Before Sara left for Seattle. Signed and notarized. I also promised to move in with her to be with her in her last days if her treatment doesn't take." She hesitated; he seemed to shrink away. "Please come with me."

"I'm not moving in with her." He was unwavering. "That woman *stole* you from me."

She glanced at the barren ground. "Rick, David is a big kid and can take care of himself. He won't be any trouble."

"You're talking like he's part of our family."

The air around them was desolate.

"How can you be hostile to this? With me moving in, Sara will have more strength to fight her cancer. She'll recover and I'll never have to pay on my guardianship promise."

"I'm not going to live in that house with that woman."

"Have it your way. But if you're not leaving me, if we're together I'd like you to stay with me."

He took a deep breath. "Does David know you're pregnant?"

"How could you even think that? I wouldn't tell anyone anything. No one except you and my ob-gyn office knows it."

"Not even the guy who fucked you?"

"Rick, please don't be crude."

"Our secret."

"Not unless you told someone."

He whistled dismissively. "I don't talk about our private life."

"Then how come Jay approached me about my *mutilating* myself. You told him."

"That's different. I was worried for you health. Those cuts are crazy and weird and you shouldn't have done it."

"But you told him."

"Jay got you pregnant. I wanted to make him feel guilty."

"It's not Jay. It's not him. Please let's just stop your pushing him on me. You don't know. No one will ever know."

"So the guy who got you this way doesn't know it?"

"Especially him. There are secrets worth keeping for life."

"Yeah, you and me, the gatekeepers."

She realized that their situation was dreadful. She'd not encountered it in the chick lit or romances she sometimes read for relaxation. Maybe *The Scarlet Letter* came close? But this was life, real life, and her effort to get over her doubts, failures, retractions, and repetitions. Her heart took a plunge. "First I'll stay with Sara, and then we can decide what's best for us. I'm giving you a way out of this mess. We can separate. Why don't you take it?"

"The easy way out? It's easy for you to say that. You don't love me as much as I love you."

She didn't believe that was true. She didn't say anything.

He grunted. "I'm some kind of a caretaker to you."

"No, you're not."

"You can take it or leave it, and I have to deal with it. "

She didn't answer.

They returned to the plane and were soon on the outskirts of Anchorage. The Chugach Mountains were awesomely present, and the waters of Knik Arm and Turnagain Arm visible as they circled a wide sweep before landing.

chapter 14

They landed at Ted Stevens Anchorage International Airport without further incident, returned the rented Cessna to the air club, and checked into a hotel. Emily switched on the laptop she carried everywhere and signed onto the hotel's wireless. I had sent a new e-mail. The subject line blazed: "I need you."

It made her squirm. I was precocious, already taking New School classes even though I hadn't graduated from high school. Looking back at myself, I realize that I'd been a pain in the ass, too smart for my agemates, and made myself a target for resentment.

She clicked on her photo archive to bring up my pictures. One closeup showed dark amber irises and wide eyebrows. Another shot pictured me standing broad-shouldered next to her. My faintly dimpled chin asserted a boyish maturity and my arm slung over her shoulder marked an early casualness with women. The third picture showed me with my high school drama and art teacher, Sister St. Ambrose. I held a papier-mâché shield marked with the Star of David and Sister held a cross and a sword in a pose mimicking St. Joan of Arc. We were warriors, one a nonobservant Jewish student and the other a Catholic who had dedicated her life to Jesus.

Emily took a deep breath. She couldn't identify the wellspring of her attraction to me. She loved Rick. A reasonable, well-paced love, until the fundamentalists captured his mind on the issue of birth control. Her affair with me made no sense and had set her emotional life on edge—passion that mixed the ridiculous, the illicit, and the immoral. The force of it was terrific, the sort of thing that drives people to elope, or go insane.

She looked at the subject line again. "I need you."

"Angel?"

She turned at the sound of Rick's voice.

"I'm no prude," he said, looking past her. His pale gray eyes showed a determined mood. "I'm a hardworking man who wants to have a family."

They had made a contract—they would not talk about having more children, and here he was already questioning it, revising it, amending it.

"Who said you were a prude?" She fumbled with her computer and erased my e-mail without reading it. She checked her cell and saw my number. She erased the text without reading it and then voice mail without listening to it. And finally, as Rick went on about something, she blocked my phone number and was ready to give Rick her undivided attention. She saw him gazing at her. Several clouds were brilliantly white on the horizon behind him; a few had encased the mountaintops. Maybe they were getting somewhere.

She felt a sudden modest pride in her sexual attractiveness and his desire made her feel whole. There was hope for their marriage after the baby was born. "You don't know this, but before this pregnancy you had made me pregnant."

His eyes started to glaze. "You destroyed my child?"

"I miscarried."

"You never told me. You never said anything about the most important thing in our life."

"What could you have done?"

"We could've, I could've—"

"We tried."

To satisfy his religious scruples she had at the time started to use a set of color-coded fertility cycle beads that looked like small polished ovaries, to count the days she couldn't conceive. They wouldn't have sex during those twelve fertile days marked with white beads, and a couple of days on each side for insurance. The approach was simple, natural and safe, but it was far from perfect, a crapshoot in fact. Either her eggs were exceptionally robust or his sperm were.

"But you didn't abort." He was suddenly sunny.

"Yes, I would have had our baby. Your baby. I wouldn't have given it up for adoption."

"That makes a difference. That makes a big difference."

"But you want me to give up *my* baby."

"Must we talk about it now?"

She shrugged. After the unplanned pregnancy, she had used a Magic Marker to mark off five additional beads on each side of the twelve-day fertility window. There were then twenty-two days on which not to have sex, and often the remaining good days were iffy, either due to a flu or a cold or anxiety-filled evenings, her dancing injuries, and their finances. All combined, it spelled the death of desire.

"This is powerful." He was beaming. "You didn't abort. I wish you'd have shared that with me earlier."

"There was nothing you or anyone could do about a spontaneous miscarriage. You had your problems to deal with. I didn't want to pile on more problems. "

"I thought we were closer. I thought you'd have told me."

"Oh, honey." She felt closer.

"I still want to throttle the fuckin' guy."

He was coming to terms with his unconventional marriage. He was the consort, and he still suspected Jay of being the father. He touched her forearm with the four hash marks. She told him the cuts in her arm affirmed life. "One of them is for you."

"I have to share your body with three other hash marks?" He clenched and unclenched his hands.

"One of them is for the unborn baby and one is for Sara."

He looked at her forearm. "It's the unknown hash mark that blows my mind."

But the tension subsided. After a decent night's rest she danced twice the next day to complete her commitment. That night they took a commercial red-eye flight to JFK.

chapter 15

By the time the plane reached its gate, her sleep-deprived eyes were set in half-moons. Her domestic plan was unchanged: she was moving in to live with Sara for the duration. But Rick, now that he was earning good money, didn't want to surrender their Williamsburg apartment and he didn't want to live with Sara. When the subway stopped at his station he held Emily. "Take care of yourself," he said, sounding formal. He wanted to hold her longer but the soft-padded doors began to close. He waved goodbye as the train pulled away. She took her seat and yanked her suitcase closer to her feet. They'd said they wouldn't separate, but the heavy weight of her suitcase made her feel as if they'd agreed to a trial separation anyway.

On the wall of the train a hospital advertisement showed a smiling woman with thick eyebrows and worried eyes claiming that she had received the best cancer care in the world. It was the same hospital whose doctors had sent Sara to Seattle for a marrow transplant. Emily looked away from the ad. The rattling sounds of the subway seemed to be tunneling into her soul. The silence Sara had imposed on their relationship contributed to a lingering sense of uneasiness and uncertainty. She stood up, eager to get off as the train slowed at Nostrand station, and then, breathless, she pushed her way out as soon as the doors opened.

The early-morning coolness didn't stop her from sweating, and by the time she'd reached Sara's brownstone her underarms felt wet. She climbed the wide steps and let herself in without ringing the bell.

"Sara, I'm back!"

The silence was crushing.

"I'm back," she whispered. The walls absorbed her voice.

She dropped the suitcase and took the stairs that led to the ground floor. The spare oxygen cylinder kept at the bottom of the stairs near Sara's sickroom had been taken away. The medicinal smell, part stale bread and part chlorine, had not dissipated, and the sliding pocket doors to Sara's basement room were wide open.

Not wanting to disturb her if she was sleeping, Emily descended in stealth-quiet steps, grimacing when the old wooden staircase creaked. Sara's room was unlit and the window shades pulled. It took a moment for her eyes to adjust. She jumped when she saw me sitting on the floor. I didn't have shoes on and my cheeks were smudged. She dropped to the floor and sat back on her heels. She didn't have to ask what had happened. My mother had planned it all. She had imposed a curtain of silence, returned home to die, and managed her exit with painkiller prescriptions she had been saving.

Emily was overwhelmed by an infinite exhaustion.

"Oh, honey," she said.

I turned away. "You didn't answer my e-mails. You didn't take my calls." I spoke insistently but quietly and with a hint of anger.

She slid closer on her knees and attempted to hug me.

"Don't touch me," I said.

"Your mom *wanted* me to stay away."

Sara's willfulness was all too obvious. She had curtained her illness to shield Emily from grief in order to keep her focus on dance. Emily rolled up the shades. She was angry that no one had taken me under wing while she was gone. "How come they all left you?"

"I told my uncle that I was staying with a friend until you came back."

"You lied."

"I did." An army of lies had to be dealt with in life.

"I'll make you something to eat."

She went to the kitchen, where breathing was easier. The refrigerator was nearly empty, the scallions and lettuce soggy, the carrots forlorn, the basil black. She checked the eggs and saw they were past pull date. There was applesauce and sour cream that looked okay. In the pantry the potatoes were good, though starting to sprout.

A blowtorch must have seared Emily's heart—mine too. It was painful for us to go on with the routine of living. We tried. She peeled the potatoes and crumbled a matzo in a bowl and chopped half of an onion and grated four small potatoes together. She waited until the oil in the pan was smoky before adding large dollops of the mixture. The smell of frying permeated the air.

My anger at her for blocking my calls and texts receded. I explained that my mother's death and the funeral had been compressed into two days. Her artist friends had come to the service, but my father, Alex, long-divorced from Sara, couldn't be found.

I sat at the kitchen table. I wore a tight black T-shirt and black jeans. Despite the grief, I was awake to her attraction, the contours of her body.

It's clear to me now that there's no peace treaty anyone can enforce when it comes to desire. I couldn't help thinking it was all in the seeing eyes, all surface, no substance, no depth, all of us condemned to this narrow passage of liking or not liking, desiring or hating, a Darwinian struggle for sexual selection, for fitness, for survival, competing to the end of our days—the essential nature of mankind.

She served me the potato pancakes on plates my mother had fired in a pottery kiln. I held Emily's wrist a moment. My attractiveness must have troubled her. "Look, enough of that," she said and pulled her hand away. "What we did we'll never mention, never do it again."

"Sex?"

"Never."

She suppressed the new adult image of me that her mind responded to. I was still a minor and her job was to help me make my way in the world. We had some financial leeway, a safety net—my mother owned the brownstone she had inherited from my grandfather mortgage-free. Emily took a seat and we talked about practical issues: the rent, the house, savings, and my future school expenses. The noise of her scraping her chair on the floor broke our uneasy tension. My job was to be the obedient boy she was guarding from harm. "I'll raise the college money for you. Your mom's art, you know. We'll sell it." Relief flooded her voice. She was in charge and was doing good works.

"Mom's been trying to sell her stuff for years." I gestured toward the rooms upstairs. "She's got a warehouse full of stuff."

"We're going to sell it. She's got the MoMA PS1 show coming up. That publicity will help us. Rick and me, we're going to move in and pay you rent to spread the cost of living here." Her enthusiasm gave us both a lift.

"Who's going to buy her art?"

"There will be buyers. Jay Bradbury for one. He's a soft touch."

"Because he loves Sara's art?"

"Because he loves me."

This was a slap in my face. I must have immediately soured. "I'm supposed to worry about you and a geriatric guy getting it on?"

"No one is getting anything on."

"The fat slob."

"Well, I suppose a slim seventeen-year-old might think Jay is geriatric and fat."

The sexual tension came swinging back, obliterating her good intentions, crumbling will, and spiking desire. She brushed back a lock of hair on the side of my head. I pretended not to care and went back to eating my pancakes. I was at that age of becoming, testing, seeking, observing, and arranging events to my own liking. I took out my cell phone and read the text I had saved, defining the word *taboo*: "An object, place, person, or action in which 'holiness and pollution are not differentiated.' A brotherhood of the subversive and the good." I put away the phone. "You haven't touched me in weeks."

"It won't happen again. Not in the way it had happened." She was as calm as a peach sitting on a windowsill in morning sunshine. She felt she had the upper hand now. She was grieving for my mother and had a family purpose, a guardian duty toward me and a debt to be repaid my mother. She gave me a light kiss and took the empty plates to the sink.

Desire is endless, she wrote in her journal, desire for shoes, blouses, or jackets. Desire for more, for newness, for youth, for wealth, for anything more perfect, for life, and for sex. She was determined to break her desire for me. Her body and her mind were focused on nurturing new life barely formed. She was too busy with dance and with life to allow me to upset her hopes and ambitions.

She put away the plates and called Rick. He had reached their apartment okay, had showered and shaved, and was in his car on the way to the Bradbury plant in Red Hook. The reception was cutting in and out as she gave him the bad news about Sara. He said he was sorry to hear that. His words of condolence were warm but she hung up dissatisfied. Mourning, like love, was a personal thing with a depth and a height and a weight no one can measure for you.

chapter 16

She asked Rick to come live with her at mother's brown-stone until her estate could be settled, but he resisted, in part because he continued to believe that Sara had stolen Emily from him, and my mother's influence even in death remained strong. He also came up with additional excuses. He was now too busy. He was away all of the time. He usually stayed over-night with Emily only two nights a week. He said it would be a hassle to sublet their Williamsburg place in a down market, but inconsistent with that, he urged her to help him look for a house outside the city.

Her desire for me continued to terrify her. She wanted to have Rick close, a permanent reminder to keep me away. In that respect Rick was preventative maintenance, her insurance policy against defaulting on her moral values. There was always some new excuse for not giving up the Williamsburg lease. The latest was that he was traveling out of town on company business so often that he had to keep it because it was located more conveniently to airports.

In the morning after one of his nightly stopovers, Emily said, "My carrying a baby makes me feel sexier making love to you."

"I wish you'd found another way to feel sexy."

She reached across the breakfast table, fingers knitted into his. "We'll put this behind us. You'll be a great dad."

"Yes."

"Can you make that vote of confidence in us a bit more enthusiastic?"

"I'm here for you," he said.

It didn't take an anthropologist to figure him out. Closed social groups were always less interested in adopting from outside the group. He'd grown up in a small town, with a small circle of like-minded friends. And in her case, she knew few Lithuanians who had adopted. Like many who lived in former communist countries, they preferred to support orphanages. She hated it that many Chinese women, along with the women in the democratic subcontinent, used ultrasound to identify female fetuses in order to abort them. She wondered how the Japanese approached adoption. She wondered how the conservative and orthodox Jews managed. Jews believed they were God's chosen people. Did they ever adopt the non-chosen gentiles or black children? Americans, on the whole, adopted with great fanfare and freedom and faith in the human ability to change and embrace goodness. Americans rose more easily above the divisive issues of race and culture. She was hoping that Rick would get with the program.

"If I died in childbirth, you'd give my baby away?"

"No one dies in childbirth in America today."

This was not true. Fortunately, childbirth deaths were a rare occurrence. She continued to worry. Other than Rick, she had no one. No parents, no stateside aunts, no uncles or grandparents. No family outside Rick. She wanted him to love her child as he would love his own. The image of herself as an empty nautilus shell cast out by a turbulent sea came back to her more frequently. She would tumble along the shore, the grains of sand abrading her.

chapter 17

She rescheduled her class for young dancers and juggled gym workouts to free more time for rehearsals. Her schedule was overloaded and the two dancers who had danced with her in the previous year said they were no longer available. She asked her best student, Melissa, to dance at Jacob's Pillow, and she was also trying out a new male dancer. Melissa was an excellent dancer, but the male dancer wasn't working out and her performance date at Jacob's Pillow was fast approaching.

We were both unusually busy. I was coming to the end of my school year and I wanted to do a Euripides play as the graduating class's penultimate effort, but the sexual themes I had chosen were getting pushback from the school's administration. Given how busy we were, there was little time for much else. No time for bad behavior on my part and not much reflection either—not until my teacher, Sister St. Ambrose, sent this message to all of us:

When I looked for a companion to climb a mountain, I re-
alized that hardly any of my friends were suitable—One
was too phlegmatic, another too anxious; one too slow,
another too hasty; one too sad, another too happy; one too
simple, another more thoughtful than I would like. I was
frightened by the fact that one never spoke while another
talked too much; the heavy deliberation of some repelled
me as much as the lean incapacity of others. I rejected some
for their cold lack of interest and others for their excessive
enthusiasm.

Emily had a panic attack when she read Sister's take on
Petrarch's famous advice. Was Sister alluding to an ethical
mountain Emily faced?

Sister St. Ambrose was old school—confident in her
knowledge and tolerant toward other faiths and nearly always
on my side. She was in her sixties, a trained classicist, her face
peach and pink. You couldn't help but like her. As a twenty-
first-century woman, she embraced gays as church members,
spoke of love, peace, and grace, and supported economic justice on earth as well as happiness in heaven. She agreed with
the civil rights leader Susan B. Anthony who said, "No man
is good enough to govern any woman without her consent."
And Susan B. Anthony said that in 1895.

Sister called Emily to have a teacher conference. They held
it casually, walking in the rectory garden. "What's wrong with
David?" Sister asked. "Our Spoza."

Emily cringed inside. "Hmm, his mother—"

"And her being so young!" They seated themselves on a

bench. "Her boy had behaved, and now he's become a wild thing."

"A wild thing?"

"He's a provocateur! He's staging our graduation school play and he wants me to give him the go-ahead to stage *Hippolytus*. You know that one? In which the queen falls fatally in love with a boy?" Sister paused to let that sink in. "A big *no* was my answer. So, you'd think he'd quit, but no, not David. Like a shrewd prosecutor he offers to drop *Hippolytus*, provided I let him run Racine's story of ill-fated Phaedra proposition-ing her stepson. A play modeled on the luckless woman in Euripides' *Hippolytus*. Can you imagine Dr. Wilson reading either of these filthy plays?" A pair of squirrels chasing each other ran across the path. This brightened the sister's mood. "David is a challenge! Not one out of a hundred of my stu-dents can distinguish Euripides from Racine. They're reading the honorable sex-free longing-imbued *Twilight* series and the delightful *Harry Potter*." She spread her arms heavenward. "What to do with David?"

"Ask him to stage *Our Town*?"

Thornton Wilder's play was one of Emily's favorite American plays. Some critics called it sentimental, but she found it tragic. "I can't imagine David offending anyone by staging *Our Town*."

Sister beamed a "thank you" as if a new and more effective prayer had been found. "That's good. That's very good."

They parted, and Emily took the subway to her ob-gyn clinic in the East Village. The clinic visit was uneventful. Everything appeared to be normal. She patted her stomach, thinking how sweetly the curve of her baby's backbone nestled inside. The life within made her part of a greater cosmos, extending her solo flight on Earth. She felt a sudden, pleasing, reticent pride as a future mother.

chapter 18

At home that evening Emily switched on her laptop. She checked my school blog and followed my tweets. The ambient awareness of my sexual existence plagued much of her day and troubled her evenings. She didn't want to admit to herself how powerful her obsession had become. She followed my schedule carefully and was moved by my moods and silences, by my lame wit and enthusiasms, and at times, when she was completely unaware of how her mood shifted to mimic something I did, she mimicked me.

The floor upstairs creaked on account of my presence in the house. The old brownstone was in need of repairs, even desperate for them. In her journal, she called it *The House of Sounds*. Her sounds, Rick's sounds on the nights he slept over, and my sounds—too many sounds.

The best possible outcome for her situation was to have me out of the house on a full scholarship by fall. She sent me an instant message asking about my early college applications.

I messaged back, but on another subject, denying her the adult power she wanted: "Hey, check this out! Tell me if Charlotte Brontë wins in the manhunter category. Jane Eyre has to be the world's most celebrated sexually aggressive teenager. A mind-blow in the extreme writing category until *Wuthering Heights* came along."

Emily made a note of this in her journal:

> *David was at it again, he's at it and at it and at it, saying that Charlotte Brontë's teenage protagonist orchestrated the death of a man's mad wife in an attic fire to open the way for Jane Eyre to win her man. He keeps on pushing me with his art and artifice. Rick, by instinct, is slow to reveal himself, by training cautious, and a good and loyal man. There is no madness in him until his intense shift to right-wing Catholicism. As for me, I don't have time to read all the books David is reading. But I've got my own insights, and I worry about the consequences. I think David is toying with me, teasing me. I'm an object that has sex to offer.*

She suppressed an urge to run upstairs and have it out with me. She was, and preferred to be, an open, affectionate woman who loved bright colors and the latest shoes. Concealment wasn't her game, and now she had so much to hide. Her separation from Rick was not doing her any favors. Upset and intrigued by my seduction—and susceptible to it—she called Rick to encourage him to join her full time.

"Angel, I'm going to be tied up at the plant in Hoboken for a few days. I booked a motel room." He was a busy man.

She tried again. "I need your adult company."

"We'll talk later." He was in a rush. "I love you, honey," he said to end the call.

She ignored the "bing" on her computer indicating another e-mail missile from me. She sat fuming for a while. She wished Rick would drop the price on their old apartment, take a loss on the lease, and come live with her.

She climbed out onto the fire escape for some fresh air. Perfection in life, perfection in dance, perfection in health, in marriage, in birthing—all of it seemed tantalizingly close and absurdly distant. She carried a tiny fetus, no larger than a pea, a sweet pea that was partially mine. I would later theorize that it was this baby that made me seem so attractive. Gathering her will, she rubbed the marks on her arm, maddened by her inability to stop thinking about me.

The warm air whispered a breeze, and a late-night carousing starling was cackling at his neighbor as Emily lost track of time. A half-hour went by before she climbed back inside, picked up her laptop, and went upstairs to inventory my mother's work, stored in a large room next to mine. As she worked she noticed a booklet she had not seen earlier. She glanced at a yellow highlighting inside: "We are, all of us, sentenced to solitary confinement inside our skins." I had highlighted a note by the playwright August Strindberg writing on *Miss Julie*.

What did Strindberg know? she complained in her journal. She was exposing herself with her choreography, showing others what might happen with passion torn. Strindberg was a man who'd gone insane. Another "bing" shot to her ears, and then she heard her cell phone. I was calling her, pursuing her. She wrote in her journal: *Stop beating on me. Stop it please. Stop for my sake.*

She distanced herself by staring at her own image in a full-length antique mirror my mother had kept. She was without false modesty in rating herself—she was fortunate to have a body that was limber and beautifully proportioned. She had great turnout and strong ankles, and her movements were precise, graceful when she wished to glide. She wasn't afraid to fall and didn't have the tiny, narrow hips that could have restricted movement.

I knocked on her door and went in without being asked. I had put on a frog costume she had designed. Inoffensive and charming, her earliest choreography had a redeeming familial quality. Audiences had loved it. The new work was alive with doubts and insecurities. I collapsed into the only upholstered chair in the room.

"How come you can't sit without sprawling?"

I took off the frog head but didn't change the scattered arrangement of my legs or arms. My wide-eyed expression faked innocence. "You're supposed to kiss the frog and turn him into a prince."

She refused to do it. I wiggled out of the costume. I was wearing a T-shirt and jeans under the costume. In her journal she said I was divinely good-looking.

"I got kicked out of religion class today. Dr. Wilson was sitting in for God as our interim teacher. Our Million-Buck Doc slumming among us dollar-a-day kids. He cozied up to me after class, a sort of man-to-man thing guys are good at, and told me I don't have to call him Dr. Wilson. I can call him Doc from now on." I tried to keep the deadpan look of a stand-up comic. "He said they changed the name of the Holy Ghost and started calling it the Holy Spirit because the faithful got confused on Halloween night."

"He did not?"

"Ask him."

"Stay away from him. You're asking for trouble."

"Okay, let's look at the upside. They can't excommunicate me because I'm Jewish and then there's this thing with Dr. Wilson as an evangelist. He needs me as a potential convert. I'm solid. A precious commodity. There's no downside."

"You're annoying him."

"Yeah, it's a smorgasbord out there. Sex and God and everything confused."

She admitted that God could be gauzy and hard to pin down. Was He mean-spirited and jealous, or was He kind and sort of absent-minded? Instead of creating order among people, He made bigger messes out of the chaos He had inherited. He allowed murderous enemies worldwide to remain triumphant. And why did He punish her with an unwanted attraction for a boy she'd rather not be involved with? It was enough to despair over.

I started to strum air guitar. "*My* God is better than *your* God."

"Don't be a prick, David."

"What's that supposed to mean?"

"People should keep their personal God private, like they used to keep their sex lives private."

"Private sex lives? What, with the Internet? Not a chance. No more chance than keeping somebody's personal version of God private. We've got a real God glut out there. Mega-stadium glut. Every believer is pushing their own version of God. I mean, like they're looking for bragging rights? A disaster happens and some dumb preacher says God is calling down retribution. You get lucky and win the Lotto and some dumb preacher says you have to thank God. In God We Trust. Right?"

"Have some respect."

"I do. In fact, I'm proposing a Brownie point term paper to Sister St. Ambrose, *Variations on the Theme of Compassion*. The way I see it, if *my* God is to become supremely compassionate, *He* has to kill off the competing gods selling competitive compassion. So it follows that the most compassionate and successful God is also the most murderous."

"You're going to get kicked out of school."

"I'm graduating."

"They'll do something to you."

"Yeah? I doubt it. The honors classes are easy. I've time on my hands."

I must have looked soberly smart, my dark hair curled. Her journal reveals that the unwanted warm feeling she had experienced returned. Her feelings, unwanted, derelict, were offensive to her sense of good order. Her mind screamed against it and her body was deaf. She pinched her arm to make it go away. She was awakening to something not only attractive but also dangerous in me, to something that compelled her toward the dangerous in her choreography—she told her journal that she feared I had a more than a touch of malice in my heart.

"Let me show you a dance I'm working on," she said, and tried a short, faltering step, reaching for balance in an awkward phrase. She wrote in her journal:

It's not true that everyone can be graceful, or smart, or successful, yet we believe it, a wonderful myth, a social myth embraced by Sister St. Ambrose looking for talent within each student.

Early on in her work she had won a prize for being the "most entertaining" dancer. So many prizes were awarded— for best dancer, best solo, best duet, best music, best acrobatics, best new-newcomer, best costume—that she was bound to win something. She won early praise, and then she shifted toward the humorous, a dance called *The Frogs*, floppy and amazingly athletic, obviously homage to the Aristophanes comedy that she danced in a fluttery full cover-up costume so complete that the audience couldn't tell if a man or a woman was dancing. This was a step forward for her, away from romanticism and the childish sentiments of earlier dances. What she was attempting now was even more challenging.

She tried a sinuous sequence in *Kiss*. It set up internal vibrations that made marking time difficult. She stopped dancing. We watched each other silently.

"David," she said.

"I know," I said.

"I don't want you to have any girl other than me."

"Can you dance without clothes?" I asked.

"I don't think so."

She did not say anything more. She was feeling uneasy and uncomfortable and pleased with herself. And then she felt my hands at her waist. She wrote in her journal that they were soft hands, palms caressing and lingering. She moved a foot forward and then the other, repeating a passage from *Kiss*. She still had her back toward me. I did nothing. She kept her back turned and waited. She waited longer. She didn't know what was going to happen. I didn't know what was going to happen. The wait seemed eternal. I felt we were united in a way that surpassed lovemaking. I took her hand and kissed each finger, and though I was eager to continue, she turned and placed her palm on my chest. This was gentle, not a rebuke. But we went our separate ways.

chapter 19

The idea of sin entered her life. She actually was quite free of sin before me. She had believed that an artist had to live a placid and complacent life, free from distractions, to have the peace of mind needed to create in fanatical freedom. Previously there had been nothing melodramatic to disturb her. And then it all changed.

I hadn't yet encountered John Keats' famous discovery of Negative Capability, of which he wrote, "Shakespeare possessed so enormously…when man is capable of being in uncertainties, mysteries, doubts, without any irritable reaching after fact and reason…" But in our separate ways, Rick and Emily and me, we were on the cusp of this exploration.

Although I pushed on the quarrelsome tangents questioning faith, I actually wasn't too interested in religion when I was young. Eschatology, theodicy, and the birth of evil were subjects that bored me, and heaven and hell were too big to bother to learn. But devout Catholics, nurtured by their catechisms, knew even less than I did and the religious angle gave me an edge over my classmates that allowed me to make a name for myself. I'm not sure I would have bothered to learn any of it if I'd gone to a public school.

Around this time I did one of my most outrageous acts of resistance at school—I wrote a term paper about sin. It caused a scandal and provoked Dr. Wilson. Here are several pages in which I was experimenting with voice. Some of it sounds juvenile to my ear today, some of it is too simple and too reductive, some of it is okay, and some of it is earnestly highfaluting, and you can skip all of it if you want to get on with the history of *Morning Light* uninterrupted.

The Story of Sin

In the beginning there was no sin in the world. God was a-hustling somewhere else, fixing chaos, or just keeping out of trouble, and in no mood to watch out for sin. He'd already done His rib trick with Eve ripped out of Adam's chest (I wonder if they gave Adam morphine), and then a-thinking and a-worrying that He'd made an imperfect thing, God got angry and kicked the both of them out of heaven. By and by there got to be more people on Earth. Not knowing 'nough about sin and left to their own, people worried about doing good or bad, and they worked and worked to avoid the bad. But bad was not sin, at least not yet, bad was simply bad.

So like so many things on Earth, sin had to be created from scratch. Moses got a good start on the project. He delivered the Ten Commandments, ten bad things to avoid, and from then on the Greek ideas about good and bad behavior began to change. It wasn't just bad to go a-lusting after your neighbor's wife and murdering the guy standing in the way—it was now offensive to God and therefore a sin.

Sin was a more complicated thing altogether, vastly more complex than bad behavior. It kept you out of heaven and punished you in purgatory. Or even, it sent you to hell, and punished you forever. The saintliest folks would still have to go to purgatory for a spell. No one liked it. Anxiety set in. Guilt. Grief. Terror. Fear.

Christian clerics devoted themselves to sin work. Distinctions had to be made. They added charcoal flavors to sin, and made larger casks to hold larger quantities of sin. Some of the sins were identified as mortal—damnable and punishable for an eternity under unrelenting torture unless you got some grace from God.

Some sins were only venial, maybe like pot smoking, or not washing your hands after going to the bathroom. But more things became sinful, even thoughts, and then you've had to think like crazy on how best to avoid thinking that could be sin. Before the invention of sin thinking wasn't bad, but now it became a rat's nest and an everyday worry for Church members.

Things got into a real mess. Bad behavior has no known cure, 'cept the paddle and a little learnin', but fortunately there was a big-time cure for sin that required a powerful new medicine called grace. It was a controlled substance locked up in God's safe. You couldn't get free from sin without getting grace.

The distribution of grace and the administration of sin became a complex bureaucratic effort. But the thing about bureaucracies and hierarchies, they always over-reach and want to grow bigger and bigger. To grow bigger they needed more sinners.

Catholic theologians came up with a powerful new way to increase the number of sinners—they theorized that everyone was born bad. Everyone was already a sinner, except Jesus and the Virgin Mary, and of course God, if you want to ignore God's many sins. This was a big big blanket endorsement of sinfulness, an' covered everyone human on earth with sin.

Sin became like napalm, once fired up and spreading, it stuck to your clothes, you couldn't get away from it, wash it, cut it, or avoid it, not by any natural means—you burned with sin and suffered, unless—and here the fix came in—unless you got a saint or a priest to help you get some of that hard-to-get grace from God. You had to plead for it, grovel and beg for it, pray for it, and pay for it. It was a hell of a bad situation.

The demand for priests skyrocketed. They were as confused as everyone else why God should make sin a birthright and plentiful, and grace so skimpy and expensive. They kept on exploring and explaining it, making up new theories. They had plenty of work to do. It got pretty hairy, really complicated, the complications came in Satan, matters occult, exorcism, virgin birth, saints and miraculous interventions, limbo, all that hocus-pocus, like making the body and blood of a martyr into a consumable and an edible thing—they called it transubstantiation. The word was so long that people were afraid to ask about it.

But the basic facts were simple: From day one God

gave everybody "original sin" without a fee, but you couldn't get grace for free.

The average person couldn't understand any of it. But as plain as anyone could see, this wasn't fair. They relied on priests to explain, and the priests had to do a lot of fancy dancing. And you'd better listen to them because if you didn't they could set you on fire like a hot dog on a stick, like they burned the guy who translated the Bible into English. They said this form of fiery persuasion therapy was okay, because God was merciful and He only tortured people to make them believe it.

After the priests complicated bad behavior and made it over into sin, they also mystified grace, making it harder to get. The sin market exploded with miscreants, and the demand for priests kept growing. The priests needed places to live, food and wine to sustain the hard work of forgiving people their sins.

Maybe Jesus could get by with His offerings of simplicity and love, bread loaves and fishes, and the wine He made at Cana, but to get the priests to love you, a simple hardworking stiff, was another task altogether. The priests were high maintenance even though celibate, and many of them were vain, loved sartorial splendor, loved women, loved comfort, loved art, loved wine, and even sometimes loved their progeny—natural-born children who knew them as "uncles." Actually, that part of the clerical life, their pleasure in life on earth, I liked. The priests were *Human, All Too Human.*

The price for maintaining them went up over the centuries. The things they needed weren't cheap—garments got fancier and more expensive, houses of worship, too. Great artists were hired. The churches needed servants and the houses needed maids and butlers. The people, those who worked and struggled and fell ill and went broke, learned to keep paying their priests because they controlled access to God and grace, and things were so bad that many of the faithful wanted to leave Earth and go to Heaven.

Who could blame them?

You couldn't tell where a sinner might crop up so an angry God punished indiscriminately, often with plagues, wars, and economic disasters. The scale of His divine killing was way over-the-top when compared to wimpy sins of mortal sinners. Some people began to think that God had died, was dead, or they started to think of Him as Evil.

Despite this circumstantial evidence that God was neither just, nor kind, nor loving, most people worked on the principle that they'd rather work with the devil they know, rather than the one they don't, and they defended God despite His violent ways. They said it was your fault that God was so violent, actually a sadist. He was punishing you for your sins.

The priests grew more powerful and creative in selling the idea that you, everyone, your mom, your dad, your children, your cat, and your dog deserved to be punished. Original sin, it was your entire fault.

Not everyone was willing to admit this. Some of them were then convicted as witches, and were burned. But priests also developed better sin antidotes, antivenom vaccines to make the cost of sin less painful. The best of these were delivered in prepaid insurance plans to get you into heaven with a reduced punishment plan in purgatory, no matter how much of a miscreant you were.

This "indulgence" as they called it was an innovative idea, much better than subprime mortgages and financial derivatives are today. The priests loved it.

Church officials were the only salesmen authorized to sell indulgences as sin-clearance items—pain-reduction products that didn't need current FDA approval. Indulgences were unregulated and grew into a big project, profitable, a growth business you'd keep in your portfolio. Especially since it was tax-free profits. Today's preachers fill stadiums when they put on their sin-clearance sales.

My conclusion: Lack of knowledge has always been kind to the powers at play, but if the product works for you, even if it's only a placebo, take it.

Well, that was my paper, giving my one-sided view of both sides. I had sent a copy to Dr. Wilson and soon there was rumor afloat that they wanted to kick me out of school. You'll have to hang around and read a bit more to see if they did.

chapter 20

The secrecy Emily imposed over her feelings made her consistently jumpy. It wasn't only her single act of bad behavior with me that caused her stress—Christian guilt and grief, remorse and atonement. The ancient Greeks never worried about that stuff. They hated to lose and they loved to win. The admired perfect forms and lovely bodies. They loved vitality. We got the Olympics from them.

But Emily had to deal with Christian guilt and grief, remorse and atonement. Melancholy was also present. Those "little deaths" that novelists sometimes talked about. I don't think they actually have melancholy in heaven. In fact, I don't know what they store up there—billions and billions and billions of souls I suppose. But on earth we're running out of space, and the climate is going weird on us. On earth we've got limits, choices, decisions, time and space. And we have to decide if we should start taxing churches for selling their various products.

On account of the baby, she no longer sipped the occasional glass of wine, and she had never done pot or drugs. She chewed gum instead; no matter how childish it made her look, it relaxed her. Unable to vent her worries to colleagues, or her dance coach, or Melissa, and disappointed in her attempt to reach out to Sister St. Ambrose, she needed to unburden on someone. She set about sharing her secret with a priest in confession. Though she wasn't especially devout, she recalled some of the Catholic rituals she had experienced in her youth. The act of letting in fresh air, confessing, admitting, regretting, would lead to atonement and forgiveness. Perhaps even peace.

Just then she got a text message from me: "I miss you. Do you miss me?"

"Like I miss a torn cartilage," she answered, powering off.

Her decision to confess to a priest wasn't free of worries. She didn't want a local priest who knew her to hear the worst things she's done, not even the kindly Father Dan. She needed a stranger to hear her out.

On Saturday she entered the neighborhood church through a side entrance and hesitated at the baptismal font in the vestibule. Ever since her youth she'd had a sketchy relationship with the organized Church's power symbols commanding obedience. It wasn't really *her* religion. It was an accident, like finding a coin on the road. She was born in Lithuania and in that country—except for a few Protestants, and a remnant of the formerly large Jewish population—they were nearly all Catholics. She believed that if she'd been born in Israel she'd be Jewish, if born in Saudi Arabia she'd be wearing a Muslim chador, in Utah she'd be studying the Book Of Mormon and becoming a lawyer or getting an MBA, and in India only God knows what wonder-filled religion would have consumed her.

Had she been given a choice, or had she had access to a broader education, she would have assembled a collection of fine devotional pieces from Buddhism and Taoism. But she was stuck with Catholicism. The male clergy seemed to be imposing something on her, a gender-based idea of sin; females were more sinful, obviously so, or at least it appeared that way to some men. Ecclesiastical authorities were demanding something from her without having a clear idea of her resources, her hopes and possibilities, without actually caring much about her purpose and meaning on Earth, except as a baby breeder and divinity worshiper.

The clergy, understandably troubled by earthly sensual matters over which they had little control, sublimated their passions into a devotion of ethereal bodies in heaven, which no one could see, and from where no one returned, except of course Jesus, if you wanted to believe that.

To win a prosperous life in the hereafter, the clerical men in charge levied a huge earthly admission fee. They demanded that she abandon her intelligence, give up science, throw away education, surrender free will, and imprison intellect, and accept by rote whatever priests tell her is true—often naive priests, badly educated priests, and sometimes even stupid priests.

She was troubled by it. Despite all these reservations, she wanted to confess, to prostrate herself as priests do in Rome. Her willfulness, her work ethic and her ambition, made it all the more difficult, but this once, just once, because of the trouble she had in dealing with me, she wanted a priest's help.

Standing uneasily in the vestibule, she paused to reconsider because she wasn't fully convinced she was sorry for her sins. The lack of urgent contrition could ruin the guarantee of a clean sweep and a pure soul after confession. She decided to take her chances nevertheless.

She had not been to church for some time and noticed a change. Below the intersecting arches in the entry there used to be a beautiful statue of St. Teresa she had admired. The woman's representation had been so fine that St. Teresa's nipple showed under her robe. Dr. Wilson had been so deeply offended by the work's physicality that he had spent his own money to buy a mutilated St. Sebastian to replace her, substituting a tortured male for a sensuous, innocent, perhaps orgasmic female. The mix of fear and piety and money among prosperous male believers had altered what used to be a faith of great and alluring simplicity and collegiality among the followers of Jesus.

Overcoming doubts, she went forward and genuflected at the center aisle before crossing to the other side. She glanced sideways to see if she recognized anyone she knew. A visiting priest was sitting out his sin duty in a darkened booth with a tiny light glowing above it. This was good, the essential stranger she needed to hear her sins. Nowadays, confessions could be made in a well-lighted office or out in the open for everyone to see, or in one's heart when a general absolution was available. But she was determined to scrub her soul in keeping with the older tradition.

She paused, trying to remember the rules. The formula she remembered required her to say, "Bless me, Father," and then mention the amount of time that had elapsed since her last confession. Could she actually admit it had been twelve years? Not since she was twelve years old and had discovered the joy of self-pleasuring that she didn't want to admit? It would take a week to catalog all her sins properly, provided she could remember them. If she forgot them, could they be forgiven? And should the first sins be confessed first? She might never get to her most recent sins. She decided to cut to the chase: me.

Steeling herself, she entered the confessional.

"Bless me, Father, for I have sinned," she whispered, not mentioning the amount of time that had passed, and hoping it would go unnoticed.

The priest, apparently waking from a snooze, made a sign of the cross and turned his head to listen. His profile looked severe, lean and unforgiving, more Calvinist than Catholic. The average age of priests was now north of sixty. She had hoped to find a rotund and corpuscular man more sympathetic to human weakness, perhaps a man who enjoyed the sensual pleasure of roast dinners and fine wines, the archbishop perhaps, someone who loved magnificent robes, sumptuary pleasures, golden staffs and orbs and chalices fixed with jewels. Nevertheless, she whispered in a monotone her gravest sins. Recent sins. Her face was warm and she assumed it would look shamefacedly red with her skin breaking out, had there been more light.

She confessed to having had sex with me. Admittedly, she skittered around the subject by substituting the word *desire* for *sex*. She did use the word *intercourse*, but said it in such a way that it might suggest a conversation that hadn't involved bodily fluids.

She spoke quickly and didn't mention pregnancy because that was actually God's gift to her. She rather liked the conceit of a virginal girl giving birth to Jesus. No mess. Less bother. She wondered if a Virgin Mary today would have gone a step further by hiring a surrogate's womb. Possibly so.

The belief that Mary was a virgin was up in the air until nearly four hundred years after Jesus' birth. Some of His followers believed Mary had to have had sex, and others did not. Men assembled to judge the facts and argue the case. Women were not invited. Many artists used underage models for their paintings of the Virgin Mary. Attractive and forever youthful. The men liked that. Some of the debaters believed this underage pregnant girl was the site of carnality, but after much discussion the Virgin cohort won the day and formulated a rule that proclaimed her a virgin. The purists had won, giving rise to today's Marian devotees. They then ordered everyone to believe in Mary's virginity, and it worked magically for millions of people, who learned to worship not only Mary the Mother of God, but also virginity, too.

"How do you desire this boy?" the priest asked.

"What do you mean, Father?"

She didn't want to be more precise. Religion worked on imprecision, on mysticism. She had not anticipated running into a priest who wanted the facts.

"How do you desire this boy?"

Didn't everyone know what desire meant? "I want to have sex with him, Father."

She wrote in her journal that she didn't like calling the man "Father." The apostles had not been called *Father*.

There had been women apostles, too, and no one had called them *Mother*, until later on when we had Mother Superiors in charge of convents. The prophetic powers of language worked almost exclusively in favor of the men in charge. Hundreds of years into male-ordained evangelical work, Church leaders came up with ever more sophisticated ways to dominate women and make them subservient to the men of the assembly.

"How often?" he asked.

She was startled. Was this man an accountant?

"All the time."

That was the worst of her sins: those terrible sins associated with thoughts. Given most everyone's wayward mind it was impossible not to be sinful—the Church knew it, and used it as a powerful tool to dominate naive believers. But she had no envy to confess, no greed, no gluttony. She didn't think ambition was a sin, although it might be an accomplice.

"Why do you desire him, my child?"

His question immediately rankled, and she withdrew slightly from the grille. For one thing, she didn't think she was a child. She was self-made, with some help from Sara. Furthermore, "why" wasn't supposed to be part of the confessional protocol. She glared at the priest's profile, not softening any because he was old. The elderly, as much as the young, had an obligation to learn something new every year, even if it meant relearning what they once knew when they were young and had forgotten. This man had clearly failed the test.

"I'm not a child," she said. She didn't cotton to the passivity encouraged by clergy, especially passivity among women and girls, leaving things to be decided by God and His male priestly delegates.

The priest nodded with an infinitely portentous air. How could she explain what she could not explain to herself? Darwin? Sexual selection? All that dry stuff? The need for sex was not a bit player in *The Human Comedy*. But there was more. She had constructed a weird aura around my youth, she noted later in her journal.

"I think I love him," she said. No one else made her feel as exciting, singular, blazing with magical interior lights. The priest shifted his weight, and the shellacked confessional creaked with generations of age-old weariness.

"Love him without touching him," the priest advised.

That was how one loved God and the Virgin Mary and St. Anthony and St. Magdalene after she'd become a saint. It was a wonderful and a terrible way to love—untouched.

The priest gave her five Hail Marys and five Our Fathers to say in penance. The light sentence disappointed her. The Church honored believers who suffered pain and martyrdom, and she suddenly realized that she had martyred herself to Rick. She had to be punished for having an attractive body. Despite centuries of sensual Church art, Bellini and Michelangelo, the Church frowned on female sensuality in all things except birthing. To be beautiful was a gender-specific sin among Rick's like-minded believers. She added a note later, about men seeing themselves as Odysseus battling Circe, Scylla, and Calypso. That must have been the reason why Dr. Wilson had to replace the statue of St. Teresa. Men liked women, the curves and indentations, the taut flat places, the voices. Nature's subtle narratives of attraction were hard to resist, but all of that could be sinful, and so they beat up on themselves and sometimes on their women, too.

The priest asked her to pray for strength, and to send money to the poor children worldwide. And for this last she admired the priest and the Church. There were so many poor and ill and persecuted on Earth, and evangelical organizations tried to be helpful. She said her Act of Contrition, a ritual prayer starting with "O my God, I am heartily sorry..." She murmured it all the way through, hoping she actually meant it.

After her confession she experienced a floaty feeling. The sacrament of reconciliation added power to her soul. She had flushed the gunk out of her body and left the confessional feeling clean and absolved from sin, but once again she was alone.

chapter 21

That weekend Rick sublet the Williamsburg apartment and moved in with Emily. She was relieved to have him join her, and he in turn was aggressively optimistic that they could survive her "indiscretion," as he now called her pregnancy. His optimism was a shield he fashioned out of a collection of bad events. Working for Bradbury Container had renewed him and he must have felt ready to take on new challenges.

He gave her a tour of the Red Hook Bradbury plant to show her a new six-color Miehle press that could "print cartons faster than Jesus could count angels." He was called away to meet his purchasing manager, and Emily went to see Jay Bradbury, to sell him art my mother had crafted. He told her about a hyperexpensive half-block-long corrugating machine they were looking to purchase. It produced linerboard from which corrugated cartons were made. He offered a poetic line. She recognized his attempt to flatter her. And he, too, was called away to a meeting, and she used the interlude to text me: "Jay told me that 'no man is an island.' What is he talking about?"

"John Donne," I texted back. I supplied part of Donne's *Devotions upon Emergent Occasions*, which I found on the web:

> ...all mankind is of one author and is on one volume; when one man dies, one chapter is not torn out of the book...No man is an island, entire of itself...Any man's death diminishes me because I am involved in mankind: and therefore never send to know for whom the bell tolls; it tolls for thee.

Your ancient beau might be hung up on Hemingway, who stole the tile of his book "For Whom the Bell Tolls" from Donne.

Jay controlled the Bradbury Foundation and had used some of its funds to finance her choreography. The grant was enough to pay her newly hired dancers a small stipend through the end of the Jacob's Pillow festival. Grateful and indebted to Jay, she bore his flirtatiousness as the necessary price of doing business with him. And she did it with good humor. Years earlier, he had leased her an apartment in Manhattan. He had fixed her up with a snazzy red convertible and he had taken her to fine restaurants and wonderful Broadway musicals. Despite these gifts, she had walked out on him without notice, leaving the keys to the car in the empty apartment. Jay, though married now, held a long, silent, despairing grudge against Rick.

Her sudden departure had the effect of making Jay's loss seem enormous, insurmountable, a love that one pines for. And now, thinking about it in her journal, she knew she could have prepared him better. Had she remained with him longer to allow his low tolerance for boredom a natural course, their relationship might have faded gracefully. As it was, he was devastated.

Given this background, and Jay's attentions, it didn't surprise her that whenever Rick brought up Jay in conversation, he did it in a tone suggesting a rival. She tried to calm Rick's uneasiness with several carefully phrased dismissive remarks about her time spent with Jay. But no matter how many times she said that she had no interest in the man, Rick, having already absorbed a blow, was wary, and believed that Jay was the baby's father.

Things never go perfectly as planned, she fretted. She hadn't expected that by approaching her former boyfriend to do Rick a favor, she might be asked to return a favor of a different kind. It happened after they'd met a second time with Sister St. Ambrose and the financial committee that included Page and Rick. They'd met to discuss the school's annual fund-raiser and Emily was taking a break with Jay in the school cafeteria.

"What makes you so smart?" he asked, cupping his Styrofoam coffee cup. They were sitting at the end of a foldaway table.

"Smart?" Her voice was lighthearted and hurried; she had to interview a dancer shortly. She checked the time on her cell, erased the "pls don't ignore me" message from me, and smiled at Jay.

"You've got killer assets," he said, squeezing the cup.

She spilled some orange juice, and wiped her fingers on a napkin. Pointedly she said, "Jay, I'm not good at sexual baiting and I don't think my looks have killed anyone yet."

"No one but me." His eyes tended to be watery and they seemed to be especially liquid now.

She believed this was the right moment to make it clear to him that she wasn't going to offer him a personal payback on whatever he considered to be his investment in her. "You can do better than me."

He leaned back and his chair creaked noisily. She pushed on, smiling, mixing in light banter. "You're turned-on to me because I'm unavailable. The moment I divorce Rick you'd dump me."

"Divorce?" he asked, raising an eyebrow.

And then Sister St. Ambrose came over with Rick and Page and Dr. Wilson. They agreed to meet one more time, and said goodbye.

Emily got into the car with Rick. "I'd hate it if you're carrying *his* baby," he said.

"Let it go. Let's have something to eat. Stop being grim."

"Guys like him want to eat up the world's fuckin' resources by fathering tribes."

"He doesn't have kids."

"Which only makes him more aggressive."

"I'm not one of his brood bitches."

The harshness of this remark would haunt her later. They were crossing the Brooklyn Bridge, when Rick, troubled, asked, "You didn't mean that? The thing about 'brood bitches'?"

"Oh, let's drop it, let's just drop it."

"I would like to hear a bit more respect for my position. The Pope had announced a total ban on artificial contraception for the faithful as far back as 1968."

"Yes, I've heard he's infallible." She added cheer to her voice.

"He was speaking as *Pope*."

"He didn't have a womb to bother him." Her voice was even more cheerful. The absurd question of infallibility was centuries old.

She made an extra notation in the margins of her journal. Popes at one time weren't infallible and got lots of pushback on dogma. That made governing the faithful difficult, so like clever executives and legislators everywhere who are uncertain of their power, the bishops convened a bunch of like-minded ecclesiastical officials—a kangaroo court—that then declared Popes infallible on canonical issues. This wasn't democracy, but autocracy works in China, Russia, corporations, and among dozens of tin-pot dictators worldwide, and also works for the majestic Catholic Church.

Until she brought up infallibility she'd never before questioned intellectual ideas, swallowing them whole. They weren't her business. But a question can be as dangerous as a bomb to the established order. It must have been this moment that Rick realized she was no longer "one of the faithful."

Emily said in her journal that she didn't know what possessed her at times. This conflict showed up in her work; it showed up in the dances she choreographed. She explained them one way, but her choreography indicated something else. As a famous observer of such matters, D.H. Lawrence, once said, "Never trust the teller, trust the tale." Twenty years later, I was following the tale and looking for the truth in all this. Life seemed to me to be nothing more than a half-truth in search of an answer as we journey on.

This questioning attitude was my mother's gift. Sara found much that was beguiling and true and beautiful about the American character. No country on Earth showed as much generosity as America did, and no country would have adopted Emily as readily. Emily loved the enthusiasm for angels and vampires and ghosts and zombies and power prayers. She liked it that Americans loved authority but took such great pleasure in pulling it apart. She was fascinated by America's passion for pills offering long life, sexuality, brainpower. She liked all the "how-to" books, the books on zero-down deals, on making it, keeping it, looking good, looking out for #1, having great sex, seeking nirvana and peaceful relationships, and she even liked the granddaddy of them all, Dale Carnegie's *How to Win Friends and Influence People*.

The country's affection for grandiose projects and mesmerizing pursuits to make all things larger had taken a hit lately, but my mother's best student, Emily, loved the country's vitality and unbridled energy, the confusion and conflict. She loved America.

chapter 22

One night, after an exhausting day of rehearsals, she came home late, got her Epsom salt footbath going, and before she could relax heard Rick rattling the front door to let himself in. This was a bad sign because it meant he'd been drinking and he couldn't find the keyhole. She dried her feet, switched on the night-light for him, and dressed in her nightgown went to wait in bed. Rick ambled in wearing his light raincoat. Without taking it off he slumped into a chair and she sat on the edge of the bed.

"You smell like a brewery," she said.

"We hit a few places."

"You've been going out with Jay more and more."

Their socializing was unexpected, given their management disagreements at work and Rick's suspicion that Jay had fathered her baby.

"Is Jay being impossible again?"

"Yeah." Rick's voice wavered.

He was a hard-charging, middle-class guy who had impressed Jay's now-retired father. Jay never rushed anywhere. Never had to, and never would, and the world of inherited wealth would forever cradle his life.

She waited for more.

"He's still carrying a torch for you."

She got out of bed and put on a robe. "Jay is an old, *old* beau."

"He's fifty-two and healthy as a lark. I tell you, it's almost sad. He hasn't gotten over you."

"It's unfair of you to say that." She adjusted the pillow higher against the headboard.

"Hey, what do I know?" Rick said. Retreating under her skeptical glance he added, "Okay, I was the youngest VP at Bradbury before the bug took me to start my own company. I guess I shouldn't have done it. I mean, gone out on my own."

He had been his usual optimistic self. That's what had motivated him; he saw only success. Nothing left to chance. Each thing itemized and evaluated. The fact that he had failed in an extravagant personal collapse and a catastrophic business misjudgment was unexamined because failures are not studied and therefore invisible in America; the only visible alternative is success. I was startled to see Abraham Lincoln quoted in Emily's journals: "Men are greedy to publish the successes...but meanly shy as to publishing the failures... men are ruined by this one-sided practice of concealment of blunders and failures."

But that, too, was the American way—the idea that you can't fail, along with the dream of being your own boss, and it remains irresistible. She remembered the franchise sales-men who had persuaded Rick to abandon the safety of a sal-ary. They were as slick as seals and had promised unlimited profit in a protected territory the size of Nebraska. Rick should have known better, but skepticism wasn't part of his nature. That's a funny thing about optimistic guys like Rick—they're easy converts, easy sells if the right sales pitch comes along.

As I read her journal, I imagined just how painful this pro-cess was for the both of them. She was beginning to suspect that for all of Rick's carefully stage-managed self-control, there was something devastatingly incomplete within him that required the cult of optimism to keep afloat. To be self-employed in any profession or art takes an enormous amount of courage that most people prefer not to test. To search for your own personal God is equally demanding. Insecurity and uncertainty is always troubling. And to work at great mental heights, without scaffolding or a safety net or harness, is scary. Rick didn't want to plunge into the unknown. He glanced at her journal on the night table. "I bet you tell that damned thing more than you're ever willing to tell me."

"That's what journals are for."

He got up and was weaving as he picked it up. "Is the guy I want to kill in this thing?"

She grabbed the journal out of his hands, threw it into the nightstand, and locked the drawer. "You're no killer."

Her husband didn't have the instinct; he was a diplomat, a negotiator, a cost-analysis guy. And she was grateful for it. She loved the outrageously criminal movie *Bonnie and Clyde*, but she had no interest in having a husband like Clyde Barrow. She rubbed her abdomen, feeling for her baby.

Rick's face clouded. "Jay is annoyed that you stood him up last night. Supposedly, you canceled on him and his wife without calling them."

"Oh." She covered her mouth. She'd forgotten.

"How come you didn't tell me you were going somewhere with him?"

"I wasn't going anywhere with *him*." She had been unwilling to see Jay alone. "Page had asked me to show them around the downtown performance scene. They think I have the keys to the edgy arts community."

"He's pissed."

"I forgot. I didn't think it was a firm date. I'll call Page and apologize."

Rick pried one eye wider with the help of his thumb and forefinger.

"I don't like you drinking so much. You haven't done it before," she said.

"I wasn't such an ass-kisser before."

She wrapped her arms around herself. "You're not an ass-kisser."

"Yeah?" He looked into her eyes for more reassurance. "Thanks a bunch, Angel. You'll be proud of me yet. You see, Jay is pissin' an' moanin' about the state of the world. I push myself away from the bar, get up, wobble, and say, 'I had enough to drink.' I start to leave. Jay gets up and stops me. He says, 'Have another drink.' All along, we've been buying rounds and splitting the tab half and half, even though I can't afford my half nearly as well as he can afford his. I look at my empty glass and think I can handle another one. I reach back to his dad's generation and say—"

"Hit me again," she said.

"You've got that right, Angel. I'm tight."

The colloquialisms still confused her: *tight* as in cheap, *tight* as in close friends, *tight* as in drunk, *tight* as a nut is tight on a bolt.

Rick toppled and caught himself. "I have no will power, right? Yeah, I say to the ol' wallet, 'Hit me again.' I don't say 'okay'; I don't say 'yes'; I don't say 'all right.'" Rick covered his mouth as if he was about to reveal a secret. "So I'm purring and purring at Jay. I'm a real pussycat. I'm hoping that he offers me my old VP title back now that I'm doing the same work I did before, the title his dad gave me. I say, 'Jay, I'm better than you at some things.'"

"You offended him?"

"No way. Jay has a fail-safe shit-reversal circuit. If I say shit, he hears sugar."

Rick went to the bureau and took a bottle of wine from a drawer. "Want some dago red?" His social instincts favored inexpensive wine over Châteaux Lafite.

She shook her head.

"I'm wasted." He screwed off the cap and took a drink from the bottle. "Jay asked me if you could use another Bradbury Foundation grant to fund your Jacob's Pillow gig. I don't think he cares diddly about dance, but he keeps asking about you. If you sold soybeans, he'd be asking me about the price of soybeans. It's not that he asks me directly, not exactly. He slides it in sideways, like, 'You think we can get Emily to find more time to help Page with the school auction?'"

"Rick, please stop worrying about Jay."

"Once burned, twice careless?" Rick cranked his head to one side, thinking it over. "Did I get that right?"

She heard an edge in his voice that she had not heard earlier, and she sensed an undercurrent in her own willfulness as well. She was sorry, but there was more to life than endless atonement. "Please let it go."

He was now muttering. The words weren't aimed at her but at the chair that was "in the fucking way." The bureau was fucked, too, and the lousy doorframe that caught his elbow. She got him his pajamas. He put them on and then, weaving, lurched to take hold of her.

She couldn't stand the smell of whiskey on his breath and she couldn't bear his touching her that moment. She pushed him away and he tumbled onto the bed, his legs hanging over the edge. *Wasted—a perfect description.* He made an effort to get up, but after a few more "fucks" aimed at the universe, he discovered that his legs were without traction. He folded his hands over his chest and closed his eyes. She moved his feet all the way up on the bed, and before she was finished he was snoring.

chapter 23

She switched off the light and slid into bed next to Rick but felt dislocated and wide awake. She tried to lull herself to sleep. She needed more sleep when she danced a heavy schedule. She fretted silently. Then, turning practical like she did when faced with a difficult sequence of steps in a dance movement, she broke the task into smaller parts. She ordered her toes to wiggle and then rest. She spoke to her ankles, calves, and legs, telling each part to relax. The autohypnosis made her drowsy but not sleepy enough. She lay awake next to Rick, listening to him snore.

She tried to understand the countless fragments surrounding her life. The intimate dance landscape, her many passages, her dumping Jay, her questioning Rick's fundamentalism, her queries about marriage, her moods, her bond with Sara, her puzzling over me, and her regrets.

She was developing a suspicion that her dance coach didn't like her work. That in itself wasn't a problem. Dances and dancers were wonderfully different. You simply learned to avoid people who didn't like your work. Besides, she'd learned tons of useful craft from people who didn't like her, but now she needed someone to love her work in order to grow. My mother had been the one who provided support.

Her coach, Langston, had once been an outstanding dancer, and now as a teacher past his own prime he offered good advice, and on occasion he offered excellent advice, but a resentful undercurrent spoiled many teachable moments, and a touch of envy like mold on spoiled food—a catty remark, a cynical observation—could be poisonous when it caught her in an unguarded moment.

She wasn't one of his favorites. She had not told him of her invitation to debut at Jacob's Pillow because she was afraid he would be resentful and become angry with her. She'd invited me to come to a workshop as an observer. I was quick with a conclusion. "Why are you taking lessons from this guy? He doesn't like you and he thinks your dancing sucks."

"Sucks," she said, "Totally sucks?"

What a thing to say, a terrible and useful word, so proud of itself and so fully, energetically dumb in its sweeping certainty. But *sucks* aimed at her choreography? She was offended. She had a special gift, a way of arranging movement that deepened an audience's involvement. It wasn't only her steps—it was also *her*, some inner spirit on display.

When she was younger she had created dances spontaneously. In Lithuania dancing was about the happiness to be found in groups and social inclusiveness. Individuality wasn't encouraged. Her beginnings were rustic. She wasn't one of the exquisitely confident children who start their early training in ballet. Dancers like her start out slowly, and if talented, they eventually begin to chaff as part of the group. There was pride and vanity in it, too. She was a contemporary dancer, a modern dancer, and not a ballet dancer, but with either the classical or the modern, each dancer went through a long apprenticeship.

Professionalism had taken over since the early days—lessons, coaching, practice to erase habitual faults and extend range—and once she'd become professional, the margin for mistakes became narrower. Mistakes still occurred, regularly, because she kept trying new things. She was not afraid to try new movements. The effort to give pleasure to an audience took work, a huge amount of it, and it could be painful, as when her foot swelled and needed ice packs. But the fun of a new achievement never faded, and there was pleasure in the work itself.

She hadn't read Langston accurately because he was as hard to pin down as Jell-O. She should have been alert to the fact that his Delphic pronouncements could be taken to mean anything, but she had assumed he was sincere because she was sincere. At any rate, sincerity had failed her, as it often fails sincere people, because they can't believe that other people can be fundamentally different. They love to say, "Deep down we're all the same," even though anthropologists have demonstrated that this isn't true. She lay awake thinking about Langston's duplicity as noise rattled down from my bedroom upstairs. The floors were thick, but recent plumbing repairs had not yet been plastered over, leaving exposed sections.

She heard me rearranging my sheets, and then she heard another sound that had all the clarity of muted strokes, faint, but strokes that were persistent and annoyingly steady. She had seen a movie in which the incomparable actor John Seymour Hoffman was playing a character pleasuring himself. It had repelled her and captivated her. *The House of Sounds.* What did she actually know of desire? Her journal contained a few answers and many questions. If she believed I was making love to her in my dreams, she suspected that I couldn't get enough of her.

She had started to choreograph dances perfumed with desire. Yet she felt utterly and hopelessly uninformed. Not about the mechanics but about the aura and the penumbra. She faulted her Lithuanian upbringing. Rick's sensual knowledge wasn't much better, advanced by celibate priests at a Jesuit high school who had their own inner St. Augustine to deal with. It was likely that many of his teachers were as afraid of sex as the American Shakers had been, but unlike the Shakers, the priests did not join in ecstatic communal dancing with women to set themselves free.

So much for ignorance, so little teaching, she wrote in her journal. She listened to my sounds upstairs. She could start her own blog: *The Innocent Page, The Foolish Page, Artless in America.* She glanced at Rick, nearly comatose from drinking. She liked skinny guys, but he was a skinny mess and the wrinkled and rumpled coverlet made him look like a baby beluga.

New problems at work were plaguing him. The company had thirteen plants across the Eastern seaboard, making folding cartons for the food industry and corrugated boxes for every industry that needed them. The company's products were, by their nature, green, recyclable products, which was a good thing.

She glanced at the ceiling that needed plastering. She needed relief, Rick needed relief. She felt for her baby and decided they could both handle sex. "Rick," she said, accepting his booziness. She lowered her voice. "Rick, make love to me."

She didn't think he was awake but he responded to her touching, and then to her closeness. *I'm ridiculous,* she wrote in her journal. *Sex is ridiculous. It makes fools out of people.* But the sensation compelled her. *In sickness and health.* There was nothing stopping her from leaving him, from divorcing him, from running off with an underage kid, or a man like Jay. She arched her back and then a sudden spasm came, waves, electric. She lay becalmed afterward until she fell asleep.

chapter 24

In the morning, Emily awoke feeling refreshed but with the flush of sex still lingering on her skin. Her passion calmed, she was now worried about her baby, thinking she might have to scale back on an energetic sequence of steps in one dance to keep the child safe.

She made breakfast. The circles below Rick's eyes looked puffy. He apologized for getting drunk. He wasn't into substance abuse, and last night was the first alcohol-fueled stumblebum display she'd witnessed in years.

Rick spooned his soft-boiled eggs. "What's up, Angel? Why the sad look?"

"Oh, sad?" She didn't know it was showing. "I'm sad? Well, hmm, I don't know. I guess it's this Langston business. He tore me up over a dance I had choreographed."

Rick enjoyed dance, but not too much, and she could barely stop herself from yawing whenever he brought up the box-making business. The Bradbury Corporation did things to boxes, corrugated paperboard and flat-folded cartons. The company printed on them and packed them off to customers, competing with companies that made exactly the same kind of boxes, with paper bought from the same suppliers, and sold at the same prices. In fact, executives at competing companies had just paid a huge fine for price-fixing, but didn't admit guilt and avoided jail time.

To amuse Rick, she asked, "How did it feel to be raped by me last night?"

"You didn't?" He sounded sedated and charmed.

"You were out of it."

He shook his head to express his doubts, and his voice gained authority. "Guys can't get raped if they have, you know, if, as you say last night, if, like they—"

She raised new concerns about Dr. Wilson. "Wilson is becoming a real pain in the butt, harassing David. He hauled David into the principal's office for using the word *erection* in a sexual funny way when he pitched a play."

"I don't like using that word either."

Of the many words associated with intimacy this was one of the least alarming. It reminded her of scaffolding near a building under construction. "I guess it's not in the New Testament, or the Old Testament, too."

Rick laughed. "Are you into Bible studies?"

She hummed a little tune. She felt a sudden return to longing, disturbed by the idea that it's repetitive and without end. Their inability to talk frankly about sex haunted her.

"I know what you're thinking," he said.

"You do?" She waited.

"Some crap Sara dumped on you. For me, I don't see anything wrong with Jesus' Incarnation, Atonement, and Resurrection." He was citing the core principles of Christianity.

"Rick, you're so lovely as an innocent." They were both innocent and self-censoring, each in their own private ways.

"I know what's going on," he protested. "Just because some of the Church's teachings about sexuality hurt some people, it doesn't mean that everything they teach is evil."

He was doing something very un-American, becoming more introspective. Not a huge amount of reflection, but a little was seeping in under his ironclad convictions. She got up from the kitchen table. An orphan breeze from the open window rippled her blouse. *Am I swelling?* She looked closely. But rebelling against secrecy, the effort not to look pregnant, she said, "We never talk about my pregnancy."

"What do you want me to say?" And then in a voice she would never forget, he added, "I'd like to kill the guy who made you pregnant." He gave a high-pitched laugh, and said he was "just kidding," but the line between honesty and humor was invisible, and she translated his words into a clear warning.

She went upstairs and laid out an assortment of clothes on the couch to see what she had to wear to the upcoming school auction. She sorted through the cascade of brocades, sheers, sequined dresses, shawls, and low-cut gowns, some beaded, some hand-tied, others woven of fine silk thread and pashmina wool. She loved fabric for its sensuality. She brought out Sara's black dress and held it in front of her, striking a pose. She couldn't tell what part of her life was ending, and which part was beginning.

Rick came up unexpectedly. "We"—he stammered and straightened— "we really, really, should make a plan to have some of our own kids after you—"

"Don't mess with me, please."

At twenty-four she was nowhere near having the AMA code stamped on her medical file to indicate the birthing risks of advanced maternal age. She inspected a pair of flats and put them down and molded another dress to her body. She didn't mind thinking of her body as a tool. She honed her body as carefully as a master woodworker sharpened woodworking tools. Her stomach was still flat, but in her mind it was bloated. She wondered how the last trimester would look on her. Her curved and chiseled places showed an added pound with the sensitivity of a jeweler's scale. She puffed her abdomen out to mimic an advanced pregnancy. *I'll be a puffball on stage.*

She heard the door slam as I left on my way to school. She worried that I hadn't had breakfast yet. Rick was ready to go to work and came to say goodbye. His white Pima cotton shirt and fine-combed wool suited him well; a red and blue regimental silk tie made him look sharp. They kissed but a look of distress hovered in his eyes. She gave him an extra hug and his cheerfulness returned. Her knight, *riteris* in Lithuanian, charging off to defend the Bradbury Castle and make good order out of fouled production lines. On the way out he reminded her she had a date to see Page Bradbury that day. "A rich day for you," he said, amusement in his voice.

chapter 25

Page Bradbury had invited her to a leisurely spa session for "girl talk." And Emily had to figure out how to dress for the occasion. She had no trouble feeling attractive in front of men, but she didn't want to be too attractive for Page. Some women are extremely wary of other women, especially pretty women. Better to look like a poor church mouse. Emily decided to dress down.

She went to her studio to teach an early-morning dancercise class, and then, still worrying about Page, she changed out of the sexy tights and leotards and put on a pair of work jeans that had a full crotch and sagged in the rear. She buttoned a boring blouse, slipped on an oversize knit-cotton sweatshirt, and purposefully left her hair unwashed and in disarray. She made a few calls, checked for new messages, ignored my message, read Rick's "I love you," and then, without showering, headed out to meet Page.

She swiped her MetroCard in the aluminum turnstile slot. "Please swipe card again at this turnstile," the readout advised. She swiped it again but did it slowly; she swiped it slower still. People were backing up; the city's irritation gathered force behind her. She swiped it quickly and failed to get through. She tried another turnstile and passed. It was a small victory, a slot of one's own, and it made her feel better.

Warm subway air preceded the train into the station. She rushed down the left side of the stairwell to catch the train, and boarded in the nick of time. The train squealed in the tunnel before reaching Union Square. The air conditioning failed to keep ahead of the mugginess and the body heat from shoppers and late-morning shift workers heading into Manhattan. The subway got moving. Her shirt stuck to the small of her back. Inside the crowded subway car she saw a man sitting with an empty seat on each side of him. He was detached from everyone else, soaping his underarms with an empty bottle. He lifted one arm and rolled the bottle in his armpit, and then, switching arms, he cleansed his other armpit. He looked intense and very busy in his cleansing action. His movement gave her an idea for a new gesture she could use in dance. He rubbed his head afterward, and then his chest. He must have been thinking that he was coming clean in some way. She doubted that he saw his obsession as clearly as she did.

The idea that she was falling in love with a boy terrified her. It made everything else permeable because she could no longer judge emotions close to her. Her self-doubt and confusion leaked into other relationships and she became suspicious of people's intentions toward her.

She arrived late at the spa near the Chelsea Piers late, took a robe from an attendant, showered, and joined Page. She was a good-looking woman in her middle or late thirties, with exceptionally beautiful skin, green eyes, and blond hair tightly wound in a bun. She gestured toward a second tub alongside her own. Emily let her robe slip and, bracing herself on the rim to test the temperature, inched forward.

"I can see why Jay had a thing going for you," Page said. "You have a beautiful body."

"Oh…" Emily let herself down slowly. The praise felt like a poison dart.

Page's climb from chief bookkeeper to the wife of a wealthy man had given her attitude sickness, a crazy kind of moneyed insecurity. And now, waging an assault on Emily's privacy, she pressed on, "Jay can't get me pregnant. I can't get my man to give me a Bradbury baby. I want to have the baby his dad would love."

Her remarks were blatant and the shock of them landed like a punch. But the next thing Page said was impossibly bad. "Did he get *you* pregnant when you guys were dating?"

"Nope," Emily said. She tried not to blink.

Page's gaudy temperament and trash talk, and the Bradburys' wealth, had made her a force in raising large sums of money for good causes. This confident woman could talk to the governor and the junior senator, and yet was reduced to a frenzy about birthing a Bradbury baby.

Her breezy intimacy continued. "Men, what a messed-up piece of work they are. Jay's dad—now, there was a man, a mensch." She paused. "I know. He's ill and out of it at his

Florida place. But, did Jay tell you? He trusts me. His dad gave me the power of attorney to vote his Class A Bradbury shares." She seemed pleased with herself. "In a showdown, I control the Bradbury Corporation. I could fire my husband, kick his butt good." She slapped the side of the tub.

"I'm grateful Jay hired Rick."

"I told him to do it."

"Oh? Thank you."

"Hey, don't thank me. Jay's old man told me to do it. The Oedipal thing, you know. He doesn't trust Jay to make good decisions. I don't trust Jay to make good decisions either. He floats, he circulates, runs here and there, does this and that, cracks the whip to organize trivia, misses the big picture, and he can't stick to any one thing. He drives the staff crazy. Rick has been a lifesaver for us. Steady. Boring. Persistent. He's made a huge difference in an extremely short time." Her aggressive intimacy was in full bloom.

Emily lowered herself into the oozy, primordial warmth of the bath. Only her neck and head remained visible. There had to be a dance in this, a passage from birth to death, the ever recurring. She bridged the social uneasiness by asking Page about Jay's dog Lady, an Irish setter.

"That dog!" Page exclaimed. "I bought Lady a diamond-chipped leash and collar. On Madison Avenue there's a great doggie shop, so after a spat with Jay I'm looking to make up with him and I walk in and say, 'I want one of those and one of those.' It was less than two grand for the pair." This was trickle-down economics at work. Page had escaped her working-class roots.

Emily didn't answer, but turned to look at her, signaling disbelief.

After a shower-and-steam session and a towel wrap, the massage took forty minutes. The smell was mildly medicinal, herbal and spiced with orange. The session ended with a satisfying flourish of towels. Emily got up, felt wobbly, and caught the warmed granite table to steady herself.

"Are you okay?"

She was slightly dizzy and worried: Was the bath too hot for the baby? It nagged and nagged her. "I have to go."

"Oh, don't go yet! I wanted to show you the exquisite jewelry I just picked up for a song at Tiffany's."

"I'm running late." She promised to see Page and Jay the coming Thursday evening, and went to get dressed.

chapter 26

The following day, Emily rehearsed *Scent* with Melissa. My mother's spirit seemed to hover nearby. Emily's copies and approximations of other choreographers' styles had given way to something new—her own style.

Scent was primordial, inexplicable, daunting, confined to stark moves and startling gestures, palms twisted outward, ankles twisted inward, jittery movements far removed from the gracefully balletic *Swan Lake*.

Melissa, eagerly awaiting Jacob's Pillow, was taken in by the new work. Their mood was high. They changed into street clothes and Melissa fixed her hair with two jeweled chopsticks to highlight her youthfulness. The novelty was lovely, and Melissa's oval face and gently slanted eyes echoed her partially Asian heritage. She helped at school functions and the both of them had volunteered to participate in Sister St. Ambrose's art outreach program. They drove across the Williamsburg Bridge to attend a session at the Met.

"BMW," Melissa said. She extended both arms and pointed toward the Brooklyn Bridge. "Gimme a *B*." She said it like a cheerleader. "For *Brooklyn Bridge*." She moved her arms upriver. "Gimme an *M* for *Manhattan Bridge*." And with arms straight ahead, she said, "Gimme a *W* for *Williamsburg Bridge*, and what have we got? BMW."

"You've got a car fetish."

Melissa puckered her mouth. She was gorgeous, almost incorrigibly attractive, sparkling and mercilessly spirited, industrious, and talented, too. A stage mom had cajoled her into dance, prayed to God for help, and then married a rich guy who paid for Melissa's move to New York. Her mom thanked God for a miracle. Then, after nailing a two-year stipend from the rich man, mother dumped the useful man and went back to the Midwest, where she married her third husband.

Melissa, vibrating with energy, moved a chopstick away from her brow. "I'm seeing a guy who actually *drives* a BMW." This sounded like a coup, but no more details were forthcoming.

They had extra time and parked on Delancey to shop at an eyeglass store. Melissa selected a light frame with delicate oval-shaped lenses. She inclined her head at various angles to see how the pair looked on her. "Do they make me look older?" She let it slip that her new man had a few years on her. "My mom married *up* with older guys." She made a goofy face. "Like mother like daughter."

"So what's with this new guy?"

Melissa tapped the bridge of the glasses to fit them closer to her face. "He likes me. He's interesting, and it's like, you know, like I'm adding polyphony to a song." This was expressed with such awkward insincerity that it had to have come verbatim from something the man said to her.

"He's a musician?"

"He's married."

Melissa looked at the frames again. "I don't want to look *too* old." And then defensively, "You were young when you were with Jay."

"I'm not old now."

"But you were really young."

"Jay wasn't married."

Melissa bridled a bit, and her voice took a slightly querulous tone. "You're talking as if you really know what it feels like to be in love. You're too much of the ice girl to let yourself fall for anyone dangerous."

"Rick is safe," she agreed.

"Is he also exciting?"

That dropped like a brick—exciting and safe? The two didn't go together. "So you think I'm an ice girl?"

"Well, you know, you're kinda formal. All business. Discipline. This step and that move, on the mark."

"It's the way I grew up."

Melissa stepped over to a Dolce & Gabbana display case. She checked the eyeglasses closely and decided to buy frames with nonprescription lenses because her eyesight was in fact 20/20. She wanted to look serious and intelligent for her older man. They got back to the car and headed uptown.

Emily said, "You're really putting on a show for this BMW guy?"

"We're sort of, you know, exploring. I'm hoping we like get to know each other better, even if nothing happens."

"What's happened so far?"

"Um—"

"For your sake I hope nothing much happens."

They were driving uptown when Melissa opened up again. "Before you go negative on me, let me tell you what I went through." She started talking about a former boyfriend, an agemate, a poet she had dated for a whole year, a century in the life of a teenager. She said they went to a poetry reading in the Village one night and he recited a cycle of poems that started out with, "I don't love you, I can never love you, I don't even want to be your friend." She coughed and cleared her throat. "Was this his poetic persona speaking? I sat, stupid and smiling, until he finished. And then with a knowing smirk on his face, he went to sit with another girl. So it's like I have this empty chair next to me, advertising, letting our friends know for the next half-hour in a very crowded room what he meant by the poem. Every minute was screaming at me." It smashed her up. She fled to the basement where the recyclables were collected, thinking she was trash.

"So what did you learn from the experience?"

"Not to trust anyone when they talk about love."

How could Emily not trust Rick? She trusted him openly and implicitly, totally, completely, and yet they did not agree on so many issues.

Melissa, recovering from her sadness, said, "The other thing about older guys, they really think they're lucky to have you. Like you've been gift-wrapped or something." She paused. "Don't nag. I'll be all right."

chapter 27

They found a parking spot, a nearly priceless luxury near the museum mile, and scooted right in. They hooked up with a dozen students being escorted by Sister St. Ambrose to the Greek and Roman galleries at the Met. I was among them. From her journals I learned that my amber-flecked eyes felt like sunshine that day. I may cringe at some of my antics, but at the time I was trying everything in my limited repertoire to get her to go to bed with me again. She wrote that my youthful face could have been sculpted in antiquity, firm mouth and full lips. The worst part of her attraction, besides her melancholy guilt, was the effort she had to expend to conceal it.

Sister St. Ambrose came over and greeted her with a wink. "Now you'll see." She nodded in my direction, indicating the "wild thing" she'd called me, and we moved on to another gallery. Her theme was indeterminacy in art. She directed us to a painting of a woman dressed in shimmering gold robes. "An example of Orientalism in the age of colonialism." The oppressive colonial politics of the time was easy to miss because the woman in the painting was beautiful.

Everyone admired it, even me, but I was insufferable, too—a pedant's delight. "Ovid says everyone has at least one physical flaw."

Sister gave Emily a knowing nod, as if to say, "Here he goes again!" Then turned to me. "The spirit and soul are always beautiful, uncorrupted by bodies." We looked closer at the brushwork—"coruscating" was how Sister described it.

"But if you want to stop loving someone," I interrupted, "you just focus on a physical flaw." This remark annoyed Melissa, and probably the rest of the class, too. She laughed to show her contempt.

"You are flawless," I said.

"And you are a pretentious kid."

Both of us smiled. She was right, but it wasn't what I wanted to hear at the time. According to Emily's journals, this insignificant museum event pushed her already difficult attraction for me toward a full-blown obsession: she was afraid to lose me to Melissa.

"Miss, you'll have to stand back," a guard warned Emily.

Her face was too close to my face and we were both too close to the painting. She felt the guard's authority intensely and was unable to speak for a moment. "I'm a little mixed up, a little cuckoo," she said, falling back into immigrant diction, back into a child-state she loathed in herself.

"What's the matter?" Melissa asked.

Emily held a hand to her forehead as if checking for fever. "There's nothing the matter," she insisted. Her emotional life churned with the effort to stay away from me, and it was taking a toll, stealing her energy.

The guard made sure everyone was wearing museum admission buttons. Emily squared her shoulders to show it clipped to her collar. She couldn't bear such close scrutiny, the horrible suspicion of others. She was afraid they would find out about her derelict passion for me.

"This painting," Sister Ambrose began her lecture, "called *Salomé*, painted by Henri Regnault, shows how love can alter art. One day the painter saw a girl with extremely dark hair in Rome who attracted him. He painted her head and called her the "peasant woman." A year later his fondness grew and he enlarged the painting to bust size and called it *Study of an African Woman*. Like Dante's love for the sixteen-year-old Beatrice that Dante had seen only once, this painter's love kept growing for the girl he never saw again. He added three sides to the painting and painted a seductive woman he called Salomé. The original Roman girl who inspired him was long gone from the picture. Regnault had a magnificent new girl that he had created. The final version got raves at the French Salon and he was suddenly famous." I was amazed by the Sister's knowing engagement with art. Then came the spin—

"Converts to Catholicism can learn to love God in the same way, starting with small, private moments and expanding love for Him from panel to panel until He enters the inner soul. And as St. Paul says in his letter to the Galatians, 'There is no longer Jew or Greek, there is no longer slave or free, there is no longer male and female, for all of you are one in Christ Jesus.'"

I liked what she said about St. Paul's letter. Sister insisted that you had to come to the Lord not out of servile ignorance or fear, but with love. I liked that, too. The sister's lecture on Regnault's panel-by-panel obsession and step-by-step ascension to fame animated Melissa. "Do you think I'll be famous?" she whispered to Emily. She was talented and beautiful and eager to raise her performance above the infinite grains of sand that held her close to the beach with other beautiful girls.

"You look warm enough to melt snow," Emily reassured her.

"No, talk to me seriously."

"She is serious," I said.

"Hey, mind your own business."

"You must like me." I wanted her to hear the irony.

She wrinkled her nose like a basset hound sniffing out a challenge. "I don't like you nearly as much as you like yourself."

"Funny," I said. I didn't want to be sidelined, but I didn't snap back. In fact, I did like her.

We left the corridor gallery and squeezed into a small elevator where Emily brushed up against me. Her touch set my heart to beating faster. We got out and entered the Rockefeller Wing, pausing before a glass case protecting an African power figure adorned with metal scraps and studded with hardware, nails, hinges, screws, and bolts. I was mesmerized by it. The pain, the complexity, and the power of one's religious beliefs were perfectly united. Sister St. Ambrose tapped my arm and informed me of Nietzsche's famous dictum:

"If it doesn't kill you, it'll make you stronger."

Sister winked because she didn't like Nietzsche's ideas. A proper and devout God-fearing minister father had raised him, but Nietzsche rebelled. In place of the mysticism of the hereafter, he believed in the primacy of life on earth and the urgent need to make the most of it—a challenge that's more demanding and uplifting than our wish to escape Earth by going to Heaven.

We entered the area that displayed large canoes and carvings. The Rockefeller Wing had been one of my favorite places after my mother first introduced me to it, but it wasn't as popular with the public. Perhaps the silence had a too-delicate weight inside the gallery, a coloring, a pale pink-tinted gray-white, a shade too light to be seen in bright lights of the city. Affecting a casualness I did not feel, I asked Melissa to sit with me on the floor in front of a Melanesian canoe as Sister St. Ambrose addressed the group. "Missionaries converted pagans—"

"The missionaries killed everyone," I whispered to Melissa. "By spreading European diseases." Later in life I would add, by spreading faith-based ignorance, too.

"David," Sister St. Ambrose demanded, "please let the class hear you."

I repeated my statement to no special effect, because the kids were giggling among themselves. Sister St. Ambrose went on about the carved Melanesian poles facing the canoe. "We have no right to call this society a *Third* World society. It's tribal of course, but…"

The penile carvings on the Melanesian canoes were ornate and very large. Sensuality must have been a troubled issue for them also. This wasn't a subject endearing to Catholic schoolteachers. Sister's authority and fearlessness awed me. Some schools would dismiss a teacher for far less. Wilson had run an article called "Museum Smut" in the diocesan magazine and received many supportive comments and e-mails.

The rough territory between smut and sensuality kept many cartographers busy, and each person seemed to need his own handmade map. For Dr. Wilson, it was all of one thing, sex was smut, perhaps regrettably enjoyable smut, a position taken early by Catholic theologians, St. Augustine prominent among them. The conception of smut gained power as the centuries rolled on, and priests became holier if they avoided the unholy parts women offered. This Church-inspired misogyny gave birth to popular pornography as surely as Prohibition gave birth to speakeasies.

Melissa's short skirt had hiked higher to show the underpants triangle. Why had Melissa chosen a tartan skirt and white socks that made her look like a schoolgirl? A dart of jealousy made Emily uneasy. The girl was too attractive for words.

Sister St. Ambrose glanced at the curatorial card and mispronounced the tongue-twisting tribal names associated with the poles. She was ready to move on. We all got up quickly and followed her out, trooping through halls that displayed medieval and Renaissance paintings, mostly religious works because the Church had had the money and the power and paid its painters well. The sister said the images they painted were "books for the illiterate."

You can make people believe in anything, I realized. Nail-studded power figures to protect you, whale-size penile carvings to safeguard your boat, virgins to save you, and love everlasting. People can believe in silly, harsh, dangerous, even horrible things. They can believe they're superior Aryans and infallible leaders, and if you have the power you can force others to make believe they believe in what you believe. A lot of the world's energy was aimed at making people believe one thing or another that they did not want to believe, and museums were full of art that was once propaganda.

We ended the class in the Robert Lehman Wing. Everyone gathered before the Balthus painting, *Nude in Front of a Mantel*. The young girl in the picture appeared to be pleased with her reflection in the mirror.

The painter had been obsessed with girl models. His Japanese wife had looked adolescent into her forties. (At least at a distance.) Hundreds and hundreds of good-looking women walking Madison Avenue wished to look younger. Many men underwent eyelid lifts to look less droopy. Sister St. Ambrose didn't discuss the primal forces behind an unending search for youth. People wanted to be like the species of jellyfish that can grow old and turn round and then grow young. Almost inconceivably so, but researchers tell us it's true.

Like most savvy teachers, she tried to gauge what was safe to teach her young students. She wrapped up the lecture by inserting a new subject, the use of complementary colors. She dismissed the class afterward, and the students broke up to leave the museum. Sister huddled with Emily.

"I noticed that David shows real affection for you."

"Um, I'm nothing special."

"You are—you must be."

She felt uncomfortable under the Sister's scrutiny.

"What I mean is that Spozo's behavior today lacked his

usual outrageousness. You can change his life. He could make a difference in the world."

"I'll try my best."

And if you ask me my opinion, she did.

chapter 28

She recorded this incident among many others in her journal, highlighting it in blue, but the more she talked to herself in those pages, and the more those pages seemed to talk back to her, the deeper the pathos they seemed to reveal. From her journal:

> Rick insists on romance, on symbols of fidelity, dinners out, on flowers. He insists on tradition, endurance like stone. No wasted moves or backtracking. He is always full on and full in, the warrior-knight defending the borders. Occasionally I see doubt creeping in. Occasionally I see him rub his Brown Scapular he wears for good luck and for protection. I tell him that he should let me go and within six months someone else will come along. He takes this as a challenge and is now more eager than ever "to stay the course" with me.

When I read these lines they gave me a chill, and my heart went out to both of them. And now when I think about them, which is often, I'm as divided in my opinion today as I had been unbending earlier. I suppose Rick and Emily were blessed and condemned both at once. They supported each other, and they couldn't understand each other. Rick was stuck in the cult of optimism, hiding behind iron-sided clichés and fixed pieties, and Emily, unknowingly at the time, was like me—we were the searchers, advancing incrementally beyond our failures.

They were more vulnerable than I had been. She loved the solidity of Rick's beliefs, but when she looked at her own life, she saw no such thing as a God fixer looking out to help people in need. She didn't see a fixed career path, a fixed nature, a fixed fortune, a straight line to good performance. And she believed that there should be such a thing.

I was fortunate in many ways that they were not so fortunate. I wasn't stuck to a catechism. I had my mother to teach me and she had borrowed ideas from Isaiah Berlin, who believed that from the *Crooked Timber of Humanity*, nothing straight could be made. You see, my mother liked athletic boys but she vehemently disliked ignorant boys and had pushed and pushed for me to learn more. She arranged classes for me that few kids my age would have attended.

Emily imagined my future and wrote about it in her journals—my future without her.

He will see my face in other women's faces. He will hear my voice in the sound of other female voices. I will become the memory spreading across the many folds of his life to reflect his youth and adolescent promise, and then I will blur in his recollection, the woman of his youth, the first love, the first extended sensual experience, my memory absorbed into his future adult relationships—an attraction that forever whispers its intimate sounds.

chapter 29

The following day, Jay called Emily and asked if she had had a chance to inspect Sara's art and see if there was anything more he could buy on the company's dime. She promised to get back to him. She was working on her choreography and tried to keep dance separated from her personal life, but the personal life had invaded her choreography. At this late date before her appearance at Jacob's she was experimenting again. She had been known for elliptical, lyrical work that now became jumpy, jumbled, and acrobatically willful. The sparse look was complicated and distressed. She stripped a new dance to staccato gestures, but it was claustrophobic, and then she fled the restricted movement to try baroque in another dance. The individual steps stumbled and lagged, got twisted up in details and looked crooked when the whole thing came together. If art was intuition under house arrest, she had not found the house to live in.

Then suddenly and mysteriously, as if it had always been fated, Jacob's Pillow gave her a more prominent time slot to perform at the festival. Things were beginning to happen in her career. She set aside the raw things she wouldn't have time to rehearse. Melissa's unspoiled airiness worked beautifully in *Scent* and *Kiss*, but Emily was still looking for a suitable male dancer to dance *Trio*, and the time to find one was impossibly short.

She briefly considered Langston but instead of getting *behind* her choreography, he wanted to get on top of it and reduce her style to his style. Her craft and her willful confidence had become his enemies. Instead of advancing her work in areas in which his own mostly balletic experience fell short, he insisted on pointing out her work's shortcomings in comparison with the whole world of dance since Louis XIV.

This was a burden no new choreographer could carry. It reminded her of the difficulty she had in learning English. Her early mispronunciations amused teachers, her misspellings irritated them, and she took her whacks from superior spellers, who invariably associated bad spelling with inferior upbringing and slacker indifference.

It's hard to do good work that pleases everyone, but it's even harder to please yourself, and it gets harder as you get better. She called Langston to inquire after male dancers he knew without telling him she had been chosen to dance at Jacob's Pillow. Their conversation was short, and as events would show, completely misdirected. He recommended that she see Dylan Correa.

She asked me to come along. The subway was less crowded riding against rush-hour traffic, and when we exited on Canal

Street, the street vendors looked bored because the afternoon crowd had gone and the evening crowd heading for Chinatown restaurants or Mulberry Street Italian eateries had not materialized yet.

We turned up Bowery and came to the Correa Dancers space, located above a restaurant supply house. A man with a French accent greeted her from a window. He said he was Dylan. His short hair was as curly as mine, but his was bleached gold, the roots fashionably dark. He buzzed the door open and we climbed the wide stairs to his studio. A number of dancers were present. They gave Emily a quick and indifferent inspection and continued to practice.

Emily had not spoken directly to Dylan but had relied on Langston. This led to confusion as she took off her jacket and slipped out of her cargo pants, ready to dance.

"Ah, you are a *dancer* as well!" Dylan's surprise was friendly.

She was taken aback. She had come to audition him but Dylan, she realized, had gotten the message wrong and assumed she had come to apply for a spot on *his* group. She decided to play along. He showed her where to stand and how to place her feet. He was older than she was, and his bright-eyed politeness cornered her into a strangely unprepared, almost complacent moment. She felt like a novice again, knocking on doors. She glanced at me and I shrugged.

"We'll dance this phrase together," Dylan said briskly.

He was quick and slender and extremely graceful. I watched him demonstrate a sequence, and he watched Emily repeat it. She wasn't in her best form and not as alert as she usually was. She had had a bout of morning sickness and was eating saltines to quash nausea. She stumbled badly. A dancer nearby tittered.

"You don't have to be ashamed for me," Emily said.

A huge amount of practice had gone into making dance, and much of the work was inevitably futile. What's more, even though she'd been a dancer from the age of five, she found it difficult to talk with dancers. Their personal gossip left her cold; the constant career chatter was even chillier. Some dancers needed an audience in order to do their best, she could dance without an audience, and dance with the same intensity, but even so, she needed to see other dancers dancing to measure her own ability. She needed to see the work of other choreographers to mark her progress.

"Honestly," Dylan interrupted, "you dance with what we say…" He looked at the stained ceiling and addressed muses unseen by her. "You're holding too much back, not letting yourself go. You won't know how far to go until you've gone too far."

She tried to absorb his words without a change in her expression. Yes, she was holding back. All her life she had held back, but not when she was dancing. She let it all go when she was dancing, but she wasn't doing it for Dylan.

"I didn't know you were a dancer," he said, almost as an afterthought. This unsettled her further.

He took her aside and instructed her to make her movements a little thinner, a little longer and stronger. He was extremely kind. He hesitated "Maybe…" He hesitated again. "Maybe you're too bright and too perky? You know what I'm saying? We're looking for a darker quality. A muted edginess."

He tugged at the ragged edge of his lemon-colored shirt. He clearly had no clue that she had come to audition him.

"What did Langston say to you?" she asked.

"He recommended you for fund-raising work. Development."

"For development work?"

It suddenly became clear to her. Langston had thought so poorly of her dancing and choreography that he had recommended her for office work. She explained why she had come. Dylan looked at her as if she was one of the nut cases stalking the Bowery, and then they both laughed. To perform at Jacob's Pillow was Dylan's biggest break yet. He accepted the invitation.

chapter 30

Emily had found her male dancer, but she was still upset because she had stumbled in front of his class. One awkward move in Dylan's studio had brought years of good work to a clumsy finish. This incident, an inversion of her recent success, made her fearful. She could be admired in one situation and spurned in another. Something within her accepted this instability, but she didn't like it. No more than anyone else did. It terrified her to think she was a step away from failure anytime she moved a foot forward.

Her pregnancy filled her with a complicated anxiety. She was suspicious of every muscle spasm, tenderness and soreness, and change in appetite. Her ob-gyn had given her the green light to continue dancing, but another doctor could have just as easily put her on an extensive not-to-do list. In addition to no wine, no unpasteurized cheese, no pepperoni, no sushi, all of which she accepted dutifully, the one other thing a cautious doctor could have said to her was to avoid exercise that pushed her pulse above 140 bpm. She would have had to give up dance.

"What's the matter?" I asked as we stood on the subway platform on the way home after our visit with Dylan Correa. I was carrying her gym bag.

"I don't know," she said, testing her mood. "My stumble back there knocked me off my pace. I feel like I'm pushing when I need to be letting go, pulling when I need to be floating."

The subway car we entered was crowded and we had to stand separated from each other. She felt her stomach furtively, thinking back to the spa date she had with Page and wondering if Page had persuaded Jay to go to a fertility clinic.

"How about going to Coney Island?" I asked. "Just to have fun?"

She said okay. We held on to a pole and she looked up at me. The shadows under my eyes were deeper. I was studying like crazy in my advanced classes, organizing like mad to get into college. The theater had become my lifeblood. She probably saw my high forehead and cheekbones and amber-flecked eyes all held together by a promising youth who would have a great future, my features changing, growing stronger—or maybe she saw just a pain in the ass.

I had gotten Sister St. Ambrose to read Thornton Wilder's essay in preparation for staging *Our Town*. Wilder argued that there's something deeply unsatisfied and unrequited in the American character, a yearning that never stops searching for love and youth, not because it is lost as in Proust's search for lost time but because it can never be found in the right proportion.

"We're all longing for something or someone to come along," I said. "I got in trouble in school on the subject. Dr. Wilson was pitching ethics and faith at our religion class and was going on about St. Augustine. I turned to a girl next to me and told her that St. Augustine believed that male erections were the mark of original sin. That freaked her out."

Emily acknowledged my smile. "And you were hauled into the principal's office for using the word *erection*."

I nodded, my curly hair dancing. "She complained to Dr. Wilson."

"You didn't have to repeat the word *erection* several times."

"Nope."

"But you did."

"I did. I was trying to be constructive. It was my way to lower the alarms that the thing causes."

Three subway stops later enough people stepped off for us to sit next to each other. I sat close, intimate, my thigh touching hers and warmth invaded me. Maybe such feelings belonged to the natural order, maybe she felt them, too, but natural or not, allowed or forbidden, I loved it.

On the Brooklyn side of the East River the subway car raced along the underground track as it inclined upward, and, like a whale breaking water, the cars breached daylight, rising above the rooftops. I took her hand, and she, hesitating at first, her fingers on fire, pressed my hand in response.

The subway ride terminated at Surf Avenue. We got off the train and skirted a young crowd cruising the carnival atmosphere. Nearby the abandoned roller coaster looked like a python in search of prey. The rusting parachute jump stalked the sky. We were seeing the old Coney Island, a ramshackle area that city planners hoped to rebuild by the time you read this. I stopped in front of a shooting concession. Standing mute, she saw the huge rabbits I was eyeing. I slid a bill toward the concessionaire.

"I'm going to win you something."

I wanted a prize to give her, to amaze her, to make her proud of me, but all she wanted was for me to be next to her. I picked up an air gun chained to the stand, my left hand gripped the front, and my cheek on the stock, I pumped out ten shots. Puffs of compressed air disappeared and the chain-driven ducks rattled on undisturbed.

"I'm not having any luck."

"It's not luck," the concessionaire told me.

Even here, shooting ducks as close to sitting as I was likely to find, I had to be calm and steady. Not too quick or too eager, nor abrupt or angry, and I had to move the sight steadily in font of the moving target. We watched a customer walk away with a large stuffed rabbit.

I had ten more shots, and now I had to be very careful. I let loose in a fury, the shots arching high and then low. Nothing hit, nothing won. The chained ducks kept chugging along as I shoved a crumpled bill across the counter for another setup. The concessionaire took my money, glancing at Emily. She gave him a baleful look.

I shot the next load without hitting a duck. A line of sweat marked my forehead. The air smelled of oil-greased puffs. Emily felt badly and tried to make light of it by giving me a reassuring smile. The concessionaire took back the rifle in apparent disgust with me, and laid it carefully on the carpet-covered counter. "Ma'am," he said, "some young bucks get to shoot their ducks easily. Looks to me like your boy has got to call down an artillery barrage."

"Shut up," I said.

"Oh, don't be a sore loser," Emily said.

I jerked my arm out of her grip. "Why do people love a good loser? I want the prize." I was combative, assertive, and proud. I had to win her a prize. My voice had grown confident despite the bad shooting. She knew what I meant: *You're my prize. I want you.*

"Let's get some cotton candy," she said.

"You're dissing me."

"David, don't be a sourpuss."

We turned onto a street leading to the boardwalk. She paused at a shop window displaying shorts, sun hats, and sunglasses. She went inside and I followed. She checked the racks and didn't like the orange, the lavender, or the many black outfits. She chose instead lime-green pants, a color she had never worn before, and retreated behind a curtain to try them on. Not sure of her taste, she came out to show them off to me. She pulled the low-hugging material at her hips and smoothed the seams. "What do you think?"

"Your boy likes the tank top," the salesgirl interrupted.

"I'm not her boy."

Emily tried on a set of small earrings and then chose larger hoops. Her jump from a perfectionist on stage to a consumer of beauty and fashion products captivated me. She inspected lacquered shoes in the window and asked the clerk for size seven. Her arches were strong and a terrific aid to her dancing. The clerk found size seven and a half and she put them on. My voice reached for a lower register. "The leather is scuffed."

The shoes were shopworn, or had been returned, but she ignored the scuff marks and asked the clerk to put her old shoes and clothes in a bag because she wanted to wear red high heels and new clothes. The clerk went to package the items. "Why are you buying the shoes?" I demanded. My tone wasn't the least conciliatory. "I wouldn't waste money on someone's old shoes."

But the shoes reminded her of the dancer in the movie *The Red Shoes*. When she was breaking away from Lithuanian folk dancing, her first love, she found Fred Astaire and Ginger Rogers, and later *Red Shoes* deepened her love for dancing. According to the movie, a dancer who relies upon the dubious comforts of human love will never be a great dancer. They say that's true for all artists. None can be good if they're loved so much as to be fully satisfied. But I'm gonna quarrel with that.

We went outside. A car with a cracked muffler clawed at the evening silence, and a bunch of young men, windows open, arms hanging out, yelled something stupid at her and one of them gave a stinging whistle.

"You're dressed like a streetwalker."

But she often wore different costumes to allow her to enter the emotional space of people she wanted to define in her dance. "You get out of the way if they come back at us."

"You want me to run?" My voice had a mocking edge.

We faced each other and the accordion-wide space narrowed. It could never be so good, she must have been thinking, never anything so fine as this moment of romantic illusion.

I picked up on her gestures, the way her hand went palm up at an uncertain angle. Her walk was now my walk. I was losing my swagger and working on poise. I repeated the words she used when she spoke to me. I mussed my hair and had started to apply a bit of wax to it to mimic how she did her hair in points. And she felt different, too. There was something mutual in the air between us she had not experienced before. She felt my rhythm in her own breathing; my scent permeated her in a pleasing way. I felt as if her heart was beating inside my rib cage. I pulled her palm to my chest. "Feel it?"

"Yeah, what are we going to do now?"

She was churning inside and kept pressing my hand. Her confusion felt immense. "We could dance," she said, "call ourselves *The EmilyDavid* dancers." Her romanticism was gliding beyond reason. "Yes, like the dancers Ruth St. Denis and Ted Shawn coming together as the *Denishawn* dancers." She was happy.

"I would love that," I said. "We're not that different. You're only a few years older than me. We could be together."

"Ted Shawn was the founder of Jacob's Pillow," she said. Her excitement skipped along. "But I think your mother might not have wanted us to."

"You're wrong. She only said I had to wait for the right girl to come along."

Young love, I was thinking later in life. How beautiful and adorable and flawless in its illusions.

She glanced at the abandoned roller coaster that had once hurtled cars on screeching rails, riders screaming. She felt the same scream-like turbulence rising within her and she wanted to scream, not because she was thrilled but because she was afraid.

chapter 31

That weekend, Emily and Rick met their social obligations by going sailing with Page and Jay. She had asked me to come, but I was busy with *Our Town* rehearsals, so what I write here, I lifted from her journals. They docked to have dinner. The Bradburys had discovered a new place that catered to their whims, a restaurant built with ancient timber to give it character. Actually, Emily said that it looked like a firetrap. It was a place I would see later. The wooden floors in the main building creaked and the red seats and red curtains absorbed too much light and made the room dim. A tall, husky-voiced server came forward to show them to the private outdoor dining area in a garden protected by a large canopy. They inspected the faux-medieval table next to a propane-fired barbecue. Uncooked food was kept in a small refrigerator and the condiments were handy. The air smelled of sesame oil, ginger, and lemongrass. It was a place where you could grill your own food if you wanted to. The idea behind the restaurant was roughing it, though there was no roughing involved.

Page asked a server to bring them the fixings for gin and tonics and when he did she took the bottles and told him they wanted to be alone. She began mixing the drinks, adding an expert flourish she had learned when she worked as a bartender during a now-erased portion of her earlier life. Emily asked to have only tonic. Page gave her a don't-be-a-wet-blanket look.

"I quit drinking," Emily said. "To keep my energy high and my weight down."

Page feigned a look of wide-eyed jealousy. "Does all this mean you're pregnant?"

Rick's head seemed to ricochet away from those words. He shot a murderous look at Jay.

"How could I dance pregnant?"

Emily's remark was accurate and misleading. Page sighed, and poured the drinks and handed her a tonic. Page raised her glass in a toast.

"Have another drink," Jay said.

Page had had several by now. She swished about, giggly with drink, organizing Jay's grill.

"You don't have to do that," Jay said. "Darling, I'm competent to grill sausages."

Page sat down to keep her balance. She pointed a pair of tongs at Emily and Rick. "You guys are probably wondering why my big barrel-chested man is being so quiet today."

"They're not wondering about it," Jay said. He arranged the utensils the way he had them arranged before Page took over.

"Yes, they are wondering. They want to know why hubby

and me went to a fertility clinic." She was in an aggressively intimate mood.

"They don't want to know that. You mind giving me back the tongs?"

The business of wanting and having kids, of birth and decay, percolated uncomfortably.

"Jay," Page demanded. "We can tell them, can't we, babe?"

"Darling, please stop braying about having kids."

Page stewed silently.

Jay attended to his cooking. He held up a skewered sausage. "Eating Pennsylvania sausages can kill anyone inside of a year."

"Farmer's sausage," Page corrected him. Her native Southern lilt hardened. "Friday was the best time of the month for us to have sex."

"They don't want to know that." Jay's eyes betrayed his embarrassment.

"La-de-*da*, there he goes."

Jay rearranged the sausages on the grill. Page waited for him to say something and not getting a response, she went on. "I married a Master of the Universe. You know those guys? Up in Manhattan high-rises? The Big Bonus guys. Golden parachutes. Swiss accounts. The Hamptons. They're supposed to have millions of sperm just squirming to conquer female territory. So what do we find out at the clinic? My hubby has a makeshift hundred thousand or so in a shot. It sounds like a fortune, but it's small change."

Jay appeared to be straining to maintain his good humor. She gestured to columnar stones that served as a stagey land-scaping backdrop. "I like those rocks, babe."

"Darling, it's basalt," Jay said. "Columbia basalt. The restaurant owner told me he had them shipped in on a railcar from the Columbia River Basin." He paused and added doubtfully, "Priapic, I suppose." His tone and manner were peaceful. Age was taking its toll on him. Page took a sip of her gin and tonic and got up and did a pelvis-thrusting stay-in-place dance. She then turned to Rick and Emily. "Why are you two lovebirds so quiet?"

Neither one answered her. Rick shrugged, and Page went on without hostility. "I'm supposed to keep a chart of the good days to have sex with Jay and snatch that baby from cosmic oblivion. Big joke, right? The playing field is tilted against me." She sipped from her glass. "You guys know that us gals have only four hundred eggs to squander in a lifetime."

"They don't want to know that," Jay said.

Page nodded her head. "That's right—four hundred eggs. From day one we have to watch those eggs. A single basket and a bunch of eggs. From first menses to menopause only four hundred eggs. One a month, sometimes two a month. We can't go squandering them on jerks."

"I like that joke, darling," Jay said.

He didn't take offense easily. Page acknowledged his calmness with a dismissive hand gesture. "Nothing wrong with *me*. No rotten eggs inside me. I could be an egg donor, for God's sake. Freeze them. Sell them. I tell you, it's his sperm." Her unguarded openness was fascinating. She turned to Emily. "Why are you so jumpy? Every sound makes you pop a little."

"All this talk about fertility," Emily protested.

"I'm having a hard time getting pregnant," Page said flatly.

"But I'll bet if you crossed a street and so much as looked at a guy, you'd get pregnant."

"I hope not."

Jay was dishing up the sausages. Emily wasn't hungry, but Rick looked alarmingly eager to eat. They were in a quagmire of emotions. Rick stabbed his sausage and chased bits of meat to the edge of his plate. Page had her green eyes half-closed, probably to dwell on some unhappy thought. Emily imagined a dance with four dancers in search of meaning in their lives. Had the Bradburys not been so generous in supporting her choreography, in hiring Rick, and in supporting my college fund, she would have found some excuse to avoid them.

chapter 32

That week Emily delivered two of Sara's jewel-like boxes reminiscent of Joseph Cornell's work to Bradbury, and felt Jay's eyes eagerly seeking her own as he asked his accounting manager to cut her a check. She took the sum in hand and they went into the hallway.

"Doing anything this afternoon?" Jay asked. "If you can spare some time, I've got a fun project for us. We can do a candy shoot."

"What's a candy shoot?"

"We hit a few stores to study competitors' packaging." Jay had an art director to do that kind of work, but she didn't call him out on it. "It's a blast," he said. "Forensic consumer studies." He brushed his hair three times, his fingers leaving a trail.

She weighed the disadvantage of saying *no* and deciding there was less risk in saying *yes*, she accepted Jay's invitation. He walked ahead, bullying his steps down a short hallway to the art director's office to get a camera. He came out with a camera bag and guided her past the alert receptionist, bending her head to avoid looking at her boss heading into the late-afternoon sunshine with an attractive woman who wasn't his wife.

They stopped at a grocery store and photographed a selection of Brown & Haley boxed candies that occupied a shelf carrying eight or ten brands. Jay photographed the candy exactly as it appeared, some boxes orderly and fronted on the shelf, others haphazardly disarranged by roving hands. The art director's focus group would study the photographs later, compare it with their competitor's copy, and evaluate the transparent wrappers and the glued-on gold and ruby medallions announcing "NEW! 30% MORE!" The art director would then confirm these findings with another group of shoppers who wore retina-tracking devices to record their eye movements while shopping. Research to help Bradbury clients dominate shelves. Jay photographed product at three more stores without taking a break. They were standing in front of the last store on Jay's list. A breeze rustled Emily's hair.

"Dinner?" Jay asked. "If Rick doesn't mind you coming home late?"

"Rick is in Baltimore. You know that."

Jay offered an innocent look.

"Jay, you're a sweetheart, but I don't want to start anything new we would regret."

"Dinner with me won't turn you into a tart."

She smiled. "I've never known you to be so needy."

"Can I just license you for an evening?" His grin met her smile. "Just for one evening?"

She measured the amount of politeness required to rebuff

him. Jay had no power over her talent, over her work, over her ambition or her future, and unlike Page, Emily felt no magnetism in the Bradbury name. He was as cuddly as a stuffed toy, growing fluffier each year. Pointedly, she checked her smartphone. This alarmed him.

"Don't call Rick."

"I'm calling a friend."

She texted me to say that she was in Long Island and that I should fix myself something to eat. I texted back: "D u know Walt Whitman ws born n Huntington?" I added several lines of Walt Whitman I had saved:

> I Sing the Body electric…To be surrounded by beautiful, curious, breathing, laughing flesh is enough…I do not ask any more delight—I swim in it, as in a sea.

The American mythical open range that could lure a person like Whitman to travel beyond his or her station was fizzling in Huntington, where most people lived contentedly within the range of big-box stores. She showed my message to Jay, intending to impress him with my college abilities.

Relieved that she wasn't contacting Rick, Jay was also unimpressed. "Business guys don't get to do the fancy dancing stuff."

"But you tried?"

He was evasive and looked away.

She listened to a peculiar shift in his tone, backtracking, uneasy, as if fleeing some inadequacy. She texted me: "Your benefactor says business guys don't read poetry." She held up the phone to show the message to Jay and asked him to complete it. Jay stared at the screen; his fingers cut several new grooves in his salt and pepper hair. She got another text from me before Jay could think it through: "Have a gd time. I'm on a hot date myself!"

This startled Emily. I was ripping at her heart, forcing her to think she was losing me. She held her breath, and then flipped the phone shut. She was instantly tense, wondering why I had kept my date secret from her. She caught sight of a young man walking away and his broad back made her think it was me. It took her breath away.

"What's on your mind?" Jay asked.

"I just had a mental blip."

Suddenly deflated, upset that I was seeing another girl, she felt a panoramic futility in her secret attraction. Jay remained oblivious to the tension. She knew exactly where he was heading and what he wanted that night.

"I'm not going to sleep with you, Jay."

Her voice remained level, not cold and not warm, a little on the hard side but softened with a smile. Jay's eyes were starting to look jellied, lazy. A look of resignation announced itself in a shrug of his shoulders and his smile faded, hiding wonderful teeth, square, porcelain white, and glistening, alarmingly attractive for a man his age.

"All right, let's have dinner," he said.

Jay drove her to the city, to a restaurant on the Brooklyn side of the East River. He rushed a martini and ordered another one, and chatted aimlessly and expansively. She kept her phone on the table. In a wistful, exhaling admission, he said, "No, no,

I shouldn't think marital boredom would be enough to have you cheat on Rick."

She sipped her glass of orange juice and ordered a tofu dish; he settled on a porterhouse steak. His table manners were fine-tuned to the sawing of meat, vigorous, but he now seemed distracted, and the pieces entering his mouth were not so much a carnivore's delight as chewy, businesslike work.

Eating in silence, she glanced at the amber-gray evening reflected in the East River. Jay motioned to the server to bring him another drink. His speech was slurred. "I have a vision," he said. He went on to say that they could have had a good married life together, but when she remained silent he once again retreated. "I guess most everyone I know today has a vision of one kind or another. Politicians, gurus. You can't get a bowl of soup in this town without getting the soup server's vision about what's wrong and what could be made right in this town. Even Rick claims to have vision about what needs to be done at the company."

She made a face to show her loyalty to Rick.

"So, may I return to my Emily vision?" Jay's voice began floating somewhere beyond her hearing. The shimmering river had turned into a black surface reflecting Manhattan. She felt her abdomen surreptitiously and thought about me.

Jay kept talking. "…sympathy…pious soul Rick…Page was quickest gal in the Bradbury accounting department to balance a man's ledger, the quickest… "

Emily wondered where I was at that moment. It hurt her to think I was on a date, and a chunk of jealousy lodged in her heart.

Jay got up. Tilting a little, he wandered off to the men's room. He came back looking better. They finished eating and the server cleared their plates. "You're right," Jay said, "I shouldn't surrender to sentiment." Dropping to a whisper, he leaned forward. "What if I offered a donation to the organized good helpers of your choice in your name?"

"Charity is your new bedtime strategy?"

He nodded. "You're not weakening, are you?" Then he glanced out the window. "Not likely. But if you change your mind, there's the United Fund and the Red Cross."

She would have preferred Doctors Without Borders, Human Rights Watch, or Amnesty International, but she remained silent. He signaled for the check. "So tell me Emily, why do I want you around?"

The unthinkable came back to her. This man she'd dismissed as an incurable bed-switcher had deeper feelings for her. "You're still in love with me?" Her voice was high, uplifting, and incredulous.

"Now, now, now." His speech slowed. "Love is a loser's game. I *like* you because—" He looked out the window. "You're respectful, kind, loyal, hopeful, friendly, helpful, bright, informed, and, at the moment, unlikely to go to bed with me." His voice was raggedy and low-pitched from drinking too much. His eyes had reddened into a disconcerting gaze. He asked for water and the server brought him water along with the check. He drank slowly. "For you, it was orange juice after sex."

She didn't want to be reminded. She turned away from the intimacy he was offering and reached for her phone.

"What are you doing now?"

She gave him a sharp look.

"You really don't have to call Rick," he said, his anxiety speaking. "This is between you and me." She held for four rings before my voice mail took over, but she didn't leave a message.

"I wasn't calling Rick."

Jay perked up. "Would it be terrible to suspect that you, dear protector of the lost art of dance, and I, master of our great BCC Empire, are being spurned?" He pushed away from the table. "If this is our last goodbye, how about us visiting our old haunts in the city? They were never the same after we broke up."

chapter 33

She had a theory about Jay's marital life. Without a strong woman to guide him, Jay was a foolish man, and like all foolish men who looked to strong women to rescue them, he resented Page's influence and looked to affairs with other women to restore his sense of manliness. He stuck his hand out to signal the valet outside the restaurant.

"You're not driving," Emily said. She felt like a caretaker.

Several cabs had lined up; she motioned for one and the driver drove them to a bar in Manhattan they had once enjoyed, a bar that hadn't checked IDs closely back then. The fun Emily remembered had emptied from the place; the rapturous dancers on ecstasy had moved on, and the staff was older, the clientele, too. Emily went to the ladies' room to call me again. I didn't pick up so she texted me, "u be home by TEN tnight." She returned to find Jay sitting on a barstool next to a woman, apparently, a self-invited friend.

"What's coming down?" the woman was asking.

"Nothing is coming down," Jay said. He looked ruffled. He was trying to keep his head up, which appeared to be spring-mounted, weaving in faintly elliptical pauses. "I'm a dunce on a stool waiting for nothing to happen to me tonight."

"Hey," the woman said, getting up, her tone heated and cracked. "I'm not wasting my time on a souse like you." She ambled away.

"What happened to friendship?" Jay said. "I was being nice."

"I need to get you home."

She had done all she could and felt motherly now. She recalled what Page had said: Jay's father didn't trust him to make good business decisions. That's why he'd given Page power of attorney to vote the family shares.

They went out to the street and Emily packed him off in a cab to Grand Central Station for the train north. She then flagged a second cab and found herself wrapped in a feeling that comes over you when you've had an expensive dinner, been out on the town late, and had a lousy time. Why had she bothered?

chapter 34

Her heart sank when she discovered I wasn't home. Rick was still away in Baltimore. She switched off the lights inside the house and enclosed herself in a delicate privacy. She rolled the shade up and was surprised to see that it had just begun to rain. The rain left a shine on the sidewalk and the streetlights sparkled. The sound of it on the window calmed the havoc inside her. She was like a moth fluttering in the shadow of her own thoughts, battering to find a way out.

She retrieved her journal, a spiral school notebook, one of a dozen red notebooks she kept separate from the Lithuanian journals in green covers. Her thoughts pushed on each other, demanding changes in her life. She wrote in an unpunctuated broad sweep of emotion, not noticing the time. The sound of the rain kept lulling her into a deep personal unfolding. The urgent need to master new work lost its grip. Her fear of miscarriage faded, her adulterous affair lost its urgency. She felt suddenly without ambition and without desire. Layer on layer of tension curled away. Careerism and dance, her thoughts about Rick, seemed to vaporize, along with her thoughts about me, and then at last she was pleasantly alone with her baby. She wanted the baby. She loved her baby.

Washing up to get ready for bed, her eyes bright and without deceit, she wondered how she had landed in such a deceitful place. She had transferred the love she felt for Sara to me, but something desperate had happened in the translation that she could not reveal to anyone. If there was a higher helpful spirit out there, this was the time she needed it.

She settled in for a night of loneliness. *A date? David is out on a date?* The peacefulness she had just experienced took a sudden jolt. She started thinking about me out on a date. Who was I with? What was I doing? Who could it be? She was unprepared for this development. *Wasn't it true that once a man learned to make love to a woman, it was easier to love other women?* she asked her journal. She kept worrying, fearing that I had fallen for one of my agemates, a girl who was prettier, sillier, and much happier. These thoughts kept her awake until I came home at two in the morning. She didn't greet me, but at last she could sleep.

Restless, she dreamed of a whirlpool with a baby at the center, and waking in panic she feared she was miscarrying. She rushed to bathroom. In the bright light she saw her flushed face. Like Balthus's Japanese wife, she might look adolescent into her forties, but overwrought at the moment, she felt disfigured by age and by worry. She observed herself. There were no lies in the small pores of her skin; the lies were all in her head. Trembling, she removed a tiny amount of concealer she had missed. Nothing seemed awry; the baby was tiny and safe, and the tenderness of her breasts was normal. She went to bed pacified.

On waking in the early morning she felt exhausted, tense, and irritable, and an opposing energy shook her. She was angry at me for coming home late without calling her in advance. She didn't tell me that. Instead, she demanded that I clean up my room, take the garbage out, and get a decent haircut. She became dictatorial to keep the chaos within her from usurping the order she needed. She scolded me for leaving my clothes in a mess in the laundry room. It offended her that I seemed carefree and amused by the sudden onslaught of order. I touched her shoulder and she slapped me savagely hard. Then she shrank back in alarm at what she had done. Her journal said this:

> *I'm suddenly a wild thing, an ugly thing in David's life.*
> *The Wicked Witch of the West. I'm the "older" woman*
> *he can't rid himself because I'm also his guardian.*

Her heart took a leap as she studied my glowing red face. "I shouldn't have hit you." She was Maya in the play I was writing, and now she had become Medea, vengeful beyond human reason, angry unto death. Her edginess receded but her longing and the fear persisted.

She blamed herself for her weakness, but offered me new advice. "Why don't you do more *boy* things with your dramatic personas? Take up with Tom Sawyer and Huckleberry Finn. They kept away from girls."

"I don't have to copy anyone to be like me."

My flaming-red cheek was a shade lighter, and we made peace with each other. I promised her I'd read more Mark Twain. Over time I tried to channel my inner Huck Finn, but I never got as good as Huck Finn, not even close.

chapter 35

After this encounter, two days ran badly. She was really afraid that I was seeing someone regularly. I didn't volunteer to tell her otherwise. I saw her distress as giving me an upper hand. In the days that followed, in an attempt to make sense of her emotions, she cut herself loose from any fixed idea she ever had about sex, about sensuality, about desire and jealousy, about will and the moral superiority of abstinence, about career and misfortune, about Rick and having children, about talent, about the ways in which she had dealt with ambition, and the fact that everything ends. She cut loose from any fixed idea about life itself.

There was an uneasy excitement and a new rush of energy at her dance rehearsals with Dylan Correa and Melissa. With Jacob's Pillow looming, she cut back on everything other than rehearsals. She eliminated her Langston workshops and quit going to the gym. Her focus was on Jacob's Pillow.

She refined basic dance elements with secondary details. She rearranged the music tracks and borrowed ideas from Christo and Judy Chicago and Barbara Kruger and Jenny Holzer for staging. She had by now long rebelled against the full-body coverup costumes that had earned her a family audience, and chose the revealing tightness of minimal clothing.

She had no idea where her dance appetite originated, a hunger never satisfied. Like all things it would end, perhaps after a bad spill and a broken pelvic bone, maybe arthritis, or a blue, swollen ankle and a badly reset toe. But for now, she was still unafraid, and audiences responded, sometimes by whistling and stomping and handclapping.

She'd been rehearsing *Trio* when the air conditioner went on the fritz again. Saturated, they danced in wet costumes. In *Trio*, Melissa was a vertiginous, whirling Pan-like character, and Emily danced Echo, mesmerized by Dylan. The three of them reached an electric intensity.

They were on their last rehearsal of the day when Page Bradbury showed up. Emily was thrown off her mark. She couldn't defeat the emotional demons allied with a woman who remained suspicious of her.

"So this is the fabled Sara-and-Emily studio," Page said.

The transformation from Sara's art studio to Emily's dance studio wasn't complete, but with the mirrors, a CD player, and two cases of bottled water, it was getting there. Sara's art was at one end of the storefront. My mother had worked in acrylic plastics, switched to painting and soft sculpture, and finally added photography. Though much of her work was controversial, there were a number of beautifully made, inoffensive, and wistfully ambiguous objects that stood the test of art appreciation without inserting quarrelsome political ideas or gender-bending allusions.

"Page, what brings you to the low-rent district?"

Page looked exhausted, suddenly worn. She said she had just seen her parents, who had returned from an overseas mission. "They're holed up in a single-room efficiency."

Page was their only child, born in Brazil, where her parents had spent most of their middle and late years working as missionaries but had been expelled for preaching something similar to liberation theology and moved on to Nicaragua and eventually to Mexico City. Page had rejected their life of unrelenting poverty.

"And now that they're sick and have worked outside the country all their lives, they don't have Medicare or Social Security." The bad news was choking Page. Emily put an arm around her, trying to calm her. Melissa and Dylan, uncomfortable, said they were ready to go. They said goodbye and left.

"Mom and dad—"

"But they have you."

"I offered."

Page needed a handkerchief and Emily handed her one.

"They said they don't take wages from sin, meaning me. They asked me to leave." She straightened and tried to breathe.

"What did you do to deserve that?"

"I married a guy they hate."

With so few things to startle me about Christian life, this really did.

Page forced herself to sound happier. "We could be better

off and good friends if Jay stops mumbling your name in his sleep."

"Oh, no. Please." There was no wiggle room to denounce the unconscious. "Look, I'm sorry. I'm not contributing anything except dance to this situation."

Page wiped her nose. "I'm afraid. I'm afraid. I'm really scared." She glanced around and saw Sara's works in progress, eternally postponed.

"I wish I were you. I wish I had your talent, your ambition. I wish I could make things. I used to be bold and I had a future running something big, but I ended up running Jay. I hope to have a Bradbury baby to make his dad happy."

She hesitated, folding the handkerchief. "Sorry, I'm oversharing. I should stop." But she didn't. "I don't have your appetite; I don't want to work as hard. I like shopping. I like buying things. I wish I could be like you. Instead I'm Bradbury's wife. That's all I am. I caught my man, and now that I have him and the money and can do something with it, the two most important people in my life won't talk to me." She became calmer. "Well, babe, forgive me for falling apart on you like that." They parted on a wistful note, kissing each other on both cheeks.

chapter 36

Emily was beautiful and kind, lively and on the verge of a career breakthrough. For my part, I had, for a long time, had a crush on her. I didn't realize this, or imagine it, or think about it because I thought I was quite someone else at the time—I believed I was mature for my age, and that I could challenge Rick as a rival. My coming-of-age grew into a passage of assertive teenage years because I felt superior to adults, and in fact I had an advantage. I had a mother who admired intelligence and wanted me educated.

That didn't mean that I delayed other pleasures. I started staying out late and this had an unsettling affect on Emily. I wasn't into football and I wasn't into soccer. Girls, other girls, several girls, came into my life. It didn't help Emily's private mood that Rick, working intensely, had to be away two and three, even four days at a time to give outlying plant managers face time. It was in this confused and estranged turn of events that she decided to search for my father, Alex.

Years earlier Emily had met my father and had liked him. He had shown hustle and zip and even though his projects failed amid grand explanations, there was always a new project around the corner. The awful fact was that Alex had abandoned me at a most difficult time for my mother, and for that he remained reprehensible.

Emily knocked on my door

"What?"

"Can I come in?"

"No."

"What can I make you for dinner?"

"Nothing."

She remained standing at the door. "I bought us fresh tomatoes and bread, and there are cucumbers. I can make a veggie sandwich." I remained silent. "I can open a can of vegetable broth, sauté the celery and onions and steam the rice and toss in the fish to make us a soup."

She heard me stir behind the door, and that was enough to encourage her. In the kitchen she diced the celery and sliced the onions and julienned the carrots, remembering to add a shallot to power the sautéed aromatics. In a separate pan she seared the cod. By focusing on cooking, she managed desire she could neither satisfy nor escape.

A half-hour went by and the kitchen filled with cooking scents. The smell was maddening to anyone hungry. She made a vegetable roux and added it to the soup. Though not perfectly saturated with flavor, it was ready to eat. She knocked on the sliding doors with her stirring spoon. "Are you coming out?"

A rash of teenage suicides had made the news recently and she was suddenly afraid I might harm myself. Her heart seized up for an instant. In a panic she pushed the shank of the spoon to pry open the inside latch.

"What?" I asked.

"Why are you torturing me?"

The horrible fear about my suicide receded. I don't know where in the world she got that fear. I'm not self-destructive. At any rate, she persuaded me to come and eat. She was badly equipped to analyze her own feelings. Fear, desire, guilt, and grief loitered below the surface in a confusing complexity.

"Come on, sourpuss, don't be a grouch." She looked for common ground that was outside sex, outside winning or losing. "Why did you name me *Maya* in your play?"

I explained that *Maya* is a word used to describe a sensory illusion that transcends life to reach spiritual lightness. Lightness is the ideal, not heaviness or pain or torture. Bigger is not better, and size doesn't count in this spiritual world. "The name predates Christianity by two thousand years."

There must be easier ways to approach lightness, she wrote in her journal. She suppressed a wish to tell me she was carrying my baby. She hadn't been able to transcend anything in a Maya-like fashion. There had been no epiphanies in her life, no lightning illumination, no points of light. It was slogging footwork, step by step, one thing after another, but often the passage was exciting, ambitious, occasionally full of dread and aloft on panic, her Icarus moments on waxen wings too close to the sun. It was all work. Dry work. Steady work. Repetitive work. She couldn't imagine using pot, mescaline, alcohol, or nightclub ecstasy to build dances. But she relied on mysticism, love, and possibly orgasm, along with dervish-like stomp dancing to get her into the mood.

"I think that you're making a Maya-like journey," I said.

"It's work and work and more work," she said. "Some talent, but mostly work."

"Oscar Wilde said his genius went into living and his talent into work."

"What's with this Wilde thing you've gotten off on?"

"I'm testing Sister St. Ambrose's patience."

"You're testing mine, too. Let's move the rest of your mom's stuff from the house to her studio."

We went upstairs to the bedroom that was used as storage space and rooted around, organizing Sara's art. We packed the small-scale models of larger art pieces my mother had made and placed the maquettes into corrugated boxes. We then carried the boxes to the storefront studio Emily had taken over as her own studio.

The aluminum-framed glass door rattled, and a lemony, encaustic smell escaped into the street. Envelopes and fliers were scattered below the mail slot inside: a Brooklyn Academy of Music program, a Skowhegan flier, theater-discount fliers from the Atlantic Theater Company, the Classic Stage and Signature and Playwrights Horizon and New York Theater Workshop and other mailers. Sara had taken me to every Off- and Off-Off-Broadway theater in the city, and they had kept her on their mailing lists.

We dropped off the boxes and came back for more things to carry. The second trip was quicker because the boxes were lighter. Inside the studio, Sara had hung a staged photograph showing Emily costumed in the guise of a female circus rider in skintight, muted mauve-pink and pallid blue dots.

"It's a hot picture," I said.

The compliment made her recoil. I couldn't yet understand how some women could spend so much effort to be attractive, and cringe when told they'd been successful. I would learn later—hot can go cold too quickly. Hot would not carry her through middle age. Hot can be used to insult a woman's intelligence. There was also the wish to be perfect in natural ways, and "hot" implied hyperventilating artifice. She wasn't into radical feminism, but social and cultural issues simmered quietly in the background.

We organized the objects in the studio, encaustic blocks and a hot plate for melting wax, a boxful of notions, brightly colored ribbons, and buttons made from bone. There were leftover pieces of fabric from Sara's soft sculptures and odd metal pieces and even a rusted cast-iron plate with a ball-bearing sleeve. Each item Emily touched brought Sara to life, at least for an instant. She worked swiftly and then suddenly stopped and turned to look at me.

"What's the matter?" I asked.

"Why are you seeing a girlfriend?"

She had hoped to sound matter-of-fact, but she couldn't. I said I wasn't seeing anyone special. To her mind I was being untruthful. We continued working, her mood darker. She felt my mother's intelligence everywhere in the room. She owed Sara everything. Sara had strengthened her, engaged her brain, and made her confident of her direction in dance. But now

Emily was dealing with something else, sexual energy—partly lust, partly need, partly hope.

"I don't want you to sleep with anyone except me," she said.

"But you won't sleep with me."

"That's true," she said.

She would surely put her eyes out were we to do it again. Only later did I realize that I had dismantled the framework on which all else stood, her sense of society, her belief in strong values, her will to manage her life. She clenched her hands into fists, and the warm feeling she was experiencing went away.

"I don't want you bringing up the subject of sex anymore," she said.

She felt slightly bitter toward me due to my nervy insurgency. Her alternating moods produced a current that powered her imagination and at times weakened her will. She didn't want to be toyed with, played with, and she worried that I might betray her in public, making her an object of scorn among my agemates. My loving another girl put a spike in her heart, and from then on something seemed to change.

chapter 37

On Monday I went to school for a rehearsal of *Our Town*. Rick, fighting flu, came home early and offered to help Emily finish organizing Sara's stuff. "Christ, what a mess," he said on his first trip carrying stuff to the studio. The mail carrier had dumped a fresh bunch of mail through the slot in the door. Rick got down on his knees to help sort the mail. He separated the first-class from the bulk mail. "I know she was your best friend, but she wasn't a blood relative, not even an in-law."

"I loved her."

She didn't know what else to say. The commonplaces came to mind—shared values, mutual goals, and similar sensibilities—but all these, she realized, were inadequate variations of the thing called love. What she liked about love was how hard it was to define, as difficult as defining art. Sometimes you love someone who loves the same things, or they learn to love the things you love, or you love someone who loves you.

Or sometimes you have no clue why you love somebody—it's simply there. Her journal reveals:

> *Love is a matter of chance. Good luck or bad luck. In Lithuania we don't rattle on about love as Americans do, because as soon as you want to hold it firmly in your hand, make it a prison, it's lost.*

Rick continued working solemnly as if at a requiem Mass, moving the corrugated boxes to clear the dance area. They were at the far corner of the studio, where most of the art was stored. A consignment shop had promised to take Sara's fun art. These were pieces Sara had made and sold under a pseudonym to museum shops to finance the ambitious studio work that found fewer buyers.

"She never figured out how to make a living," Rick said. He was as badly informed about artists as many people are, but he thought otherwise. "A management guy like me could've made a difference managing her finances." He put aside a bundle of mail and inspected the room. "She should have run a market survey and organized a focus group." That approach was practical and commercially wise; it sold movies and frozen-food dinners, but it had made no sense to my mother. She lived on tangents and on air currents, and the work she made was one-off, ephemeral like pollen.

"Sara could no more make product than a butterfly can build a high-rise," Emily said.

Rick chuckled uncomfortably. "She almost left her kid destitute on account of it."

He was wrong. I had lived a young adult life richer than most kids experienced.

He dusted his slacks and looked around. "She wasted a huge amount of her time in this studio."

Sara had been introspective by nature. She could quickstep through a short, intense period of social life and then return to making art. Emily kept sorting my mother's stuff, but frustration gnawed at her as she worked. She disliked Rick's sure-thing analysis. He would not attempt anything new unless it was guaranteed, insured, fail-safe. "Sara attempted works that no one else had tried. She was looking for accidents, for good accidents."

"Accidents?" Rick shuddered.

Emily glanced at her husband and held his gaze briefly.

He went on quietly. "Accidents? I don't like 'em."

The messy scrambling and lurching about he had experienced earlier in his career had receded. He was back earning a high salary, and his refurbished confidence had a sassy energy that got on her nerves.

"I don't think you heard what I was trying to say," she said.

He looked at her questioningly.

She searched for something close to his experience. "The discovery of penicillin was an accident, and the paper copies we love? The process they used to call *xerography*? The guy who discovered it didn't know what to make of it. It was an accident. We need to encourage such accidents."

Rick's blank look answered her. He believed in unidirectional planning, in goals, in step-by-step powering on to overcome resistance. Freewheeling had nothing to do with his thinking. Life was one thing, business another. Unspoken between them was the blame attached to her pregnancy.

She put on white curator's gloves and went to the lateral file to sort Sara's large-format photographs. Sara had photographed Emily many times. One large photo showed her lightly wrapped in seductively flowing lace, another costumed as Seurat's *Circus Rider*, and in another she was dressed in a formfitting jacket and tight pants made from a patchwork of colors like something a clown might wear. My mother had loved these photographs. They made Emily look special, accomplished, admirable, and desirable.

"Is it all right to blink?" Rick asked.

"You've never told me I was beautiful."

"Angel, everyone knows you're beautiful."

"But you never *told* me that."

"I'm, well…well, you know, I'm only a husband."

"I'm a woman. I don't think I'm ugly."

She saw Rick straining to come to terms with her photographic images. He liked tradition and order and rules, and he liked flowers, but he disliked romantic language. He disliked displays of emotion. He disliked all this talk about beauty. He said it was vanity.

Beauty might be high heels to some and G-strings to others. Beauty was a hazardous substance, and fleeting. One thing to one generation, and another thing to another generation. His devotion to Marian virginal beauty did not adapt easily to living beauty, but Emily danced because she believed it was a beautiful thing to do for her audience.

She removed the cover from a large-format Cibachrome

transparency portrait that Sara had taken of her and placed it on a light box. The work was artfully staged. Sara had applied dramatic makeup to Emily's face. The eyelashes were thick with dark pollen. She was shot from the back in the nude, looking over her shoulder. A set of fertility-cycle beads was tied in a hangman's noose around her neck. She remembered feeling good posing for Sara.

"Say something, Rick."

"What's the point of showing your..." He looked bewildered.

The slips and evasions between them made her furious. Their early disagreement about birth control was only a symptom.

"I like the picture," she insisted. "I posed for it after you made me pregnant and before I miscarried."

Rick ran his fingers along the side of his trousers. Dots of sweat rose on his forehead. They were caught in something outside their grasp that was sliding across their marriage. He puffed up slightly, as if absorbing the humidity. "I don't know what you're rebelling against." He leaned on the lateral file. "We're lucky. We're luckier than most people."

"Rick, we grew up so poorly informed about ourselves."

"Angel, you expect too much."

"I do, I do, yes."

He gestured at Sara's unsold art. The red and yellow fabric sculptures were arranged in an assortment of puffy forms. He touched a soft sculpture and recoiled.

"What the hell is this?"

"It's a velvet vagina."

He hunched his shoulders and looked embarrassed.

"Sara was paying homage to another artist, Yayoi Kusama. MoMA had her work on display."

He glared at the soft sculptures. "Homage, you say? Sara had to copy this? There's nothing here I want to see. Nothing that's going to sell worth a damn! What Sara needed was a good critic to tell her where to go with this stuff." Straight to hell, he had to be thinking.

chapter 38

They went back to organizing the space but the unspoken was out. Rick detested my mother's values and the influence she had had over Emily. He didn't want his wife to echo that influence. He was ready to move on. His gray eyes flashed as he grabbed her forearm and pointed out the four scars she had chevroned on her arm. "You're cruising toward madness."

She switched to a bright smile, her knockout smile, and broke the confrontation with an effervescent tone in her voice. "Sweetheart, you can be so tender and so easily wounded by sex."

He reeled back. "You think I don't like sex?"

"Rick, you're afraid of sex. You've never been comfortable with my body. You really really should've gone into the celibate priesthood. There's nothing in the Catholic canon to make us feel good about our sexual nature." Her voice was firm and it was his voice that started to flutter.

"Maybe we shouldn't believe everything our priests and bishops tell us?"

This was the first inkling of doubt he'd ever displayed.

I'm not sure if this small exchange between them was the wedge that set Rick to thinking "outside the box" as his business associates liked to say. But it could have been. By my count that was the second time he expressed doubt toward Church-approved authoritarian positions he had held sacred until now.

"You heard what Dr. Wilson is doing?" Emily asked. "He's forcing all the lay teachers at school to take 'fidelity' oaths. You've got to believe the whole nine yards, or you're not a Catholic anymore."

"We don't want heretics."

But he had taken a step back; the fight had gone out of him and his hands were limp at his sides.

"Okay, too much yakking about sex," she said, her tone conciliatory.

He made a joking move to cover his privates. That made him look silly, and they both started laughing, but she laughed reluctantly. The sexual jokes among Catholic men tended toward grossness and coarseness on account of their shame about sexual experiences. She tried her own joke. "Did you know that men used to parade with costumed penis hats at ancient Athenian festivals to celebrate their virility?"

His face lighted up. He wiped away tears of laughter. "You want me to march with a dick on my head?"

"No!" She put a hand to her forehead, laughing more. "That would be fun."

He hugged her and they twirled around. He blinked, partly blinded by the intense studio lights, his face anxious. "We're talking again. We'll go to church together." His voice was straining to get a magical hold of her. Her assertive man was pleading for his spiritual life, for them to stay together, sweat sparkling on his brow. He glanced at her belly. "If God wills it, I'll carry His cross." He touched his scapular.

He would do the right thing, she realized. His faith demanded it. She didn't want to disappoint him now, and she didn't want to be estranged from him, so she agreed to go to church with him. Nevertheless, the space between them had altered. Power had shifted. She could make him afraid, and she could dominate him. Instead of feeling triumphant, she felt deflated, her power pinned down to an obligation to be kind. She had depended on his protection, shelter, and companionship, and now it seemed they'd switched jobs.

He darted toward the door, eager to escape my mother's studio, and his hip caught the corner of a file, twisting him into a painful spin on the way out. Emily put away the photograph and shut off the lights. She would have to call a window washer. The studio smelled of artists' materials, the encaustic and the paints. She felt my mother's presence and stood still to make the memory last longer.

"What's keeping you, Angel?"

She saw his silhouette outside.

"Nothing, sweetheart."

Her head ached and the floor seemed uneven where it was even. She felt a slight pain in the abdomen, straightened, moving slowly, stroking her stomach until the pain receded. *We're the walking wounded. Both of us crippled, one by faith and the other by nature.* She locked the studio and they walked to the neighborhood church, entering through the side entrance. Once inside, the street noises fell away.

Rick knelt before a statue of the Virgin Mary. He folded his head into his palms and murmured his prayers. She allowed him pray undisturbed. But she was unwilling to kneel in front of the plaster-cast deities that had ruined her marriage, and she remained standing. She was planning a change in *Trio*, thinking about new dance music, and trying to keep the chaos within her from drowning her in fear that she might miscarry.

chapter 39

The intensity leading up to Jacob's Pillow was spiked with fear for the health of her baby. With no relief possible until her performance in late August, her days stacked one on top of each other into a solid block of tension. On Tuesday, however, she took time off to deliver the remaining noncontroversial pieces of my mother's art to the Bradbury plant. Jay noticed her outside his office and motioned for her to come in and sit down. He was talking on the phone. She had caught a fleeting reference to surgery and waited for him to finish. Jay was ample and robust. She couldn't imagine him ill. He hung up and asked the front office to hold his calls. He knew she had overheard him. "So, I was at the doctor's office, right?" His voice was matter-of-fact.

"You?"

"The call I just took? That was from a plastic surgeon."

"But Page has such beautiful skin."

Jay placed a finger over his mouth to indicate secrecy. "It's me—I'm talking about me."

Before she could speak, he shushed her with a motion that looked like a referee's time-out signal. "The plastic surgeon's receptionist ushers roly-poly me into a pink consultation room. The doctor comes in. His white frock is immaculate. He begins by looking at my skin. You'd think he was inspecting an ancient violin, thinking that every crack and fissure dates back from the fifteenth century."

She held her tongue. Jay represented a subset of America, and every phrase, every detail filled her with more curiosity. He let out a huge sigh and bounced his eyebrows up and down in an effort to be funny, but his humor was heavy. She had heard from Rick that Jay had nearly demolished his father's once-thriving company. Jay was a man who loved toys, a collector of expensive musical instruments he couldn't play, like Niccolò Amati violins. Rick had told her that Jay had complained about a Stradivari he couldn't afford on his inherited allowance. His father, though ill, kept a tight rein on his finances and used Page as his son's overseer. Jay had gotten a luthier to sell him a Guarneri on the cheap. He'd scrambled the company's books to pay for it.

He gave her an eager look. "You think I'm feeling sorry for myself?"

"Yes."

"Let me finish," he said. "The doc gives me a mirror to hold and look at myself. He puts his thumbs on my brow and moves my skin this way and that. One moment I look popeyed and the next moment a little seedy, a little sinister. The doctor says, 'It's your eyes. They're *pooped*.'"

She did not want to comment, but Jay went on, expecting

her to sympathize. He wanted her to see the joke time had played on him despite his daily regimen of nutritional pills, evening primrose oils, resveratrol, Lipitor, aspirin, huge doses of vitamins, alkalinated water, and a trainer at the gym.

"I ask the doc if he could use a word other than *pooped* and he says, 'How about *weary*? You like *weary*?' 'Uh-huh,' I say. Then I tell him I like this girl who doesn't look the least weary. I've liked her a long time."

Her wince stopped him. "Jay, I was a kid back then. Let go of it."

"Ever hear of divorce?"

Neither one blinked for a very long time, but when one of them did, it was Jay who had to look away. A gravitas entered his voice. "You're sitting in *my* office, so I'm going to tell you the rest of *my* story." He was giving her a lesson in the metrics of aging. He was giving her a lesson in the powers of possession. He possessed money not earned by him, and he wanted to possess her as well. "The doc tilts my chair so my head is sloping down like some guy about to be drowned on a water board. Gravity pulls on my skin. I look fresh. The doc tells me, 'That's what a good surgeon can accomplish.' I say, 'This is vain.' The doc says, 'You wear nice clothes and you comb your hair. You don't call it vain. Cosmetic surgery is maintenance. Like putting new air in your tires.' I tell him I haven't come to grips with thinking of myself as a flat tire. He looks at my profile again. He says, 'I want you to be happy.' He gives me the large mirror to hold again. I'm thinking happy is a long way away. Happy might need more work than surgery can deliver. A new set of genes. A dad who doesn't think I've run his business into the ground. A wife who can give Dad the grandkids he wants."

Emily jumped at the chance to be supportive of Page. "The fertility clinics do amazing work."

"Tell me about it. Doctors are now doing away with lust and mating XX and XY chromosomes in petri dishes. Page thinks I'm dull. She's been around. You see, my darling wife, my beloved, is six years older than she claims to be. It's not all my fault we can't have kids."

Emily searched for something sympathetic to say, but that inner thing she'd gotten from Sara, that inner guide, the ability to pause before speaking, held her back. Only the insane say and do everything that comes to mind. But it looked as if there would be no more young Bradburys to frolic through their inheritances. Jay was a lousy businessman and a living testament that high inheritance taxes could helpfully level the playing field to get rid of stale wealth and give a new generation a chance to rise on merit rather than the divine right of money.

Jay had other ideas. "You were wrong to leave me years ago, but we can fix the damage by getting together again."

"We were together only a short time."

"You said you loved me."

She wished he hadn't remembered that. She had said it, but she was a teenager at the time, and grateful to be rescued from working in an old folks' home. She believed that expressions of love at such a young age shouldn't count as much as they do later. But she didn't like to think of herself as a heartbreaker, so she smiled her knockout smile to let him know they could be friends.

He tapped his desk sharply. "Let's do a replay."

Not in my lifetime, she wrote in her journal. "Jay, a face-lift isn't going to change a thing for you." Her voice was smiling, but not a spark of romance remained for her.

He didn't listen, or maybe he listened but didn't hear. He responded to the smile. He said he was looking forward to seeing her dance, looking forward to the school auction as well, and he invited her to join him and Page for another sailing weekend. She said she would have to check her schedule.

chapter 40

She didn't want to go sailing with Page and Jay, but Rick arranged it and invited me. Emily reluctantly canceled a rehearsal to make herself available.

The *Miscellaneous Expense* was sailing under wind-vane autopilot; the mainsail and the jib were as tight as airplane wings. It was late in the afternoon and I was near the bow, sitting on a deflated raft and petting Jay's Irish setter. The sun sparkled on a slant on the water, and it was warm. Perfect sailing weather. We were all in T-shirts and shorts, Page in tight shorts. Jay chatted about motivating optimism at work. Apparently, sales had crumbled—crashed in fact—and the way to overcome this disaster was to pretend it hadn't happened by layering peppiness and optimism and preaching teamwork. Tension was brewing because Rick wanted things to be done one way and Jay another way. Jay had scheduled a company paintball shooting contest to encourage a fighting company spirit, and to show Rick who had the upper hand. Rick thought it was a waste of time and money. Underlying the tension was Page's support of Rick. Jay didn't like that at all.

The sailboat heeled as the wind picked up. Emily sat next to Page on the windward side. She was wary of morning sickness and had brought a box of saltines in case seasickness made it worse. She chewed several crackers.

"You are pregnant, aren't you?" Page said. "You quit eating cheese and raw fish because you want to avoid food-borne diseases."

"Uhmm."

"I wish I was as young as you are."

"How are your missionary parents getting along?"

Page said she'd gone to her parents' landlady, swore the woman to secrecy, and paid on her parents' rent. "When the landlady told my folks a stranger paid their rent, they took it as a sign from God. They thought it was a miracle." She removed her baseball cap; her blond hair streamed to the side of her head. "I'll need a miracle to have a baby."

"How is that going?"

"I don't know yet. We're now thinking of gestational surrogacy, paying some poor woman who needs the bucks to carry our IVF baby for us."

"You sound bitter."

"If I hadn't married Jay, I'd be looking at my uterus as a profit center, too." She made a shimmy with her hips. "Maybe my vagina as well."

Emily had hoped to go light on drama that weekend. "Let's see what the guys are up to."

The guys, as it turned out, were talking about profit

margins and bottom lines and the advantages of printer slotters and rotary cutters in reducing costs. Boring, laborsaving, moneymaking stuff.

"We're hungry," Page said.

Jay suggested the restaurant they had gone to before, but instead of using the outdoor barbecue, they would eat in the dining room this time. The wind picked up, the sails ballooned and flew us across the bay in a half-hour. We docked in front of a smaller sailing vessel. The restaurant's red banquettes were cushiony, the waiters witty and attentive. The five of us ate a great meal of fresh cod caught the same morning, but Emily ate little and was restless, thinking of a troubling sequence in *Kiss* she wanted to revise. I went to the bathroom and the next minute she felt her phone vibrating. She took it out to read my text message: "Boring."

"I'm heading out with David for a walk in the dunes," she announced.

I met her outside. She said she felt alive and in the spirit of giving and living and nurturing. We made our way toward the dunes. She half-listened to me going on about Dr. Wilson wanting to convert me to Catholicism. He was breaking the solemn promise the diocese had made to my grandfather, excusing me from mandatory religion classes and church attendance. I wasn't upset. There was nothing written in stone. No contract. People died, changed their minds, or forgot what they'd said. On top of that, I wanted to take religion, and for a time I even worked on independent research. "Whenever Sister doesn't call me *Spoza* she calls me *Baruch* or *Bernard* because Spinoza had used both names, the Jewish

Baruch and Christian Bernard." I liked the ecumenical force behind that.

> *Not to laugh, not to lament,*
> *not to curse, but to understand.*
> — Spinoza

"Baruch famously believed that God was everywhere and in everything but totally indifferent to our needs. So, like, we shouldn't bother Him with our prayers, but in the last class I took with Dr. Wilson, he was teaching us how to develop 'power prayers'."

"He's at it again?"

"Yeah."

"I thought he'd given up on you?"

"Not exactly. He's adding new persuasion points."

She stretched her arms to embrace the sun. Those good feelings that made my presence troublesome and dear were warming up as we walked to a clearing. My shoulders were wider than hers and she felt petite next to me. She liked it that she was carrying a baby with my genes and my mother's genes, and she was growing more optimistic that her unconventional relationship with Rick might work out after all.

We took a path to a crest in the dunes and then down the other side of a long sloping hillside. The festive sounds from the restaurant receded. I swung my arms and then swung them higher as we walked. The sun was heading toward evening and the slanting rays turned her face to gold. We stopped to look at the view below and heard Jay's dog barking on the docked boat. I shrugged off my shirt. Electricity ran along my skin.

"Oh," she said. She liked the sunny day well enough and didn't want to complicate it. "You can slip your shirt back on. You look like an underwear ad." She turned away.

We made our way back to the *Miscellaneous Expense*. Lady greeted us with slobbering, tail-wagging enthusiasm. Emily went below while I stayed on deck, petting the dog. The others were taking their good sweet time returning to the boat. The dock lights switched on and we heard Page's voice. She was behind Jay and the both of them were unsteady. Rick was pointing at the boat and Page was into a dramatic hand-waving gesture at something Jay had been saying. They were animated and loud and intoxicated. Only after Emily had quit drinking on account of her pregnancy had she noticed how much alcohol they all consumed.

They climbed aboard and continued to behave badly, acting noisier and noisier. The skipper of another boat approached the *Miscellaneous* and asked if he could dock. Jay was willing to surrender his space and Page jumped the gun on him. She cranked up the diesel and slammed the gearshift forward. The instant Jay shouted, "Whoa," it was already too late. The prop wash was boiling seawater astern. The trouble was, the boat was still tied to the dock.

The restaurant's deck hands came running. Page swung the helm hard left and the vessel skewed, squeezing the boat's rubber fenders flat against the dock, grinding the side of the boat. The deck hands shouted for her to stop. One of them managed to get her attention and Rick took the helm. The wind had picked up and the stainless steel rigging whistled. It was getting cold, but the chaos was under control. Captive to civility, I felt I was watching several sets of misbehaving parents.

In the distance we heard the long mournful rattling sound of an anchor dropping. I glanced at the weather vane at the top of the mast and saw the seven stars of the Big Dipper in celestial harmony. They were shimmering and beyond my or Emily's, or anyone's reach.

chapter 41

Her clinical tests showed nothing abnormal, nothing to indicate birthing trouble. The bouts of morning sickness persisted, but they weren't as severe as some woman experienced. Her doctor held up a thumb to illustrate the size of the fetus, a little guy small enough to go all the way to Jacob's Pillow cushioned in the comfort of amniotic fluid. The peculiar thing about being so happy, a state she liked to share with others, was that she had to keep her happy state, her pregnancy, a secret. Had anyone told her she would one day slink around hiding her happiness, she would have cried out in disbelief.

As I looked at these passages in her journal, I was struck by the extraordinary amount of life packed into several months. Rick was piloting a newer and quieter airplane Jay had leased for the company's business. That weekend he was flying her to the Bradbury estate to dance at a fund-raiser. He had also arranged to meet two Hartford private-equity guys. The Cessna slipped through the air. The land below was layered with cloudy threads running to the outer edges of sight. Rick pulled on the control yoke and the aircraft nosed up. It was a fast plane.

"Are you trying to make me afraid?" she asked.

"Nothing frightens you."

She was pleased to hear it.

"Jay said you were *this* close." Rick twisted two fingers together, his voice full of envy.

She was horrified. What miserable new thing could now rob her of happiness? "My former boyfriend and my husband are dishing about me? Did you tell him I'm pregnant?"

"I did not."

"Can I tell the world it's our baby when I start showing?"

"What else can you say?"

Alarms were ringing. "What's the matter?"

"I've been thinking more and more about you carrying Jay's kid. I'm like one of those stupid birds not watching my nest as a more clever bird drops its egg for me to hatch."

She felt a sharp pain. "But it's *my* child, honey. Forget about Jay. I'm not carrying his child. He has strong feelings for me but the only reason I stay friendly with him is on account of your job at Bradbury. The moment you quit I'll never talk to him again." The noise surrounding wanted and unwanted partners and children made it hard for them to hear each other. They flew on without speaking.

They landed at Westchester County Airport and picked up a company car left for their use. Rick wanted to see the house they'd lost in foreclosure after their personal bankruptcy. She didn't want to see it, but she didn't want to argue. Her edginess sharpened as they drove closer to their old neighborhood.

Rick parked opposite the house. It was a big house with enough dormers to make all seven of Snow White's dwarfs happy. But there wasn't much original design, for all the eaves and intersecting rooflines. The house had been built from standard structural parts assembled by mass-market production architects doing high-end homes. Though Rick had been wasteful with money that had once been plentiful, no amount of money guaranteed good taste.

"Ladies and gentlemen, a moment of silence, please." He gave a solemn wave and she could almost hear him think, "Ladies and gentlemen, there I was on top of the world before it all went *poof*!" But he wasn't good at making jokes, and his theatrical enthusiasm for the lost house made him sound momentarily shallow, as if getting it, making it, and keeping it had been his sole aim in life. His true calling was as born-again Catholic. He probably could live on alms, waiting for miracles. And maybe he would have done that had he not fallen in love with her and needed a job.

She felt disconnected with her past. The house was a fossil. "We owned this place?"

"We were happy," he reminded her.

She remembered the pleasing smell of newly dried wood in a house under construction. She remembered the excitement of a roof going up. "And then our happy house spirits fled and left us with an underused hotel lobby." She'd meant to amuse him by saying that, but he looked offended.

"I liked the house, and I still like the house. You liked it, too, until Sara told you she didn't like it. That's when you decided not to like it."

"It's big, but it's not a pretty house." The chimney had a grotesque half-twist in the brickwork that made it look like a squirt of whipped cream. The house no longer interested her.

He turned off the ignition. "What if we were to move back to the old neighborhood?" He sounded an enthusiastic note.

She was shocked. "We can't afford it." She wasn't sure if he was earning enough to hire a landscaper, a cleanup service, and the craftspeople needed to fix all the things that go wrong with a large house.

"You have no idea how much I'm earning now."

She made a face meant to say, "I'm not moving back here, ever."

Rick tapped the steering wheel, his fingers trembling. "Okay. You don't like the house anymore. I'll call up one of Sara's old pals, say, someone like Rem Koolhaas or Frank Gehry." Sara had not been friends with either architect. "I'll ask which one of those high-priced geniuses will work for a client making a go of it on a manager's salary."

"Rick, please. Let's just see if we can survive this weekend."

The neighborhood was beautiful and the trees a hundred years old. Stability and continuity were awesomely present, but Emily felt like an outcast in a neighborhood she once called home. She was relieved when Rick switched on the engine and started to drive.

chapter 42

They drove along the spaciously curved road that led to the Bradbury house. The sun-dappled leaves filtered light onto the slate roof, where the light mingled with green shadows. Jay and Page greeted them, and Jay immediately asked Rick to meet the Hartford financial guys. Page took an hour to tour the gardens with Emily.

Page persisted in courting her and had invited her to ladies-only lecture events, most recently by a leading horticulturalist flown in from Seattle, and then there was the luncheon to raise money for Darfur women. But the mood was cooler between them today and Emily felt uneasy. Page kept circling back to the problem of having Bradbury offspring.

"Jay's dad is going to kick the bucket soon."

Page's eyes were glistening, and it struck Emily that she might have started to cry had not the men joined them. As soon as Jay showed up the change in Page was immediate and striking. She mixed herself a drink and very quickly had another drink and became peevish and weary in a private struggle with Jay that made it uncomfortable to be with them.

"How much did our boat cost us, babe?" Page asked. There was contempt in her voice. He told her. She laughed at the enormous amount.

"It's a business expense," Jay said. "The feds allowed it."

The wealthy are different from you and me. They hire lobbyists and lawyers and tax accountants to pass laws and make rules to keep them rich.

"Your dad would've gone crazy if he'd learned of it," Page said.

"He did learn about it. You told him."

"Well, what if I did? You should've told him yourself."

Jay took charge of the grill and Page had another drink. They all chafed in silence until Page said, "What is it you call me when I've had a few?" She raised her chin to dare him to say it. "Mean?" she asked.

"You're not mean," Rick cut in, "You're one smart woman."

Page pulled on Jay's shirtsleeve gleefully. "Jay, just remember our Rick here is a keeper. I hope he'll remain bushy-tailed and happy, unlike my dear VP so sadly gone. Yes. Sadly. Jay, what was the other man's name?"

"You called him a Young Turk," Jay said, his mouth and his jaw tightened.

"Yes," Page recalled. "He graduated from Princeton, didn't he? Not like my Jay baby here. Neither Yale nor Harvard would have Jay, not even Wharton for heaven's sake. How low can you go in admissions? A *business* school turned my babe down? That's like Grand Central Station not letting you in."

"She never finished college," Jay said.

"What are you two arguing about?" Emily was exasperated, unable to get at the source of this strange public anguish, but fascinated by it.

"Jay, tell her why we're arguing."

Jay stopped working the grill.

Page made a squiggly line in the air to underline something that had escaped everyone else. "Oh, dear. My husband is ignoring me. Now it's you, Emily, and me. Us women. Über*babes*. Sisters."

Emily heard a pungent undertone. "I'm upsetting you?"

Page cocked her head. "A wise man once said it's good to keep your friends close and your enemies closer."

"I'm your enemy now?"

Emily couldn't help Jay's obsession with her. She pretended to find a joke in Page's remark and checked to see what time it was. "David, Dylan, and Melissa must be at the train station waiting for me."

She excused herself and left.

chapter 43

She found Melissa at an outdoor table working her laptop. I was inside the station playing video games, and Dylan was touring the town on foot.

"You're looking flushed," Melissa said.

Emily gave her a wry grin. "I've been working overtime being nice to our wealthy benefactors." She took a seat. "Our benefit performance will be the first time anyone has a clue what we're doing with our Bradbury grant."

She crossed her fingers. She wanted the audience to like *Scent*, the only dance to be performed at the benefit. Her new dances were provocative and touched emotions she had never attempted to display on the boards, anger and envy, possession, desire and despair. Unlike classical elevation, extension, graceful bending and unbending, and beautiful ethereal flights suspended in air, her work had become earthy, scented with passion. Not only were these dances unexpected, but they also were different from everything she had choreographed earlier.

She was nervous about showing them in public, but thrilled to do it. "Anyway," she said, "how is your new boyfriend, the BMW guy?"

"He said I'm his muse, but I didn't understand what he was saying, not exactly." Her springy voice furled back into itself. "You think I'm way out of line calling him at home?"

"Why don't you ask his wife what she thinks?"

"That's funny," Melissa said grimly. "She actually answered the phone and I started babbling." The slanting sun tinted her hair with an auburn glow.

"What did she say?"

"She said, 'Calm down.' But I kept talking and talking and she called him over to shut me up."

"What did he say?"

"He wants to see me."

Emily was certifiably blind to the chemistry in her own affair but acted the knowledgeable older sister. "Please, dump the guy. He'll only give you a headache."

"Easy for you to say. You'll be with Rick a thousand years from now."

"I hope so."

I came over and kicked a chair out from under the small table and straddled it.

"What's up?" Melissa asked me without interest.

"I'm trying to get a girl character pregnant in a play I'm writing," I said, my eyes bright with provocation. "You have any advice?"

Emily held her breath, thinking this was the moment I had chosen to betray her in public. A lump formed in her throat and she couldn't speak, wondering how I managed to guess her condition, which I wouldn't know about for another twenty years.

Melissa leaned close to my face. "You're a depraved kid."

We quarreled. I accused her of being a dance idiot. She told me I was seriously dumb.

"I hope you guys are having fun," Emily said. Her voice was tight and complicated. But she shouldn't have worried—I had no clue that she was pregnant, let alone with my child.

We had an hour to kill before they had to get ready for the benefit performance. "Yeah, let's be constructive," I said. I gave Melissa an *Our Town* script and persuaded her to read a few lines so I could practice my Stage Manager role. I stepped off distances and blocked out the action by arranging newsprint under small stones to mark our positions. Dissatisfied, I stepped off a new distance and stuck another piece of newsprint under a stone.

"Can't we just read the lines?" Melissa asked.

I moved the stone a few inches. "Thornton Wilder actually didn't know a small town like Grover's Corner. He made it all up."

"I don't care. Can we please read the lines?"

Melissa stood straight-backed, her feet turned out, her body bending and unbending as she practiced a step out of *Scent*. Her vitality was exciting, her eyes languorous and sweet. Her body a plantlike extension, a long neck that made it seem as if she was weaving her torso and limbs in aquatic, underwater slowness.

Still dissatisfied with the marks on the floor, I moved them again. "People don't get the play the way Thornton Wilder meant it. He was a cosmopolitan guy, and he wanted to show

how a conformist, small-minded place like Grover's Corner made people want to escape it."

Melissa intervened. "Sister St. Ambrose asked you not to mention all that. You know your problem? You're pushing all the time. Jumping borders."

"Bullcrap—I'm easygoing."

"Easygoing? You're about as easygoing as a sewing machine running at top speed. You don't have a clue when to stop."

"I only try to annoy people I like."

"Like me?"

"And others."

"Dr. Wilson?

"I love the guy. No one pays as much attention to me as he does. He invited me to join the Catholic Charismatic Renewal movement and I had to tell him that I can't go because if I fall for the charismatic thing, and then start seeing God in all those flames rising, it could burn my eyes out."

Emily snorted in annoyance. "That was calculated to annoy Dr. Wilson."

"It did. I didn't say anything disrespectful. I have my opinions and the Doc has his. He keeps on bringing up the term paper I wrote about sin. He keeps poking holes in my argument."

"You're wasting his time," Melissa said.

"Maybe. I bugged him even more when I pointed out the tiny percentage of agnostic Jews nailing down so many honors, including Nobel Prizes."

I remember the moment when I said this to Dr. Wilson. He wasn't really angry. He said he would have liked to have lived a life that could have won him a Nobel Prize. It was a moment of innocent closeness between us, and he moved toward kindness by giving me a small gift. I found a card he had given me and showed it to Emily and Melissa.

"He gave you *that*?" Emily did not believe it.

"It's a pretty card. I love it." The card, *Mater Purissima*, pictured ethereal clouds surrounding a beautiful woman holding a child. "I told him that Catholics depended too much on pictures. They grow up looking at statues and paintings, the gorgeous stained-glass windows, Michelangelo, Caravaggio, Raphael, and Bellini, sculptures and pictures to make God concrete and easy to love. They don't have to think; all they have to do is look at the icon and believe. But us Jews, you see, we have this Yahweh no one has seen. And we're not supposed to say his name. He's difficult to grasp, an abstraction, a mysterious force that we're supposed to experience. It's hard work. You Catholics get a ready-made divinity dressed in robes you can touch. No heavy mental lifting required. No practice in abstract thinking—you walk on easy street and the mind tends to get complacent, so you don't win as many Nobel Prizes."

Melissa laughed. "Who needs the prizes when we have heaven?"

"But I've got Earth," I said.

chapter 44

That evening Emily and her dancers performed at the benefit. Her dance was one of three acts staged for Page's fund-raiser and the last one to be performed that evening. A stand-up comic had been invited to deliver a monologue on his Catholic grammar school days, and a local church choir sang a cappella.

Emily sensed that her dance wasn't meant for this audience, a crowd of open-faced, sober gentlemen and ladies. Expecting disaster, she was grateful the Hartford guys had called Rick and Jay away to discuss the legal language in the Bradbury financing package. Taking a deep breath, she flew onto the stage to dance with Melissa and Dylan, but the magic she had felt at rehearsals felt clunky. She couldn't see the audience clearly due to the lights aimed at the stage but she imagined stony-eyed people sitting still and grim. Against all the rules and warnings not to use flash photography, a camera flash blazed and nearly tripped her.

The curtain dropped at the end of the dance and the sound that followed had the still quality of undisturbed stone. Then, politely, a few claps popped up and scattered like popcorn. She was embarrassed to go out to take a bow, but she did, raising Dylan's hand while Dylan held Melissa's. In sweat-soaked costumes, they escaped behind the curtain and hugged each other for comfort.

Back at the Bradburys, Page was at her hostess best, guiding people to meet other people, introducing the monologue comedian, who had gotten the most applause, urging servers to accommodate guests with drinks and small snacks. She wasn't drinking herself that evening and came out to the patio where Emily had gone to escape the guests. Fireflies were zippering the night, and ground-hugging garden lights cast a muted light onto the paths.

"I really bombed, didn't I?" Emily said.

The chirping crickets seemed to agree with her. There was the faint smell of roses in evening air.

"Crickets," Page said. "What do crickets know about dance?"

They walked toward the part of the garden maintained as a rose garden. Emily saw a Japanese beetle lifting its iridescent green-tinted carapace. "Sara grew a few roses and she could never kill the beetles. Rick said she should have called it a beetle garden."

"Funny, that's what Jay's dad called my rose garden. A beetle garden."

"You seemed very upset by his being so ill."

"I was. I am. He gave me my big chance, and he was the most modest and handsome man I knew. A gentleman. He didn't think I'm a witch—"

"Who thinks that?"

She gestured to let it go. "Jay's dad thought I was genuine and the best office manager he'd ever had. No one ever praised me like that before. Not my folks, not ever them. Especially not them. I was a sinner to them. I was stubborn and needed lots of punishment. Mom believes in punishment as therapy, punishment to please the Lord." They walked a few feet. "He's getting worse, you know. Jay's dad. It's not going to be long now."

"You'll miss him?"

"You bet."

Page went back to tend to her guests but Emily skipped the reception. She went to bed and didn't wake even when Rick returned from his meeting. In the morning she boarded the Bradbury plane with Rick at the controls. They flew home without incident.

chapter 45

The following day Emily went to Dylan's studio to rehearse the piece that had bombed upstate. Melissa and Dylan had been at it a while. Emily slipped into her rehearsal clothes and made a few tweaks in her choreography. Energy and fearlessness marked her dancing. But that day Dr. Wilson was like an angry witch occupying a corner of her mind. He volunteered his professional services at my school twice a month, and he volunteered extra time to teach one of the divinity classes. The latest confrontation had come when he told me he wanted to pull me out of *Our Town* to punish me. My sin paper still rankled him.

Emily had made an appointment to see him at school. Instead of jeans she wore a navy skirt, and a navy jacket over a white blouse with a single strand of fake pearls. She wanted to be taken seriously by him. The skinny nurse who helped

Dr. Wilson was in the office and had her back turned as Emily walked in.

"How's our gravity-defying dancer doing?" Dr. Wilson asked.

"Just fine."

She was determined to be professional but not especially friendly. A smile might be okay. She took the seat he pointed to and smiled stiffly.

"Dr. Wilson," she spoke briskly as if she had a sequence of steps to finish, "I have to ask you not to interfere with David's spiritual life." She was sure I had a spiritual life, but not one easily organized to follow rituals provided by churches and synagogues.

The nurse stepped back from the file cabinet. It seemed to Emily that the three of them took a deep breath. A flick of the doctor's head, barely perceptible, directed the nurse to leave. Her slim figure faded on the other side of the frosted glass.

"Yes?" Wilson said.

The doctor's habit of steepling his fingers into a temple was maddening. He pressed them together and made the tips of his fingernails white. Emily spoke slowly. "Aren't doctors men of science and trained skeptics on things they can't prove?"

He collapsed the steeple.

"David is a secular boy. Sara didn't want him baptized."

"A sprinkling of holy water? That's worrying you?"

She hesitated. She was a believer, loosely defined, but she felt that others should be free to choose what they wanted to believe. Embarrassed by his unwavering stare, she wasn't sure how to continue. There was something in his eager and pious eyes that made her cautious. She couldn't place the look exactly. A shrewd look? Maybe it was only a look of pride, too much money, and easy power. Few parishioners realized that Dr. Wilson contributed more money to the school than Jay and Page Bradbury did. He had made a fortune in real estate that he developed for medical professionals, and believing that Jesus had anointed him with great wealth for a purpose, he became evangelical in the extreme.

"You're meddling, doctor, and I care. You're adding stress to the life of a boy already under immense pressure after the death of his mother."

The doctor steepled his fingers again. "What about saving his soul?"

"He'll save it in his own way."

"Are you serious? I don't think you're the best person to make that decision."

"I'm his guardian."

"That's only civil authority." He dismissed it with a wave of his hand. "God's authority is divine."

He then pulled out a photograph someone had taken of her dancing *Scent* a few days earlier. Her body appeared to be suspended from wings. With good shoulders, firm muscle, sinuous narrow waist, straight back, legs tapered, she looked light and yet strong. "Naked," he said. Her costume was minimal, tight, and flesh-colored. "You should leave dancing to tramps."

"You didn't like my choreography?"

"I didn't see it."

"But you're judging it?"

"Why not?"

His smile annoyed her, but she didn't want to quarrel with him. She remained a nominal member of the Church to please Rick. But she saw, as I did, that belief has no boundaries, no required proofs, and no defined standards. She waited and Dr. Wilson waited. She decided to speak first. "Rick and Jay and you are friends and I'm an outsider from Lithuania."

"That was the last pagan country in Europe, wasn't it?"

She refused to be sidetracked. "You probably think you're being helpful."

"You have to learn how we do things in America."

"Yes, you punish a lot. You make criminals out of people who don't agree with you."

"I don't need a speech."

The steepling and the smiling were equally maddening. She didn't know how to go on. She had learned to defer to professionals. She had been raised to respect authority. Her mother had taught her that politicians could never be craven, police are always fair, priests are never immoral, bishops never devious, judges never corrupt, cops never lie, prosecutors never break the rules, social workers are always wise, and government officials have been elected to help people. The last thing she said is that doctors are no fools. Her mother had committed suicide.

Emily drew herself up, and then very softly, almost reluctantly, she said, "I'll decide if David needs your help."

Dr. Wilson retrieved a letter from the file that contained her picture and looked at her directly. "In cases of moral turpitude—" His voice was calm, his eyes penetrating.

She became cold with fear. "What are you saying?"

He placed the letter on the desk. My father's distinctive handwriting marched across the page, and Wilson read it aloud: "I hereby appoint Dr. Wilson as my son's spiritual guide…"

She recovered her authority. "Alex? I tried to find him."

"My lawyer tells me Alex should have been consulted on David's guardianship."

That could be true. She wasn't a lawyer and Dr. Wilson was part of the governing class. Dozens of his college friends were now wielding serious power—judges, prosecutors, legislators, officials, administrators, trustees, and directors.

She refused to be bluffed. "As David's guardian I demand that you stop. I'll sue if you don't stop meddling." The confrontation came out all of a sudden, and she was surprised she'd said it.

"You don't want go to court. Courts are expensive."

"Rick will back me up."

"Courts take time away from everything else and no one has fun."

She was still. It shouldn't be so difficult to speak to authority. It shouldn't. The people who have the governing tools and make the rules don't like to listen to you. She made a move as if getting ready to leave.

"I'm not finished," Dr. Wilson said.

She sat down again.

She weighed Dr. Wilson's threat. She didn't speak.

"You can go see David's father yourself," he said.

The doctor checked his cell phone address list and wrote Alex's number on a prescription pad. He ripped the page from the pad and handing it over, he promised to pray for her.

She felt a sharp spasm, and then nausea came over her. She bent forward slightly to get it under control. She took the slip of paper and forced herself to say goodbye politely.

chapter 46

The school bell rang and the building erupted with the sounds of students changing classes, metal stairs booming, kids rushing, school bags swinging on their shoulders. I caught up with Emily. "Hey, are you avoiding me?" It wasn't that I was shy, but I wasn't as forward as I'd pretended to be. I was still climbing a young adult barrier, a new adult reticence around sex, and the awful insecurity of knowing that you're not yet the person you'd want to be.

"I just read *The Picture of Dorian Gray*," I said. "A character in it says that it is 'self-denial that mars our lives.'"

"Oh, hokum bilge. You picked up that malarkey at a Catholic school?"

I quoted another Wilde line: "'The only way to get rid of a temptation is to yield to it.'"

"And you're working on it?"

"What do you think?"

She dismissed my remark with a wave of her hand. "I just learned that your father is back."

The hallway echoes flattened, and my eyes blurred. "Dad, dear ol' Dad."

She bit her lip.

"Dad, dear ol' Dad."

"Stop saying that. He's probably sorry he messed up. He might have been a good dad given a chance. "

"He's had years to try."

"You're unforgiving, aren't you?"

My voice brightened. "Come with me to talk *Our Town* with Sister St. Ambrose." I took her arm to convince her that she should, and we entered Sister St. Ambrose's spare and tidy office.

"Well, look who we have here," Sister warbled pleasantly. Her skin had a pliant texture, and her creamy complexion gave her a glowing appearance, but the Sister's bad eye sometimes made it difficult to look at her steadily.

"I'm acting as David's dramaturge," Emily said to lighten the mood. She was determined not to let Dr. Wilson ruin her day. Just then, Wilson, apparently leaving for the day, poked his head inside the office and asked Sister to step into the hallway for a chat. Emily kept her hands clasped between her thighs. I moved restlessly in my chair. Her journals indicated that her attraction to me persisted, baroque at times, like an overly fussy dance sequence, but it felt lean this time, private.

The sister didn't come back for awhile. When she returned, her keen and usually open face was clouded. She clapped her hands in a gesture that was more extravagant than the occasion called for, a noisy let's-get-to-work clap. We started talking about the technical business of staging the play, but something had happened outside and Dr. Wilson seemed to have been the cause of it. All of us were aware of it but pretended otherwise. I asked for additional spotlights with louvered fronts.

Sister, perhaps biding her time, touched her rosary absent-mindedly. She showed us a mock-up of the yet-unprinted program. "David, I've removed your reference to Thornton Wilder's uncertain sexual orientation in the program."

"That's settled?" I asked. I think my eyes must have widened.

"It's speculative. Even if he was gay, which no one knows for sure, we wouldn't want to mention it because it would upset our parishioners."

She was wrong on the facts and right about her audience.

"Did you leave in the thing about him going to school in Shanghai and living his formative childhood years in China?"

"Simplicity, simplicity, David. We want simplicity. Don't complicate the story."

She stopped, and none of us knew what to say next.

Life as we know it is the most complex thing any one of us will ever face, as complex as growing up, as complex as a marriage, as complicated as faith and its discontents. The worship of simplicity had made Rick a SMART guy—Specific, Measurable, Attainable, Realistic, and Time-bounded—narrow, a man choosing to live his life in voluntary self-confinement.

I tried to make my point: "Wilder said, 'I am never free of a sense of inadequacy; I feel that I am forever dry when warmth is called for, and warm when judicious impersonality is called for.'"

Sister sighed, "We are not going to muck about in doubts and uncertainties. Thornton Wilder served with distinction in North Africa and Italy during World War II. He was promoted from captain to lieutenant colonel and won a Bronze Star. Now those are facts you can give the public with confidence."

"But the play is ambiguous."

"We'll fix that."

"He said: 'Religion is the emanation from an extinct star.'"

"We'll ignore that."

Sister was one of the best-educated people in the parish. She carried her learning gently and used persuasion rather than top-down commands when guiding her students. She continued tinkering with the beads on her rosary. "I might as well tell you what happened outside in the hallway." She lifted her hands in surrender. "Dr. Wilson said he would pull the play's financing if it didn't illuminate our Catholic values. To start with, he wants only people of faith to participate in the play."

The threat of losing money hung over us. I sat on the edge of my seat. "But you'll protect me, won't you?"

The sister's silence was stony, adrift in discomfort. I went on about Thornton Wilder. "He was separated from the mainstream. Things come out of that, an ability to see different points of view. He allowed Emily Webb to die in childbirth, and in the hereafter she reflects on some gloomy things. Life, she says, 'It goes so fast. We don't have time to look at one another.'"

"The hereafter is a joyous place," Sister corrected. "Thornton Wilder was a happy man. He was honored, loved. He won three Pulitzers. He became part of our culture. We can stress happiness instead of alienation."

"*Our Town* wasn't meant to make us feel good."

"We'll lighten up the ending," Sister said. "Miracles do happen."

"The play echoes with religious doubts all the way through, disappointed love, American loneliness."

"We'll have none of that," Sister said, patient, serene. "We're cutting the Simon Stimson character altogether. He's not likeable. What's the point of the town drunk and suicide snarling at us, 'That's what it was to be alive.... To move about in a cloud of ignorance.' None of us want *that* to happen. We have Jesus illuminating a path for us."

My face must have been coloring. "There's more to a play than just having likable characters."

"Let it be. Let's move on." Sister St. Ambrose was working hard to control the narrative.

My face must have been glowing by now. "Maybe we should add a triumphal sex scene at the end of *Our Town*?"

"Don't be rude," Emily said.

She sounded priggish, but in her journals she revealed herself otherwise. She'd taken the Bradburys to see Tennessee Williams's *A Streetcar Named Desire* on one of her Thursday-night culture trips. A reviewer had noted that Thornton Wilder had seen the play back in 1947 and in a comment "delivered like a papal bull" had complained to Tennessee Williams that a "lady" like Stella couldn't possible have married a "vulgarian" like Stanley Kowalski.

Tennessee Williams reflected on his colleague's inability to grasp these characters. Wilder, he decided, "has never had a good lay." Emily added three exclamation points for emphasis: *Like Wilder!!! That's Rick for you!!!* She seemed to be unaware that she was also criticizing herself. She elaborated with a quote from Samuel Steward, Gertrude Stein's young friend, who claimed to be Wilder's lover: "Thornton always went about having sex as though it were something going on behind his back and he didn't know anything about it." *Like Rick, tho Rick is hetero,* Emily wrote, and then, perhaps several years later on rereading her note, she must have reconsidered, and made another note in tiny letters barley legible: *Not only birth control kept us away from each other. I loved perfect male bodies too much to love Rick as passionately*—the remainder was unreadable.

That note caught my attention. I've heard women jolt at some innocent thing that put them off—this guy had thin fingers that made them shudder, that guy had loopy ears that made them laugh. But when I was sitting back then in Sister St. Ambrose's office vying to control my production of *Our Town,* I couldn't have imagined as much.

Sister puffed a little breath. "David, you have the gift of a skeptic and we are believers here." She smiled. "God bless you."

A silent prayer appeared to pass between the Sister and the picture of St. Teresa of Ávila on her desk. The saint was pictured wearing her Brown Scapular. Some Catholics believed that if you wore the devotional scapulars honoring the Blessed Virgin Mary, as Rick had been doing, the Mother of God would come down from heaven on the Saturday after your death—Saturday was Mary's birthday—to yank you away from the flames of purgatory and pull you straightaway into heaven.

Sister rapped the table gently and went on. "Aeschylus won more prizes than anyone in classic Athens because he showed us how to act honorably in bad circumstances." As simple as this drama theory was, Sister made it simpler. "Don't show it like it is, David. Show it how our divine Jesus wants it to be." She paused to give me time to think it over.

The birth of the divine, virgin or otherwise, remained hard to explain to laypeople. They had to take it on faith because creation myths are plentiful. Zeus swallowed the pregnant Metis in order to gestate her fetus in his thigh. The birth child became the dance and wine-loving Dionysus. Not satisfied with just using his thigh as a womb, Zeus put his head to good use too, and gave us the irresistible Athena born out of it. There were other ways to give birth to divinity—spirits, even elephants, give a hand in many religions, and then there's the Virgin birth-child Jesus gestating inside Mary, preparing for His divinity on earth.

For Emily the birth of a dance came shrouded in similar mysteries. She was thrilled by the unmatched work of Vaslav Nijinsky dancing *Le Sacre du Printemps* set to Stravinsky's *Rite of Spring*. This work had inspired her to read Euripedes' *Medea*—a story of revenge about a mother who kills her children to punish her wayward husband—and she read Euripedes' *Hippolytus* as well, to locate passions to drive *Scent*.

"Have I lost you?" Sister St. Ambrose startled me.

My attention returned to the task at hand. The Sister's attitude remained affectionate, but the agreeable mood was flickering uneasily.

"I was thinking—"

"Faith is feeling," Sister corrected.

"We can't discuss—"

Sister glanced at the picture of St. Teresa. "David, realism isn't attractive to us. We find it hurtful, even damaging. Mysticism is okay with us. We don't want to dwell on transubstantiation like you do. Let it just be. We don't want to know everything about Jesus. That's hubris. We want to *experience* Jesus."

"How?"

"Without thinking it."

"A lobotomy might help." My voice was intemperate.

Sister remained tranquil.

"Forgive me, David, but if you keep pushing like that, a reputation like yours is going to be hard to change once people make up their minds about you."

"What reputation have I got?" I asked.

"That of a loner."

"I'm a Jew in a Catholic school."

"You make too much of it," Sister said. "We're not questioning your heritage. St. Paul was a Jew. Jesus was a Jew. We're together in Jesus. We believers believe. David, you can join us. Theater is a community project, and that's why we teach it and encourage it here. *Kibbutz*, as Sara must have told you, also means 'community.' We learn to discuss things and work things out together. That's what *community* means to us. We want you to be part of our community."

"As long as I hide the person I am."

"That would require a lot of work," Sister said.

"To censor myself?"

"A drama too much," Emily added.

I said nothing. All of us appeared to have signed up for the Legion of Censorship.

"Spoza," Sister said.

Her voice was seductively affectionate and I wanted to belong to her clan, to surrender and rely on communal protection, if only I could. My mind kept going its own independent way and I was helpless to stop it from wandering.

"In a letter to a friend, Wilder said, 'I'm one of the most extreme goers-alone I ever came across.'" My voice felt stronger. "*Our Town* is a tragedy. Emily admits the mistake of living. That's why the play lingers, why it stays with us."

"Nonsense. We are together in Christ and in love."

Sister's voice was calm and insistent. She was ready to move on. "Tragedy doesn't work for us Catholics. None of that teaching about fatal flaws or unrecoverable bad actions does us any good. By accepting Jesus and the Holy Spirit and the Virgin Mary and the sacraments, we always have a happy ending." Her peacefulness and tranquility were dauntingly in evidence. Sister shifted her gaze to the framed picture of St. Teresa. "St. Teresa's father was a *converso*. You know what that means?"

I shook my head to say *no*.

"He was a Jew. David, you can become one of us."

Sister was persuasive. I wanted to belong. I didn't want to be the isolated youth, the standout in the land of the faithful. I took some comfort from the fact that one out of five Americans chose "none of the above" when asked to select a religion they practice.

"Converted Jews became the chief targets of Inquisition torture."

"Sad, sad history. The Church has apologized for its crimes."

"If I can stage *Our Town* my way, you can baptize me."

Emily was startled. Sister looked suspicious. I was being dishonest, disreputable, and speaking quietly. Emily frowned, her expression a warning, but I went on, "Afterward, you can put me on the torture rack to make me recant and admit to lying about my conversion."

Sister shook her head. "Oh, dear. We would never hurt you." The icy grip of her good eye silenced me. "It's your free will."

"My free will?"

"You may go now."

"What about our final rehearsal?" I asked.

"We'll manage to get through it."

"But you need me."

"You're free to go."

Sister rose from her desk. There was a dignity about her that was difficult to intrude on. We took the signal to leave and left.

chapter 47

Outside, Emily grabbed the handrail to steady herself. The sun was like a fire stick in her eyes. A wave of nausea lingered just briefly, but at the time I was too self-absorbed to notice her pain.

"What happened in there?" I asked. "Why doesn't she want me at the rehearsal?"

"Sister fired you. She threw you off the play."

"No she didn't. I'm the smartest kid in her class. She can't replace me."

"David, the smartest kids don't have much fun. Everyone is afraid of them and they don't get much help. You bombed. She'll use your understudy."

"Then the hell with her."

I pushed back tears as we crossed the schoolyard and I bolted ahead, a grim expression on my face. Emily shouted after me. Her left ankle felt tender. She hesitated, but then she saw me stop near a fire hydrant and she caught up with me.

We were in front of a garage converted into a space to sell freshly killed poultry. The birds' necks had been slit and the birds were hung on hooks to drain. The warm air, the dirty wet straw, and the poultry droppings formed a detestable humid odor. Death dominated.

"What's the matter, kid?" the poultry man asked me. He was middle-aged and unshaved. He wore a bloodied apron and was having a smoke outside. His yellow teeth matched the skin of the plucked birds hanging from the ceiling.

"What's it to you?" I said.

The blood was ripe in the straw.

"What's it to me?" He spat on the sidewalk. "What's a young kid like you—"

"I'm not a *kid.*"

"Hear, hear." The man gave Emily a look and then flicked his cigarette into the gutter. He got up from the crate he was using for a seat. "Nice boys shouldn't sound so full of hate."

I was startled. "That's not me. I don't do hate."

"You're not so tough," the man said.

We left the poultry man. She proposed that we take her car to Prospect Park and the Brooklyn Botanic Garden to breath fresh air. She drove to Atlantic Avenue and turned left and found a parking spot near the Brooklyn Museum. She had studied plants to inspire her early dance-making in imitation of natural forms. She wanted to show me the lily pond. We went around to the back of the museum and entered the garden. On the surface of the pond I saw my unhappy face, my anger boiling.

"I want to be as wicked as Iago," I said.

"You'll grow up to be as miserable as Macbeth."

I couldn't forgive the injustice done to me.

She looked away. Perhaps my amber-flecked eyes made her uncomfortable, or maybe she was retreating from my anger. I've been writing playlets and skits since elementary school. My enemy was no longer single or double but cumulative and broad, the hated others who were keeping me from my calling.

"David, Sister isn't a bad person. She likes you."

"I like her, too. A lot of good all that liking is doing us." I grumbled on about being misunderstood. "Did she protect me?"

Emily decided just then to call Sister St. Ambrose. They chatted awhile, and then, still on the call, she turned to me. "Sister wants to know if you want your name listed on the program as producer. She's asking you to come to the rehearsal to help your understudy."

"To hell with her."

"David says, 'okay.' He'll come." Emily ended the call.

"I'll do it for you," I said. I would do anything for Emily. We went back to school and I refused to act the role of the chastised student. I was now the executive, the producer in charge.

Several nuns, a number of students, and a few lay teachers were present. There was no opening curtain to start the play. The understudy stood onstage in a spot I had blocked out. Taking license that Thornton Wilder wouldn't have allowed me, I'd chosen a girl as my understudy. She wore a fedora, a kind of Casablanca Bogart touch. "This is good," I whispered. Had she used a straw hat to indicate the simpler era of *Our Town*, the play might have been lost to nostalgia.

We watched the opening action. Sister St. Ambrose showed up in a crowd scene. She got a laugh from the teachers present. It was silly, and I slumped in my chair in disgust, whispering that I wouldn't have allowed it.

The student playing Mrs. Gibbs was charmingly matronly in her studied movements, but even her gray wig couldn't disguise her youthful vitality.

The scene moved on. Here were the Gibbses and the Herseys, so many of them in one cemetery, in one county, in one country. The good feeling among the people in Grover's Corners made me feel especially lonely. All of Emily's family was gone, and those few who had survived remained in Lithuania. The density of family was missing in her life.

The Stage Manager moved events along smoothly. I whispered a compliment about the understudy's delivery. I hated to admit how good she was and how quickly she had taken over. She described how it felt on the days when you're first in love and like a sleepwalker you couldn't see where you were stepping, and didn't hear the people trying to catch your attention. Emily sat still, mesmerized in her affection for the play.

After the rehearsal, Sister left quickly and the auditorium emptied. Emily joined me at the concession area in the back of the auditorium. I was deflated. My help wasn't needed. No one wanted me. "What's the matter now?" Emily asked.

I gripped her small wrist; my fingers were cold from the Coke I'd been drinking. "You haven't touched me in a long, long while." I traced the now-healed scars she'd made. She felt her pulse quicken.

"You're in my heart," she said. "You're in my journal every night."

"I don't know if I can believe you. You're avoiding me. How about letting me read your journals?"

She had given me several carefully expurgated sections, and now I wanted more. I always wanted more. I wanted to pry into her mind and embody her in my play. But she was leery of granting me more access to her thoughts, some of which changed from day to day.

"Why don't you just make it all up?" she said. "Imagination can change people's lives."

"If I'm making it all up, I'm never quite sure it's honest and true."

I suppose every art has its craft to distinguish it, and whatever I had learned from Sister St. Ambrose could be used badly or well. Emily saw me grappling with the push and the pull of creating a play that would resonate with an audience, and she was trying to understand if I was old enough to be the man she'd imagined me to be. She gave me another small section to read from her journals.

held on to the pages for a week but when I returned them, Emily didn't believe I'd gotten past the first three pages. I said I was disappointed with the small sample. There was nothing physical in them to make the action bounce. It was all about feelings and moods and thinking and worries and doubts, the inner music of life—which was most of what we live for, but I was too young to know that.

As I look back, the reason I needed fireworks to make my play work onstage was the absence of emotional fire within the play, and by extension within me. Whatever I lacked inside, I had faithfully reproduced its absence in the play *Maya*.

As a kid I liked action movies. I thought there wasn't enough *pow* or *bam* in her life because my own emotional life was too hooked on bodily notes and moves, and distractions. In contrast, Emily's new dances were ethereal and were winning praise from her peers for evoking something beyond the moment of expression. She wasn't just into a funny, crowd-pleasing, family-oriented, frog-costumed stuff any longer. Her visual metaphors added longing and desire. But when I was seventeen, I needed more *pow* and more *bam*, as in *pow pow pow* and *bam bam bam*. The movies had lots of it. And that's the way it was for me when I was growing up.

Emily would have liked to talk about her dance with Rick, with Father Dan, with Sister St. Ambrose, even with Page or Jay, but each was busy in his or her own way and saw dance as something both lovely and frivolous. She talked with Melissa and Dylan, but that was about a phrase or an unusual movement, the pieces used in construction. The underlying architecture, the final language, and the ultimate landscape surrounding the House of Emily she shared with no one. She was as public in her presentation as anyone could wish, and as private as the moon resting on the other side of earth.

Rick, working late, harried at times, getting by on little sleep, was frequently out of town. After negotiating a new labor contract and securing a much-needed credit line for Bradbury, he'd become an essential ingredient for the company's survival. People outside the company—suppliers, bankers, and customers—preferred dealing with him. He was always ready to listen, willing to make commitments, and he was reliable. He was so busy that on some days it felt as if he had dropped out of Emily's life altogether, and for a while the tension over her having and keeping another man's baby diminished.

There was less time to fret over her pregnancy, and with Jacob's Pillow approaching she'd finally found her path into professional fulfillment. She was shocked to hear Rick say,

"Angel, let's move out of Brooklyn." He'd found a house in Westchester County.

"Moving upstate would take me away from dance." The dance scene was in Brooklyn and Manhattan.

"But you don't *have* to dance. And in your condition—"

He meant to be kind, but she was hurt. Her condition was dance. They started quarreling. Rick broke it off and said he was late for a meeting. It was hard for either one of them to keep up an interest in each other's work. They tried and often failed. Elements of dance were instinctual, a taste for rhythm and song pressed into movement. She made sculptures in air, painted hues in space, wrote melodies on the floor. Rick manufactured folding cartons and corrugated boxes. By design, the boxes were meant to confine things. His industrial engineers clocked wage earners' work with stopwatches and computers. There was no music in it.

"Rick, do you still love me?"

"Angel, I couldn't live without you."

He said this with such determined affection that she had to catch her breath. They embraced in a hug that pulled her off the ground. She struggled to get free out of fear of hurting her baby. This caught him off guard. Their bodily miscommunications were more frequent. But in general, they were too busy and too committed to their individual careers to do much sleeping together, though, she wrote, the flame was still there.

"Rick, if you love me, then please pay attention."

He threw up his hands.

"I'm good at things you've never paid attention to," she insisted.

The fault line separating them wasn't me, though I was part of it. The gaping space was her desire to make something of herself in the larger world outside marriage, but he was satisfied to have a woman at home.

"Please don't ever ask me again to quit dancing."

"But you're chasing waterfalls and windmills."

His newfound confidence was stark and powerful. She heard his voice rushing off to the next meeting, and she let him go without a kiss.

chapter 49

A few days later Rick drove her to the plant at Red Hook. She'd hitched a ride with him to deliver a piece of my mother's art that Jay had bought. She was surprised to see Jay waiting not in his own office but in Rick's office, and was struck by his new hairstyle. He had gelled or moussed his hair and arranged it to look spiky messy. This was a far cry from his careful, tidy, old-school corporate look. It was as startling as seeing Madonna or Lady Gaga in a three-piece business suit. There was immediate tension in the air. His dog, Lady, typically overjoyed at the sight of a human hand, remained lying at Jay's feet, her feathery rusty-red tail twitching side to side like a cat's.

Jay removed his feet from Rick's desk and came forward. The gesture was assertive, even hostile. She felt an immediate apprehension. They heard the croaking of a noisy frog in the landscaped quad that separated the office complex from the manufacturing plant.

"What the hell was that?" Jay demanded. The weeds outside the office had been cleared and new landscaping added.

"A frog. Two frogs," Rick said. The quad had been a trashy yard before he had restored the wasteland. The croaking grew louder. "What's up?" Rick asked. His outward calmness would have been remote had it not been for a telltale clenching of his hand. The tension at work had been rising. Page consistently supported Rick as the brighter man to lead the company, but Jay, jealous of Rick's recent achievements, was becoming combative.

"You know what's up," Jay said.

There was something in Jay's tone that made Emily look at him with a quick and questioning razor-sharp glance. His slacks were pressed and pleated, but the waistband had expanded beyond its recommended pressure. Jay wasn't acting like the teddy bear she had known and enjoyed. Instead he was taking on a warrior role she deplored. He stalked across the room, and Lady sprang up to run after him. Another croak from the frogs, and he swore at them softly. "You need to rethink your approach to sales and manufacturing," he demanded of Rick. There was something stagy in his delivery, as if he hadn't had enough time to rehearse. "If our competition grabs Island Foods then we have to kiss our vegetable-packing people goodbye." He paused and both men turned to Emily.

They were talking about peas and cauliflower, but she suspected they were fighting over her. Jay seemed eager to show her what an inferior man she had married. She fixed Jay in her sights to stop him, hoping her cold glare would do it. Jay looked sheepish but then he went on, newly determined.

Whatever else was happening, Jay was in no mood to listen to anyone. He spoke with dramatic gestures. "We've got to kick some butt."

Lady trotted from under his feet to lick Emily's hand. Willy-nilly, she was being sucked into an intracompany fight. On her previous trips to deliver Sara's art, she had seen a banner hung over the main entrance. "Only the Motivated Need Apply." A surreal apocalyptic urgency and fanatical dualism swept the company as her life spun haphazardly into the men's orbit.

Open disagreements were banished and secrecy reigned. A straw poll indicated that seventy-five percent of the employees supported Jay's strong-arm approach. They had to kick butt. Flags were unfurled and martial music played in the lunchroom. At a lunchroom rouse-the-troops meeting on a previous visit, Emily had seen a clerk stand up. "We're with you, Jay," the man had said, his docile face breaking into fragments of silent hysteria. One of the other clerks then put her arm around him, and a weird thing happened: Both clerks raised their clenched fists above their heads. They were going to be winners.

But Jay's earlier business decisions had turned out badly and Bradbury was losing several major accounts. Some employees had turned against Jay but most wanted to stay the course— the hammer always looks more forceful than a scalpel—so the craziness continued.

The company paintball shootout organized to teach fighting values was taking place that weekend. Everyone signed on, either as one of Jay's Commandos or as one of Rick's Foragers. The hunters and the gatherers were to have it out. Some people snickered at Jay's Napoleonic overconfidence, but everyone feared him, especially now that Page had become busy with philanthropic work and didn't come to the office. The worse things got, the more Jay insisted that he had been right all along and no one was going to persuade him otherwise. He invited Emily to come to the paintball shootout.

They drove to a forested area in New Jersey. Combatants had trained using computer combat games. They carried air-powered paintball guns, water, and ammo. They wore goggles and each had a belt hung with extra paintball canisters and CO_2 cartridges. Shouts and rebel yells rolled. The rules required a person to play dead if a paint shot marked him or her. The shots stung and could break skin if fired at close range. The rules also required combatants to stop shooting once a person was paint shot.

Jay was an easy, ample, and slow-moving target. When the shooting started, Rick nailed him on the arms and chest almost immediately. Jay collapsed and slid ten feet. Rick called for a cease-fire. Despite the rules calling for combatants to stop shooting the fallen, a flurry of shots kept hitting Jay as he lay sprawled on the ground. The violence was startling. "Shoot the bastard again," someone yelled. "Shoot the son of a bitch." By then the company had laid off a third of its employees by embracing outsourcing, and many of Jay's employees were seething with submerged hatred for their flag-waving boss who didn't give a damn about them but wanted to earn more money. It was a brutal thing to realize that class warfare was alive and well in America. Incensed and blinded by the heat of the battle, his own team members were shooting him.

The games were called soon after. The fun had been short and now they had to deal with dirty fatigues, grimy hair, and splattered paint. On the way home, Emily, Rick, and Jay stopped for dinner. Once seated, Jay lifted the edge of his shirt to check the dime-size bumps stitched across his skin.

"That's leadership. I was out in front of everyone," he said.

Jay pulled his shirt down to cover the spots.

"Your own guys shot you in the back a dozen times," Rick said.

"You want me to humiliate myself, don't you?" Jay asked.

No one answered. Rick found an envelope in his fatigues and handed it to Jay.

"What's this?" Jay asked.

"It's my resignation."

Emily held her breath. Rick had been updating his resume, but she hadn't thought he would go so far as to quit. She applauded him silently.

"You can't leave me like that," Jay said. "We're in the thick of it."

"I'm clearing out," Rick said, "You've got two weeks' notice."

Emily had not seen the two men sitting opposite each other like this, one man large, the other compact and tidy, the large man melting like a chunk of butter left in the sun.

"Don't be a quitter. I need you."

"If I stay, you become the chairman and your new job is to go golfing every day."

Jay's wattles jiggled. He pushed the resignation letter toward Rick's side of the table. Rick looked neither surprised nor relieved, nor even satisfied. He took his letter back. They ate very little and afterward drove a half-hour before anyone spoke. It was Jay who broke the silence. "I need a pit stop."

chapter 50

Jay's departure from Bradbury headquarters after the paintball shoot had unintended consequences. He had lots more free time. Either out of a need to avenge himself, or strong feelings for Emily, he used this extra time to pursue her with renewed vigor, sending her flowers every other day—chrysanthemums, roses, ranunculuses, gladiola, lilies—and signing the cards, "Jay, a dance fan."

She didn't like cut flowers, stems hacked, scents frozen, blossoms without insects to cross-pollinate them. She dreaded the delivery van coming because it upset Rick. She rushed home from rehearsals to get there before he did to take the bouquet from the top of the steps and run it across the street to an elderly lady who loved flowers.

Outwardly, an eerie normality descended on her relationship with Page and Jay. She continued to escort them to Thursday-evening events downtown. Sometimes Rick came along. That evening they were all seated at the Joyce Theater.

Emily was next to Rick, and Rick was next to Page and Jay. They were like fragments of air held together by the force of silence until Page finally whispered, "Is that Paul Newman in front of us with his wife and children?"

Emily's mood lifted on seeing the Newman family. Her humor came back to her. Here they were, "Newman's Own," as the labels on Newman's brand of supermarket food products proclaimed, in this case his children and his beautiful wife Joanne Woodward. Married thirty-five or forty years? It was an eternity. How did a celebrity marriage last despite the availability and diversity of partners working in Hollywood? They looked peaceful and happy together. She was proud to sit behind them, and felt an extra bit of pride in her own marriage. She wanted it to get past the stormy weather and bad karma and endure.

The curtain rose to show two tall women, standing entwined on stage. The dancers shifted back and forth like leaves suspended in air. Emily felt lightheaded to see them dance so beautifully. It was such a gift to dance well, a gift of good fortune to the audience as well. She felt sudden love for the dancers. At intermission she praised them.

"You liked it?" Page said, skeptical.

Emily had admired the intimate twining. But now she remained silent.

"You guys," Rick said, embarrassed to be caught in the middle of a cultural disagreement.

"Us guys," Jay agreed. They'd gone downstairs to buy refreshments.

Jealousy flamed in Rick's eyes. He still must have believed

Jay was his rival and the father of Emily's baby. Emily plunged to rescue them from a miserable evening. "They say Nijinsky climaxed into a scarf at the 1912 premiere of *Afternoon of a Faun* in Paris."

"He jerked off?" Page said.

"They say."

"What a waste."

Her efforts to become pregnant had come to nothing. There was something in Jay's semen or maybe her uterus that was hostile to IVF-implanted embryos. To overcome this defect, she and Jay had signed up a gestational surrogate as the next step. Page had her eggs removed surgically, and Jay surrendered his sperm to a test tube. The clinicians scored a number of hits they then implanted into the hired woman's body.

"Oh, isn't it wonderful?" Emily said. She was happy for them.

"So far, so good," Page said.

With abundant house help and a huge house, one of four houses the Bradburys owned, why should they bother with the fuss of child birthing? A surrogate mother was a terrific idea, a logical idea, inexpensive, too. They could afford to be generous. No pricy tuition was required. No healthcare coverage, except for birthing. They didn't need to hire a college graduate; they didn't need a high school honors student, or a homecoming queen, and they could pay better than Walmart.

Page would suffer no pain, no stretch marks, no nausea, no sagging breasts or loose folds to deal with after bearing children. The rich are different. They can hire the poor to help spread their genes. There were other benefits, too.

"Our surrogate is a non-drinking Baptist. I can drink all the alcohol I want while she carries my baby. What's not to like?" Page asked.

"Does that make the surrogate a prostitute?"

"Huh?"

"Sara did a series of photographs on surrogate mothers."

"Prostitute," Jay whinnied, cutting short his laugh.

No one said anything. The carpet was thick underfoot; the buzz of the downstairs refreshment crowd was soothingly distracting. Page sipped her wine. Rick looked uncomfortable.

"I wish I'd met your precious Sara," Page said.

"An outlier," Rick said. "Way outside the box."

"Prostitute? Our kid being born of a prostitute?" Jay asked. "Where the hell would Sara have gotten that idea?"

Rick nodded. "This girl Sara—"

"—What's the difference between renting a womb and paying to use a vagina?" Emily asked.

Jay giggled. "That's a creepy way to think, even twisted."

Entitlement glowed in Page's eyes. She had left the low-rent districts. "Our surrogate gets paid—that's all we need to know."

"She doesn't sleep with me," Jay agreed.

"That's right. That's perfectly right. What's not to like?" Page finished drinking her wine.

Emily moved past it. "Did you guys know that choreography's roots come from Greece? *Khoreia* means 'dance,' and *Graphein*—you know, as in German but from the Greek—it means 'to write.'" The end-of-the-intermission chimes struck. *Thank God. Back to your neutral corners.* "Choreographic," she added. "Dance writing."

At the end of the performance they decided to walk to a nearby restaurant. They came to a storefront selling sex toys and sensual adventures. Low-wattage spotlights cast magenta and buttercup spots onto two mannequins bound together with leather and chains and various studs and bolts and rods. Emily would not have known how the objects were worn had they not been tricked out on the mannequins. She felt that her small-town Lithuanian naiveté was showing. Page snickered, worldly, knowledgeable, and Jay sounded a bombastic note. Rick said he was disgusted. The items must have looked profane to him and they all walked faster and crossed the street.

"We're hoping…" Page leaned toward Emily. "We're hoping you'll remain our downtown event guide after you do Jacob's Pillow."

Emily said she would have to check her schedule. She wondered if this was yet another attempt by Page to keep her enemies closer than her friends in order to watch them better.

They stopped to eat a light meal. Page's voice was low-pitched and conciliatory. Her eyes, however, continued to waver between fear and anger on account of Jay paying so much attention to Emily. According to her journal, Emily was thinking about me when she saw a youth, a dark-haired youth with curly hair and a girl outside the restaurant.

Melissa? A searing blindness overcame Emily. *It had to be Melissa.* She watched the couple hailing a cab. It was a warm night and many people were out and her view was partly blocked. Her throat tightened and panic seized her heart. The couple started to run toward the cab and Emily rushed out just as the cab was pulling away. She watched the cab careen through a changing light. She did not actually see the passengers inside, but she was sure she had caught me cold. She was wounded, bruised, and in pain. She came back to the restaurant, her heart pounding.

"What's gotten into you?" Rick asked.

"I saw a dancer I knew."

She could not get me out of her mind, and obsessed with this new fear, she couldn't make out what Page or Jay or Rick were saying, but she nodded her head as if she was listening with avid interest to every word.

Rick drove home after dinner and she walked ahead of him into a darkened house. Her heart was thumping again. She switched on every light within reach. Without taking off her coat she rushed to my room to confront me about my going out with Melissa. I was quietly sitting at my computer.

Her jealousy leaked away. "It's way past your bedtime."

"I'm looking at a soft-porn DVD I got at school."

"At school?" She grimaced and turned to leave.

"You don't have to look." I adjusted the sound higher. "They're really cool naked pics of someone you know."

She blushed. *Melissa, Melissa.* She had an adorable figure. *It had to be Melissa. How she hated that girl!* She glanced at the DVD label on my screen. "*Thai Ecstasy?*"

"You have to double-click on the thumbnail."

I gave her the mouse and she double-clicked. The image popped open to show Dr. Wilson naked with two Asian girls who looked barely eighteen.

"My God," she whispered. "Where did you get this?" The

image of the man and his porn was like a weird hologram that refused to match up.

"I lifted it out of Dr. Wilson's case after getting my booster shot."

The man who had put himself in charge of the school's porn patrol, the most devout man in the parish, had just been reduced to a lustful smudge. She looked out the window toward the dark night for a word to describe her anxiety.

"There are twenty-six images on the disc," I said.

"And you—"

"You want to see the rest?"

"David, I've seen enough."

chapter 51

The next time Emily saw Dr. Wilson's balding head she was preoccupied with the logistics of her group's trip to Jacob's Pillow. Wilson was physically unchanged, yet he didn't look the same. He was somehow transfigured, perhaps disfigured, the same guy, but tarnished. They were both attending the long-planned school fund-raiser. She joined him and others inside an enclosed display booth to see a calla lily photographed by Mapplethorpe. He wasn't a photographer Emily had expected to see at a Catholic school auction, but a calla lily offended no one. "Thank the Lord every penny serves our school," Sister St. Ambrose said reassuringly.

Framed alongside Mapplethorpe was a large black-and-white picture called "Fun Picture #3" by Sally Mann. In pictured a nude torso of one of her kids. The anatomy was ambiguous because the figure's head and lower abdomen were cropped. A glistening liquid drop slithered down a slender belly. Rick leaned in for a closer look. "Is it a girl? It could be a boy." It was beautifully photographed.

"Chuck," Jay said to Wilson, "can you help us sex this picture?"

Wilson should have known from the pelvic formation but the figure was adolescent and the doctor evasive. Without offering a logical connection, he began talking about unisex cherubs in medieval church paintings. They never showed genitals, he said. The artists vying for commissions from Church authorities had erased gender. Dr. Wilson managed an approving tongue click. He went on, cupids in secular paintings, anatomically identical to cherubs, did show their male gender.

One of the guests mentioned the Catholic artist Henry Darger. He was a well-intentioned artist with a kindly take on girls. Darger attended Mass every day and died in the 1970s. On his death, his landlady discovered a lifetime of artwork stored his rooms. He had created an entire charming world of forceful Vivian girls, fighting malevolent forces.

"He just got one detail wrong," the guest went on. "His Catholic education was so desperate about sex that he came out of the parochial school system a functioning ignoramus. He outfitted the girls with penises."

Several chuckles interrupted the guest. "Inconceivable," someone said.

Someone else said that was a whole lot better than the erotica Jeff Koons made in picturing his wife, and nowhere near the inciting vulgarities created by the Chapman Brothers, London artists. Darger was all-American, and Midwest bred.

"He drew what he knew," someone else said.

"Sincerity is the hallmark of a good artist," another guest added.

As I read these lines in Emily's journal my thoughts went back to Rick. Sincerity was his trademark. Earnestness was his calling card. He didn't pretend toward anything. His soul had been committed to Marian worship and virginal goodness, and the real-life beautiful female he'd married suffered by comparison.

Sister fanned her face. "It's absurd to explain Catholic education in Henry Darger's terms. We operate some of the finest universities and field powerfully learned teachers, some of them Jesuits. You don't have to be Catholic to be stupid or obsessed with sex. Marcel Duchamp was holed up in his Manhattan walk-up distributing straws around a female nude figure for fourteen years and nobody laughed at him. The Philadelphia Museum of Art displays his enigmatic assemblage *Étant donnés* behind a solid wood door with a double peephole."

"Yes, yes," someone said, impatiently. "But Catholic bishops are in the forefront pushing retrograde ideas, condemning contraception, censoring sex education."

Emily felt her stomach. *You can be educated and still be stupid in romantic matters*, she wrote in her journal.

Sally Mann's photograph was strictly cherubic and could be framed within a Raphael painting without offending anyone. But even in its innocence, there was something in the torso that compelled physical feeling.

"What do you think?" Jay asked Emily. "Is it a turn-on?"

"None of us are immune to visual excitement," she said, her voice neutral.

Dr. Wilson cut her a look he quickly covered with a smile. Emily waited for someone to say something different. They all kept their own counsel, and the silence embarrassed her. She was too easily shamed, too quickly subdued by fear of what others might think of her. She went on, "People like looking at nakedness. Or something close to nakedness. I'm making a career in dance partially because people enjoy looking at me dance in skin costumes." The shattering silence that followed scared her. She wrote in her journal that she should have stayed away talking about female bodies and said something about Michelangelo's sculpture, the nude *David*.

Dr. Wilson's eyes held her for a critical moment, as if they were sharing a secret. She wondered what had led him to record his unexciting performance on a DVD. His endowments were far from beefcake. And now, Dr. Wilson in evening dress, in tie and silk lapels, didn't look nearly as dominant as he had once appeared. He, too, was a prisoner of sex.

Jay seized his arm. "How do you treat the folks you get to come to your place upstate?" A medical journal had quoted Dr. Wilson's research. He treated obsessive-compulsive sexual dysfunction. Wilson looked over his shoulder to make sure there were no children nearby. He said studies showed that half of college males have an immediate sexual response on seeing a nude female picture. His voice edged lower. "We use images from the Abel Assessment for sexual interest to grade our erotic responders."

"Erotic responders?" Emily said.

"Science," Dr. Wilson said.

"Chuck," Jay said. "I don't know any one of us guys who can't get it on after a little encouragement."

Jay was good in seizing attention, but the group's focus remained with Dr. Wilson. "We wire their genitals to a ple-thysmograph." He paused to let his listeners visualize sexual responsiveness harnessed to science. "It's trickier with women. We use optical laser measurements." The doctor was earnest as he went on. "When we get the response we're looking for"— there was another slight pause to let people imagine it—"we bust it up with noxious smells. Aversion, you know. It imprints the memory."

"For Christ's sake," Jay said. He avoided looking at Emily. "You mean half of our college guys should be in jail?"

"Men," someone said.

"No, women, too," a woman's voice added.

"It's simple," Jay laughed. "All of us should be in jail."

That was the problem the Church faced: how to deal with the human condition.

Wilson raised an eyebrow and resumed his easy, confiden-tial tone. "We can use chemical castration if they let us. Or we ask patients to imagine their intimate acts broadcast on a billboard. It scares the heck out of some of them, but then you have the narcissists who enjoy seeing themselves on a bill-board." He shrugged.

Jay, clearly annoyed, turned to the Sally Mann picture. "Chuck, you didn't answer my question. We don't know for sure if this picture is of a *girl*."

They were rounding the corner of an androgynous mystery.

"So," Page intruded, "if a straight college guy gets a rise out of this picture thinking it's a girl, and then we discover it's a picture of a boy, does that make him gay?"

They stared at the slender belly, but no one ventured an answer. There were things you simply didn't discuss in a country where legislators in half the states were busy legislating new restrictions on individual freedoms in matters of privacy and reproductive rights. Instead the guests talked about the high minimum bids for the photographs on auction, which segued into a joke about trickle-down economics.

chapter 52

"Sister," Jay said, "you're our classics scholar. True or false: Aristotle and Plato kept slaves?" Sister St. Ambrose said that Aristotle, the master of democracy and a practical man, had kept as many as thirteen slaves. Plato, the republican elitist, had gotten by with six.

"Thank heavens we dressed up slavery," Jay said.

Rick gave him a questioning look.

"We no longer call working people slaves," Jay explained. "We call them wage earners."

It took a moment for Sister St. Ambrose to catch the joke. She didn't laugh.

But Rick was on fire. "That's dumb." For him work wasn't only a wage but freedom to choose meaning in life. Page produced a wooden clapper to cut the conversation and signal the last round of bidding.

Emily and Sister St. Ambrose left the bidders and took the

path to the gazebo. The Sister had a prayer book and a pen-light. She talked warmly. "How's our dance mistress?"

"Persecuting myself."

Sister whistled merrily to overcome the melancholy tone. "I've been feeling guilty about David," Sister said. "He should be in the play. He should be our Stage Manager. Maybe Reinhold Niebuhr was right—none of us can brandish power without guilt."

"I won't force him to falsely become a Catholic."

"Then you should find David's father and make him an ally. Dr. Wilson keeps bringing up the letter Alex had given him."

"That thing can't be enforceable?"

"By the time you finish arguing over it, our staging of *Our Town* will be over."

Emily had put off looking for Alex. But now, realizing that Sister was happy to undermine Dr. Wilson's stubbornness, Emily decided to put Alex back into her tight schedule. Just then they heard a rustle on the path and I came into the gazebo. I was playing with several younger guests and dragging a thread behind me.

"What in the world?" Sister asked.

"They pulled me into silly game," I said.

Wilson's daughters entered the gazebo next. One was strong yet delicate, and in the dim light she could have been mistaken for a handsome boy disguised as a good-looking girl. The other was a fair-haired and a chubby, lovely young creature with large eyes. She was taking up a thread I'd left behind. "I'm playing Ariadne," the innocent girl said. She balled the thread and the three of us ran down the hill.

"He'll be a lady charmer, our Spoza."

"Yes. Isn't he already?"

"You know the Ariadne story?" Sister asked.

"Should I?"

"Every woman knows that story."

Emily was silent. There was so much bombarding her that year, so much to learn, so much to do, so little time. She wished she could turn herself into one of Marc Chagall's flying figures to escape.

Sister paused as if seeking permission to continue.

"Go on," Emily said.

"Here's the gist of it: Ariadne, a king's daughter, falls in love with Theseus and goes against her father's wishes by giving Theseus a gold thread to lay down in the labyrinth so Theseus wouldn't get lost after killing the Minotaur inside the labyrinth. He succeeds and they flee together. Then, having gotten what he needed, Theseus abandons Ariadne."

Was the Minotaur the devouring sexual nature of mankind? Emily asked her journal. *Is my own fate to be Ariadne and predestined to a bad end?*

It had gotten dark and the moon was nearly full. Sister St. Ambrose admired it. In a voice filled with wonder that must have taken her back to her own early childhood, she said, "The moon is the symbol for Diana, the pagan goddess of chastity."

Emily wished that the goddess Diana had been there for her when she needed chastity's help.

chapter 53

It struck me on my journey through Emily's journals that the unexpected events in her life, in my life, and Rick's life, and the actions we took to face them or avoid them, and the consequences we failed to consider, could be easily dismissed as ignorance.

Someone could just as easily say we had lived twisted lives. Much of what we did was ill-informed and badly chosen, but all of it was earnest and authentic—my coming of age, Emily's growth as an artist, Rick's struggle to keep his religion. We came into the world expecting one thing, worked feverishly to achieve our varied goals, and discovered that life was something other than what we had anticipated.

Most people have no idea how twisted and volatile and angry and sensual and fantastically imagined the Bible narrative remains. Emily's journals show us sensuality and its discontents, and her questioning of deep-rooted beliefs. In her heart she was always seeking to right the world's wrongs, but the world got ahead of her.

When we got home, Emily demanded that I return Dr. Wilson's *Thai Ecstasy* disc to him. She believed that blackmail was a greater evil than a man's erotic wanderings. She didn't want me to watch the disc either. I agreed to return it.

The following day I had a brief and tense meeting with Dr. Wilson. He was rattled, and embarrassed, too. He called me a thief. He said I had invaded his privacy. He said that I didn't know my place in the world and I wasn't obedient to authority, that I was rude. I took up issues I had no right to raise. He said I asked too many questions and asked the wrong questions.

He didn't think he could trust me, and he was right. Nevertheless, that same day he went to see Sister St. Ambrose and demanded that she reinstate me as Stage Manager in *Our Town*. He made it all sound as if she had disenfranchised me and now he was correcting her error. Afterward, there was no more talk about converting me.

I was happy to be restored to my rightful place as the Stage Manager. In fact I was thrilled. Paul Newman did a great job as Stage Manager. A noted dance enthusiast who had edited the magisterial *Reading Dance* had taken a youthful shot at the role. I was joining an honored tradition, that of the trustworthy narrator.

On the night of the school's staging of *Our Town*, Dr. Wilson, his wife, and their two daughters sat next to the Bradburys in the first row. Emily and Rick were a few rows back. She caught Jay's glance as he turned to look at her. She tightened her mouth to suggest disapproval and he looked away with a sharp snap forward.

Our Town is set in an imaginary New Hampshire town, and had been performed all over America to raves since it premiered in 1938. Sister St. Ambrose had the school pay a fee for permission to stage the play. I quoted a few things in the program that were taken from *Some Suggestions for the Director*, written by Wilder. He wanted his Stage Manager to sustain a knowing distance, at once sympathetic and dry and understated to engage theatergoers in a tale of regret and tragedy—a three-act evocation of people's lives, youth, marriage, and death. The close observer of narrative styles should see that I've chosen to play the role of Stage Manager in *Morning Light*, too.

I walked onstage and the audience quieted. I explained how I had married many couples in my day and had asked myself if I believed in marriage, and paused, and then offered the opinion that of the millions of marriages, only a rare few are interesting. Of course I know now that every marriage is interesting to the married party, and I was discovering that Emily's marriage to Rick was one of the more interesting marriages.

Emily was enthralled as she listened: here was the unfolding of life in all its majestic, slow passage. She felt her heart jumping. I was no longer a youth acting an adult role; I was a man speaking of manly things.

"Angel," Rick whispered, "you're crying over a silly play?"

She wiped her eyes and straightened her jacket. The top of the proscenium carried a crest with a mysteriously beautiful image of the Virgin Mary molded into cheap plaster. The play went on and Emily went on watching, listening, and though she'd seen the play several times, she was still hoping for a happy ending. Her attention broke when she imagined her baby had kicked—*it's too early, too soon*—but panic seized her. She reached for Rick's hand and he whispered, "Your hand feels clammy." She was afraid to get up and sat quietly, waiting for her racing heart to still itself. The organist played Mendelssohn's "Wedding March" as the couple on stage rushed forward from the back of the auditorium to get married. I announced a fifteen-minute intermission.

The audience clapped enthusiastically, thrilled by the high quality of a high school production. Emily rose to her feet. The auditorium shifted underneath her and she wondered if Rick could hear her heart pounding, her emotions blistering. Gasping for breath, she felt something wrong. She swept past Rick to get to the aisle and then ran to the ladies' rest room, where she fainted.

When she came to she felt unstable, her mind detached. She didn't recognize Jay trying to help her off the floor and screamed at him not to hurt her baby. He retreated, and the next thing she knew, three pairs of hands were holding her up as she heaved into a sink. There was blood on her forearm; horrified, she had an awful premonition, thinking that she might be losing her baby. And then, with several people helping to steady her, she saw that the blood had come from the cut that had embodied Rick, torn open.

chapter 54

Her sudden illness frightened everyone who knew and loved her. Jacob's was around the corner. Her ability to recover from colds, flu, and strained and pulled muscles was a gift, part mental gymnastics and part hurry-up work methods, but no one had ever seen her pass out before. Everyone near her had heard her scream about not hurting her baby. People wondered if stress had unbalanced her. Rick, traveling to Boston the next day, called her three times to check on her.

Her emotional landscape remained cluttered. Jay kept pestering her but getting a restraining order against him wasn't an option. She came up with a desperate plan that wasn't more desperate than the plans clever people invent at the point of desperation. She invited Jay and Page to see the extreme performance artist who had inspired her to make those cuts in her forearm. They entered Performance Space 122 and took their seats before an altar-like setting shrouded in incense smoke and illuminated by candles. Jay made a joke about Rick being too busy to spend an evening with them. Page told him to keep quiet.

The murmuring sounds of an uneasy audience heightened the tension. Two performers entered the stage, an androgynous youth who looked ghostly and a robust man in a robe that gave off a priestly aura. The robed performer held the youth's arm firmly and pierced it with a sharpened lance the size of a knitting needle. A communal gasp went up from the audience. The youth rolled his eyes under his lids. There was no mistaking the imagery, a body transfigured into a bleeding St. Sebastian.

"Weird show," Page whispered harshly. People turned in her direction.

"You don't get it?" Emily said, her eyes ablaze with deceit. She had already frightened Jay with a fainting episode during the performance of *Our Town*, and she hoped she could finally get rid of him for good by appearing to go off the rails.

Just then a dozen dancers flew onstage and whipped themselves with sharp hydra-headed points as they whirled. The tips tore into the dancers' flesh, their backs welted over and lacquered red. The audience's psychosexual embers fueled the drama. At a pause in the performance, Jay looked startled and Page, suddenly self-possessed and a bit righteous, looked worried. They both looked at Emily, as if seeing her for the first time.

"I love the pain," Emily said. She loved no such thing. Jay looked at her slantwise. The priestly figure had started to push another lance into the youth's arm.

"Jay, *look*," Page hissed.

They sat mesmerized. The lance exited at the back of the youth's arm and caught the flickering candlelight. It seemed as if no one was breathing. A black performer had entered the stage and sat on a sawhorse with his back turned toward the audience.

"Look," Emily whispered. She pulled up her sleeve to show them her four scarification marks. "I did it, too."

Page got up. "Jay, let's go."

"No, stay. I can make the cuts bleed!" Emily squeezed the torn scar to show them.

"What are doing?" Page asked, alarm in her eyes.

"I want to stop myself from sleepwalking through life."

"Jay, let's go."

The audience seemed to inhale all at once. The priestly figure cut a line across the black man's back, and then he cut another line, and another line, the blood spreading on black skin. The intoxicating ritual was beyond ordinary pain. The Bradburys took their seats again.

At a pause in the performance, Page asked Emily if the stress of getting ready to dance at Jacob's Pillow had gotten to her. Jay chimed in on how it had to be tough to work a body so much. The inquiries were kind but frosty; their former openness had shut down.

"This show isn't good for you," Page said. "It's deranged."

Jay tried to get above it. "Different strokes."

"Move it," Page said to Jay. She was again ready to leave and Jay's hooded eyes and overall reticent manner showed that he was ready, too. He was fast retreating from Emily, which was what she'd hoped for. She made a motion rubbing her arm in a backhanded rubbing way, recalling the insane man in the subway who'd brushed himself with a bottle. Jay and Page looked at her in an odd, slanting way, and then got up in a sudden, quick move and left, looking back several times. Emily remained sitting on the edge of her seat and watched the performance all the way through to the end.

chapter 55

After the PS122 show, and in the days just before Jacob's Pillow, Emily worked harder to make her choreography vivid. She shortened the languid phrases and inserted a few laconic elbow and hand gestures into *Trio*; and instead of a singular curve in *Kiss* she tried to disrupt expectations by speeding up a few beats and adding unbalanced moments. As she was growing as an artist, her personal life was crumbling. The immediate source of pain was Melissa.

Melissa had let her hair grow over the summer and had braided it, pulling it back into a bun. This highlighted her face and showed off her fine bone structure and smooth skin. Her cheeks sharpened the oval shape of her eyes. The cumulative changes in her appearance also made her look older. To Emily, the reason for all the changes was obvious—I liked older girls and smart girls and Melissa was older than I was. If Melissa was Emily's rival for my affection, she was a beautiful rival.

Emily checked my blog to see if anything revealing had been posted and found nothing. At a rehearsal, she asked Melissa to describe the movie she'd gone to see with me on a recent school-group outing. Melissa answered without hesitation, mentioning the shadowy lighting in the restored film noir. Emily's suspicion lingered. She was a prisoner of jealousy rather than a warden in charge of her incorrigible heart. In a fit of high-mindedness and a wish to get beyond the personal, she went to look for Alex, in the hope of packing me off to live with my father. She called him at the phone number Dr. Wilson had given her and found that it had been disconnected. She then went to look for Alex at the East Village café where she had first met him and Sara.

At that time, the café had been a haven for artists in need of financial help and a hangout for rich kids struggling to look working-class poor. The dress code extended to engineering and logging boots sized to fit the smallest urban foot. The café had changed since those days. The working-class poor had been pushed out. The trust-fund kids had graduated college and had found useful internships and uptown apartments. There was more dust on the floor and the old oak tables had been replaced with steel-topped ones. The entryway was still the place to post personal fliers and an orange one read, "Stressed OUT male seeks l-a-i-d back roommate to share expenses. Tidy females preferred. Geeks may apply. Call Alex."

Three or four tabs with the phone number had been torn off the bottom of the flier. Emily asked a Hispanic woman behind the counter if she knew the person who had posted the flier. The woman described a slack-limbed male with a tiny scar on his lip. *That's him.* Emily was nearly certain of it. She ripped a tab from the sheet and called the number and recognized Alex's voice. He said he was available to show her the apartment if she came right away.

She walked the three blocks quickly. Expecting her, Alex had left the main door unlocked. She entered the building without ringing the bell. Her throat was tight and her mouth dry. She felt like a secret operative as she climbed the stairs to the fourth floor and knocked on Alex's door. She heard rustling inside, as if someone was scrambling to hide things. "Oh, my God," Alex said as he opened the door. His arm came forward as if to catch his balance. "The adorable Emily!"

He had shoulder-length hair and had lost weight since she'd last seen him. The small cut on his upper lip showed up as a white line. He twisted his head for a better look at her, and suddenly embracing her, he asked about Sara. On hearing that she was dead, he started to cry. Emily, too, was overwhelmed by the memory of my mother.

Alex recovered. "I'm so sorry. I've been meaning to visit David. But you know how it is." He wiped his brow.

She didn't know how it is. She knew she would never abandon her child.

Alex was handsome in an Orphic skinny way. Emily had known him as an emotional man Sara kept saving from disaster. He was an adult who hadn't lost the child within, and that wasn't a good thing. In the words of women trapped in such failed rescue operations, Alex was a lovable loser.

A whirlwind had picked him off the ground when he was young and landed him early recognition as an indie filmmaker.

He had been poised for success, shy, but also arrogant in expecting it, and feeling entitled. He was mistaken. After his first film, most every project he started turned out badly.

"We need to talk," she said.

She forced a smile to make him understand that she was not blaming him for the past. But her silent appraisal rattled him. His complexion deepened as he pointed a long and delicately formed finger at his own chest. "Things are finally working out for me." He was getting the financial backing that he needed to produce another movie. He had an option on a literary property, and had lined up bankable stars. "Just a couple of loose ends left to tie up."

She was still outside his door. A slurping sound from inside the apartment intruded. "What was that?" she asked.

"Ah, that." Alex had a lazy, nasal way of speaking. "The drain gurgles when someone flushes upstairs."

He let her in. The studio apartment was small. A folding door hid the two-burner gas range set above a thigh-high refrigerator. The bathroom was located in a tiny closet next to the kitchen. The shower, sink, and toilet occupied a space just large enough for four opened pages of *The New York Times* laid out side-by-side. She tried to ignore the things that needed to be picked up off the floor. He looked around, his eyes wide open. "It's a mess here."

"It must be tough running an indie film operation."

He snorted, buoyed by her words. "My former beautiful wife and I never did see eye to eye on that issue. But we had a great relationship. I couldn't stop saying *yes* to her and she couldn't stop telling me what to do and how to do it."

"Be honest. She supported you."

He was unruffled. "I loved Sara."

"Are you with anyone?"

He shook his head and smiled. "I'm subletting from a camera operator who's working temp in Texas. He's subletting from a financial guy with a three-year lease. A freaky house of cards." He asked if she was serious about renting a room share.

"Yes, I want him to live with you."

Alex's face brightened. "For sure. I'm thrilled. He asks about me?"

"He never talks about you."

He cocked his fingers next to his head to mimic the hammer of a revolver hitting a bullet chamber. "I'm glad you're not going soft on me." He asked her to take a seat and then sat next to her. His knees looked like knobs on skinny poles. "I'll make it up to David somehow." He took a deep breath. He was being tender and caring and yet managed to look very needy. She was getting to dislike tender-hearted men.

"You're not religious. Why did you write that letter authorizing Dr. Wilson to look after David's spiritual life?"

"He pinned me to the ground."

"He did?"

"Well, not exactly."

She remembered Dr. Wilson rubbing his thumb and forefinger together to indicate the useful warmth that money provided. Alex made the same gesture.

"I was short on the slippery stuff."

She asked him to write another letter rescinding his original letter. He said he would. She offered to pay him. He refused.

He said he was going to get paid a bundle soon, and was closing on a deal in L.A. He had been heading out the door when she called. He picked up his bags and smiled helplessly. She followed him out and they exited to the street. A "don't walk" signal told them to wait and they stood alongside a seafood restaurant that displayed live fish in a window aquarium.

"I'll bet the fish think they're only visiting," he said.

The light changed. He promised to call her in two days max, and said goodbye, and he took a right as she kept going straight.

chapter 56

By her own generous measure Emily was: (a) a good guardian, (b) a secret lover, (c) a regretful breaker of marital vows, (d) a passionate dancer, and (e) a caring person. She was also a woman tied between galloping horses that were tearing her in half.

My appeal—an attraction that seemed to combine excitement and worry—bedeviled her. She could almost predict it: sometimes down to a trickle when she was absorbed in a dance or worried that her pregnancy had begun to show, and then suddenly blooming like an infectious disease colonizing her body. This colonization, as she explained it to herself in her journals, happened most often after she'd exchanged sharp words with Rick. It didn't have to be a full-blown argument, just some slight disagreement, from which she recoiled as her mind fled from Rick toward me.

She didn't want those intimate back-and-forth feelings to go on. She wanted clarity, an open road toward a visible goal, not the prevailing fogs and mists and mirages, so finding Alex had raised her hopes that she could finally manage to extricate herself from a pileup of unwanted emotions, a pileup of jealous feelings, of love and regret, and worry.

That day, she knew that I had just finished a class at the New School and called to ask me to meet her at Washington Square Park. I got there before she did and she found me sitting on a bench near the arch. Desire glowed openly in my amber-flecked eyes as she plunked herself down next to me.

"David, I have to give you up, honey." She felt intense warmth toward me. But she'd made up her mind. She didn't want to live with futile regret and remain in hock to the broken boundaries marred by longing. She was not sleeping well, not eating well, she felt fickle, critical of Rick, and jealous of Melissa. She got up from the bench and extended her hand in a formal gesture. "David, sweetheart, we have to put this behind us."

I didn't take her hand. I suppose my eyes dilated. A car with a bad muffler passed and then there was silence except for the song of starlings. I went on ignoring her goodbye gesture. She remained standing. A warm breeze filtered a musky smell from gingko trees along the north sidewalk. It was hard to force a youth taller than her to bend to her wishes. A few moments passed and she felt silly standing and sat down again. For all the authority she carried on the boards when she worked with Dylan and Melissa, she felt herself dissolving into a lovelorn girl when she was with me.

Another minute passed. The corners of her eyes tightened as I recited from memory a line from a play by the nineteenth century playwright Georg Büchner: "'I wish I were part of the air so I could bathe you in my flood and my waves could break on every ripple of your beautiful body.'"

"What are you saying?" She was touched.

"You shouldn't even think of leaving me." I spoke softly. I wanted to hold her and have us disappear into each other. How could she think of spending her life without me?

Her voice wavered as she tried to make it sound calm. "I want to be your mom, not your girlfriend." This was not true. As with all her efforts torn in half by indecision, she wasn't sure what would work, but she had equivocated too long and now moved ahead forcefully. "You've got to leave."

An aggrieved look probably made my jaw tighten. I got up and walked away. She watched me leave, my easy confident stride, my figure receding and becoming smaller, and wondered if she would ever see me again.

chapter 57

She hailed a cab to get to Dylan's studio. After snapping her tie to me she knew that nothing except a bad injury could stop her dancing. Nothing mattered other than dance. She was a tigress and she was a sylph. She was impossibly directional and she was ethereal, she was ambiguous and perfectly clear, she was a mystic and she was real. She conquered pain and space to build dances for a new generation of dance lovers.

She rehearsed *Trio*, in which Melissa was no longer Melissa but a force in spring and Dylan was Dionysus. The three of them were alive in a sinuous bond and repetitive loss. *Trio* felt exhilarating and she went home elated; her work was good, her partners terrific. They were disciplined and creative and ready for Jacob's Pillow. They wrapped up very late at night. She climbed the stone steps to the main entry to my mother's house. She and Rick had continued to pay rent, set aside for my college expenses. She was surprised to see a light on in the front room. Rick had come home.

"I thought you were in Boston," she said.

"I did some personal stuff for us."

Struck by his vigorous appearance, she saw again that there was nothing better than success to make a man look handsome. There had been times she could look at Rick and not see him, when she could listen to him explain something and not hear him, but now he was alive again.

"I'm sick of living in Sara's place," he said. "I'm sick of using her linens, her china and stainless." His tone was earnest. "Everything here reminds you of her. She was this great woman you worshiped and I'm just an adjunct business nuts-and-bolts guy."

"Rick, Sara will never take your place in my life."

He wasn't listening and looked about. "Like I'm supposed to owe her something? The junk she planted in your mind could drive anyone crazy."

Her tender mood shifted. She lowered her voice and placed a hand on her abdomen. "Please stop looking at me that way."

She hadn't intended to sound harsh, but he clearly regretted that she wasn't carrying his baby. He was moodier too, sometimes short-tempered, smiling less frequently and more direct about wanting her to do this or that or some other thing at home.

And there was something else, something she wasn't completely sure about. He kept observing her at a slant, not only for signs of advancing pregnancy but also for faults, for weakness, for mental illness. He asked her how she was feeling too frequently in a tone of a raised eyebrow, suggesting that her answers could not be trusted.

She wondered if Jay and Page had infected him with their fear that she was going mad, going "off." He noticed her scarification cuts more frequently, commenting how the four scars marred her white forearm.

"I want us out of this dump," he demanded. He pointed to the water-stained fleur-de-lis-patterned wallpaper peeling off the wall. "The mold is probably messing with your head."

"Messing with my head?"

"You're still obsessed with Sara."

She turned away. She was just weeks away from performing at Jacob's Pillow. Why was he undermining her confidence with new accusations? "I need to bathe my foot." Later, dressed in pajamas, she found him lounging in the upholstered chair. His eyes were clouded in thought.

"Out with it," she urged.

"Sara's afterglow is obliterating me in this house."

She sat silent at her dressing table, her laptop and cell phone in front of her.

"We don't have to live so far below our means anymore." Vanity and pride were getting a grip on him. "The Hartford guys came through with a fresh round of money and Bradbury is no longer in danger of defaulting. It's humiliating to hide my home address from my business associates because I'm afraid to give them a bad impression about us living in a low-rent neighborhood."

She felt as if a nerve had been ripped out of her. "The only impression that concerns me is the one I make onstage."

"I don't believe you."

She went silent, and back to her laptop and started to

revise her schedule. She was unable to stop thinking about my whereabouts. She clicked on a picture thumbnail and my face filled the laptop screen.

Rick had thrown off his jacket. "There's a Sub-Zero refrigerator and the Wolf range and stove, a built-in wine cooler and a Miele ventilation system installed in the kitchen…"

She listened to everything he said and heard nothing.

"I found a classy real estate agent who knows her stuff. The agent gave me a subdivision map, the CC&Rs and a slew of comparables…"

Emily checked and rechecked her phone, waiting for a call from me, and then, unable to wait any longer, she called me and got my voice mail. She left no message.

"You think David is okay?" she asked.

"Angel, haven't you been listening? The bank is willing to do a short sale on the property. We'll get it at a third less than the folks paid for it three years ago."

"Oh? I'm not moving, sweetheart."

Just then her phone started to vibrate. I had texted: "I'm at massage prlr in Chinatown." She looked at the time—11 p.m. The alarms couldn't have been louder. Anyone in Manhattan could figure out what kind of massage took place at 11 at night.

"U COME rt home," she texted.

I didn't answer, and she imagined me trembling with illicit pleasure. She texted a number of messages—"you're not that kind of boy," "home," "we'll talk"—but there were no more messages from me. She glanced at my picture, the brow, the eyes, and the full lips. It was terrible to think that another woman had possessed me.

"Honey," she said to Rick, "please turn down the lights."

They went to bed and she closed her eyes and kept seeing my face before her. She couldn't fall asleep until she heard me come home at two in the morning.

chapter 58

In the morning she felt she hadn't had enough rest. Rick was observing her more closely every day. His face was inscrutable, hiding secrets from her. He was definitely quieter with her, less demonstrative. His eyes suggested suspicion, or perhaps wariness. He avoided talking about dance, and she avoided talking about business. Not a word about the baby.

At times the silence between them was healing, and those times Rick's decency and loyalty amplified the guilt she experienced. This led to mutual evasiveness that became oddly contagious and appeared to be gathering strength, as if they were adversaries maneuvering for advantage in a potential divorce. Yet she didn't want a divorce. She wanted him to stay and affectionately placed Rick's hand on her stomach to engage him in the project of parenting. He recoiled, pulling his hand away as if from battery acid.

One morning Rick accused her of being bipolar. She then cut back on elation in Rick's presence, and she stopped talking about her fatigue when she was tired. She wondered if he saw something she couldn't. *Mental illness?* She was under suspicion. *Does a person see mental illness coming, or only see it in the rear-view mirror departing?* She was afraid to admit fragility, including the recurring wish to be taken care of, a yearning for safety and security. Maybe she could enter a new and happier phase with Rick if she could get me to stay with my father. *Maybe, maybe, maybe?*

At breakfast she told me that her decision to send me off to live with Alex was final. "Dad, dear ol' Dad," I said, repeating my caustic mantra. "Has he returned your phone calls?"

"I'm seeing him today."

This wasn't the exact truth. Alex had not called her, but Emily had gotten more information from the Hispanic woman at the café about Alex's involvement in running a video store in the East Village. It was past the morning rush hour and she took a cab there instead of the subway.

"What!?" Alex said on seeing her. He was at the counter helping a customer check out a Blu-ray disc. He finished ringing the sale.

"Why a video store, you ask?" His voice was strangely muffled. He leaned against a battered display rack.

"You were supposed to be in L.A."

"I'm busy right now. Come by in an hour and I'll have that letter you asked for."

"I want David to move in with you."

"For sure, we'll chat."

Startled by the inconsistency of a supposedly big-breaking A-list indie producer clerking at a store, her palms had turned sweaty. She left the store, nervous and eager, crossed the street, and found a doorway to hide in. She waited ten or fifteen minutes, and half expecting it, she saw Alex leave the store.

She followed him. They passed sidewalk booksellers, incense vendors, and DVD pirates doing business at their portable stands. She disliked her own eagerness to catch him. She was fifty or sixty feet behind him, and Alex was getting away, sidestepping people and dogs and then turning at the corner. He hustled down a less-crowded street before turning north on Avenue D, or Avenue Death, as it was then known among real estate people.

He strode past a bodega and stopped in a doorway. Her breathing was under control as she walked up and said hello. Alex startled and held a hand over his heart. She tried to act as if nothing strange was going on.

"You scared the bejesus out of me," he said.

"You were going to see me." She felt provincial for having to say such an obvious thing.

He offered no excuse. "You want us to stand here and get mugged?" He motioned for her to follow him to his place. He had moved to a loft share, he said. The apartment sublet must have been a scam, she realized, but she didn't confront him. She felt her feet dragging heavier as they climbed higher and her suspicions got thicker. She could barely drag herself up the last flight of steps. *I'm the biggest fool on Earth.*

Alex opened a heavy metal door on the fifth floor and they entered a large, dingy space. He slid the locking steel bar to shut the door from inside. They were not alone in the loft and someone was coughing violently near the back windows.

Blankets and bed sheets were strung up to separate tenants from each other.

"You own the video store?" she asked, troubled by the run-down loft. She tried not to show her nervousness.

"Does it look like I own anything?" His manner was sweet. "I'm a clerk."

Without the least sign of remorse, he admitted that he had not flown to L.A. but had moved a few blocks to find cheaper rent in an illegal loft shared with five tenants. He found two beers in the communal fridge. She said she was not drinking. He motioned for her to take a seat on a threadbare, broken-down couch. A police siren invaded the loft and overwhelmed the sound of coughing.

"You're still working in pictures?"

He tapped the beer can against his forehead. "I'm a piece of my own work all right."

His alternative reality didn't mesh with what she was seeing. "You're a small-time fraud." All his skinny parts looked ready to fall apart.

He sipped his beer, his pupils dilated in the dim light. He complained that Netflix and the web were killing the video store and might put him out of work. He was bothered by it, but not too much.

"Are you happy?" she asked.

"I do all right." His eyes looked enormous. "How much can you pay me to keep David?"

She couldn't imagine Alex encouraging me to make the most out of my life. Silently, she changed her mind about sending me away. "I don't have any money to spare."

"Then I can't take David."

"You don't love him?"

"He was collateral damage from my relationship with Sara."

She decided not to be critical. They talked fondly about Sara and then it was time for her to go. She went outside into the blazing daylight and called me.

"Did you get to dump me?" I asked.

"I'm working on it."

But there was no getting around the fact that her good intentions had come to nothing. She was where she'd started, in the middle with no way out.

chapter 59

Just before leaving for Jacob's Pillow, she moved into a protective pre-performance zone. After a jumble of rehearsals, staging changes, and costume and stage makeovers, she was ready. Her ankle, thank God, didn't hurt. But there was still plenty to do. Paying bills, organizing and checking last-minute staging changes.

Peaceful was out—she was too excited with nervous anticipation, but something hopeful had entered her life that was hard to describe. Despite the mounting tension, she felt extremely lucky to go to Jacob's Pillow. They drove in Dylan's van to Becket in the Massachusetts Berkshires. They'd packed it full, and the roof rack was loaded with tied-down suitcases and boxes of staging materials.

Scent was meant to be humorous, a witty piece that had flopped when danced in front of a humorless church audience. She had tweaked the work in several telling ways, expanding a few phrases and pruning others. But even in its funny parts, it was an erotic piece. Desire combating will, passion over captivity. It was three minutes shorter and a trial showing in the East Village got more laughs, but in contrast with her earlier work, it also made the audience profoundly uneasy.

"You okay?" Melissa asked before going onstage.

"It's a flu or something. Punches me out." The spells lasted only an instant. She pushed aside the discomfort and mentally prepared herself for the stage. The next minute they were on and the crowd's enthusiastic response began the moment they appeared.

She'd crafted new movements, using her hands, folding and unfolding, in a language her body had not spoken before. The terrible jealousy she felt toward Melissa as a rival was transfigured into intimacy on stage. Melissa was beautiful, and the costume Emily had designed for her pushed her beauty in an extreme direction, in a kind of neo-German Expressionism with exaggerated and colorful stage makeup and artfully tattered pencil jeans, high boots, and bustier top.

Emily wore scarves of white, flowing silk and her midriff was exposed, accented with gold-white paint. Her smallest movement signaled vitality in a sequence of bends and turns, unpredictable, uncomfortable, uncertain. The audience kept clapping throughout. They came to the end of the piece and were taking their bows. Melissa pointed to her hand in Emily's. "My hand?"

Emily blushed. Sensitized to touch and scent and sight, sleepwalking in a mist called love, she felt more affection for everyone.

"Could I have my hand back?"

Emily didn't want to let go of the warmth; she didn't want to be alone.

"My hand?"

She released Melissa's hand. Nothing in her Lithuanian past had prepared her for the discovery that affection could be contagious.

Coming off a great afternoon's work, she felt terrific. She regretted that Rick and Jay had been called away to talk to the Hartford guys again, and had not been able to attend the afternoon performance. But they made it back in time to see *Trio* danced that evening.

chapter 60

In the evening the curtain lifted to rap music filtered through a background of "Clair de Lune." A pleasant ripple of applause ran through the audience. Stage lights spotted Melissa, her eyes sparkling, and then moved to Emily, the anguished waif. The music shifted, sampling tracks from Stravinsky's "Rite of Spring," staccato and insistent, violently demanding, and then retreated into languid drifting steps, lost, mad out of mind. The applause rose in waves. Excitement ran through the dancers as well as the audience—Emily had shattered the old, had overcome her reticence. Sara would have loved to see her breakthrough.

The dancers accepted four curtain calls, gloried in them, grateful, luxuriating, and when the applause died away they lay flat on their backs in the wings offstage, drenched in sweat, saturated in their affection for each other, and for the audience now seemingly far away.

Breathless with excitement, Emily met Rick backstage.

She was relieved to have made it through without harming the baby. Sweat stuck all over her, and she felt a fleeting anxiety. "Well, what did you think?"

He cleared his throat and jingled the keys in his pocket. "Charming," he said. It was the least negative thing he could say.

At the party that evening she saw him from a distance, working the reception room. *He wants his own children,* she told her journal, *a bloodline, essential for feuds and tribal wars.* He'd grown more reserved, careful and polite, making nice with his soft gray eyes, always slightly pale, the color shifting in bright sunlight. He liked to be nice, and the nice inside him hid the violence it clothed. It was killing him from the inside.

She saw the end of nice. Her body caving to age, she and Rick retiring to a ranch house in a gated community set among palm trees. It might take forty years. Only thirty if she was unlucky. There would be nothing to trip over, nothing hard to fall on, everything on one level. His International Rotary flags he loved to collect would sit brightly in a rack on the fireplace mantel. There would be days for golf and tennis and they would own a fancy golf cart and join the hiking seniors. This would be the good life at the end of life. She loathed it and feared it.

Page came over. "I'm glad you kept up your dancing! You looked *gorgeous*!"

Emily smiled uneasily. She saw me across the room and was distracted by a wish to be with me. "You think so?"

"Are you all right?"

"Yes."

"You sound angry."

"I'm sorry, I'm unwinding."

Dancers were supposed to be happy party girls, wacky and fun after hours. And many of them were happy and wacky party girls. But others were not. Her friends outside dance had no clue what it took to keep dancing. Never enough money. Never enough time. Life with injuries, bruises, blood on her toes, muscle strains, and sprains. There were enough divine feet competing in dance to make everyone else feel clumsy. It would have been wiser for her to become a bank clerk. And it paid better.

"Keep it up," Page said and went off in a whirl of loud cheer.

Rick came over and Jay joined them. Jay was cheerful and had a drink in his hand, but looked somehow plundered, as if Page had plucked his feathers. "Emily, that was unbelievably good! *Incredible* to see you so sexy." He gave another cheerful burst of appreciation, proclaimed a need to give the "young ones" encouragement, and ambled off to the buffet table where Melissa and Dylan were talking.

That evening Emily was a celebrity who had overcome her unpromising beginnings. But her post-stage euphoria crashed and something different asserted itself. She could slam herself to the floor and slam herself against Dylan's body in *Trio* using Pina Bausch's dance language to express the dodgy movements between jealousy, longing, and guilt. But now that she had to face her own life in the quietness of the ordinary, she felt depleted, and was looking at jealousy, longing, and guilt.

chapter 61

The next morning I slept in, Dylan left for Manhattan in the van, and Emily went for a walk. Something felt not exactly right, she reported in her journal. Not cramps but a fluttery feeling, perhaps only the downshifting mood she experienced after every major event. Some of the dance steps had been difficult to perform, a shock to her body. Maybe she'd danced more assertively than her ob-gyn had intended. On the other hand, she had also held back. She put aside her anxious thoughts.

The lodge cleanup crew came to rake the lawn and collect party tailings. The landscaping people descended to do their chores, and the private grounds lost their sense of privacy and privilege and began to look like a public works project. Melissa chatted with Emily and then took the shuttle for a lift to the station. Emily and Rick went to have brunch with the Bradburys in the Rhododendron Garden. Jay had a near fetish about doing his own grilling that summer. A server had dropped off a dish of fresh salmon to barbecue, and Jay, taking up his cook's role, maneuvered the fish onto the grill.

"I wonder if these are Atlantic or Pacific?" Jay asked.

Page nodded her head icily. "You should be asking for *wild* salmon. Very fertile, you know. Those big fellas in the Columbia River have to dodge hot utility discharge. The dams try to stop them and the poor suckers scatter their little eggs and their seed in panic." She paused. "Seed? Is *seed* the right word, Jay?"

"It's called *milt*," Jay said.

"Whatever. Poor little darlings. They're so disorganized." Page counted the fingers of one hand, and then the fingers of the other hand and then started to count them all over again.

"Is it months or years you're counting?" Jay asked.

"Weeks. It's all about gestation." She was in a viperous mood and sipped the drink Jay had handed her.

"Page is a sweetheart," Jay said. "Once you get to know her."

"Jay, did you tell Rick anything more about our last VP?" Page glanced at Rick, who had stopped eating. Page went on, "Yes, he was darling, divorced and good-looking. He and I, unlike our serious-minded Rick here—well, we *talked* a lot."

"I fired the guy," Jay said.

"For inappropriate behavior, wasn't it dear?" Page turned to Emily. "The dearly departed VP was too handsome and too bold for Jay's taste." Jay gave Page a blackened piece of fish. She broke it up with her fork. "Did you have to make it with that girl last night?"

"Leave her out of this." Jay kept busy at the grill.

"That was *inappropriate* to mention, wasn't it?" She seemed unsure. "My big Bradbury man likes to use the word *inappropriate* a lot, don't you dear?"

"Darling, let's cut it out."

"Inappropriate, inappropriate," she insisted.

"You want more to eat?" Jay asked.

"Why," Page brightened alarmingly. "I have more curves on my body. I'm more seasoned. I think I'm even more sensual than she is."

The intimate coarseness between Page and Jay upset the garden's peacefulness.

Rick laughed abruptly and nervously. "You're so funny."

"Did you hear that, Jay? Rick said we are *funnee*."

"Enough, dear," Jay warned her.

She dismissed the warning with a gallant wave of her hand. "Tell them, Jay! Your Daddy wants us to give him another shot at the world's gene pool before he passes on. A clean-living, good-looking surrogate we found. We'll give your dad a kid who'll ace Harvard. That could mean something to him since Daddy never went to college. He thinks my vital eggs are spunky enough to pull it off for him."

"He's always liked bimbos," Jay said quietly.

"Me?"

"You."

"You're crazy. I was the old man's office manager. Wasn't I, babe? Managed myself and a clerk, didn't I?"

"You managed."

"He liked me real good."

Jay stopped working the grill, and without raising his voice said, "She fucked my father."

Rick shifted his weight in his chair. "Is there something I can do to help?"

Page burst out laughing and then continued softly. "You can be so *agreeable*, Rick. And Jay, well, he likes agreeable people. Little ol' me, I get bored with nice people. Isn't that right, Jay? I could never, ever be a snob, not like you, dear, sniffing wine like you've invented it." She paused to take a drink and appeared to be close to sobbing. "Did you have to do it with that girl last night?"

"I told you to leave her out of it." Jay put down his tongs. "The trouble with Page—"

"My eggs are hot to make children."

"You'll like kids," Rick said. "We're planning on them ourselves."

Emily grew alarmed. Rick's sincerity rattled her. He must have been on fire with hate for his boss, but he was acting like a friendly guy. He fixed his gaze on something in the grass and seemed unable to stop himself. "Sure, we struggle at times. Have our doubts. I'm even thinking that we should renew our vows."

Page was keening softly, pulling petals off a lacy pink rhododendron bloom. Rick didn't know how or when to stop. "But it's nothing serious with our relationship, nothing a couples retreat can't cure. Nothing a few power prayers can't help fix. We'll have a child to prove it to you." Rick believed in God, in justice. He believed it would soon be his turn to have good things happen to him.

"Rick, please don't say anything more," Emily pleaded.

Page stared at her empty glass. "Rick, baby, you are a sweet, sweet man. Are you the only one here who doesn't *know*?"

"I beg your pardon? Know what?"

"Melissa is my husband's mistress."

Jay kept silent, absorbed in scraping the crud off the grill. Page sniffed at her food. She looked at Emily.

"We'd better get packed," Emily said, suddenly rising.

"I'm sorry," Rick said. "We're sorry."

Emily shook her head. "No, we are not sorry. We had nothing to do with it."

Rick must have realized he had blundered. Prosperous, idle men like Jay Bradbury were collectors. They collected support groups, invitations, business ventures, houses, art, they collected praise, and sometimes they went into politics. Jay had collected Emily early on, and now Melissa. Rick must have been seething inside.

Page gestured for them to let it go. Jay turned the gas off and sliced orange wedges for everyone. He was unruffled. "Darling," he said to Page, "will you please pay the contractor for the work he did on our Kennebunkport kitchen?"

"Yes, dear," Page said. She wiped away her tears.

chapter 62

Rick left early. Emily stayed behind to spend time with several dance colleagues. She'd accepted Jay's offer to use his company car. She'd thought that I had gone back to Brooklyn with Dylan. I troubled her when I showed up, smiling brightly. We went to see Sam Shepard's *Buried Child* playing in town that evening. The theater seats were so closely spaced that it was impossible not to touch the person next to you. Our arms shared an armrest. I suppose she tried not to think about me as the father of her child, but she was charged, flushed. I could almost feel her vibrating with excitement. At a coffee shop afterward, I said Shepard's play was about corruption and renewal, birth and unintended consequences. She didn't care to hear about the play's intricate structure and wasn't listening. "So we're taking this trip?" I asked.

She was startled. "What trip?"

"A while back you said you'd like to tour New England with me."

"I did?"

"We'll never have another chance."

"Let me think about it."

"Strictly platonic." I think I actually meant it. I wanted her near, to be with her.

She was thinking about the baby—there was nothing more, nothing else, nothing less that she cared about. We returned to the lodge and went to our separate rooms. The fieldstone lodge had old-fashioned charm. Each room had a flush toilet that looked a century old. Each room came equipped with outdated answering machines. The bed was wonderfully plush however, and she melted away into a deep and restful sleep. When she awoke at ten in the morning I was gone. She was actually relieved not to see me. She wrote a note and slipped it under my door: "I won't be back until after you've gone to bed tonight."

But the note said nothing about love and she needed to say more. She wanted to tell me she was carrying my baby, her baby, our baby. She wanted to tell me she loved the baby and she loved me. Resisting this impulse, she felt disappointed by her own timidity. Her boldness on stage had fled and she was again a lovelorn girl who wanted to talk her heart out, say something meaningful, something urgent, something dear and permanent. In the titanic battle between willfulness and desire, the latter was winning. She called my room and talked to the answering machine.

"David, listen to me, hi. I'm freaking out. I don't know if it's the play or what…ah…maybe it's just that my life is really messy, but David, ah, are you listening? Okay, so this is the deal. I don't think I can keep myself levelheaded. I need to be by myself to clear my head."

She hung up. Her face felt hot. Her heart was plunking along as though she'd just come offstage after a dance. It was crazy. She wanted to say, "I love you." She wanted to tell me she was pregnant. Her heart pumped fiercely. She called back.

"David, I'm trying to have really healthy relations, you know, and it's not healthy for me to be married to Rick and emotionally involved with you, not as anything other than, like, a friend, and I definitely consider you my friend. That's all. Pretty articulate, huh? Okay, maybe I'll call you later, maybe I won't. I don't know, I just don't know, that's all, okay? The other thing is that I want to thank you for a really beautiful time and for the play last night. It was good."

She scolded herself for sounding childish. She hated to see herself falling apart and resolved to get a grip. Her baby was uppermost in her mind. She took a deep breath and turned up the enthusiasm in her voice.

"David! I know what we'll do. We'll stay friends. I'm okay with the New England road trip. We're going to visit Walden Pond! I always wanted to. We'll take a room with a kitchenette. And guess what—I'm cooking for you, okay? You've been taking care of me, listening to me going on about dance, and I need to take care of you better. That's all, bye."

Her voice had become calmer, but with two messages down she still felt misunderstood. Maybe the trip was a bad idea and she should cancel it. She called again.

"David, it's Emily. Just kidding about taking the trip together! I want you to erase all my messages. I'm sorry, I'm so, so sorry. It's a quarter to three in the afternoon and you're out, I guess. Today has been a crazy day. It made me cry. I guess I'm going to say I don't know, I don't know, I don't know, because I don't know what I'm thinking and what I'm feeling. I've been calling Rick and been unable to reach him. So that's what I'll have to deal with tonight. Okay? So…maybe I'll see you later. I'm sorry I called and babbled at you. I love you, sweetheart. Bye."

chapter 63

The next morning, she put on a fresh shirt and loose-fitting jeans and went to have breakfast with me on the patio of my room. She confirmed our New England road trip. She was ready to go. Her hands shook when she went over the maps to show me a way to Concord and Walden Pond. She felt terrible about having recorded so much emotional confusion on the answering machine in my room and kept wondering what I was thinking. I must have appeared indifferent, almost cool to her. I didn't yet know how inconvenient love could be, how it intrudes and tangles a mind. She hadn't planned to fall in love with me, and hadn't planned to go to bed with me, and now, still torn and attracted to me, she gave me a sidelong, unhappy inspection.

"I want to hang with Melissa awhile," I said, to break from her gaze. "She's holding over and teaching a children's dance class here."

"Oh." Emily was stunned. "I thought she'd left by train."

My eyes were shadowed from lack of sleep and Emily couldn't help wondering if Melissa had kept me up.

"You don't mind?" I asked.

She felt as if she was being destroyed. She took a deep breath. "Not at all. Nope. I hope you guys have a good time together." But she was afraid Melissa had pulled me into her orbit. Emily's skin seemed to peel in pain. Her admired dance colleague had morphed into an omnivorous sexual being. She looked for clues in the way I spoke, in what I said, in how often I looked at her and for how long I kept her gaze. *He doesn't care for me anymore!* She blamed her pregnancy starting to show and wished to be as slender as Melissa—willowy, striking, irresistible. She was lost in those thoughts.

"Are you with me?" I asked.

"I'm listening," she said, feeling a sensation of fullness. "Did you listen to my messages?"

"What messages?" I had no messages on my cell phone. I didn't bother with the room phone.

Tightness gripped her throat. "Nothing. Forget it."

I wanted her to read my *Maya* script and handed it over to her, the breeze riffling the pages. I also wanted to shower and left to do so. For a moment she couldn't move, couldn't blink. It was terrifying for her to admit a new truth—she suspected that I was falling for Melissa, and knowing this, her emotions blinded her. She couldn't let go of me.

She started reading the script I had handed her and her face drained. My intention had been to dramatize her vulnerable ambition, but I'd been young then, and had not yet explored the teachings of the director Harold Clurman, or the magnificent Stella Adler collected in two volumes edited by Barry Paris, and in my version of Emily she came off distracted and flighty, a beautiful face, a wonderful figure, obsessively sexual, juvenile, painted over to appear bright and peppy. She was offended by the debonair way I had copied from the several small journal sections she had entrusted to me—willy-nilly scattering her throughout my script. She went inside to give me an earful but the shower was running and she decided to wait. She saw the tiny light on my answering machine blinking, and realized that I had not listened to her messages. They now made her cringe.

She pushed the play button and was startled to hear Melissa's voice asking if I wanted to go out with her. She seemed young on the phone, hesitant, rushed, but she had an extremely vital voice. Her own messages started to play next. Emily's heart beat very fast. She pushed the erase button and then pushed it a second time and third and fourth, erasing all the messages, especially her own distraught ones. She had to get me away from Melissa. *As fast as possible,* she told her journal.

She heard me turn the shower off and shouted through the closed door that she'd be ready in ten minutes, and still, she was afraid that Melissa might call. She pulled the phone cord from the phone jack and went to her room to get her packed bags, eager for us to escape Melissa.

"Don't bother drying your hair," she shouted. "I've got my bags ready."

"But were going tomorrow," I said, from behind the closed bathroom door.

"*No*. We're out of here."

"Can I charge my cell phone?"

"Forget it. Let's go."

She tapped her foot impatiently even as I carried her bags and loaded them in the back of the car Jay had left for her use. She wanted control; she wanted to flee Melissa, and she felt better as soon as we got on the road. She nudged the accelerator and slipped a CD into the player, punching up the sound on Marianne Faithfull's *Broken English*. Despite the heartbreaking lyrics, her fearful mood receded. She had me all to herself and would not let me pass easily out of her life.

An hour later, she'd turned off the main road and circled a lake. It had gotten windy by then, and the steady rhythm of waves came up short on the steep banks. A switchback took us to a hilltop that had been shorn of trees for a clear view of the lake and the mountains. Two cottages were on the west side of the main building of the bed and breakfast she had booked. She claimed a key to a cottage, and I hauled the bags and put them against the Empire chair next to the couch.

The cottage had one bed. The pillows and the comforter were in yellow buff, and trimmed with lace. She raised the temperature on the thermostat and hesitated in a pinch of uncertainty.

"A queen-size bed?" My tone was questioning, lost among the vagaries of desire. I was neither salacious nor eager to go to bed, and this disoriented her slightly. She had imagined my hands all over Melissa.

"You don't want me?" she asked.

"It's not that."

"What?" She was afraid.

"I don't have a condom. What if you get pregnant?"

"Silly," she said, tousling my hair. My shyness was unnerving her. She plumped the dawn coverlet.

We stepped out onto the porch and admired the view and the pink hawthorn. The breeze was feathery and moist. All along I had taken the initiative, but I think I was nervous now because she was taking charge, and she was terrified by fear that she was losing me.

"We'll visit Walden Pond first," she said, her voice unnaturally high.

We took off immediately in order to avoid going to bed. She drove with her window open. At the pond, which was actually a small lake, there were cars parked bumper to bumper. We strolled to a stone ledge overlooking the water. Children were all over the paths.

"Kids," I said dismissively. We walked on in silence.

The native chestnut trees were gone at Walden Pond, but the ragweed thrived. The new timber growth was spindly and the brush sparse and acid rain had thinned the birches. She froze—what if I would never see her again after this?

I was chattering, going on about Henry David Thoreau. "The guy kept three chairs at his house at Walden Pond to prevent people from coming and bothering him. He said one chair was for solitude, the second for friendship and the third for society. What most people don't know is that it took him five years after he left Walden Pond to write his book."

"Which chair will you save for me?" she asked.

I laughed, my voice capricious.

She balanced herself on an embankment. I followed. To keep her from slipping I circled her waist. There was permission in her breathing and in the air around us. I let go and we walked single file across a jagged stone surface to a cedar walkway. The sun caught the shine in her dark hair as I took her outstretched hand and our fingers entwined. We were alone and the surroundings were quiet except for the crackling on the path underfoot. The site of Thoreau's cabin had no foundation, no rude logs or mossy shingles to show where anything had stood. There was only a stone mound on the ground to mark the site. We felt all alone and all together and extremely happy. She was with the man she loved, the man who had fathered her child. And I, at seventeen, felt like a man.

chapter 64

We returned to our cottage, alert to each other's breathing. Her restored optimism was amazing, but she didn't know what to do next. We slipped past each other, bruised by uncertainty. I locked the bathroom door and she heard me shower a second time that day. I came out in my briefs and she noticed that I had sprinkled talcum powder between my toes. I put on a billowy white shirt and combed my wet hair. I was afraid that she'd scorn my new adulthood and rebuff me again.

"Are we going to make it through this?" she asked.

She skipped past me and showered and came out wearing her chrysanthemum-patterned robe. I stood waiting. "You smell so *nice*," I said.

It was dusky by then. She turned off the lights and pulled the blinds up so we could see the beautiful garden outside, and sat next to me. She touched the tiny creases at the corners of my eyes. My breathing had turned adventurous as she removed her robe to get into bed. For an instant she thought she felt the baby moving, but she couldn't tell for sure. She grew bolder, snuggling closer.

Her mouth felt lush, the taste warm and sweetly saline. The movement was slow, hypnotic, tender, and insistent. Her head was in the crook of my arm, her eyes partly closed as we lay together making love.

The next morning we were up early. I wanted her again. She had been alive to desire the night before, sexually exhilarated, knowing the appeal of her body, but she could not do it again in the morning: she was thinking about Rick.

It's one thing to have sex and another thing to live a satisfying life with a lover. I must have looked angry. My long eyelashes stood out as they always do, but my eyes were hard.

How quickly unwanted moods spread from one body to the next, she wrote in her journal. She wanted to satisfy me to make it peaceful and good between us. She went on as if nothing had happened. She went on with the things she had to do. She wanted to buy a larger-scale road map for Massachusetts and Maine. She needed to call Dylan and ask him if he was available in the fall.

"Do you have any laundry you want done?" she asked me. I said I was okay. She went to wash up and I came in to nuzzle her neck and press myself against her. But she didn't want me to paw her as she washed. She pushed me out and closed the door.

By noon we were in Boston, where we stopped to shop. I stopped being sullen. We talked more. She bought a suitcase at a discount store and she bought another nightgown, a white, floaty baby-doll gown. She bought me a package of briefs and a pair of jeans and two shirts. She picked up a black cotton sweater for me on impulse because it made me look older.

We would eat alone that evening, she decided. She would cook me the meal she had promised. At DeLaurenti's grocery, we discussed what to buy and then we embraced in a narrow aisle. That's the wonderful part of new love, the touching and the embrace and the curiosity unsatisfied. She felt my knee press into her as we rocked in place, holding on to each other until a customer came along and Emily broke away to study a bottle of cold-pressed Tuscan extra-virgin olive oil. She read the label three times to steady herself.

In the car, we were more intense and loose-handed with each other, but I got in the way of her driving and we had to stop petting. She wasn't as clandestine about showing her need for my love and touched me as much as I touched her. She was more eager to go to bed with me than she had been a day earlier.

Despite our excitement, we had trouble finding new lodging. I pointed to a motel with a nearby landing strip. It was a desolate place. She squinted at the reader board. "Efficiencies!!! Book Two Nights For The Price Of One. Free Breakfast. Rent By Day, Week, or Month."

"I'm surprised they're not renting it by the hour," I said.

She laughed.

The one-story building enclosed a U-shaped courtyard. She liked the neon palm tree on the office roof. Its slender tubes of pink, white, and green lighted up in a sequence to make it appear that the fronds were moving up and down.

She denied reality and reached for fantasy. "Let's pretend we're having a honeymoon," she said.

She booked a kitchenette suite for one night. The meal she prepared in the late afternoon was excellent. The small room and the tiny kitchen became saturated with the smell of lightly spiced olive oil. She did not burn the shallots, and her tomato sauce had a delicate flavor. We ate slowly, tasting uncomplicated flavors.

"You're wearing fresh makeup," I said. The artfulness of it made her look younger, and I liked the subtle color variation at her eyes and her cheeks.

Later, in bed, I said, "I like your scent; I like how you smell. I like us together."

She kept her body warm against mine, her legs loosely twined around me. But again, Rick wandered into her thoughts, and the baby, too. She wanted to escape the inevitable confrontation with Rick. She kept seeing herself as one of Chagall's floating figures flying free out the window.

Cirrus clouds textured the sky, and the sun was below the horizon, but it was still light. I was vaguely aware of a shadow moving past the partially curtained windows. She noticed my uneasiness. I got out of bed and pulled the shade down.

"Who was that?" she asked.

"I can't tell." I shrugged. "Some spook. What do we care?"

She surrendered to my fingers, but something within her remained tense and she couldn't lose herself in lovemaking. She slipped on her clothes and went to the office.

"There was someone outside our cottage," she said to the clerk behind the counter. The clerk handed her a small sealed envelope. She opened it and was stunned to see Rick's handwriting. "I didn't come to spy on you," she read. "All the

Bradbury cars have GPS. I tracked down Jay's car in the hope that Page and you and me could have a fun weekend together. I didn't expect to find you alone with Jay." He obviously had not seen who was under the covers. She felt a horrible pain in her side.

She went out and opened the driver's-side door of Jay's car, amazed to see all the extra dials and switches and buttons that she had not bothered with. The small GPS control panel was above the rear-view mirror. She switched off the transponder.

Back inside the cabin I had showered and stood naked in front of the bathroom mirror, combing my hair to get at the dark strands stuck to my neck.

"What are you thinking?" I asked.

"I'm thinking I don't have the will to give you up."

But she didn't tell me about Rick and her heart was racing on account of it. She was afraid that Rick might have killed me. She went to the kitchenette for a glass of ginger ale. *It's not that things just snap into place and make sense*, she wrote in her journal. She walked to the complimentary buffet to find a box of cereal and called Rick. He was piloting the Cessna when he answered. She expected him to condemn her and he had every right to, but instead he asked if she was feeling okay. His passionless words made her angry. She was fucking a boy whom he'd mistaken for Jay, and he didn't care? Incensed by Rick's calmness, a sudden warp in her thinking blamed him for everything.

"Angel," he said. His tone was flat, probationary.

She waited. She felt a queer, quiet danger lurking in the silence between them. Her hands trembled and her breath caught in her throat. She imagined lurid headlines: "Deranged Husband Kills Wife's Boy Toy." She needed to think clearly. She couldn't leave me, but she still wanted Rick, stability, peace, and a future together with him.

"Don't do anything foolish," he said. An air-traffic controller wanted his attention and he ended the call. She went back to our room with a fresh pack of cereal, and a sense that things might not be smooth ever again.

"You're very pale," I said.

She checked the mirror. She was naturally pale. Her skin had a bright ivory tone that set off her color-changing eyes. They weren't exactly night eyes or sleepy eyes, but at the moment they looked charred. "I'm sick to my heart," she said.

"I can't see your heart."

"That was Rick who saw us in bed together."

"No," I said, alarms going off.

"Except he doesn't think it was you. He locked onto the GPS in Jay's car, and he thinks it was Jay." She hated the onslaught of technology, the loss of privacy.

"What do you want me to do?" I asked.

"I don't want you hurt."

She was calmer now and still trying to figure out what to do, grateful that Rick had gotten it wrong and thought it had been Jay. This was the end of something she had been unwilling to face, but she saw no new beginnings.

chapter 65

We drove all the way home to Brooklyn that night. She dropped me off at a friend's home. "What if he smacks the shit out of you?" I asked before I got out.

"Rick hasn't hit anyone in his entire life."

She promised to call me that night to tell me she was safe, and then she went home. Rick was watching TV and said "hi," and asked if she needed help with the bags. His calmness was so normal that it felt surreal. She said she would unpack her own clothes. She didn't know what else to say to him because he acted as if nothing had happened.

"I'm going downstairs to make myself something to eat," he said.

"We have to talk."

Rick made a strange laughing sound and went downstairs. She followed him. He started clattering about in the kitchen, shoving the pans and pots as if they were clubs meant to harm her. She tried to calm him.

"Jay," Rick said, "the fuckin' weasel!"

He hated Jay; hate was blooming, rising, binding him. He suddenly hated the wealthy. He had to be thinking of them as privileged assholes who earned one hundred times more than he did and paid less in taxes, the ones who wore American flag pins in their lapels but sent their investment money to China, the ones who preached patriotism but outsourced American jobs to India and the Philippines. He hated all of them. They bought congressmen and senators and screwed American families by sending jobs overseas. He hated how they inherited things and how they lied, and how they lorded it over everyone else. He hated Jay for stealing his wife.

Rick turned around and stood slope shouldered, his arms spread wide. A pan was dangling from one hand like a tennis racket. He pounded the cabinet with it, breaking a knob off the door.

"Don't. Please don't." She was afraid.

"That fuckin' asshole with all his fuckin' money. The dumb son of a bitch who can't figure his way out of a paper bag."

A terrible cramp came on and sent her shivering. She braced herself against the wall. Rick slammed around, tipping the table and sending a vase shattering. Her cramps shot to her lower abdomen. She felt as if her spine was twisting inside her.

His face had turned livid. His voice was unnatural. He hit the sink with the cast-iron pan, breaking the porcelain. "How did it happen?" he shouted, breathing in short, sharp bursts. "Where is the fucking feral bastard tonight? Fucking Melissa now that you're pregnant?"

He shouted about having to give up sex. He came closer, the pan in his hand. She could smell his rage. She felt an abdominal cramp and cried out. He became suddenly quiet. His face went smooth, pasty, brows arched, eyes fixed. He was staring at the linoleum floor.

She looked down, too, and saw blood pooling. The blood didn't seem to have anything to do with her. It belonged to someone else, somewhere else. And then she saw blood on her Nikes, on her white socks. She gripped the jeans at her crotch to stop the bleeding. Blood soaked her hand. She lifted her hand to her face, and then she screamed.

chapter 66

Rick called 911, and emergency guys came and drove her to the hospital. The doctors performed a D&C and she was kept overnight. As she was leaving, a nurse said, "It was a girl, if you're interested."

She didn't answer.

Darkness the likes of which she had not experienced came over her, a sadness that was impossible to lift. Rick, his rage broken, was struck dumb with guilt. He stopped going to church. He stayed home from work to be helpful. She told him not to bother. He was nothing to her now, a blank, a cipher. She didn't speak to him and she didn't want to see him.

She ate very little and lost weight. She continued work in her studio, sketching movement on a pad. As her substance melted, she believed that her dancing was soaring. It seemed to her that she was no longer tied to ligament and sinew and bone and that she was dancing better than ever. But with Rick out of town, she began to cough badly and was unable to walk down the stairs and called for my help. Her muscles were sore and she could not tell if the soreness was from strain, or the aftereffects of miscarriage.

I might have suspected something wrong, something unspoken, but I was a kid—a smart-ass, ignorant boy—and unaware of women's issues. She didn't tell me anything about her pregnancy or miscarriage. She canceled her classes, quit the gym and was moody, but she wanted to continue dancing and asked me to help her get to Dylan's place in Manhattan.

Dylan took her aside. "You're scaring me. You have a terrible look on your face." She checked the mirror and saw nothing different. Her heart was beating faster and her breathing was shallow, but she felt perfectly fine. Dylan suggested she take a break from dancing. She told him she was perfectly all right. Nothing wrong at all, she insisted. "It's only a cold."

She took my hand and we left. Her breath came in leaps and trailed off in whispers as we rode the subway and got off near West 28th Street. We walked the two blocks of the flower district on Broadway, and she wanted to buy a flower to bring to my mother's grave. Among the palm plants and the ferns for sale, she saw two caged finches. She was startled by the bright-colored halo that surrounded their plumage. She described it to me as two beautiful butterflies chasing each other, even though she didn't have the correct rhythms of speech to express it.

"David, don't be a sourpuss. Just look at them!"

"I don't see any butterflies." My voice was halting.

"Just open your eyes, sweetheart, and look at them!"

"You sound like a bird yourself."

A new awareness rattled her. She was depending on a boy to give her comfort during the most stressful passage in her life. There wasn't a single halo anywhere. She jerked her hand out of mine and pirouetted to prove to herself she was still a dancer. Her wedding band slipped off her thin finger and clinked as it hit the sidewalk.

She didn't see where it had fallen and got down on her knees to search the weeds next to the building. The wedding band had been important to her. She liked to see it on her finger, another band on Rick's finger, proud and resolute, an affront to Jay. But a terrible knowledge came over her, a biblical emphasis. She had tortured Rick enough and decided to leave him. She was doing what was best for him. Rick was fit and intelligent and had a great job. Someone would scoop him up quickly if they divorced. They had done each other a terrible injustice and there was no way to make amends. She sat down on the sidewalk near an entryway, and braced her back against the building. She pulled out her cell.

"Hi, Angel," Rick answered. The high note in his voice gripped her.

"I'm divorcing you," she said.

"Angel, you're not feeling well."

"I don't want you anymore."

"We'll talk about it, Angel."

She ended the call before he could say more.

"About time," I said. "About time."

I was a foolish young man brimming with advice about matters beyond my experience. I kept looking for her ring along the cracks near the fire hydrant.

"Forget about the ring."

I kept looking anyway, pulling crabgrass, brushing aside cellophane and gum wrappers, flicking away cigarette butts. I found the ring lodged between the pavement and the granite curb.

"I don't need it anymore."

I pocketed the ring. She pulled herself together and said we'd better catch a train home before rush hour.

chapter 67

She didn't call a lawyer. A dragged-down feeling she had not faced in her life continued to exhaust her. She rubbed the scars on her arm for prolonged periods and was overheard saying she wished she were dead. Many in the parish had heard that she'd lost Rick's baby, and some of them sent her cards, and some brought meals. When I asked her about it, she said that the rumors were crazy and that she'd never been pregnant.

Sister St. Ambrose called to inquire and offer comfort, and knowing Emily to have a sense of humor, she tried to cheer her up with jokes from the ancient world. Apparently, the Egyptians believed that the body's organs were individuals with moods and quirks and angry moments that jerked them around inside the body from belly to head as they looked for a place they liked better. The Greeks had other funny notions. The uterus, Plato said, was an animal within an animal, moving angrily about. Smart men got it wrong any number of times.

Even St. Augustine, who should have known better, believed the devil was located in the uterus and caused hysteria.

Sister St. Ambrose wasn't the only one concerned. Page called Rick and set up a conference call with Dr. Wilson. Wilson told her that severe performance stress could set off a string of major psychiatric and psychotic events. The doctor speculated that Emily's intense preparation for Jacob's Pillow, and her unexpected success there, could have brought on feelings of emptiness afterward, similar to postpartum depression. "At my facility we evaluate the physical events. Does the patient have a brain tumor? Has she had a history of depression, maybe a bipolar condition? Is this a singular aberration? We do good work, you can send her here."

Rick held his tongue, but admitted to Page later that Emily hardly spoke to him. Once Emily had said, "You're a ghost to me." He believed that Jay had ruined his life, and his bitterness toward Jay increased exponentially.

On a beautifully clear Wednesday evening, two days after Rick's conference with Dr. Wilson, Emily climbed to the roof of my mother's brownstone and stretched her hands above the street. She believed she could fly like the goddess Nike. A soft breeze blew hair from her brow. From her high perch she saw Rick walking home from the neighborhood church where he had just told Father Dan to go fuck himself on account of all the lies Father Dan had preached about a merciful God. Rick's break with the Church was as sudden as his charismatic conversion had been earlier.

He strutted a little, swinging his arms. He picked up a chestnut fallen from a tree near the rectory. He considered its shape and then he dialed a number on his cell phone. Looking up, he saw her on the roof. His face contorted in a grimace. He shouted for her not to jump and ran toward the house. He hated Jay for driving her insane.

He was out of breath when he got to the roof and pulled her away from the ledge. He asked if she'd taken the medicine Dr. Wilson had prescribed.

"Who?" she asked warily, sedated.

"You need a rest."

"Rest?" She echoed his last word as if doomed to repeat the last sound of each sentence. They climbed down the creaky ladder. He gave her a double dose of medication and she went to bed.

Rick sat brooding. A sketchy doomsday idea started to take form. He would get his revenge on Jay, he would punish the bastard, but he wasn't sure how or when. He called Page and said he was now more worried about Emily. Page promised to help and they cooked up a plan. He hung up. Later the next day he talked to Emily and set the plan in motion.

"Angel, Jay and Page want to take you to their favorite Chinese restaurant."

Her eyes dilated alarmingly. She was still groggy after 16 hours of sleep.

"To help you over a rough spot," Rick persisted.

"Chinatown?" she asked.

She wasn't hungry, but she agreed to go and changed into Sara's navy skirt, white blouse, and pearls. An hour later she and Rick were seated with Jay and Page at a Chinese restaurant on Pell Street.

Revived by the drive, she saw her face glowing in the dining room mirror. Her clothes were neat, but her hair was unkempt. She listened inattentively as Jay and Page went on about the troubles they had remodeling their house in Maine. She noticed that Rick hardly spoke. A few beads of sweat were bright as mica on his forehead. He glared at Jay. Page complained about the slow service. The lazy Susan moved food around a circle of tension.

No one was having a good time eating the crabmeat dumplings and Page splattered sauce on her silk blouse. Surprisingly, she didn't break out in profanity. She balanced her spoon on the edge of her plate. "Emily, honey, you don't look too hot, babe. Jay and I have talked about it, and we'd like to do something for you. Wouldn't we, Jay?"

Rick was seething at Jay, loathing the man and all his privileges, but he didn't say anything. By then a vengeful plan must have come into sharper focus.

The medicine Emily had taken made her extremely woozy, yet she saw very clearly the intricate orange and white shades of beer-battered shrimp, and smelled the steaming Lion's Head pork meatballs. She listened to the chattering TV near the cashier's counter and wondered idly why cashiers at so many small restaurants never ring up a sale when they make change. She didn't pay attention to the man who had just entered. He wore a dull blue uniform with "MEDIC" on the back. He looked like a man ready to pick up a takeout order.

"Please don't be angry with us," Page said. "It's irresponsible not to help you." Page turned to Rick. "Don't you think so?"

"I'm leaving Rick," Emily said to no one in particular.

Rick's face seemed to cave.

Page looked shocked. "Oh, babe. You're one sick bunny."

Emily listened as Page said dance was a huge river and Emily was a lovely, small stream feeding it. But there was nothing Emily could do to make herself leap higher or run faster, and she had exhausted herself trying.

"You didn't like my work?" Emily asked.

"Oh, it was good," Jay said.

"It's not that we're trying to put you away," Page said.

"Put me away?" The wooziness suddenly lifted and her pulse quickened.

Rick and Jay looked at Page. She took a folder from her bag and showed Emily a document with Dr. Wilson's signature on it. There was a shaded box with a large *X* and Emily's name was typed below the box.

"Needed paperwork," Page said helpfully. "A Coventry Gardens release for Dr. Wilson." The bold script at the top of the form read "Voluntary Commitment." Page held a ballpoint pen for Emily, but she must have been tense also; it slipped from her fingers and fell into the shrimp sauce. Rick retrieved the pen and wiped it off with a red napkin.

"You want me to sign this self-commitment order?" Emily asked Rick.

She remembered him as the man she'd fallen in love with. A shy and ambitious man, tending to remain silent in social groups, but competent and hard working, loyal, a man who she never doubted would look after her best interests. She looked to Jay for confirmation. "You all want me committed?"

A hush fell over the table. A muscle wouldn't quit jumping on Rick's chin.

"Coventry is a posh place," Page said. "BCC will pick up your tab."

Rick let out a deep sigh.

Emily seized the pen and in a fierce move slashed her signature twice across the bottom pages. Page handed the document to Jay to sign as a witness, and he signed it solemnly, handing it back to Page, who dashed off her signature savagely.

Rick began to sob. He wiped his face with a handkerchief that was already wet, and then he wiped the back of his neck.

"I don't think there's a just God," he said, signing the commitment papers.

Even Jay was rattled to hear this. No one had ever heard Rick say a word against God. Jay got up from his chair and walked over to whisper something to the medic. He then paid for dinner, and coming back with the medic, he stood alongside Emily's chair.

Page stroked Emily's arm. "Emily, babe, we're going to take you upstate to Dr. Wilson's place." Rick looked confused, and Page was determined.

"Tonight?" Emily asked. "You're taking me away tonight?"

"I brought you some personal things," Page said. She showed her a pink satchel. "PJs and stuff. We'll have the rest sent to you tomorrow."

chapter 68

Emily couldn't remember later if Rick had come along on the drive north to Dr. Wilson's clinic. She did remember the approaching headlights and the receding taillights stretching into blurs as they crossed the George Washington Bridge. After two days of evaluation by his associates, Dr. Wilson came to see her with a couple of aides. Wilson asked her if she was having suicidal ideations. She shrugged and refused to answer and refused to talk about the scarification marks on her arm.

She said she wanted to dance and she couldn't do it if she were dead. The doctor raised his eyebrows. "We're moving you up the river," he said. She was his prisoner. He gestured to a male nurse and a stout female assistant to get cracking. Emily carried her laptop, and the assistants carried the small suitcase Rick had shipped to her. *Up the river* could mean anything.

"Where are you taking me?"

"To a room of your own in the woods."

She was an object to Wilson, an interesting medical case. As a choreographer she was always in control, and now she was a prisoner of medical good intentions. But she sensed that there was something more to this. Her journey away from the place she had occupied as a complacent female supporter of the status quo was complete. She had become an outlier, too independent, distant from ordinary expectations, scornful of conventions, and the community Rick and Page and Jay had joined with Dr. Wilson to punish her.

As they were weighing her fate, she heard voices cresting nearby, and someone shouted that they saw a red squirrel. The voices faded, but she heard laughter as Dr. Wilson's nimble steps led the way. She caught sight of a cottage. They marched right to it. It wasn't much different from the other cottages on campus except that the windows were barred. The interior of the cabin was exceptionally neat, almost sterile. It had a double-size bed. The blanket was tucked with precise military corners. There were no pictures on the walls. Dr. Wilson, in a jocular mood, pointed to a landing strip beyond a grove of trees. "Rick can land next door."

The doctor's voice was casual, but the creepy fear that had been crawling up her spine crawled higher. Dr. Wilson showed her a key with a working end that looked like a tiny flag. "I'll give Rick the spare for your conjugal visit." The male nurse, the doctor, and the female assistant left.

"There's nothing wrong with me," Emily shouted after them. But she was cuckoo to them. She stretched out on the bed fully dressed and remained wide awake. She was calm and restless, and time seemed to be stuck in the eternal present.

She was a brood bitch to them. Secured in the cabin for Rick's sexual pleasure. The past and the present started tumbling her thoughts. When she heard a small airplane circling, she knew it had to be Rick. The prop's pitch changed as it landed, and then it ceased. After a while she heard Rick's voice and then his knock on the door. She didn't move, and he let himself in. The mattress jerked as he sat on it.

"Are you going to say anything?" she asked.

"Will you ever forgive me?"

There was no way to soften her mood, so she let his question linger in the stillness. The ceiling was patched with fresh tongue-and-groove cedar, but a few knots had popped, leaving knotholes that were darker. A mosquito and a fly had made homes for themselves in the cottage. She listened to the whining and buzzing. "I'd like it better if you stayed at a motel," she said.

Rick knelt at the side of her bed and out of a prayerful habit put his hands together. Then perhaps remembering that God had forsaken him, that his prayers had been ignored, he formed them into fists. "None of my plans have worked out for us. I deserve to be damned." He didn't blame the bishops and cardinals and the priests, even though to my view they were accessories to a moral crime. He didn't blame the structured ignorance contained in dogmas they had built over the centuries to contain human fears. He blamed himself. She remained still, counting the grooved cedar planking in the ceiling. She felt the mattress trembling on account of his shaking fists. "Pray for me," he said.

"How?"

"Help. Pray for help. I need help. I'm afraid I don't believe in anything. Not God, not me. Not us. But I tried. I swear to you I tried my best."

"You did. Yes, you did."

She reached over and held his hands for a minute until they felt calm to her touch. She fell asleep, and in the morning she rolled her head toward the window, expecting to find him sleeping on the floor. But he had left.

chapter 69

She felt better after I showed up. I stayed with the staff in their quarters and paid for my room and board by working the grounds as a laborer. We were outside her cabin, and juniper scented the air as we walked to the lakefront dock on the Coventry premises. In a fevered optimism, she became more attentive to the smell of sap in the fir, and she heard the sounds of woodpeckers pecking for insects. The wind was steady from the north, and the waves were short and abrupt against the side of the dock. Her eyes were brightly focused on the far shore. I ran my finger across the four scars on her forearm. At the time that we were going through this passage, I didn't know what the scars had meant to her—the four most important human beings in her life. She finally gave a partial explanation. She couldn't tell me that I was the father of her dead girl.

"The second mark is for you," she said.

"It's the least visible. It's going to disappear."

"I'll always know it's there."

I glanced toward the main building where she'd been under observation. "You shouldn't have cut your arm. They think you're crazy. The fat guy Jay will keep you locked up just to make sure Rick isn't distracted from doing company work."

"Rick hates Jay." She didn't explain, and stretched to embrace me. She was pleased that the fluttery good feeling she'd felt when we touched hadn't been destroyed.

Her regimen at Coventry Gardens was strict. They had a kiln and she used it to make pottery. There were expert beading classes and even a beginner's metalworking class, where she'd forged and pounded a silver bracelet that she inlaid with amber pieces. She could work with any of the crafts so long as the crafted objects had nothing to do with dance. This was a terrible blow. Dr. Wilson kept her away from dance. The governing medical principle seemed to be that dance had driven her insane, and to recover she had to quit.

She spent a portion of each day surreptitiously making dance. That was her secret, and it became my secret, too. I helped where I could. At times, I was a lookout protecting her from observers. Once, we heard Dr. Wilson approaching and we had to hurry to push back her bed and nightstand that we had moved to make room for dancing.

Our time together passed in a shuffle of openness and concealment. Her desire to dance and her fear of getting caught dancing became like breathing in and breathing out. We were cautious not to appear overly intimate, and we did not once sleep with each other. A new idea was formulating in her head. I was almost eighteen. She said I could wait until I was of legal age to resume lovemaking.

She felt as if she was getting back on her feet and thinking more clearly. She'd sent me home to pick up her wallet, her credit cards, her driver's license, her journal, and the extra cash she kept in a drawer. She wanted to escape Dr. Wilson's medical prison. I returned excited and eager to help her get away. She went to see Dr. Wilson in his office.

The doctor ran a finger along his sideburn. The midmorning light made him look faintly ghostly. He proceeded to explain the meds he'd given her.

She hadn't seen Rick in a week, and they did not text each other. So far as she knew, he was still seething with hate toward the privileged Jay.

"Rick is coming today. Will you give me a pass into town?" Emily asked.

"He should have called me first," Dr. Wilson said.

"He's awfully busy."

Wilson chuckled. "Sure. You and Rick can have an overnighter." He pulled out a pad and wrote her name on an order to give to the security guard. She was incensed that Dr. Wilson was her warden. She'd lied to Dr. Wilson. Rick wasn't coming, but telling lies in the defense of freedom was okay. She took the gate pass and went to get me. We walked briskly across the wide, grassy field and past a huge maple to get to the guard gate. She showed her pass and the guard waved us on.

I looked older to her. Something in my attitude and manner had changed in the last month. Not far from the gate we brushed lips and my mouth tingled. She was bold to let the guard see us kissing, but she was indifferent about being seen, and kissed me again. She then called Jay on her cell phone.

"Emily?" Jay said, surprised. "You've never called me on my private phone before."

She told him she'd kept the number close.

"Not close enough. How are you?"

She said she was feeling fine and she wasn't going back to Coventry Gardens. The Bradbury Corporation could save its money. But she needed a private place to catch her breath and rest. She anticipated his response: he invited her to spend as many days as she wished at his Kennebunkport place.

"I'm not staying with Rick."

Page came on the line. She asked if she could act as the honest broker in arranging a no-fault meeting between Rick and Emily. "I'll let you know," Emily said, but had no intention of doing it.

That evening she booked a two-bedroom suite and gave me my new orders: no physical sex until I was eighteen. I responded badly. I reached into my pocket and came up with her wedding band. "You may want it again."

"You're a real sourpuss."

She took the ring and packaged it in a puffy shipping envelope and overnighted it to Rick. Page was on the phone to her the next day. She said Rick was flying up to Portland, Maine, to check on the Bradbury corrugating plant and had offered to meet Emily on neutral ground. Page said she'd arranged a meeting in a public and crowded place. The Bradbury Company had leased several vacant acres adjoining its plant to a traveling circus and carnival. She'd arrange a meeting there. Emily hesitated, Page pressed on, talked about "closure," until Emily, worn down by a sense of obligation and not wanting to be ungrateful, promised to do her best to keep the date with Rick.

chapter 70

The night of the meeting I spotted Rick first. He was near the Ferris wheel that Page had identified as their meeting place. I dropped back to stay out of sight, and Emily walked up to him without his seeing her. His profile wasn't severe, she wrote in her journal, but he wasn't looking well. His skin had turned sallow and his cheeks were creased, and when he turned in her direction, she saw he was not only trim but also gaunt. He dropped the bag of peanuts he had been munching on and spread his arms, moving forward to embrace her. She lurched backward, her body recoiling from her intention to forgive him.

He wiped his forehead. "I want you with me."

Rocked by his earnestness, she said, "Let's go have a beer."

They went to a thatch-roofed beer shanty. Beers in hand, they sat beneath multicolored overhead lights strung above a long table that gave the place a festive feeling. A carousel calliope nearby added to the carnival mood.

"We used to hold hands," he said.

She impulsively reached out to touch his fingers. They were thin, even bony. "You haven't been eating." The blue lights hanging above them painted their brows blue, and the table candlelight illuminated their reflections in the golden bottle glass.

"Angel, if I had a chance to reach into our past and change our lives, I would learn to love your baby. I would be a good father, I'd—"

She turned her head and the dual image that had been reflected on the beer bottle dissolved.

"So, it's finished?" he asked. "You're still with him?"

"With?"

"Jay said you're coming up to Kennebunkport."

"You can come, too."

"I want my fighting chance to win you back."

"Don't look so grim. It doesn't suit you, Rick. You're an optimist."

Rick agreed he should look on the bright side. He had a long day's work ahead of him tomorrow, and he left abruptly. She didn't finish her beer. We drove to Kennebunkport that night.

chapter 71

The Franciscan Monastery at Kennebunkport near the Bradbury compound remains a beautiful place where Franciscans, a mendicant order famous for taking strict vows of poverty, lived in a luxurious tax-exempt communal mansion that would make a billionaire's jaw drop from house envy. Emily had booked a guest room for me in the monastery's campus dorm, and we learned that Dr. Wilson had rented a guesthouse nearby. The Bradbury compound was located a few miles away. Page had arranged the use of a barnlike studio for Emily, and Rick was assigned a private cottage.

These were the last days of summer, and a large contingent of the faithful drove up from New York City to vacation, many of them only for an extended weekend. Dr. Wilson was with his family, and Sister St. Ambrose had surrendered the urgencies of administration to an assistant in order to vacation here. The general mood I sensed was one of reconciliation, an end to bad business. Despite Emily's miscarriage she felt a growing enthusiasm for life.

At the Kennebunkport bookshop, she bought self-help books, spiritual books on mysticism, religious books, and how-to books. Once again she was spiritually connected with Sara, who was a seeker, searching for something beyond the immediacy of her art, but once finding it, she'd tried to embody it in her work. Emily read about stoicism and Sufism, she reread *Walden* and thumbed through a paperback on kabbalah. She picked up Alain de Botton's *How Proust Can Change Your Life* and his *How to Think More about Sex*. She skimmed the pages in the *Bhagavad Gita*, and read several Bible passages at the store, and back at her studio she read portions of a Catholic Missal. This was a huge quantity of advice to absorb.

The Buddhists say that the trick to having a peaceful life was to be free of desire, yet her desire for me burned. She could not explain this to herself nor reveal it to a judge, or confess it again to a priest. She'd made that vow not to sleep with me until I was legal, and with that settled, she felt free from sin. She wasn't thinking of calling a divorce lawyer because there was something holding her back, some uncertainty about love and romance, and the transience of the latter. She'd been safe with Rick. There was no safety in me, or with me, and no future she could foresee, and there was a lingering feeling that she'll never again meet a man as sturdy and as reliable as Rick. Let people assume what they had to assume, and she and Rick would deal with it.

In the mornings, she ran on the beach. The sand was coarse but the shore breeze felt good as she traced the surf washing up from the ocean. The mystics of self-denial were giving her strength. No longer depressed, she asked me, "Are you still working on *Maya*?"

"I've got new pictures, scenes I posted on the web."

She went home and pulled out her laptop to work on a grant request and took a moment to check my blog. She needed only to substitute her own name for *Maya* to read about herself. I had an author picture in the box labeled "playwright." I wore the loose-fitting white shirt I had worn on the night we made love. It was enough to set off a warm feeling in her. But she conspicuously did not invite me to join her for dinner. Avoidance, she hoped, would strengthen both of us. Just then her cell phone started to vibrate and she saw my name on the caller ID. She looked at the pile of self-help books she'd stacked on the floor and looked at my picture on her laptop. She tried, really tried, to blot out all the pleasant memories.

To her, I was more intelligent and beautiful and sensitive and competent and thoughtful and helpful than anyone she'd known. The run-up of my good qualities was so unrealistic, extravagant, and powerful that it frightened her. She was a fool, she admitted, a tender fool. Her eyes filled with tears, and it was a while before she could slow her emotions. There was no doubt in her mind that desire could overcome reason.

I called again. She picked up.

"Can I come over?"

"No."

"Hey, I'll be eighteen this month."

She hesitated, and in that brief pause I made my way toward her heart. "Okay," she said, and I came over. I had showered and we lingered in the entryway. She returned my kiss, and more followed. She was barefoot and I was wearing gym shoes. I had grown muscular over the course of the summer, and my deep-set eyes looked at her with quiet determination. I wanted her. She wanted me.

"I have about as much will power as water running downstream," she said.

We were in bed when a sudden loud knock on the door startled us. She slipped on her robe and went to see who it was and found Dr. Wilson. She was speechless. He raised his digital camera high to let her see the LCD screen. She watched him scroll through a sequence of images that showed us making love.

"Proof!" he said. He was triumphant. He turned and marched toward his car.

"Wait, please wait," she shouted. She ran to catch him.

He turned and shouted, "Transporting a minor across state lines for sexual congress will get you twenty years in prison!" Then he drove off.

I reread this journal passage several times. The forces of faith, the forces of government, ecclesiastical authorities, and government officials love to spy. Emily asked me to stay out of sight until she'd caught up with Dr. Wilson. She drove to the monastery grounds, where he'd rented his summer guesthouse. She knocked on the door and Mrs. Wilson said he'd gone to pray at the chapel nearby. In the chapel Emily found Dr. Wilson kneeling alone in the third pew, a rosary in his right hand. His male pattern baldness gave him a monk-like appearance. She eased past the huge candelabra and took a pew behind him.

"You hate me. I don't know why you hate me," she said.

He continued to pray. "Forgive us our sins—"

"Dr. Wilson, can you forget what you saw?"

"Lead us not into temptation—"

"Let me go."

He turned to face her. "You're a sexual predator. A damn foreigner." He resumed his prayers. "Deliver us from evil."

She smelled the scent of beeswax wafting from a wrought-iron stand filled with burning candles. She saw herself in the reflection of the glass. They were unblinking eyes, candles filled with loathing for women.

Dr. Wilson turned toward her. "You've got six hours before I go to the police with my pictures."

Peace and grace and love were in short supply in his heart—revenge and torture, punishment and damnation were the operating principles. The Virgin Mary looked innocent in her illuminated niche, St. Anthony wonderfully kind.

"You're a hypocrite," she whispered, getting up.

She left the chapel feeling that she'd been stabbed in the heart.

chapter 72

She went outside and felt the first cold snap of the season. It had come all of a sudden, and leaves had begun to turn crimson and gold. She saw me cycling toward her, dressed in the jeans and the black sweater she had bought for me. I, too, had an instinct where to look for her. She felt irrationally peaceful, no grief and no remorse, and the longing for me remained. She explained what had just happened. "I'll go to prison for sleeping with you."

"I'm not worth it."

There was coolness in the air from a freshening sea breeze. A lost seagull cawed as it flew across the lawn and out across the inlet on its night flight to sea. But her calmness was slowly withering because I seemed uncommunicative.

Six hours.

She wanted to be alone and sent me away. I hadn't come up with a plan yet, and I went away. She returned to her car and drove without noticing the streets. She found herself back at the Bradbury compound and parked past the caretaker's quarters. Just then Rick called her on her cell. He was on the road coming home and extremely upset, and asked to see her face to face. She had nothing more to lose. "Sure," she said. She crossed the road and sat on a bench in front of his cottage to wait for him. She stared at her hands and fingers and thought about the dances she'd made beautiful.

Six hours? What do people do with six hours of freedom?

She was startled by the pink belladonna flowers planted nearby that she'd not noticed earlier. They were gorgeously lush, and poisonous. Page must have ordered them from a greenhouse, because it was too cold for them to winter over in Maine.

Going to prison for transporting a kid across state lines to have sex—it was a good law. It could catch her twenty years. Her thoughts were scattered and she looked around restlessly. She wondered idly what a gas can was doing close to the house. She saw a paperback titled *Final Exit* on the wicker table. The title suggested existentialism, but when she opened the book she was shocked to discover it was a manual on how to end your life by committing suicide.

She read a few pages. The choices were ugly. She could stockpile prescriptions that would kill her, or she could put a plastic bag over her head to asphyxiate herself. She could hang herself or shoot herself. Thank God, she didn't want to. Page must have had a wicked sense of humor to leave the book for guests to read. Emily flung it aside when she heard Rick's car approaching.

He stepped out of the car and complained about the tourist traffic that had delayed him. His tentative voice and hesitant body language made him seem vulnerable. He wrapped his arms around himself defensively. "I'm not going to try to talk you into leaving Jay. I just want an evening with you."

She didn't correct him about Jay. There was a liturgical quality in his voice and a grave manner. He didn't look quite the same either. There was more tenderness in his gestures and his voice pulled her toward him. She stepped forward and held him, but there was no hugging back. He seemed to have turned into water running out of her hands. She saw that the fear that had brought him to ask her for a face-to-face meeting was growing larger. He kept looking past her, apparently seeing something she could not see.

"I'll change my clothes and we'll go eat," he said.

"This late?"

"Oh, let's do have dinner together."

She let him go to change. *Six hours. Why not a last meal?* She waited in a world of private patience. She was startled when he came out wearing a tuxedo. His shadowed cheeks made his forehead more prominent. "You recognize it?" he asked. Her face told him *no*. "I wore this tux at our wedding."

"You brought it to Kennebunkport?" She brushed her lips with her finger as if to remove a fallen snowflake.

"Today is our anniversary."

She caught her breath; her forgetfulness was cumulative and corrosive—first she had forgotten my birthday, now this. She felt badly. "I'm not dressed to go out with a guy in a tux."

"I don't care what you wear."

What followed was haunting. Rick wanted to look at her, wanted to smell the fresh outdoor air around her. They got into his car to go to the dinner he'd arranged. By then it was dark. Rick turned up Main Street and drove past the scrawny oak and up the coastal road. She was struck by his quiet efficiency. He did well in neighborhoods planned on a grid. They both felt safer inside formal structures.

The sky was clear above the town, but out on the coastline and near the spouting rock, the shore was partly shrouded in fog. They got out of the car and gazed at the dark sea for a time. The light from the moon made the crest on the waves look like scalloped ridges. The night air was warm and the sound of foghorns calming.

He had taken her wedding band with him and handed it over to her, pressing it warmly into the palm of her hand, and curling her fingers over it. "I still love you. Keep it for me."

"Rick, I'm sorry."

"I'm keeping my wedding band." His voice wasn't bitter. He showed her his hand with the ring on his finger. "You won't have to leave me." He sounded reassuring, but his remark confused her. It took a second for her to realize that male pride preferred to have others believe you were taking the initiative to leave, rather than the one who'd been dumped. So be it.

They both saw a coast delineated by darkening lines that grew lighter farther out to sea. They got back into the car and drove to the Cottage Inn for dinner. Rick had reserved a table in a private alcove that overlooked the ocean. She was in jeans and a jacket and was totally presentable, but felt awkward next to a man in a tux. They were eating their food silently when

Rick put down his knife and fork, reached into his pocket and gave her his Brown Scapular. "I wore this thing day and night."

"Why are you giving me this?"

"A souvenir," he said.

It was made of leather. He'd never taken it off before, not even when they'd made love.

"I'm not as religious as you." But she held out her hand.

They ate a little. The silence continued, and then he said: "Angel, I'm better than Jay."

"Rick, please don't humiliate yourself. You're fine. You'll be okay. I'm still your friend."

"You're my last best friend."

His grim eyes rattled her. "Don't use that word *last*. It sounds fatal."

"I wanted us to last."

"Please, Rick. We're okay. I've forgiven you. We'll be best friends forever."

"It's taken me too long to realize you have a life of your own."

"My dance reality?"

"No, something more than just your choreography. There's some part of our life I've not seen until now. Maybe I was lacking empathy, or some kind of mindfulness…"

They were still eating and talking quietly when the restaurant staff started closing and a server stood mute at the front door, signaling with downward glances that it was time to leave. Rick paid the bill and drove them home. They stood outside on the path to the rose garden. He looked so sad that she gave in to an urge to kiss him goodnight. He kept hugging her, patting her, touching the back of her neck, and she, troubled by the pain she had caused him, returned his kisses in a rush of sorrow. She felt a hard object under his jacket. "What's that?"

He touched the left side of his tux. "My Army .45. Licensed. I like the feel of it." He turned to go. He said he was going to say goodnight to Page and Jay before he turned in. "I would love to have more time for us. If only—"

She took a quick step backward, fearful that her own separation anxiety was beginning to show. "See you tomorrow," she said, with a cheerful spin on tomorrow.

chapter 73

She returned to her barnlike studio. I had been waiting for her. I got up from the couch and asked where the hell she'd been all this time. "Come on," I said. I came at her all in a rush. "It's late. We have work to do." I had made my plans and I wanted us to see Dr. Wilson before he made his report to the police. I seized her laptop, grabbed a manila envelope, and we left. A moment later I had the foresight to call his guesthouse. The maid answered and said that the family would not be back until later. They'd gone to see a movie. I asked which movie and then I called the movie house and got the movie run time. We had an hour to kill.

Six hours.

The hour we wasted was the longest hour in my life. The dullest and the slowest hour ever. We spent time nursing Cokes at a diner; we could barely keep eye contact. What little we said I didn't remember afterward. I did recall saying that I was going to talk Dr. Wilson out of following through on his threats. The drive to Dr. Wilson's rented house was a relief from the silence between us. We parked, and for a few seconds our headlights illuminated the front of the guesthouse. A wide screened porch ran around two sides of the house.

A full moon was out, casting a pale light on the trees and the lawn. Both of the doctor's daughters were visible in the light in the windows. One was weaving on a loom downstairs, and the other was reading. Dr. Wilson's wife was in the kitchen. She was a handsome woman and her lines were softer in the evening light. We did not see Dr. Wilson.

"What are you going to do?" Emily asked.

"You stay here," I said.

I grabbed the laptop and the manila envelope, got out, walked over, and rang Dr. Wilson's bell. The daughters sat up in the living room and the wife looked out the kitchen window. She came to the front door and released a block of light as she opened it. Emily watched as I greeted Mrs. Wilson, and soon enough Dr. Wilson appeared in the doorway. The doctor looked at me, glanced at his wife, and motioned for her to get back inside.

The night was still. I heard the faraway sound of a low-pitched aircraft droning high above in the starry sky. The night air was refreshing.

Dr. Wilson walked with me a short distance from the house. Emily saw me rip the envelope open and slip a disc into the laptop. A bright orange-colored background popped up on the screen to display *Thai Ecstasy*. Wilson staggered a little, his cheeks creased, his eye sockets deepened. Emily knew immediately what I'd done. I had lied to her and kept copies of Dr. Wilson's tourist porn. Wilson's wife came out and watched for a moment, but she couldn't see the screen from afar.

"Is that boy bothering you?" she asked. She had a flat, Midwestern way of speaking.

"It's nothing, love—nothing to worry about. Go back in the house."

A telephone rang inside and Mrs. Wilson went to answer it. She returned to the porch, holding a phone in her hand. "It's Rick, honey. He wants to speak to you. He says he's circling above us in his plane."

Dr. Wilson looked up. "What fool thing?"

I spotted the red and green port and starboard wing lights of the low-flying aircraft.

"Sweetheart," Mrs. Wilson said. "Rick says he *has* to talk with you."

Dr. Wilson let loose an expletive.

"He can't wait, hon. He says his call is breaking up. He sounds like he really needs you."

Dr. Wilson looked up. We all looked up.

"I've got business here," Wilson said. He stepped closer to me.

"Is that Emily by the car, hon?" Mrs. Wilson raised her voice. She held up the phone. "Why is Rick flying up there so late at night?"

"Who the hell knows?"

"Maybe Emily will talk to Rick?"

Emily looked at the navigation lights of the aircraft. She ran over to take the phone from Mrs. Wilson, but the phone line carried static now. Just then the sheriff pulled up in his cruiser to take Dr. Wilson's statement. I raised the laptop screen with the doctor's Thai photographs. The sheriff hailed him from a distance. "Dr. Wilson—"

"Put that thing down!" Wilson hissed.

"I have backup discs."

Dr. Wilson grabbed the laptop and flipped the screen down. The sheriff walked across the lawn. There was a pleasing smell of cut grass. "Sir, I'm here to take your complaint."

Dr. Wilson staggered and didn't know what to do with the laptop.

"Sir?"

"I've nothing to say," Dr. Wilson said.

The sheriff looked startled.

"It was a mistake," Dr. Wilson added.

"A mistake?" the sheriff said.

"I've nothing to say. I'll make a contribution to the sheriff's fund."

A shift in the night breeze brought the sound of sirens from town. A deputy sheriff pulled up and jumped out of his cruiser. We could hear his radio squawking. The deputy ran over and pulled the sheriff aside for a huddle. The deputy and the sheriff looked up at the sky.

"He's flying away from the coast," the deputy said.

Everyone waited. The sound of the aircraft was fading now.

"What are they talking about?" Emily asked.

"Hon, what are they talking about?" asked Mrs. Wilson

"Rick, they're talking about Rick," the doctor answered.

The officers walked to the deputy's cruiser and called the

air-traffic controller. The sound of sirens coming from the town's direction grew louder. We gathered around the cruiser. The deputy turned to Dr. Wilson. "Jay Bradbury was shot."

"God be with us," the doctor said.

Rick banked the aircraft, heading away from the shore. From the ground his port and starboard lights grew dimmer, and the sound of the aircraft grew thinner and fainter. Dr. Wilson's two daughters came out and looked at the sky. Everyone was looking at the sky now.

"How far can he fly?" the sheriff asked the controller. He listened to the answer as we watched the aircraft flying farther offshore.

"Is he going to turn back?" Mrs. Wilson asked.

No one answered her.

"Did you say Bradbury got hurt?" Dr. Wilson asked.

The sheriff said something to his deputy. The deputy said, "Mr. Bradbury was shot dead. His wife gave us a description of the shooter, an employee."

The sheriff indicated Rick's aircraft with a nod. "Allegedly."

Wilson's two girls were now holding each other. Emily shivered even though it wasn't cold.

"Lord have mercy," Mrs. Wilson said.

"The airport ground crew says the aircraft wasn't refueled," the sheriff said. "The tower thinks the plane doesn't have enough fuel to land anymore."

"He will crash?" Emily said.

"If he gets beyond the point of no return."

"No, please no," Emily cried out.

"The Air Force scrambled two fighters," the sheriff added.

"The night is calm," I said. "He can turn around and glide to a landing."

"Please, God in heaven, he's your child, your servant—help him, turn him around." Mrs. Wilson was crying.

The seconds ticked by. Emily looked distraught. "He'll glide. He's an optimist. He'll glide and glide and glide. He can make it!"

Winging over the Atlantic, Rick must have seen the shore lights beneath him scattered like lighted flowers. Scrupulous and thorough, he would have calculated the wind speed and the airspeed and the amount of fuel necessary to take him beyond the point of no return.

Mrs. Wilson started to pray, and Dr. Wilson joined her. "Pass lightly through this world, for it is nothing…"

"Rick, don't leave me!" Emily shouted at the sky. "I'll do anything to get you back. Anything! Please don't *leave* me."

chapter 74

The Coast Guard didn't find much—several cushions, floating aircraft debris. They didn't recover Rick's body. In the days that followed, the Bradbury caretaker let everyone know that he'd found empty cartridges in the main house that had been fired from Rick's Army .45. The clip was empty; five shots had nearly decapitated Jay. No one wanted to believe that a man as decent and thoughtful and hardworking as Rick had murdered his boss, but there was no denying the evidence.

At the time, I didn't know what to make of Jay's murder and Rick's suicide. I didn't know what pressures he'd endured. I didn't know about her pregnancy. I didn't know I was to blame. Emily and Rick—they believed that all things well intentioned end well. This was a beautiful and uplifting thing to believe in, even if we're all minnows swimming against eddies and carried by the tides beyond our ability to understand.

Summer vacations were ending at Kennebunkport, and the last of the seasonal visitors had started to pack for the trip home. The locals turned their attention to a red tide threatening shellfish. I was with Emily at a table outside the lobster shack. I wanted to say I'm sorry; I wanted the good spirits to return Rick to this world.

She tugged at a corner of the gingham-patterned tablecloth as I handed her a letter informing me about the scholarship I had won. "Oh, that's good," she said, but her voice trailed off as unspoken thoughts battered us. We hadn't anticipated the unfolding misfortune we caused. She mourned Rick's passing and regretted Jay's death. I, too, had a deep longing for life, a terrible hope to have it continue in all its uncertainty on unforeseeable paths leading to the next unknown destination.

"Sister St. Ambrose will drive you back to Brooklyn," Emily said.

I waited, uncertain what she'd say next. We were both uneasy. Emily said that she'd arranged for my uncle to take charge of my affairs. I was too stunned to react. She picked up her bag and started to ease herself up from the table. This was it? She was leaving me? I leaned forward to kiss her goodbye, but she shot up from her seat as if to avoid a blow from my fist.

And now, so many years later, when all these events should have been remote amid hazy memories, I find myself buried under a mountain of melancholy. I'm alone. I've never found anyone else who attracted me as much as Emily did. My solitary night whisperers keep repeating our intimate past: *Maybe you can make something out of these journals?*

My answer was *Morning Light*. The play opened in Seattle and was a minor success. I returned to New York and staged it Off-Broadway. But I kept pursuing the past, reliving it. I was looking for answers, seeking explanations, hoping to find the key that would make right what had gone wrong. I blamed myself foremost, and Emily, too. I didn't blame Rick.

There was an adversary guiding us toward tragedy that I did not recognize when I was young, an adversary that even now I hesitate to name. Strindberg gave us the aristocratic Miss Julie and Euripides gave us Medea, women whose natures carry the unwritten sensual code. But it's not about gender, I thought. We all carry that code. It's in the scent that we breathe and the skin we touch. Schopenhauer put it this way: "Sexual attraction is a diabolical invention for the propagation of the race by the will of the species, ready relentlessly to destroy personal happiness in order to carry out its ends." I was a willing cog in the relentless machinery that fuels sexual selection. I wanted sex; love was only a tangent. I wasn't the master designer of such things. Her journal had no answers either, not even the last thing she wrote—

> We could have dealt better with sex. All I needed was the certainty of your love, the promise that we had a lifetime to work things out. If only you had more patience with me. I never loved you more than when I became pregnant and wanted to keep the baby. I wanted to be loved; I wanted to be understood. I understand now that's all you wanted, too.

I copied this note in longhand. I read and reread it. I would have liked it had she written this note to me, but in the end I had to accept that she'd meant it for Rick. They'd loved each other with a startling innocence hard to imagine today. Instead of seeing each other for who they were, they saw what they wanted to see. They were blind to each other's individual beauty.

I searched for Emily to apologize, to explain myself, hoping to hear once again her encouraging and uplifting voice. I searched for her on the web. I looked up her former friends and associates. No dance group, no listing of choreographers, gave me a clue. I searched all the private dance school listings; I searched the names of teachers at colleges with arts programs; I searched the membership rosters of community arts organizations. I started writing letters to her I couldn't send anywhere. She was gone, unlisted, uncatalogued, not on Facebook or LinkedIn, not on a dozen other social sites. Google turned up nothing. I searched criminal records and public real-estate records. I turned over my Visa card to a handful of Internet companies specializing in background and identity checks. They searched state driver's licenses, infractions, lawsuits, crime reports, civil litigation, judgments—all to no avail.

The terrifying thought that she could have died claimed my attention. I couldn't sleep longer than four hours each night for weeks on end after this morbid thought colonized my mind. My wretched wakefulness led to another obsessive search lasting months, a search among the dead. Who would have known there are so many obituaries written, so many funerals held, so many cemeteries to locate? Once again I came up empty. I was relieved that maybe she hadn't died, and the mystery of her life deepened.

I wondered if she might have returned to Lithuania and I contacted an investigator there to find her. He kept offering me tantalizing leads—Klaipéda, Vilnius, Kaunas. He checked on a Jesuit orphanage to see if she was working there. He said that she was elusive, but he said he was getting closer. He was manipulating me. It cost me a bundle and must have bought the man a new car before I realized he was simply yanking on my wallet. I hired a stateside investigator next and he traced Emily's social security number, and I thought he'd locate her.

As I sat brooding about our past I felt Rick closer to me. I understood his hopes. He was a believer. He believed. He believed in eternal goodness. You don't have to believe in the hereafter to believe in goodness. You don't have to believe in God to believe in goodness. I believe in goodness, too. Rick went a step further; he believed that if your heart was pure you would suffer no harm. He believed that if your intentions were good you'd get your just rewards. I, too, want to believe that, but I can't do it. I shudder at his despair, the day-in and day-out pain of it, the ceaseless torment of a broken heart that he could only escape in death.

The investigator called me and for an instant I hoped that at last, at long last, I could meet Emily in an outpouring of mutual grief and regret. We would honor Rick with the affection he deserved, a loyal man worthy to live forever in our memory. But the investigator said Emily's social security number led to a dead end. She'd stopped using it years ago. She was mist, gone, incomprehensible and unreachable. She'd ditched her former identity as surely as a butterfly would have left an empty chrysalis.

It was the end of the affair for me. And now, as even more years have passed almost unnoticed, my solitary night whisperers keep repeating the last thing she said to me: *Maybe you can make something out of these journals?*

So I keep searching for a happy ending, looking, wondering, working, hoping, and moving ceaselessly into the future.

ACKNOWLEDGEMENTS

I owe a debt of everlasting gratitude to my parents, Antanas and Jadvyga, and my brother, Father Anthony, a Roman Catholic priest whose intimate knowledge of Church matters informs this book, and his best friend Antonio Aveleyra, who kept watch. I wish to thank The Writers Room in New York City, and its director Donna Brodie, for offering space to work; the late Frank Conroy for admitting me as his special student at Iowa Writers' Workshop; and the University of Arizona, which granted me an MFA.

I wish to thank writers who have written and edited books about dance, among them *Reading Dance* by Robert Gottlieb, *Once A Dancer* by Allegra Kent, *Ballet's Magic Kingdom* by Akim Volynsky, and several wonderful books by Toni Bentley, including *A Winter Season*.

Several readers contributed their insights, each in his or her own way—Margaret Sanchez, who clarified St. Ambrose Catholic School, art historian Paul Ivey, the curator Julie Sasse, gallerist Elizabeth Cherry, journalist Tim Vanderpool, and playwright Mary Rogers, supporters Eddy and Charlotte Adomaitis, friend and librarian Ina Bray, film and Yale drama teacher Marc Lapadula, the close reader and reluctant editor Jacob Knabb, my friend musician Billy Squier, poet Stefanie Marlis, and cultural guide Gregory McNamee.

I'm also grateful to many others, especially artists and writers, who shared their experiences with me, and whose lives as artists inform this book—among them the novelists Judith Rossner, Beverly Swerling, Lee Smith, Bob Houston, Jonathan Penner, Carol Orlock, and Jack Cady, the essayist Vivian Gornick, the sculptors John Davis and Earl Olmstead, designers Kelly Leslie and Siobhan Roome, the painters Gwyneth Scally, Haleh Niazmand, Olivier Mosset, Gary Swimmer, Michael Chittock, Eric Twachman, Tom Miller, Tim Murphy, Liam Everett, Vytas Sakalas, and Craig Cully. I wish to thank Emily Cooke and Doug Wagner for editing, Amanda Bauch for proofreading and fact-checking, Beth Jusino for marketing advice, and Morgana Gallaway for launching the production of this book. None of this would have come to pass without the support of my wife, Dana. To everyone, thank you.

A NOTE ABOUT THE AUTHOR

Photo by Gediminas

HOLLAND KANE is the author of the novels *Winter Reeds* and *Morning Light*. He spent his childhood in Europe and his teenage years in New York City. He served with distinction in the U.S. Army Signal Corps, handling secret government documents. Since leaving the service to join civilian ranks, Holland has been an entrepreneur, a journalist, and an editor of a literary magazine. He holds an MBA and an MFA, and makes his home in the Pacific Northwest, Tucson, and New York City. Visit him online at **www.hollandkane.com**.

WINTER REEDS
by Holland Kane

*"Kane spins a fascinating web of discoveries and intrigue,
and the surprises don't stop until the very end."*
— *Kirkus Reviews*

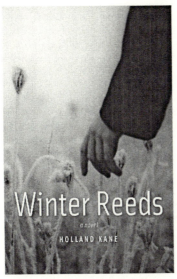

Documentary filmmaker Mike Harrison moves from New York City to a remote Northwest town to research an infamous car dealership fire. The generation-old, unsolved arson left two people dead, and if Mike can solve the mystery, he'll have a career-making movie. He's distracted though, by beautiful Katie Ames, a fellow New Yorker who's come to Hallmark County with her mentally handicapped brother, to piece together their own complicated past.

Katie's dating an architect who was tangled up in the dealership arson. The man is obsessed with Katie, and threatens her when she tries to break up with him. The next morning, the police find his dead body. Was he murdered? The medical examiner won't say.

Mike and Katie are outsiders in a town where the popular Sheriff Trout is a law unto himself, and citizens live under constant surveillance... But there's a story to be told: one that ties the arson, the dead architect, the sheriff, and Katie's missing family together into a devastating small-town scandal.

Winter Reeds Print ISBN 978-0-9858293-0-8
Winter Reeds Digital ISBN 978-0-9858293-1-5

DEER CREEK
forthcoming by Holland Kane

Author Holland Kane returns to the northwestern area he first described in the acclaimed novel Winter Reeds *for a new story about ambition, love, and secrets that bind them together.*

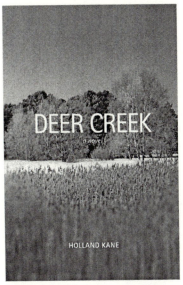

Twenty years ago, high school sweethearts Richie and Sally ran away from the troubled, violent streets of Chicago. Sally was already two months pregnant.

Of course, no one in Deer Creek knows about all of that—not Sally's husband Tom, the ambitious and wealthy mayor; not the political opponents who want to ruin Tom's campaign for governor; not the investment manager who's demanding money Sally doesn't have; and certainly not Jason, the handsome young man Richie raised alone, who believes his mother died in childbirth.

Richie still pines for his first love, but Sally's successful new life seems secure and complete. That is, until Crystal, her teenage daughter with Tom, falls in love with Jason. Now, in a twist of fate worthy of Shakespeare, Sally must find a way to separate the young lovers without revealing their awkward biological relationship and her own embarrassing past.

Deer Creek Print ISBN: 978-0-9858293-6-0
Deer Creek Digital ISBN: 978-0-9858293-7-7

CPSIA information can be obtained at www.ICGtesting.com
Printed in the USA
LVOW08s1654250913

354111LV00008B/1077/P

9 780985 829339